JAMES McGEE

An army brat who grew up in Gibraltar, Germany and Northern Ireland, James McGee became a writer after jobs in banking, sales, the airline industry, and bookselling. *Rapscallion* is his third novel featuring Matthew Hawkwood.

Also by James McGee

Ratcatcher
Resurrectionist

Eddie 'Golden' Gaynor
1925–2011
This one is for you

Chapter 1

The Paradise Street All-Night Bus Station

Peligan City was worn out and rain-soaked and the dark clouds that hung over it cast long and murky shadows. Only the city centre escaped the gloom, with its circus of dazzling casino lights and flashing billboards. Beyond that, hidden behind the glare and the smoke, were the back streets where steam rose up from the sewers like mist. There, far away from the slot machines and the car horns, the only sound was the rustling of the rain and the wet smack of footsteps as Lil Potkin ran down the road, her shadow stretching and shrinking as she passed through the yellow pools of light beneath each street lamp.

She arrived at Paradise Street out of breath and just in time to see her bus, a lumbering double-decker, chug away in a cloud of black fumes. As it passed her, the back wheel sank into a pothole; Lil recoiled half a second too late and got slapped in the face by a wave of puddle water.

'Hey!' she spluttered, glaring after the disappearing rear lights. She tried to think of a good comeback while the grimy liquid dripped off the end of her nose, but nothing came to mind, and there was no one around to hear it anyway.

She looked at her watch, and then reluctantly turned to the waiting area. It was 8.35 p.m. She had half an hour to kill and nowhere better to kill it.

As she stepped through the automatic doors,

she was hit by the glare of fluorescent tube lights. The waiting room was a grid of chipped white tables bordered by pairs of plastic chairs, all securely bolted to the floor. High-level speakers leaked electronic background music, just loud enough to be annoying but not so loud that you could actually hear what song was playing. But it was warmer than outside, and it was dry.

Lil, a wiry twelve-year-old with cup-handle ears and a belly full of ambition, wore her hair cut into a bob with a short fringe and a signature yellow rain mac. A small rucksack, containing a well-thumbed book, a notepad and a nest of chewed pencils, was slung over her shoulders.

Wary citizens avoided the city centre after dark but Lil wasn't easily scared. She'd been stalking the streets for years, looking for a story, sticking her nose in where it didn't belong, waiting for a scoop big enough to get her onto the staff of the underground news pamphlet the *Klaxon*. She'd been unlucky with her previous cases – they had both come to nothing – but Lil knew that she just had to keep at it. Her hero, the great investigative journalist A. J. McNair, once said that 'news is everywhere, if you know where to look' and Lil's eyes were permanently peeled.

The waiting room had only a few inhabitants: a couple of stubble-faced night workers drinking tea; cleaners in overalls, probably on their way to factories or office blocks; and a large family clutching suitcases, who looked like they would be spending the night there.

On the opposite wall was a noticeboard. A muddle of flyers covered it, overlapping haphazardly, like they had been drawn there by a powerful paper magnet. Lil flicked back through the notices offering services rendered and items for sale until she caught sight of a crumpled and crayon-drawn plea half buried under adverts for cheap appliance sales.

LOST TOY! Help me find my best doll. PLEASE. He has one good eye and blue

trousers. Someone has taken him and never given him back. Even though he is all I've got.

Below there was a badly drawn picture of a winking egg character with arms and legs and a few strands of seaweed-like hair.

Lil blew out her cheeks. The doll obviously meant a lot to the kid; it wouldn't do any harm to make a few enquiries and, anyway, it was no worse than her last investigation, The Case of the Stolen Bin Lids, or the one before that, The Mystery of the Forgotten Laundry Bag.

There was an address she couldn't quite make out at the top of the note. Lil gave the page a sharp tug and as it came away a horrible feeling of dread crept over her: a whisper, like the draught of a cellar door opening onto a darkened staircase. A shadow flitted at the corner of her eye; she turned quickly but there was no one there.

Everyone was right where they had been. No, she looked again – there was a new face and it was staring right at her. Sitting by the window, only a few tables away, was a boy. His skin was so pale it was almost white, and the arms of his grey sweatshirt rode up, revealing his bony wrists.

Lil felt her ears turning red and let her eyes glide past, like she was just casually taking in the room, pretending she hadn't seen him. People didn't generally look right at you in Peligan; they kept their eyes to the ground, in case they saw anything they might have to do something about. Lil wasn't like that, but it didn't mean she liked being stared at.

Putting on a breezy stride, she made her way to an empty table and sat down, ignoring the grim sensation of soggy jeans pressing against her skin. Then, taking out her reporter's notebook, she pulled the pencil from its spiral binding and flipped the cover open with a well-rehearsed flick of the wrist.

She held the flyer up as though she was copying down details and used the cover to peer over it. The boy was still staring. Lil tucked her hair behind her ears and then untucked it again. *What was his problem?* She ignored him for as long as she could, chewing thoughtfully on the end of her pencil, then she drew a big bubble question mark on the next blank page of her notebook and coloured it in.

Eventually her curiosity got the better of her and she lowered the flyer.

He wasn't staring any more. A newspaper lay face up in front of him and he was absorbed in reading the cover story with his head bowed low and a lock of fair hair falling untidily over his forehead.

A man in a donkey jacket lurched into the seat opposite the boy and took the newspaper. The boy looked up but didn't say anything. The man licked his thumb, opened the paper and shook it out. After a minute, she saw him shiver and pull his jacket collar up. He looked about him uneasily, and then without a word he stood up, dropped the paper on the floor and moved to another table. The boy watched him go.

The lighting overhead buzzed and flickered.

Lil lowered the flyer a little more. She took in the boy's tattered trainers and the frayed hems of his jeans and felt bad for pretending she couldn't see him earlier. She had been thinking about getting a hot drink to pass the time; maybe she would get one for him too.

As she stood at the drinks machine looking at the choices, Lil flipped her coin with practised nonchalance. Out of the corner of her eye she could see that the boy was looking at her again – *probably pretty impressed by my coin flipping,* she thought – and dropped the coin. It rolled over to where he was sitting.

'Fantastic,' she said under her breath, and then out loud: 'Sorry. I dropped some money under your table.' The boy looked startled as she approached. He blinked uncertainly back at her.

Lil looked at the coin and then at the boy. 'It's right there.' She pointed. 'Could you reach down and get it for me?'

Only his Adam's apple moved as he gulped noisily.

'Too much trouble for you to just pass it to

me?' Lil frowned at him. 'Fine, keep it if you want; you look like you need it more than I do.' The boy just stared, his dark eyes round. 'You don't say much, do you?'

He shook his head, swallowed and then croaked, 'Sorry,' in a voice that sounded like it hadn't been used for a while

Lil shrugged. 'That's OK; some people say I talk too much.'

He gave her an awkward smile. Lil tucked her hair behind her ears and then untucked it again straight away and returned to the drinks machine.

As she stood there, waiting while the thin chocolate was squirted into the paper cups, a cold, creeping feeling began to spread through her bones. She glanced over her shoulder; someone was standing outside the automatic doors and they were stuck on open.

She carried the two cups over to the boy's table and held one out for him.

'Is that for me?' he said, like he couldn't really believe it was.

'You looked cold.'

'I am.'

His eyes were seriously dark, almost black. He frowned at the cup as if he was concentrating really hard. When he reached out to take it Lil noticed a deep scratch across the back of his hand. It distracted her just at the moment she passed the hot chocolate to him, and she felt her skin bloom into a fresh set of goose pimples. She let go of the cup too soon and it fell through their hands, hitting the floor in a watery brown splatter.

'I thought you had it,' said Lil. 'Sorry . . .'

The boy looked mortified. He sat there completely still, staring at the brown puddle.

'It's not the end of the world,' Lil said, chucking the discarded newspaper over it and swooshing it around with her foot. 'Here, have mine.' She held it out to him.

The boy hung his head.

'Go on, take it,' she insisted.

'No!' he shouted suddenly. 'I mean, it's OK. I don't want any.'

'Sure? It's not as bad as it looks.'

He nodded sadly. 'I'm sure.'

The strip lights buzzed and went off.

Lil had never been afraid of the dark, but in that moment, blinded by the sudden blackness, her heart began to race. A second later the emergency lights came on and the room was cast in a sickly green glow. The boy was still sitting there. He looked lost. Lil thought, *He probably doesn't have anywhere to go.* She reached into her pocket and pulled out the last of her money minus the bus fare. As she held the coins out to him she noticed her own hand was trembling, so she put the money on the table and pocketed her hand.

'There,' she said. 'You can buy another one, if you like.'

He didn't take the money and Lil wondered if maybe he was embarrassed to, but it was almost time to go, so she returned to her table to get her stuff. As she made for the doors a toothless old woman called after her. 'Are you just going to leave that money there?'

11

Lil paused and looked back to the table by the window.

The boy had gone.

The night bus home was almost empty. Lil climbed to the top deck and took a seat near the front. She half closed her eyes and leant her head against the window, where it gently bumped as the bus spluttered and chugged its way along the ring road, while Peligan City crawled slowly by, skulking behind the lines of street lamps.

She looked out at the patterns of light and shadow that mapped the city she knew better than the lines on her mother's face: the disused municipal gardens with empty rectangular lakes and boarded-up pavilions; the patterned grids of the tower blocks and lines of terrace houses.

Up ahead she could make out the glow of the bonfire-studded 'Saints' area, where slums had sprouted from the skeletal remains of the old town, and beyond that the cloudy yellow glimmer of the industrial quarter whose factories spat up flumes of smoke from their chimneys.

And there on the hill, towering above everything stood Fellgate Prison, known to all as 'the Needle', a floodlit high-rise that stretched up into the sky, skewering the smog like a giant stick of dirty candyfloss.

Chapter 2

Angel Lane

The thin grey terraces of Angel Lane backed onto the railway line that led far beyond Peligan, to other, better places. Every couple of hours the blare of a signal horn sounded, vibrations rattled the windows and doors, and a train shrieked past, trailing the shunting sound of the wheels, rhythmic as a heartbeat.

Lil lived at number ten. Once she was safely inside she gave her wet trainers a good wipe on the evening edition of the *Herald*, which was still lying on the doormat. Like every employee at City Hall, her mother got a free copy delivered every day, although it wasn't actually free as the subscription was subtracted from her pay. City Hall owned controlling shares in the *Herald* – so it never ran any political stories, especially not ones that criticised Mayor Dean or any of his business associates.

Lil rescued the pizza delivery menu for the Black Pug Eatery from the day's junk mail with a smile. Inside, crumpled and slightly damp, was her own copy of the *Klaxon*, in Lil's opinion the only source of news in Peligan that was worth reading. The *Klaxon* did run political stories, the kind the politicians didn't want anyone to read, and it was always delivered in secret, in menus for the Black Pug Eatery, although anyone who bothered to find out – as Lil had – knew that there was no such place.

Lil switched on all the lights and the TV and then went through to the kitchen to hunt for something to put into a sandwich. She settled for cheese, crisps and pickle and made two rounds, leaving one lot on a plate for her mum to eat when she got home. Then she picked up Waldo the hamster's cage and placed it on the table beside the old sagging settee so she could read the *Klaxon* to him before bed.

Lil chewed her sandwiches down to the crusts as she scanned the lead story, 'Nurse Blamed for Blaze', which cast doubt on the accidental nature of the recent death of Shirley Kreutz, a psychiatric nurse who had allegedly ignited a store of nitrous oxide in the basement of the city hospital and killed herself in the explosion. Then Lil turned straight to the Rotten Barrel column for the latest instalment of a political corruption exposé the paper had been running for months now.

City Hall was leaking like a bucket full of holes, and Lil's favourite columnist, Randall Collar (it was an alias, Lil had checked), was publishing information on dodgy deals and laundered funds on a weekly basis. It was clear the *Klaxon* was building a case, but the evidence so far was all circumstantial; somehow Collar had never managed to get his hands on the vital piece of information needed to bring the mayor to account.

Lil would have given anything to be in Randall Collar's shoes: a daring undercover reporter, risking it all in the name of truth and justice.

She already had a link to City Hall: her mother, Naomi Potkin, was an archivist in charge of the Public Records Department in the Mayor's Office, filing the right paperwork in the right folders and then placing them in the right drawers, but Lil wasn't allowed to visit her at work. City Hall was locked down tighter than a drum these days and she couldn't get past the lobby let alone to the twenty-fourth floor where the public records were kept – well out of the public's grasp.

Lil cut out the Rotten Barrel and folded it carefully. 'One day I'll get the scoop on all this,' she said as she stuffed the last of the crusts through the bars of Waldo's cage. 'You'll see.'

The hamster's eyes gleamed back at her.

An hour later in her tiny attic bedroom, Lil pulled the folded *Klaxon* article from her pocket and fixed it to the wall where she kept all the cuttings of the various stories she was following.

At the centre of the newsprint collage was a portrait: a silhouette of a man's head with a white question mark over the face. Few people knew what the great investigative reporter A. J. McNair had really looked like, but a smaller version of this monochrome image was always placed at top of his newspaper column, and the *Klaxon* had used it for his obituary: McNair had been killed in a freak drowning accident a few months before Lil was born.

'What do you think, McNair?' Lil said to the head. 'Do you think I'll get a chance at a scoop soon?' She fixed the corner of the picture where the sticky tack kept coming away from the wall. 'Or maybe Randall Collar could take me on, kind of like an apprentice, or something?' The black silhouette gazed eyelessly back.

Lil heard the familiar sound of a choked

engine coupled with the whine of an exhausted fan belt, which signalled that her mum was home at last.

'I better get some shut-eye,' she whispered to herself, climbing into bed. She turned off the lamp on her bedside table, pushed the book she was reading under her pillow and curled up on her side.

A few minutes later the stairs creaked and the door opened a crack. Through the filter of her eyelashes Lil saw a shaft of light cut across the room and her mother step into it.

'Lil? Are you asleep?'

No answer.

Naomi Potkin tucked the duvet round her daughter and brushed away the hair that had fallen across her forehead before planting a soft, light kiss there. 'Goodnight, little love,' she whispered, and then silently closed the door and crept back out and down the creaking attic stairs.

In the darkness that followed, Lil pondered the strange burnt-match smell that had accompanied her mother, but that was a mystery that could wait until the morning. As her eyelids started to droop she could just make out the outline of the portrait on the wall opposite. 'Night, then,' she said quietly, and fell instantly to sleep.

When she awoke it was still dark. The moon was high, lighting the room a ghostly grey, and she was cold – really cold. She pulled her duvet up under her chin, rolled over and nearly jumped out of her skin.

Someone was standing there, in front of the window. Their stooped outline divided the blind, a stick-man shadow against the moonlight. Lil sat bolt upright and slapped the light switch on. It was the boy from the bus station.

She fought the urge to scream. Leaping out of bed she grabbed her pen from the bedside table, the only weapon she'd thought she'd ever need, and brandished it. 'Stay back!' she warned. The small, thin Biro trembled in her grasp.

The boy peered at her uncertainly. 'You can see me?'

Lil lowered the pen, only slightly. 'Are you serious?'

He waited expectantly for an answer with the fingers of both hands tightly crossed.

Lil snorted derisively. 'Obviously I can see you. You're standing in the middle of the room.'

He sagged with relief.

'How did you even get in here?' Lil demanded.

'Your – your m-mum let me in,' the boy said.

Lil gave him what she liked to call her 'Penetrating Squint'. It was a look she'd been working on.

'I definitely think that my mum would not be OK about me having boys in my room. Especially boys she doesn't know. Especially boys *I* don't know.'

'We met at the bus station earlier.'

'I am not sure that qualifies you as someone-I-actually-know.' Lil took a step towards him but he backed away. She felt a chill creep up her arms and reached for her dressing gown,

This book is dedicated to Chamali & Michael and Kalinga & Monika, whose weddings came either side of the publication of this book. All the best for your own Happy Ever Afters!

Prologue

Kumari watched the Christmas decorations slide past as they drove up streets that were all too familiar. As always, there were crowd barriers up and crowds behind them, bundled up against the cold and waving. Today's car had tinted windows, so she didn't need to wave back. Up ahead, St Kildare's Hospital loomed. The lower floors had been decorated with lights. Even though it was still mid-afternoon, it was dark enough for the lights to show. She had worked there once. How strange to be going back as a guest of honour.

It hit her properly when she saw the exit for the under-ground station. The distinctive arch above the stairs clearly visible behind the crowds lining the streets. The last time she'd come up those stairs she had been a junior doctor, craving caffeine and sleep, on the way to start a morning shift. That was the last time she had been herself.

The limo she was in turned into the hospital approach. For the first time in months, Kumari felt the claw of panic in her chest.

She must have paled because Annie said, 'Ma'am? Are you OK?'

She looked at her, wild-eyed. 'Not really. I need a minute.'

Annie tapped on the glass and spoke to the driver. The car slowed to a crawl.

Kumari drew on her lessons and took deep breaths. In. Out. Calm. She'd had lessons for everything – how to sit, how to stand, how to eat, how to speak, how to wave and even how to breathe. All those lessons, all that training, undone in a second. It would have been funny if she wasn't feeling so awful right now.

Annie was watching her with concern. 'Ma'am?'

She held up a hand. How could she explain the disorientation of coming back to this place? The fact that she panicked every time she thought about the enormity of the changes in her life. Fairy tale? Not exactly. Surreal? Definitely.

St Kildare's Hospital was so familiar to her, yet she was a stranger to it now. She knew all too well that the freshly painted, patient-free wards that she was going to see bore no resemblance to the bustling places they would become.

She closed her eyes and centred herself. No longer was she the doctor who worked at the sharp end of a crisis. Nor was she the woman who spoke her mind, regardless of consequences, because doing what was right trumped everything else. No, she was someone completely different now.

Deep breath in. Deep breath out.

She opened her eyes and nodded to Annie. 'I'm ready now.'

Drawing on all the lessons she'd had on poise and posture, she stepped out of the car and she looked up at the hospital edifice. How in the world had this become her life? She used to be so sure of who she was and where she was going. She'd come so far, it was true . . . but was it better? Was this her? It certainly wasn't what she'd planned. She glanced over her shoulder as the car door shut behind her. To think that all this had started with a simple favour. That had begun with a limo ride too . . .

Making a Difference

Chapter 1
(Two years earlier)

The Standard

Golden Globe Awards shine a light on causes that support women

They came in two by two, wearing black. This year's red carpet was given over to black-swathed actors who arrived bringing as their dates activists who supported women's causes. Each actor and activist pair stopped to be photographed together and to talk about the charity they were supporting.

Dr Kumari Senavaka was sitting in the back of a limo, which was in the queue to reach the drop-off point at the theatre. Outside, camera flashes went off like fireworks. Kumari tried not to look. She focused on her hands, tightly clasped in her lap, and tried to remember how to breathe past the tightness that had appeared in her chest. Sitting next to her was the American actress Sabine Marshall, who was perfectly poised, as always. Sabine was a few years older than Kumari yet had managed to retain her flawless complexion.

Sabine's publicist, who had coordinated all this with the publicist from the Better For All charity, was running through last-minute checks. As a consultant for the charity, Kumari was there as an ambassador for the work they did. The publicist for the charity, Kumari's friend Ruby, had responded to an urgent call from one of Sabine's people and had suggested Kumari as the best person to represent the work the charity did on female empowerment. So here she was, jet-lagged and nervous, wearing the glitziest black dress she'd ever seen. She glanced at Sabine's embroidered sheath dress and corrected herself. The *second* glitziest black dress she'd ever seen.

'Got your statement, Kumari?' Sabine's publicist asked.

'Yes.' Kumari's throat felt dry and sandpapery. She didn't dare drink anything because she was sure she would mess up her lipstick or, worse, spill it on the dress and mess up the satin.

Sabine looked over at her and smiled. 'Relax, sweetie, you'll be fine. I'll do my bit. You do your statement. We'll get some photos and everyone will be talking about Better For All before the night is out.'

That was easy for her to say – she was used to the limelight and the uncomfortable shoes. Kumari was a doctor. There wasn't much call for sequins in her day job. Or publicity.

Kumari drew a shaky breath. This was for the project. She had to do it.

The car moved slowly forward. Camera flashes speckled the windows. The car stopped, perfectly lined up with the red carpet. Sabine did one last check of her make-up. 'OK,' she said. 'Come on, Kumari. Let's do this.'

Sabine made her grand entrance to the event and Kumari followed her out of the car. Once the car door shut behind her, she looked up and her heart almost stopped.

People were looking at her. There were cameras. Suddenly, she was back in primary school again. On stage. Being stared at. Nausea threatened. She wasn't five anymore. She swallowed hard and looked up at Sabine.

Sabine's smile didn't waver, but she caught Kumari's eye. She changed her pose so that she was able to touch Kumari's elbow, indicating that they should walk down the carpet. As she turned to wave, she whispered, 'Breathe.'

Kumari breathed, but she was doing it too fast. She kept her eyes on Sabine's clutch bag, a sparkling, black diamanté affair. Watch the bag. Ignore the cameras. Why on earth had she agreed to this? This wasn't the reason she got involved with Better For All. She was a doctor. She was supposed to be out there curing people, not being photographed with some film star she'd never met until that morning.

She got through the photographing, but when it came to giving her statement, she couldn't do it. She opened her mouth, but nothing came out.

Sabine stepped forward with perfect grace. 'I'm honoured to be here tonight, and even more honoured to be here with Dr Kumari Senavaka, who works with the incredible charity Better For All. The volunteers of Better For All do amazing work. They are dedicated to improving healthcare for families in the developing world.' She looked meaningfully at Kumari.

Focus, focus, focus. Kumari drew another deep breath. Steadier this time. Ignoring the cameras as best she could, she kept her gaze on Sabine. 'Thanks, Sabine,' she said. Her voice shook. She had repeated the statement so often that now Sabine had started her off on the first sentence, the rest was there, ready to be said.

'At Better For All we are dedicated to improving healthcare for families in the developing world. Our special focus is on reducing child mortality, which can be achieved through a variety of initiatives, including childbirth clinics, vaccination programmes and setting up temporary clinics in times of disease outbreaks. We have already saved many children from painful and unnecessary deaths. We hope to save many more in the future.'

She was speaking too fast. She tried to slow down. 'We are hoping to add healthcare education to our list of projects soon, because educating girls on basic healthcare is the best way to improve the health of future generations.'

That last sentence wasn't part of the official statement. Instead it was something Kumari herself passionately believed in. Ruby had let her add it as an extra incentive for her to go to this event.

Sabine beamed at her, as though she were a best friend.

'Kumari's been working at a vaccination clinic in Lesotho,' she said to one of the reporters, as though imparting a great confidence.

They posed for a few more pictures and Kumari managed to maintain a smile for all of them. She had done her bit. Now that she had publicly linked healthcare education for girls to Better For All, they would have to take it more seriously.

As soon as they got away from the press lines, Kumari felt the vice in her chest loosen. Finally, she could take a full breath. She breathed out and felt her heart rate slow down, but the aftermath of the panic made her feel hollow and sick.

'It's scary the first time,' Sabine said. 'I remember what it was like.' She patted Kumari's arm. 'You did OK.'

Kumari decided she liked Sabine.

A few minutes later a semi-famous actor came up to talk to Sabine and despite Sabine's best efforts to include her, Kumari was ignored. No one actually wanted to talk to her. Everyone wanted to talk to the famous person.

Kumari amused herself by spotting other famous people. Her best friend, Lucy, had been incredibly jealous of her having the chance to go to the Golden Globe Awards. The least she could do was keep a tally of all the famous people she saw 'in real life'. Although, she reflected, looking around, there was very little that was 'real life' in the room.

Real life, for Kumari, meant a flight back to the UK and the start of a new short contract working at a hospital soon after that. She also had to write a pitch applying for funding for the education project she was hoping to get started. Since she was still a consultant for Better For All, it seemed best to apply to them first.

She felt another wave of exhaustion wash over her. This event was one of the weirdest things she'd done for the charity. She'd only agreed to go because she hoped it would boost the chances of getting her Boost Her! project funded.

Around her there was a general drift towards the main hall. Sabine caught her eye and motioned Kumari to walk with her. She trailed behind the actress, trying not to gawp at the finery around her. After a year in a remote vaccination clinic, the lights and sparkle and gold paint were a sensory overload.

Chapter 2

Fast Light News

Prince Benedict supports initiative to catalyse change from within

HRH Prince Benedict will be at the Better For All charity event tonight to hear pitches for future charity projects. The prince, 32, has now retired from active service and is taking on more royal duties. Although he is taking his role as patron for a number of charities quite seriously, the prince is well known for his lavish partygoing lifestyle.

Better For All, a charity specialising in bringing good health to children in rural communities in the developing world, is celebrating its ten-year anniversary by setting up two new charitable projects. The suggestions for projects have come entirely from people already working with the organisation.

'Often the people who know what is needed the most are those on the ground, working in the communities we help,' said a spokesperson for the charity. 'We are aware that sometimes the real message can get lost by the time an initiative has gone through several layers of planning. So, in order to be sure that our projects are addressing genuine needs, we have asked our own volunteers and

consultants to suggest projects to be funded. We have been amazed and humbled by the response.'

Several small grants have now been awarded to suggestions that involve only small changes to the way things are currently done.

There remains a competition for two large grants. Tonight, there will be a special pitch event where eight speakers will each be allowed five minutes to impress the board. Of these, up to four projects will be chosen to submit an expanded proposal. Two of these projects will be funded. The prince will hear all of the pitches, even though he won't be one of the judges.

The prince said, 'I'm looking forward to hearing about the innovative and practical ways in which Better For All will be bringing healthcare to children in the next ten years.'

Kumari checked the pins holding her sari in place one last time. She wished that Sri Lankan genes came with the natural ability to wear a sari, but being born and bred British meant she was almost as clueless as the next person. Her mother had shown her how to get into a sari, but she hadn't had much practice at it. The last thing she needed this evening was a wardrobe malfunction.

'Stop fussing, Kumari.' Her friend Lucy batted her hand away. 'You'll do more harm than good if you loosen it.' They were in the sparkling new toilets of the newly refurbished building of the Better For All charity. Everything smelt like it was fresh out of its wrapping.

Kumari turned and checked her make-up in the mirror. Lucy had done a good job. In the peacock-blue sari, with her hair pulled back, Kumari thought she looked like a taller, straight-haired version of her mother; she had the same high cheekbones and full mouth. From her father she'd inherited a golden-brown complexion and those vital extra inches of height, which took her from her mother's short stature to almost average.

'Ready?' Lucy asked.

As they turned to go, Ruby came in. She gave Kumari a swift glance up and down. 'You look lovely. Presentation all good to go?'

'Yes. It's all loaded onto the system.' Kumari gave her a half-hearted smile. She had known Ruby since university. They had met because some drunken guy had asked if Kumari and Ruby were sisters, simply because they were both the same colour. Ruby, half-Jamaican, half-Irish, and all south London, had soon set the guy straight. She and Kumari had been friends ever since.

'Excellent,' said Ruby. 'This evening is really important. With Prince Benedict coming to hear the pitches we should have lots of press attention for the fund, and maybe for the individual projects too.'

Kumari shot a glance at Lucy. The idea of press attention made her palms sweat. 'Great.'

She had hoped that the Golden Globes thing would help ease her nerves about being in the public spotlight, but it turned out it had just made things worse.

'Relax, babe, you'll be fine.' Ruby whipped out a tube of lipstick and touched up the scarlet on her lips. 'We've got a great line-up. Greg Frankish is doing a pitch for a photo documentary on our humanitarian work. It could open the world's eyes to what we're doing. He's so talented; his presentation is bound to be brilliant.' She popped her lips and put the tube of lipstick away. 'Hopefully, we'll get loads of donations too. Who knows? Some people might even take their lead from you and take a sabbatical so they can volunteer.'

Lucy took Kumari's arm. 'Come on, Kumari, let's get to our seats.'

'See you later, Ruby.' Kumari picked up the peacock-blue silk at the front of her sari so that she didn't tread on it. She didn't need to, but it made her feel like she was less likely to trip up this way.

'You're going to be great,' Lucy told her. 'You've practised this presentation so much, you'll be brilliant.'

The hall was already almost full. Smartly dressed people sat towards the front. Meeting the prince meant the men were in suits and the women in bright, wedding-worthy dresses. Kumari spotted a few people, less well dressed, wearing lanyards with 'Press' written on them, some of them carrying some serious photographic equipment.

'Ugh,' Kumari said. 'Cameras.' Fear clawed at her chest. She gripped her paperwork and reminded herself that this wasn't a performance. She was there to pitch her project idea for funding. She'd made it this far onto the longlist of projects. She just needed to persuade them that the project needed to be on the shortlist and she was in with a good chance of 'winning' the funding.

'You look great. You'll be fine. These people are only here to see Prince Benedict.' Lucy's voice rose a little when she said his name.

Kumari smiled at her friend. 'And you look fab. In case he's looking.'

She had brought Lucy along as her plus one for this event partly for moral support, but partly because she knew about Lucy's mad, fan-girl crush on Prince Benedict.

She saw Lucy to her seat and then gave her own name to an impossibly polished young person with a clipboard who was standing at the foot of the stage.

'Hi, Kumari.' A tall black man bounded over from the audience.

'Oh, hi, Victor.'

'Got everything you need?' Victor had helped her pull together the presentation and hone the pitch. A father of three daughters, when he heard about Kumari's project idea, he had leapt in to help.

'I think so,' she said.

'I've been looking at the other pitches,' said Victor. 'I think we've got a pretty good chance of getting in.'

Before she could reply a man walked across. 'Dr Senavaka, we need to get you on the stage,' he said briskly. He was looking at Victor, who looked back at him, puzzled.

Seriously? He had really just done that? 'I'm Dr Senavaka,' Kumari said.

'Oh,' said the man. 'It's just . . .' He checked his notes, as though there would be something informative there.

'Anyway. If you could get on stage, please? The prince is on his way, we'll be starting soon.' He pointed to the stage and bustled off.

Not even an apology. Kumari glared after him. 'How rude.'

'Idiot,' said Victor. 'Anyway, good luck, Kumari. You'll be great.'

Her anger at the other man kept her going as she marched towards the stage. How dare he assume that Victor was the speaker? Just because the title was 'Dr' he had assumed it had to be a man. The cheek of it.

She lifted up the whispering silk around her legs and climbed the steps. This evening wasn't about her. This evening was about money. She and the other people on the stage had only one job – to highlight the need and make people feel moved enough to get involved and to fund their project proposals.

She was shown to her assigned seat. There were two men already there, on their feet, chatting to each other. The older guy must be the professor who was talking about 3D-printed prosthetics; she thought his project sounded interesting. The other was . . . Greg Frankish. Brilliant photo-journalist. Well-known sleazeball.

'Kumari,' Greg said.

'Greg.' She shook hands with him and moved away from the proffered kiss on the cheek. It wasn't a big deal. When she was at university, she had gone out with his best friend for a few weeks. The trouble was, in those weeks, Greg had propositioned her twice. Still, that was a long time ago. Maybe he'd grown up in the meantime.

He looked her up and down in a way that made her skin crawl. Maybe not then. 'It's good to see you,' he said.

She forced a smile. 'You, too.'

Thankfully, she didn't have to carry on the conversation because the chairman of the charity approached them.

'Greg,' he said, slapping the younger man on the shoulder. 'How the devil are you?'

'Vince, good to see you. How's Martina?'

'Fine, fine. Just wanted to come and say hello and wish you luck,' the director said. He suddenly seemed to remember that there were other people there besides Greg. 'And everyone else too, of course.'

Kumari caught the eye of the professor and got the feeling he was thinking the same as she was. Greg knew the director. So he already had one vote on the deciding committee. She sighed. Sometimes it was like trying to push water up a hill.

Ruby came over. 'You know the rules, yes? We're trying to keep this sharp and snappy. I have a buzzer here.' She held up a tiny device. 'I'll ring it when your five minutes are up. You have to stop. No excuses.'

'Can we finish the sentence we started?' someone asked.

'No. Five minutes. No more,' said Ruby. 'And then there's five minutes for questions.'

Kumari had already given Lucy some questions to ask, in case no one else did.

'Right,' said Ruby. 'The prince will be here soon and then we can get this thing started.' She strode off to terrorise someone else.

'She's scary,' said the professor.

'No,' said Kumari. 'She's nervous. She's normally good fun.'

'Friend of yours, is she?'

'Yes.' Not as close as they once were, but still friends.

They sat down on the chairs next to the stage and waited. The professor hummed 'Someday My Prince Will Come'. When Kumari looked askance at this, he smiled and said, 'Sorry. Granddaughters.' He showed her a photo of two little girls on his phone.

'Do you have children?' he asked, then added. 'I suppose you're too young.'

She wasn't. At thirty, she was plenty old enough. Once upon a time, she'd even planned on having a family, but she had to get her career to the right place first. In the meantime, her marriage had broken down and that window had closed. She smiled politely at the professor and didn't reply.

Increased activity at the far end of the room suggested the prince had arrived. She looked across. At first, she couldn't see him, but she could track his progress by the raised arms and camera-phone flashes as people tried to record their brush with fame. She stretched to see, then felt silly. He was just a man. An accident of birth had put him in a place of privilege. He hadn't actually done anything to earn his fame. Why should she feel honoured to meet him? She was a doctor and a humanitarian aid worker. She saved lives. The professor would be giving amputees the chance to earn a living again. Even slimy Greg travelled the world photographing communities and shining the light of scrutiny on the plight of people who needed help. If anything, the prince should feel honoured to meet *them*.

She turned her head and caught Greg looking at her. The look made her shudder.

'I can tell what you're thinking,' he said, out of the corner of his mouth. 'Why should we kowtow to some tosser whose only achievement is to have rich and powerful parents?'

Even though she had just thought that very thing, she felt she had to defend the prince. 'He served in the army though, right?'

'Pah. Probably an officer. Sandhurst and dinner parties,' said Greg.

She knew that he'd done active service. She knew a great deal of trivia about the prince. You couldn't share a flat with Lucy and not know stuff.

The entourage rounded the corner and she tried not to be interested. He was just a guy. A hot guy, her hindbrain supplied. The prince's gaze looked in her direction and, suddenly, she was looking straight into his eyes. He had the most amazing blue eyes. For a second, she forgot to breathe.

The prince blinked and turned to Ruby to ask a question. Kumari breathed out slowly. Her heart was hammering. What had just happened? Had she just had a 'moment' with Prince Benedict? Surely not.

Greg made a small noise in his throat and pulled out his phone. 'I wish I had a proper camera.' He quickly framed and took some photos and showed them to her. Even at speed, he'd got a few good ones. Kumari was impressed.

'I can sell those,' he muttered and put his phone away.

Kumari rolled her eyes. 'Always on duty, Greg?'

He raised his eyebrows at her. She looked away.

The cameras came nearer and she felt her hands get clammy. She tried to find Lucy, but everyone was bunched up along the path the prince was taking so it was impossible. She looked at the prompts she had on her piece of paper. If she remembered the first line, she would be OK. Everything was going to be fine. Out of the eight pitches, four would be chosen for round two, which meant she had a fifty per cent chance that her project would get on the shortlist. That wasn't bad odds. Especially when her project was so important. This was a clear chance to make a difference. It was going to be fine.

Once the Prince had taken his seat, it took a further few minutes for everyone to settle. Ruby took to the stage. They were on a tight schedule, she explained. Each speaker got five minutes. Then five minutes for questions.

Kumari tried to focus on her breathing. Don't look at the crowd. Breathe. Breathe. She was speaking fifth, so she had to sit through a few of the other presentations. They were all so good. Greg did a nice sound bite about sunlight disinfecting while it illuminated. Something to do with his camera letting sunlight into things forgotten in the dark. Damn. She needed a sound bite. She and Victor had tried, but hadn't really come up with anything convincing. There was 'the rising tide raises all boats', but that sounded lame now she was on the stage.

'Next up,' said Ruby, 'we have Dr Kumari Senavaka, with her project, Boost Her! – empowerment through education.'

Kumari walked up to the lectern and picked up the device to click through the slides. Her presentation was behind her on the screen. She turned to the audience, the first line of her prepared speech all ready to go . . . and froze.

She stared wildly at the crowd of people in front of her, trying to find Lucy or Victor, someone to focus on. But panic made it impossible to find anything. Instead, she found herself staring at Prince Benedict. His brow furrowed. Suddenly, completely unexpectedly, he winked at her. She was so surprised that it shocked her brain back into action. Oh no. How many precious seconds had she wasted?

She clicked on to the first slide – 'The rising tide raises all boats' – and flashed past it. She came to the slide with a young woman staring into the camera. 'This is Hopeful, from Lesotho,' she said, keeping her focus on the girl on the screen. 'She was eighteen when this photo was taken. By this time, she had lost three children to cholera. When her fourth child was born, she heard of a clinic several miles away that was giving injections that stopped children getting ill. She walked, carrying her baby, for two days to get to us. Her son, Nimo, was very weak when they arrived at the clinic and they had to stay. Hopeful couldn't read or write, but she was bright. She listened to what the medics around her were saying about vaccination and started repeating it to the mothers waiting in the queue.' She clicked to a slide showing Hopeful, all smiles, with baby Nimo in her arms, and an inset of the queue outside the clinic. 'About a week after Hopeful and Nimo went home, we had an influx of people coming to us from her village.'

She clicked on to a slide with statistics. 'Hopeful became an ambassador for health. She took with her information about vaccination, about the benefits of boiling water before using it for food or formula, about basic hygiene. She used everything she learnt to make a difference. The Boost Her! initiative is about providing young women like Hopeful with basic skills for healthcare, hygiene and midwifery, so that they can help the people around them while supporting their families. By helping these girls and women raise—'

The buzzer went off, cutting her off mid-sentence. Ruby gave her an apologetic smile. Rules were rules. 'Any questions? We have five minutes.'

A few hands went up including, to Kumari's mortified surprise, the prince's. Ruby nearly fell over in her haste to get the microphone to him.

'Why are you focusing on educating girls specifically? Education is important for both genders,' he said.

What kind of a question was that? At least it gave her a chance to say the things she had missed off the end of her presentation. 'If you want to raise the general level of welfare in a country,' she said, looking straight at him, 'you start by educating the women. Women are largely responsible for the care and teaching of children outside of the classroom. A woman will pass that education down to her children. These children, both male and female, will grow up with basic knowledge that can be built on. Real change doesn't happen in a week or a year. Real change takes a generation.'

He nodded.

There was another question about mortality rates in Lesotho, which she answered and then the buzzer went off, indicating her time was up.

Kumari tried to pick up her notes, but her hands started to shake so badly she couldn't. She left them on the lectern and fled the stage.

Lucy came and found her in the bathroom a few minutes later. 'You did it,' she said, giving her a hug.

Kumari shook her head. She was still shaking. 'I screwed up. It was . . .' She closed her eyes, just thinking about being on stage made her stomach lurch. 'Awful.'

'It was a bit messed up at first, but you got it back. And Prince Benedict asked you a question. You actually spoke to Prince Benedict! How awesome is that?'

'I'm not sure it counts as actually speaking to him,' she said weakly. 'He asked a few questions to the others as well.' She remembered that he'd winked at her. And questioned her focus on girls. She frowned. 'I'm not sure he's the hero you think he is, Lucy.'

'But his question gave you the chance to talk about the long-term benefits,' said Lucy. She pulled out her phone.

'Look, I've got some pics of him. I'm hoping to get a few more. You might even get to shake his hand.'

Less than half an hour later, Kumari was standing in line with the rest of the presenters, waiting to be introduced to the prince. He walked along the line, a cameraman following him, shaking hands and saying how much he enjoyed the presentations. He didn't have any influence in the decision about who got into the second round, but she supposed it was nice of him to say.

She was still nervous. Did she have to curtsey? She tried to see if the woman two places up the line curtsied, but couldn't see.

The prince came up to her. The camera was right behind him. Kumari dropped into a curtsy. As she straightened back up, her heel caught in her sari and she pitched forward. The prince caught her, his forearms against hers.

For a split second, her eyes met his. Oh no. Embarrassment flooded through her.

The prince gently pushed her back, so that she was fully upright again.

'I'm so sorry,' she murmured.

'That's OK. Makes life interesting.'

'I'm not used to wearing a sari . . .' Now she was making it worse. 'Sorry.'

He smiled. He had a really lovely smile. Really . . . lovely. Her mind went blank.

'I enjoyed your presentation,' he said. 'My sisters are very interested in women's education.'

'And you?' she said. 'What do you think?'

'Me . . . I think it's very important. Everyone has the right to education and it's to our shame that women are still denied it.'

She was impressed. 'That's good to hear.' There was a pause that stretched for a heartbeat. Two.

Prince Benedict dropped his gaze and one of the security guys stepped forward. She realised she was still holding his arm. She released it. A camera clicked. 'Oh no. I'm so sorry,' she said. 'Again.'

'Don't worry about it.' The prince gave her a friendly grin and moved on.

Kumari wanted to hide. Her face was ablaze. More cameras clicked. She looked around, searching for a way out, and spotted Greg looking at his phone and grinning. She stared at him. Bugger. He'd got photos of her making an idiot of herself. He saw her looking at him and took another picture of her. The grin he gave her was disturbing. He was planning something. It made her very nervous indeed.

Chapter 3

Metropolitan Herald

A right royal faux pas

Everyone knows you don't touch a royal until invited to do so. And you definitely don't throw yourself at them. One young woman who met Prince Benedict yesterday at a charity event was so excited that she tripped while attempting a curtsy and ended up in the prince's arms, making her the envy of hundreds of women everywhere.

The prince took it in good humour and helped her back to her feet. The woman was so enthralled that she held onto his arm and had to be reminded to let go by his security officer.

Photo caption: Young woman who can't let go. [Photo credit: Greg Frankish]

Lucy showed her the paper the next day and Kumari sank further into the sofa and buried her face in a cushion. 'Oh God,' she groaned. 'They are going to rip the piss out of me at work, aren't they?'

'Well, yes,' said Lucy. 'Mercilessly.'

It was a rare day when they were both at home and didn't have to recover from a night shift. Kumari was working in

A & E and Lucy was an anaesthetist in the same hospital. Despite sharing a flat, sometimes they went for days without seeing each other.

'It's a nice photo of you, though,' said Lucy. 'You look all willowy and tall in that sari.'

'And stupid,' said Kumari. The picture most papers had chosen to use showed her looking up at Prince Benedict with dawning horror a second or two after he'd caught her.

Lucy didn't disagree. She picked up a different paper. 'And this one's got a really nice shot of His Royal Hotness.'

Kumari groaned again. She had met Lucy when she spent a year as an exchange student at Duke University in North Carolina. Within a few days they'd discovered a shared love of British comedy and they'd been friends ever since. When Kumari returned to England, Lucy came to visit. She loved it so much that, a year later, she applied for a job in London. With Kumari starting work as a junior doctor in London, they'd decided to become housemates once more.

'I think I might add this one to the board of hotness,' said Lucy.

Kumari peered out from under the cushion. 'Let's see.'

Lucy thrust the paper towards her. 'Go on. Even you have to admit that he's gorgeous. He's got the most amazing eyes. And that butt . . .' Lucy gave a little shiver. 'The things I could do to that man . . .'

'Thinking out loud again.' Kumari laughed.

'Sorry.'

Kumari looked at the photo. It was a good one. He was smiling and turning away. She realised it must have been taken shortly before the handshake debacle. She looked at the photo credit. Sure enough, Greg Frankish again. He must have acted fast to sell his images so quickly.

The phone rang. 'I'll get it.' Lucy closed the small distance between the sofa and the breakfast bar where the phone sat. The flat was small and mostly open plan. The breakfast bar essentially separated the little kitchen from the living room. On a good day, when the place was tidy and the sun was shining through the one large window, you could call it homely. Mostly, it was just a mess.

'Oh hi, Rukmali. Have you seen the papers?'

Kumari sighed. Her mother. Probably the second biggest fan of the royals after Lucy. She listened as Lucy squealed about having been in the same room as Prince Benedict.

'Oh sure, I'll get her.'

Lucy brought the handset over to Kumari before resuming her quest to find a pair of scissors.

'Hi, Amma,' Kumari said.

'So . . .' said her mother. 'How did your pitch go?'

'It was OK. I stumbled a bit at the start, but I think I got all the information across.' She smiled. 'I know you're more interested in what happened when I met the prince.'

'No. No. I genuinely do want to know how the pitch went. You were so nervous,' said her mother. 'I knew you would be fine. You always are.'

'Thanks. I guess I was nervous. So much so that I made a complete idiot of myself when I met the prince.'

'Yes, what happened there?' The quickening in her voice was palpable.

'I dunno. I tripped on my sari trying to curtsy and when he helped me up . . . my mind just went blank.'

Lucy shouted something about His Royal Hotness from the kitchen. Kumari pretended to throw a cushion at her.

'Well, they are very nice photos of you,' said Amma. 'Sonali Aunty said the sari looks lovely.'

Kumari groaned. Sonali Aunty, Amma's friend, lived in Australia. 'How does Sonali Aunty know?'

'It's on the Internet,' said Amma.

Which meant that everyone knew. Oh no. That meant that not only were her work colleagues and medical school friends going to tease her, all over the world people were looking up the woman who didn't know how to curtsy without falling over. 'Remind me not to look at Facebook for . . . at least a week.'

Later, she cautiously checked her phone and saw that there were several comments on her Facebook timeline. Most of them fell either into the 'Omigod you met the prince' category, or the 'Forgotten how to shake hands?' category. She decided to ignore them all. She was just about to put the phone back in her pocket when it rang.

'It's Ruby.'

Kumari frowned. It was too early for it to be a result about who had won the pitch contest. Ruby would still be working on the coverage of the night before. 'Hi, Ruby,' she said cautiously.

'Hello,' said Ruby. 'Listen, Kumari, I've got kind of a weird favour to ask you.'

Kumari sat up. 'OK . . .'

'I need you to go out to dinner with someone.'

'That's . . . who is it?' She picked up her plate with the sandwich crumbs on and walked across to the kitchen. There was no response from Ruby.

'Ruby?' she said.

'That's just it,' said Ruby. 'I can't tell you. It's a blind date. Look. I've met him. He's really nice.'

'But why does he want to go on a date with me? Why doesn't he want me to know who he is?' said Kumari. 'That makes no sense.'

Lucy, in the kitchen, had turned and was listening in.

'I know. The thing is, his . . . friend contacted me and asked me to get in touch with you . . .'

Oh, right. As if the whole thing wasn't weird enough already. 'Ruby, I appreciate you thinking of me, but I'm not looking for a relationship at the moment.'

'Please,' Ruby wailed. 'I need you to do me this favour. You owe me. I got you the Golden Globes gig so that you could seed the idea for your Boost Her! project.'

As Kumari remembered, Ruby had needed someone to go to the Golden Globes at short notice, so they had both benefited from the arrangement. But, as Lucy kept pointing out to her, most normal people would have loved the chance to go to the Golden Globes.

'You owe me. Big time,' Ruby said. She sighed. 'Besides, it'll do you good. When was the last time you went on a date?'

Kumari ran her hand through her hair and sighed when her fingers were stopped by a snarl. 'OK. OK. Fine. I'll do it. And then we're even, OK?'

'Brilliant.' Ruby's voice lost all trace of anger. 'Can you email me your schedule for the next two weeks and I'll get my . . . friend to check with Ben. Thank you, mate. You're a star.'

Kumari hung up and suddenly felt exhausted. She needed a shower and then to fall into bed. It was only in the shower that it occurred to her that Ruby's gratitude had been a little over the top. She had agreed to go on a date with a friend of a friend. Why was it such a big deal to Ruby? There must be more to this. She frowned. Knowing Ruby, this friend she was talking about had something that could influence her career. Or Ruby fancied the friend.

She turned the water off and stepped out of the shower, her mind still pondering Ruby's request. They were so different: Kumari's focus had always been on medicine and her humanitarian work, whereas Ruby was fiercely ambitious. Sometimes she wondered why they were still friends. She was just a doctor, after all. Not even a particularly successful one. Kumari sighed. She had hoped that her time in Africa would reignite her passion for medicine. In a way, it had. Seeing tears in the eyes of a mother whose baby had been brought back from the brink . . . if that didn't reaffirm your belief in the profession, nothing could. But it had also made her see just how much work there was to do. There were so many people in need and so few resources to go round.

Being back in the UK, doing A & E rotations again, she could see that resources were stretched here too, but the scale was not comparable. Just that night, she'd had a patient berate her for being kept waiting. It had taken a superhuman effort to remain calm, especially when she considered the queues of people who had waited patiently to be seen in the field clinic, often carrying children for whom the treatment meant the difference between life and death. She had already applied to go back. She could only do so much as a consultant for Better For All. Or even as a member of staff there. But if

31

the Boost Her! project got funded. Oh, then . . . then she could make a real difference.

Back in her room, her phone beeped. Oh great. More people had found her unwanted tabloid fame. Turning it to silent, she put it face down without looking at it.

Chapter 4

Rules to observe when you meet a member of the Royal Family

Don't be like Kumari Senavaka. Know your royal etiquette:

Rule 1: Don't touch them. Don't initiate a hand-shake. Certainly, don't throw yourself at them!

Rule 2: No selfies. The royals are not allowed to take selfies. You may ask someone else to take a photo, but no standing up close.

Rule 3: Show respect. Gentlemen bow and ladies curtsy to the queen. Although the younger royals don't insist on bows and curtsies, you may still want to, especially if you're meeting Princess Helena because she is the future queen.

Rule 4: Use proper forms of address. No first names please. The queen should always be addressed as 'Your Majesty' at first and then 'ma'am'. The princes and princesses should be addressed as 'Your Highness' in the first instance and then 'sir' or 'ma'am' as appropriate.

Rule 5: When the queen arrives, stand up.

Kumari double-checked Google maps. This was definitely the place. The text that Ruby had sent said, *Dress smart, but nothing over the top. Think upmarket wine bar.* So Kumari was wearing black trousers and a dressy top. Her standard going-out outfit, although she hadn't actually gone out anywhere for months now.

The bar looked small from the outside. She couldn't see very much through the windows, but it gave a gold and brown glow. She was early, but she couldn't very well stand out in the cold, so she stepped in. The place had a Moroccan vibe, with deep reds, browns and golds. Lamps with delicately carved bronze shades cast complicated patterns on the walls. A small bar, set a little way into the room, made the front look small and cosy. There were a few tables where people were sitting, talking and drinking cocktails. From here, she could see that the cosiness was an illusion. The place extended back a long way. The bar and clusters of tables had been artfully placed to break the room up, making it a series of small nooks, rather than a large, impersonal expanse. Clever.

She looked around and a waiter appeared, seemingly out of nowhere. 'Can I help you, madam?'

'I'm here to meet someone. I believe we have a table booked under the name of Ruby Codding?' Ruby had been very specific that she should give Ruby's full name when asked about the reservation.

'Ah yes,' said the waiter. He hadn't even consulted anything. He must have a full list of bookings stored in his head. Kumari, who could barely recall a shopping list if it wasn't to do with work, was impressed.

She followed him past the bar. More nooks and cosy booths. At the end of the long room, they turned a corner. These rooms were brighter. He showed her to a side room and offered to hang up her coat. She asked if, rather than take it to a cloakroom, she could keep it with her. He hung it up on a hook, discreetly tucked into a corner of the room.

'This is your table, madam. Can I get you a drink while you're waiting? We have a wine list . . .' He gestured to a folder lying on a table set with two chairs. He whipped away a red-and-gold marker with 'Reserved' written on it.

The chairs were upholstered in artfully mismatched prints. It shouldn't have worked, but, somehow, it did. It was all tremendously chic and trendy. Kumari at once felt out of place. Even in the days when she had gone out, she tended to prefer places that did a decent plate of chips or, if it was daytime, cake.

She took a seat, but didn't open the wine list. 'I'll have . . . a fresh orange juice please. If you have it.'

'Of course we have it.' He smiled. 'Would you like ice with that?'

'No, thanks.'

He gave the smallest of bows and left, leaving her alone in the room.

She looked around. There was a wall of books, all with red, brown or gold spines. There were a few tables, but she noticed they all had 'Reserved' markers on them. She checked her watch. Ruby had said eight o'clock. There was still three minutes to go. Her phone beeped in her bag.

It was a text from Lucy: *What's he like?*

She texted back: *He's not here yet. This place is well posh.*

The waiter reappeared with her drink and disappeared again. Kumari took a sip and flipped open the wine and cocktails list. She spotted the prices and nearly choked.

Carefully, she swallowed about a quid's worth of orange. Wow.

A shadow at the door. She looked up and the waiter was back. He showed someone in and took his coat.

'Hello,' her date said.

It couldn't be. It took a few seconds for her brain to catch up. She scrambled to her feet. When Ruby had said his name was Ben . . .

'Oh please, Kumari, don't stand up.'

Should she curtsy? 'Prince Benedict. Er . . . Your Highness.'

'Call me Ben.' He held out his hand.

She shook it, still too startled to speak properly. This time she made sure she let go promptly.

He gestured for her to sit and, once she lowered herself back into the chair, he sat opposite her.

'So, I'm guessing you didn't know it was me you were meeting?'

'No.' She shook her head. 'I mean, Ruby said you were called Ben.'

'Which I am.' He smiled. Such a nice smile. She inclined her head to acknowledge that.

'It's probably better this way. The whole Prince Benedict thing sometimes gets in the way a bit when I meet people who are—'

'Common?' she said.

He raised an eyebrow. 'No,' he said quietly, but very firmly. 'Who are not in my usual social circles.'

'In other words, common.'

He watched her for a few seconds, his lips pressed together. The corners of his mouth twitched, like he was fighting a smile. You never saw this sort of thing on TV. He was normally serious or smiling broadly. This was . . . different. More human. 'I think I can see why your friend didn't tell you.'

She didn't have an answer to that. She needed to up her game. She picked up her orange juice and took another few pounds' worth of juice.

The waiter appeared, as though he'd sensed a gap in the conversation. Prince Benedict . . . Ben, picked up the cocktail menu. 'Where are the non-alcoholic cocktails?' When the waiter directed him to the right page, he ordered a Virgin Mary.

Kumari was surprised. She had assumed that he'd be drinking alcohol. She tried to remember what she'd read about him. She wasn't much of a royal-watcher, unlike Lucy. All she could remember was that the prince was a bit of a party animal and had had a string of very well-groomed girlfriends. She wasn't too sure about the girlfriends, but she was fairly certain he'd been photographed dancing semi-naked somewhere.

'Is something the matter?' he said.

'You're not drinking.' Oh God, Kumari. Accuse him of being an alcoholic, why don't you? 'I'm sorry, that came out wrong. It's just that . . . I expected. Um . . .'

He looked directly at her. Startlingly blue eyes. 'You shouldn't believe everything you read in the papers,' he said.

She felt the heat in her cheeks. 'Sorry.' She looked down at her hands, one was curled into a fist, the other was clutching her juice glass like her life depended on it. This meeting was not going well. Even though she kept telling herself she was ambivalent about the royal family, here she was acting like a moron because she'd met one of them. He was just a guy. Quite a good-looking guy too, but that was irrelevant. She could do better than this. Slowly, she forced herself to relax her hands.

She looked up. So did he. They both said 'Sorry,' at the same time and laughed, small embarrassed laughs. He said, 'Please, go ahead.'

'I was going to say, please can we start again.' She hoped that didn't sound too stupid.

He smiled again. A quick mercurial smile that transformed his face into the one she'd seen so many times in the papers. 'That's a great idea.'

'OK.'

He sat up straight and cleared his throat. 'Hi. I'm Ben.'

'I'm Kumari. It's nice to meet you.'

They shook hands again. This time, it wasn't as awkward.

'So,' she said, 'why did you want to meet me?'

He looked down for a second before replying. 'Why does any guy ask to meet a pretty girl?'

'Oh.' She felt her face heat up again. That had nothing to do with him being a prince. It had everything to do with a handsome man saying he fancied her. 'I . . . I'm flattered.' Wait. He *had* just said he fancied her, right? Or had he just avoided the question?

'If it makes any difference,' he said, picking at the edge of his napkin, 'I intended to ask you out before the whole falling-into-my-arms incident.'

She fought the urge to put her hands over her face. 'I'm so sorry about that. I'm not normally that clumsy.'

'Oh, no. It was fun. Honestly, we have to do this stuff all the time and it's always the same – I mean, everywhere smells of new paint and everyone is really deferential. It's refreshing when someone does something different, like forgets their lines or fall over.'

The comment about the lines reminded her. 'You winked at me,' she said.

'I thought it might help. You seemed to be struggling a little.'

Oh. He hadn't been behaving oddly. He was trying to help. 'It did help. Thank you. If you hadn't done that, I might have wasted the whole five minutes.'

'That would have been a real shame,' he said. 'I enjoyed hearing your ideas about the value of educating women. It's something my sisters and I are interested in.'

'Oh. I see.' She didn't know what else to say.

'It sounded like a good project. And that chap with the 3D-printed prosthetics. That was incredible too.'

'Do you help decide who gets the grants?' A small flare of hope rose. Perhaps this meeting was about her project. Maybe she was going to be awarded the grant.

'Good heavens no,' he said. 'I'm a patron of the charity. I don't actually have a role within it. Even in our own Princesses and Prince Foundation, where my sisters and I are trustees, we never make unilateral decisions. It's always down to a committee.'

'Oh, I see. That's interesting.' So this wasn't about the grant. She tried to tell herself she was disappointed, but her heart gave a little skip of excitement.

The waiter appeared with Ben's drink. He checked if they needed anything and then smoothly slid away again.

'Tell me about yourself,' said Ben. 'I know you're a doctor, but I don't know much else. Why did you go to Africa?'

'I was out there vaccinating children against rubella and measles.' She'd have thought he'd know that. But then again, she did rush the presentation.

'I know that,' he said. 'I mean why did you go? What moved you to leave your job here and go and live in the heat and the mud with the mosquitoes for a year?'

'Oh. I . . . I don't know. Two years ago I looked at my life, where I was just cruising, doing what I needed to do . . . and it felt like nothing was changing. It was the same every day. I thought I'd like to make a difference to someone.' She used her straw to poke at the slice of orange that was floating in her drink. 'So I took a contract to go and be a medic for Better For All for a year. They sent me to Lesotho.'

'It must have been heartbreaking,' he said.

What? She looked up and found him frowning at a spot on the table. 'Pardon?'

'It must have been heartbreaking seeing all those people who need help and not being able to help them all.'

'But you're—'

'I'm what? Rich? Famous?' He sighed. 'But I'm so limited in what I can do. I go out there, take the eyes of the world to these places, show them what's wrong, and I try to help. But for every one person I help . . . there's a thousand that I can't.'

She understood that sentiment. She had been overwhelmed by it in the first weeks in Lesotho. Every night, when the clinic closed, and the warmth leached away, the queue of people would dissipate back to wherever they

40

were camping out. No matter how many children they treated, no matter how many food parcels they gave out, the queue never got any shorter. 'I know,' she said quietly.

Ben's gaze met hers and she saw genuine sadness. Something passed between them. She had thought they had nothing in common. Maybe she was wrong.

Ben stirred his drink and grimaced. 'And after all that, I have to turn round and come back to this.' He waved a hand to encompass the subdued surroundings and his expensive drink. 'Not that there's anything wrong with this,' he said quickly. 'It's great. It's just . . .'

'It's overwhelming and opulent, but you're used to it, surely?'

'Most of the time I'm used to it, but sometimes, when I'm just back from somewhere, I notice how extravagant it all looks.' His eyes sparkled. 'And don't call me Shirley.'

That was a terrible joke. She shook her head and tried not to laugh.

'I'm sorry,' he said. 'It's a family joke. We all love the *Airplane* movies.' He gave her a sheepish grin. Something else you never saw. Prince Benedict looking sheepish. He looked like a normal guy. A very good-looking normal guy, with perfectly straight teeth and amazing eyes . . . but a normal guy. Kumari felt her shoulders unbunch a little bit. Maybe this wasn't going to be so bad after all.

But whatever had passed between them had gone. He had killed it with a badly timed joke. There was an awkward silence.

'What about you, then?' she said, a little emboldened by the fact that even princes told terrible jokes. 'How come you're so down on being in London?'

41

'I'm not down on being in London. I live here,' he said. 'I'm just down on the sadness in the world that I can't change.'

'OK . . . in that case, what's your favourite bit of London?'

'That's easy,' he said. 'My place.'

'Buckingham Palace?'

'No. My flat. Sheesh. You really do believe everything you read in the papers.' He leant his elbows on the table. 'I'm not that guy. Honestly.'

'So the drinking and dancing naked . . .'

'OK, that bit is true,' he said. 'But I was back from active service. A few of the guys and I were just blowing off steam.' He raised his glass of tomato juice. 'But I've mended my ways, see.'

'And your girlfriend?'

'Who is it meant to be this week? I lose track.'

She couldn't remember. 'Me too.'

'Despite what the newspapers say, I'm currently definitely single,' he said, looking straight at her.

Wow. How to cut to the chase. She wasn't sure whether she liked that or not. 'Uh . . . me too.' As a second thought, she added, 'In the interests of full disclosure, I should say that I used to be married. I got divorced about three years ago.'

'You must have got married when you were . . . what . . . sixteen?'

'Ha ha. Twenty-one actually. It all went wrong after about four years.'

'What happened?' He was watching her carefully, like he was genuinely interested.

'Our careers took off and we never saw each other. Then, when we did, we realised we'd changed.' She shrugged. 'The usual story. Too young and stupid.'

'Ouch.'

'Yeah. I was young. He was stupid.'

He laughed out loud. He had the sort of laugh that belonged to a bigger man. It suited him somehow and made her want to laugh too.

As they chatted, Kumari relaxed a bit more, and conversation flowed easily. They discussed politics and food and wildlife and the books they both kept meaning to read. Ben was charming. She worked with enough doctors to know charm when she saw it. She knew guys who were genuinely nice and ones who could turn it on and off like a tap, being warm and kind to the patients and hell on wheels to the nurses. Shane, her ex-husband, had been charming.

But this guy was a prince. Charming was practically part of the job description.

She looked at her watch. Two hours had passed. How had that happened? 'I'm really sorry, but I have to go,' she said apologetically. 'I've had a really nice time, but I have to work tomorrow.'

He looked disappointed. 'Oh. OK. Not a bad idea, I suppose. I have to work tomorrow, too.'

She itched to ask what sort of work it was. Opening a new building? Playing football with orphans? Princely duties. She kept her mouth shut.

There was an awkward silence. She bent down to pick up her handbag and get out her purse.

'Oh don't worry about that.' He put his hand up. 'They put your drinks on my tab.'

'I can't let you do that.'

'Of course you can. I chose this ridiculously expensive place. I can't make you pay for your drinks. That would be . . . very wrong.'

It suddenly occurred to her that she may well be paying for her own drink through her taxes. 'Yes, but who pays your tab?'

He sighed. 'I do.' He gave her an appraising look. 'I can assure you, that's paid with my own money. I am, I believe the phrase is, "independently wealthy". So even a dedicated anti-monarchist can't object to my buying her a drink.'

She opened her mouth to argue. She wasn't a dedicated anti-monarchist. She was ambivalent about the monarchy.

'I must insist,' he said. There was a certain finality to his words.

She put her purse back.

'You know,' he said, smiling. 'Most women don't bother asking about these things.'

She could well imagine they didn't. Those blue eyes, not to mention those lovely broad shoulders . . . they could be pretty distracting. She pulled her gaze back to her hands. Not that she was distracted. No, no. 'I'm not most women.'

'No,' he said. 'Clearly not.' He leant forward. 'Kumari, I had a nice time this evening.'

'Me too.' She was surprised to find she meant it. She had been on far worse blind dates than this. She stood up.

'I'd like to see you again,' he said.

'You would? Why?'

'Because I like you,' he said. 'Obviously.' He rose too.

'But—'

'It's the prince thing, isn't it?' he said. 'Is that what's bothering you?'

She started to say no and realised that was a lie. It *was* the prince thing. 'Look . . . Ben. I don't understand what's going on here. I'm a doctor. I work stupid hours and . . .'

'You're also interesting and sharp and caring,' he said. 'I like that.'

They stared at each other. Part of her was scared and overwhelmed by the urge to run away. Another part of her was charmed. He waggled his eyebrows at her. She couldn't help smiling.

'OK, fine,' she said. 'One more date.'

He grinned at her. 'Excellent. When are you not working?' She pulled out her diary.

'You have a paper diary?' he said. 'I love that.'

'Don't patronise me.'

'Wouldn't dream of it.' He pulled out his phone and came to stand next to her. He smelt amazing. It made her think of woodland and summer. How could a man smell of woodland and summer? She focused on her diary. Pull yourself together, Kumari.

She suggested some dates and they found an evening when they were both able to meet.

'I'll send a car for you,' he said. 'I know somewhere where we can eat a nice meal without too much fuss.' He glanced sideways at her. 'I can tell you don't do fuss.'

45

He was standing very close. So close that if she moved a tiny bit, she could lean her head on his shoulder. He did smell very nice. She looked up and her gaze found his eyes. For a millisecond she stared into them and felt the magnetic pull of him. Then she remembered herself and looked away.

Chapter 5

Cause Celeb Magazine

My wild nights with the prince: exclusive interview

Cause Celeb Magazine *brings you an exclusive interview with model Emily Twist (29) who dated Prince Benedict for a short time while she was working as a society hostess in Monte Carlo. Twist was 27 when she met Prince Benedict at a party. The pair hit it off immediately and dated for around a month. Emily Twist now reveals the truth about what happened during those weeks. Turn to page 6 for the extraordinary revelations about wild toga parties, decadent excess and the now famous vodka-tasting party that led to photos of the prince dancing naked on the beach.*

Lucy was lying in wait for Kumari when she got back. 'How did the blind date go?' she said, not bothering to sit up from where she was lying on the sofa. 'Was he nice?'

Kumari didn't reply immediately. Ben had got a taxi to take her home. She had sat in the back of the car in a daze, wondering how on earth she had ended up having a cosy evening chatting to a prince. Not just any prince. The 'most eligible bachelor in the country' prince. It was bewildering and intoxicating. But she couldn't escape the feeling that she'd made a bit of an idiot of herself. On the other hand, he did want to see her again.

'Kumari?'

'What? Sorry. I was miles away.'

Lucy bounced up off the sofa. 'So, what was he like?'

'He was . . . very nice. Charming, in fact.'

'So, you liked him?'

Did she like him? He was a prince. A bloody prince. She had no place hanging out with someone like that. She was a doctor. The daughter of an overworked teacher and an equally overworked nurse. She'd grown up in a small, terraced house in Yorkshire. None of these things were compatible with going out with royalty. But did she *like* him?

'Yes. I liked him.'

Lucy clapped her hands like a cheesy YouTube sensation. 'Are you going to see him again?'

'Yes.' But only because he'd done that thing with his eyebrows. She'd always had a soft spot for a guy who didn't take himself too seriously. Mind you, that's what she'd found attractive in Shane and look how that turned out.

'You have to tell me *everything*.'

Kumari hung her coat up and flopped down on the sofa.

'Well . . .' There was one big piece of information that would blow everything out of the water. Except she couldn't tell Lucy about that. It was too precious a fact to talk about yet. Besides which, he'd asked for discretion. 'His name is Ben. He's tall. Nice shoulders. Blue eyes.'

Lucy nodded. 'Sounding good so far. What does he do?'

What did he do? Royal things. Cut ribbons, give speeches, that sort of thing. 'He . . . works for a charity.'

'What, like that Ruby woman?' Lucy and Ruby were the very definition of a personality clash.

'No. Not really.'

'What sort of a charity?'

She thought of the things he had talked about.

'Poverty alleviation in Africa, wildlife preservation, that sort of thing.'

Lucy gave her a dig in the ribs. 'So, you guys have lots in common, then.'

They did, which was weird, considering they came from such different worlds. 'I suppose.'

Lucy made encouraging motions with her hands. 'And . . .'

Kumari smiled. 'I'm not sure how well suited we are yet, but he's a nice guy so . . .'

'The crucial question though, Kumari, is do you fancy him?'

She had to think about that one. 'He's good-looking,' she said. And he smelt amazing. And his eyes were the most incredible blue. And there was something about that smile that did funny things to her.

'Ooh, I know that face,' said Lucy. 'Are you going to see him again? You are, aren't you?'

Kumari grinned. 'Yeah.'

Lucy squealed and ran over to give her a hug. Kumari laughed and hugged her back.

'I'm going to bed,' she told Lucy.

'Yeah. Me too.' Lucy grinned and gave her an excited little pat on the shoulder.

Kumari made it as far her room before Ruby called her.

'Well? How did it go? Are you going to see him again?'

She was about to give her the same answer she'd given Lucy, but something didn't feel right. 'I'm not sure,' she said.

'Aww. Did it not go well? That's a shame.' Ruby didn't sound overly disappointed. In fact, she sounded pleased.

'Ruby, I'm tired. I'm heading off to bed.' She wondered if she was going to get a thank you for going on the date. She was, after all, doing Ruby a favour.

'You sleep well, hon,' said Ruby. 'I'm sorry it didn't work out with Benedict.'

'Hmm.' So, no thank you then. 'Cheers.'

The next week passed in a tired haze of hospital beds and patient records. By the time her date with Ben came round, Kumari was a bag of nerves. She had never been interested in the lives of the royals before, but now she found herself picking up the newspapers in the staff room and leafing through for a glimpse of him. One of his sisters had worn a fuchsia coat and that week's news seemed to be more about that than anything else.

She leant her elbows on the work surface and sipped her coffee. She was in her dressing gown after coming in from a night shift. Lucy came in, all tied-up hair and sensible shoes.

'Looking forward to your date with the mysterious Ben tonight?' she said, dropping bread into the toaster.

'Yeah.'

'Nervous?'

'A bit.'

'It's no good. You have to tell me more about him.' She leant against the cupboards and crossed her arms. 'Please.'

'There isn't a lot to tell. He seems nice. He travels a lot and does . . . actually, I'm not sure what he does. Stuff to do with charities.'

'Ooh. Non-specific job description. Should that ring alarm bells?' said Lucy.

No. It didn't. Everything he did was all over the media. If only she had time to read it all. Lucy would know. She would know all about the fuchsia coat and all about Benedict. The trouble was, if Kumari let on who Ben was, Lucy would probably go into orbit and Kumari would never hear the end of it.

The toast popped. Lucy turned around to pick it up.

'Have you googled him?' she said, over her shoulder. 'He is who he says he is, right?'

Kumari had to suppress a giggle. He was who he said he was all right, only maybe a little less smooth than his public image. 'Yeah. I googled him.'

'Did you find anything juicy?'

She hid her face behind her coffee. 'No. Nothing unexpected.'

Lucy frowned at Kumari. She pointed a corner of her buttered toast at her. 'I think you like this mystery man more than you're letting on.' She bit into the toast with an air of finality.

'I'm confused, is what I am,' said Kumari. 'I don't know how I feel about him. He's nice. He's good company. But I don't think we're compatible. He's busy. I'm busy. It'll never work. That was pretty much what went wrong the first time. Shane was busy. I was busy.'

'Busy is just a state of mind, Kumari. You can work things out if you really want to . . .'

'Evidence would suggest otherwise.'

'You and Shane were never *meant* for each other. He refuses to watch any of the *Star Wars* movies, for a start. That's not the behaviour of a normal human being.' Lucy put two more slices into the toaster. It always baffled Kumari how much Lucy could eat without actually putting on any weight.

'Granted,' said Kumari.

'You've been very sketchy on details about this guy,' said Lucy. 'This is another reason I suspect you like him. I know what you're like. You don't give things up if they're precious to you.'

Kumari shook her head. 'There really isn't much to tell. Look. Let's change the subject.'

'OK.' Lucy took a bite of toast and waved the rest of the slice at her. 'Your mother called.'

Amma always called the flat instead of her mobile. Her rationale was that she didn't want to disturb Kumari if she was at work. Kumari suspected it was really because she wanted to chat to Lucy. Amma loved Lucy. The two of them would gossip for hours. Amma shared a bit of Lucy's royal obsession too. Kumari had sat through the highlights of Princess Helena's wedding with the two of them and it had been excruciating.

'And ... ?' Kumari narrowed her eyes. 'Tell me you didn't let slip that I have a date tonight.'

Lucy pulled an apologetic grimace. 'I'm really sorry. She was talking about how she was worried about you not getting over Shane and I kinda said you were dating again. I said there was no one specific. She was just happy to hear you weren't pining over Shane.'

'I was never pining over Shane. Seriously.'

'I know,' said Lucy. 'I'm sure your mum knows that too. She's just worried about you, that's all.'

Later that evening, a car arrived to take Kumari to the restaurant. It was another upmarket place that she wouldn't normally have gone to. She'd done some fine dining when she was with Shane and though she might have appreciated it back then, now she'd much rather have a takeaway and a glass of wine at home. Mind you, it had been a while since she'd been on a date. The last actual date she'd had before Ben ... oh, it had been with another expat doctor in Maseru. It was more of a farewell dinner than a date. It hadn't gone much further than dinner.

She was met at the door by a waiter who took her to a private room. To her surprise, she had butterflies in her stomach. Really? At her age? She told herself to be sensible. This relationship wasn't going to go anywhere. She was only here because she was curious.

This time Ben was already there, waiting for her. He was frowning at his phone when she arrived. He quickly put it away and shot to his feet. She liked that he stood up when she entered the room. It was old-fashioned and quite sweet.

'Hi.' He came forward. For a second she thought he was going to shake her hand again, but after a second of hesitation, he kissed her cheek. She caught his woodland and summer scent again. The butterflies intensified. So maybe she wasn't as immune to him as she'd hoped.

He pulled her chair out for her. 'It's good to see you again,' he said.

'You too.' She genuinely meant it.

The waiter appeared once Ben had sat back down. You had to hand it to places like this, the service was impeccable. She was handed a menu. She looked down at it, not sure what she wanted.

'My sister tells me their Caesar salad is very good,' said Benedict. His expression suggested he would rather starve.

'I'm not really a salad person,' Kumari said, without thinking.

He looked up. His eyes sparkled. 'Oh yes? What sort of a person are you, then?'

She met his eyes. 'I'll have the lamb.' She closed her menu and lifted her chin, challenging him to judge her.

He grinned. 'I can't stand salad,' he said. His eyes didn't leave hers.

'Me neither.'

For a moment he didn't say anything, but held her gaze. Kumari's heartbeat suddenly seemed louder. Her breath felt short. Was it hot in here?

'I think,' he said, 'I'll have the steak.' He clapped his menu shut, which seemed to summon the waiter, who took their orders.

'The last girl I went out with didn't eat real food. It was all leafy bits.'

'I see. That must have been awkward, what with you not liking salad.'

'It was. But I thought that as a doctor . . .'

She laughed. 'I do advise people to eat a healthy, balanced diet. Unfortunately, I'm not great at taking my own advice.'

He looked thoughtful for a moment. 'OK. I have a question for you – roast potatoes or Yorkshire pudding?'

'Yorkshire pudding,' she said immediately. 'Although, don't tell my mum, but I prefer the ones cooked from frozen.'

He nodded. 'Interesting.'

'My turn,' she said. 'Cream tea – cream first or jam first?'

'Ah, that's easy. It depends where I'm having the cream tea. In Cornwall, jam first. Although, in fairness, I rarely get to do my own these days. Every event that's had them has it already prepared. Usually with tiny, tiny scones.' He indicated the size.

'That's a disappointing size of scone,' she said.

They smiled at each other. His smile seemed to connect straight to her solar plexus. She felt light-headed from it. Lucy was right. She liked him more than she cared to admit. That wasn't a good thing, because this was just a dalliance to him. She didn't have time to be someone's plaything. But she caught his sparkling eyes and realised a part of her didn't really care.

Conversation flowed easily. Every so often she would look at him and notice something she'd not seen before. The way his eyes creased when he smiled. The line of his jaw. The way he put his head back when he laughed. The little details that made him a real person, rather than the oft-photographed prince she'd thought she knew.

While they were waiting for their coffee he said, 'Have you got any space in your paper diary to see me again?'

'Let me see.' She unhooked her bag from her chair and fished out her small diary. He scooted his chair over so that he was next to her and pulled out his phone. She noticed that he'd set the display to be large.

'OK,' she said. 'How are you fixed for next week?'

He peered at the diary in her hands. 'Hang on a second. Damned analogue things . . .' He put his hand inside his jacket and pulled out a pair of glasses. He put them on and looked at her diary again.

Kumari stared. She had not expected glasses. Somehow it transformed his face, making him less playboy prince and far more like the champion of the weak that she had glimpsed before. It was, she realised, unbelievably sexy. She reached up and touched his cheek.

He switched his attention from her diary to her face. His eyes looked even bluer up close. His lips curved into a small smile. She couldn't look away from it.

'That's what it took?' he said. 'I was trying so hard to impress you and all I had to do was put on glasses?'

What would it be like to kiss him? She muttered, 'I have hidden shallows.'

He moved infinitesimally closer. 'I like hidden shallows.' He moved closer still and she closed the gap between them.

It was a hesitant kiss at first. A press of lips. Exploring. His fingertips grazed her neck. His thumb traced the line of her jaw. All hesitation vanished and he shifted position to get closer. Diary forgotten, she wrapped her arms around his neck.

When they drew apart his glasses were askew. She bit her lip and righted them.

It was a few seconds before either of them spoke. Finally, Ben said, 'Would you . . . like to go somewhere else?' His lips grazed hers again and something in her melted.

She nodded. 'Yes.'

As soon as she had her coat on, he took her hand and led her out of a side door, so that they didn't pass the other diners. There was a car waiting outside. They tumbled into the back.

'Where to, sir?' said the driver.

'Cottington House, please. Let them know I'm coming over to use the bar.' Ben fumbled with a panel of buttons and the glass partition between them and the driver darkened. He turned back to her. 'Now then,' he said. 'Where were we?'

'Comparing diaries.'

'Ah yes.' He leant across and kissed her. She wrapped her arms around him and kissed him back. As the London street lights swept past, they snogged like teenagers.

Cottington House turned out to be a club that was hidden behind high walls and a secure gate.

'This is where my cousins hang out if they're staying down in London,' Ben said. 'I don't think any of them are around at the moment, but you never know.'

The car pulled up at the front. Ben got out and offered his hand to help Kumari from the car. They entered a large hall with an enormous staircase. She tried not to gawp at the size of the place. Ben said hello to the butler who had opened the door, then led her up the wide stairs.

They ended up in a bar. At least, it had a barman and an array of drinks. It was in an anteroom that led into a grand ballroom. They were the only guests there.

While Ben ordered drinks, Kumari stepped into the ballroom. It was incredible. The high ceilings, the mirrors, the chandeliers. Kumari forgot her manners and stared. How was it possible for places like this to still exist?

'Kumari?'

She turned, suddenly overwhelmed by what was happening. 'Ben, this is . . . I can't.' She shook her head. She was wearing her best dress and she felt so scruffy.

Ben stepped up to her. 'You don't have to do anything you don't want to,' he said cautiously. 'It's just a place where we can have some privacy. I'm not going to jump you.'

'It's not that. It's just . . . you're a prince. I'm just me. I'm really, really not suitable for you.'

'Really?' He touched a lock of hair by her cheek and gently tucked it behind her ear. 'Why don't you let me be the judge of what's suitable for me. All that matters right now, is whether you feel that I'm suitable for you.'

She stared at him. He was so close and he smelt so good. All she wanted to do was to kiss him again. But she hesitated.

A frown creased Ben's forehead. 'I should have eased you in gently. I'm sorry. I forget that this place can be a bit of a shock if you're not used to it.'

'A bit.'

He nodded. 'I'm sorry.' He took a step back. 'You see, the thing is, I really, really like you. I haven't felt like this about anyone in . . . well, ever.' He ran a hand through his hair, messing it up. 'I don't get to do weeks of flirting. With my schedule and yours . . . it could be weeks before I get to see you again.' His frown deepened. 'And I've completely forgotten where I was going with this speech. You see the effect you have on me, Kumari? I'm a fairly competent man but you turn me into a gibbering wreck.'

Kumari sank down onto one of the gold-and-red sofas that lined the walls of the ballroom. For a fleeting second she wondered if she was allowed to sit on it before she remembered she wasn't in a National Trust house, she was in Ben's club.

'I don't know what to say.' She had some sympathy with the gibbering wreck thing. She hadn't exactly been thinking straight either.

Ben knelt on the floor in front of her. 'OK. Let's clear one thing up. Is it me? Or is it . . .' He waved an arm. 'This stuff ?'

'Oh, it's not you,' she said. 'I like you.'

'So it's the whole prince thing.'

She nodded. 'It's a lot to . . . take in.'

'How about if we went somewhere where we could be just us? Somewhere where I'm not a prince and you're not a doctor.'

She thought about it. She did like him. He was gorgeous and charming and kissing him made her knees melt. 'OK,' she said.

'A weekend away maybe?'

'I'd like that.' Although, where would they go? There wasn't a place in the country where he wouldn't be recognised.

'Excellent. Let's try that thing where we look at our diaries and work out when we can meet again.'

'This time we'll actually get to look at diaries, yes?' she said.

'Well . . .' His face was suddenly serious. 'I will have to put my glasses on again. Are you sure you can handle it?'

She laughed and gave him a gentle shove. He laughed too, his big, hearty, comforting laugh. And everything felt right again.

'So where are you going?' Lucy sat at the end of Kumari's bed eating peanut butter out of a jar and watching her throw things into a bag.

'Namibia.' Kumari pulled out a long-sleeved cotton blouse that her mother had brought back from Sri Lanka. She waved it at Lucy. 'Too twee?'

'No, it looks nice on you,' said Lucy. 'Namibia? Is that even safe?'

Kumari threw the blouse in. 'Apparently. They had a poaching problem, but that's under control now ... according to the Internet,' she said. She pulled a face at the pile of clothes. 'I feel underprepared. And I hate being underprepared.'

Lucy nodded and popped some peanut butter into her mouth. 'Control freak,' she mumbled.

'Stop eating in my bedroom.'

Lucy rolled her eyes, got off the bed and went as far as the door. She leant against the door frame. 'It's also a little romantic, don't you think? He's whisking you away for a surprise holiday.'

Kumari carefully folded her quick-drying trousers. 'It's only five days. And he said we'd be camping.' She dropped the trousers into her bag. 'You know what? I can't handle it. I need more information.' She pulled her phone out of her jeans pocket. Ben had given her a mobile number. He had told her to be careful that it didn't fall into the wrong hands – a hotline to a prince was a valuable thing, so she'd jokingly put it in her phone as Speccy4eyes. She knew better than to call him. He had explained that the phone lived with his assistant whenever he was out on official duties, but that he checked his messages. She knew when he was in transit, because he texted her back immediately. Sometimes, if they both had some time, they'd speak on the phone.

She wrote; *Not good with surprises. Need more clues. K.*

'Is he coming to pick you up?' Lucy asked. 'Can I meet him?'

He was sending a car to pick her up. Kumari, who had been brought up to watch her pennies, rarely even took a taxi when there was public transport available. She really wished that she could tell Lucy what was going on, but it was all too new and too precious to share at the moment.

'No,' she said. 'You can't meet him.'

'Aww.' Lucy stuck another spoonful of peanut butter into her mouth. 'Can you at least show me a photo?'

There were hundreds of photos all over the Internet. Kumari grinned to herself. Lucy had a collection of photos on her board of hotness in the kitchen.

'What? What's that smile for?'

'Nothing.' Her phone buzzed. Ben had replied to her text. His message simply said, *Bring safari clothes*, and had a URL.

'What kind of a clue is that?' She clicked on the URL and a site showing a beautiful camp opened up. 'Wow.' She turned the phone to show Lucy.

Lucy did a slow motion double-take. 'He's taking you to a fancy safari camp in Africa?'

'Looks like it . . .' She stared at the text.

'Hang on. Hang on. This mystery guy takes you first to an eye-wateringly expensive cocktail bar. Then to dinner at the swankiest restaurant I've ever heard of and now he's taking you to Africa?' She stepped into the room.

Kumari glanced at the jar of peanut butter in her hand. Lucy stepped out, put the jar on the floor outside the room and came back in. She put her hands on her hips. 'Kumari, I'm not being weird, but who is this guy?'

'He's . . . a guy. I mean, he's got a lot of money, but otherwise just a guy.'

Lucy gave her a suspicious glare. 'If he's that rich we can google him.' She pulled out her phone. 'Come on. Spill. What's his name?'

'Ben.'

'You'll have to do better than that. What's his full name?'

Kumari shook her head.

'Seriously? Did he make you sign a confidentiality agreement or something . . . he did, didn't he? Oh my God, you're going out with a real life Christian Grey.'

Kumari started to laugh. 'Don't be ridiculous.'

Lucy grinned too. 'Maybe he's not taking you to Africa at all. It's an elaborate ruse to get you into his private sex dungeon.'

'No! He's not like that at all. Honestly. And he didn't get me to sign anything. He just asked nicely.'

'Seriously though, Kumari.' Lucy came and sat at the end of her bed again. 'How will I know you're OK? All this secrecy is worrying me. You've got to admit it's weird.' She was no longer smiling and looked genuinely worried.

Kumari sat down next to her. 'I'll be fine, Lucy. He's a good guy. He's just a bit wary of publicity.'

'But if he takes you out of the country and you get kidnapped, or he dumps you and leaves you out there or whatever, how will I even know where you are?'

'Lucy. I spent the last year in a medical facility in Lesotho.'

'And I spent every evening dreading what was going to be on the news. I had to friend your mum on Facebook, just so that I could message her to check you were OK.'

Kumari hadn't known that. She knew that Lucy and her Amma were in touch, but she hadn't appreciated that Lucy was so much a part of the invisible web that surrounded her. She had assumed that she'd dropped out of Lucy's thoughts while she was abroad. Guiltily, she realised that Lucy had all but dropped out of hers.

'Tell you what. I'll forward you the URL for the safari place, so that you have their contact details and I'll message you when I message my mum to say I've arrived safely. Would that help?'

Lucy nodded. 'It would.' But she didn't look convinced. Kumari sighed. 'Lucy, I wish I could tell you more. All I know is that if I'm with him, I'll probably be safer than I've ever been before.' Which was true. Ben was never without security. They were discreet, letting him have the illusion of normality, but they were always there. 'Can you trust me on that?'

Lucy nodded again. On impulse, Kumari gave her a hug. 'Thanks for looking out for me.'

'Pshaw. You'd do the same for me.' Lucy squeezed her back. 'And I'm still half convinced you're dating Christian Grey.'

Later on, Kumari texted Ben. *My friend thinks all the secrecy is because you're taking me to a secret sex dungeon.*

She got a reply back within minutes. *Damn. Why didn't I think of that? Must try harder.*

Chapter 6

The Aurora Post

Is the prince missing his days in the army?

Prince Benedict was seen deep in conversation with the manufacturers of high-octane motorbikes at the exclusive Salon Privé – the premier occasion for those coveting super-luxury motor vehicles. The prince, who left active service in the army three years ago, is said to be missing the adrenaline rush of being in a war zone and might be looking to capture that feeling through a powerful motor vehicle.

On page 8 we talk to a psychology expert who explains the link between the prince's reputed hard partying and trauma experienced by serving in the army.

Kumari got out of the car and stretched. They had been travelling for hours, first a charter plane, then the Humvee. It was early morning now and the sun was rising. She breathed in the smell of parched earth and woodsmoke, and for a second she was back in the medical camp. Except this was a different world entirely.

'Lesotho was a bit tricky to organise,' said Ben. He looked delicious in lightweight cargo trousers and a shirt. The minute they left the car, he had put on a pair of wraparound sunglasses. 'So I figured Namibia was a good compromise.'

She didn't know what to say. 'Thank you,' seemed like the most appropriate response.

He took her hand and led her towards an open-sided building where a waiter placed a jug of iced water on a table. Ben seemed to know where he was going.

'You've been here before,' she said.

'A couple of times. I like the fact that you can unplug completely.' He held her chair for her. 'And I figured you'd seen the worst of human misery in Lesotho, but there are also beautiful places like this with all this natural wonder. It's such a huge and varied continent . . . I thought it might be nice to see that side of things.'

She looked across at him, but she couldn't read his eyes because of the sunglasses. 'Thank you,' she said.

Sitting in her wooden chair, sipping ice-cold water, Kumari looked out at the savannah that stretched into the distance. They were in a safari park, she knew, because they'd driven past a sign a long way back. The vegetation was sparse, but beautiful. Here and there the vast swathes of red and brown were broken up by clusters of trees or patches of bright red and orange flowers. A breeze rippled through, carrying with it the smell of hot earth.

It was stunning.

When she was working for Better For All, she had been to the mountain parks in Lesotho on her rare days off, but she'd rarely stopped to absorb their beauty. The medical camp itself had been surrounded by mountains, but she'd barely had time to look up and admire them. She had lived and worked in Africa, albeit a very different part of Africa to this one, but not really seen it. This time, her second visit to the continent, was different. There was no background noise of people weeping. No hum of the generators. There was no press of expectation. This time, she could pause to admire a beautiful landscape and let it feed her soul.

And then there was Ben. She looked across at him. He looked different here too, more relaxed. He leant forward in his seat. 'What are you thinking?'

'I'm thinking that it's a very thoughtful thing for you to have done.' Not to mention hugely over-the-top for a third date. But then, he was a prince. Maybe this was nothing to him. Either way, she wasn't complaining. She reached over and put her hand in his. In the bright daylight, her hand looked very brown against his pink-white one. 'You didn't have to.'

His fingers wrapped around hers. He leant forward.

'Except that I did,' he said. 'In London, I feel like I've got to have eyes in the back of my head. I'm always on duty. Even when I'm meeting a girl – like that time we met for a drink. I have to always have this low-level awareness of everything around me. I can't really relax and, honestly, neither can you. Out here . . .' He waved an arm to encompass the wide savannah. 'Out here there's nothing. Just you and me. Even Dave over there . . .' He nodded to where his bodyguards were sitting unobtrusively at the other end of the hut. 'Even Dave and his colleagues can keep a bit of distance.'

She wondered what it must be like to be constantly on your guard like that. 'That must be hard,' she said.

He inclined his head. 'My family . . .' he said. 'We are in the public eye rather a lot. It's part of the job. People feel like they know us. They almost expect us to know them. We have to learn to always be gracious. Always be welcoming.'

He smiled a half-smile, as though he was thinking about a memory.

'It's not a hardship, really. Sometimes you get to meet some fascinating people. I don't mean high-profile people, I mean ordinary ones, or at least they think they're ordinary, but they do incredible things. It's inspiring and humbling and . . . quite often exhausting.' He squeezed her hand gently. 'And sometimes you meet an individual who you really want to get to know and you don't want to give your attention to anyone else.' He smiled. 'This is a place where I can concentrate on you. I know it's only for a few days but . . .'

'Thank you. I want to get to know you too.' She meant it. When they had been talking by phone or messaging each other, it felt like a normal relationship – and he made her happy. It was only when she stopped to consider that in order to be alone, he had flown her to Namibia that the whole thing felt surreal.

'Perfect.' He brought their joined hands up to his lips and kissed her knuckles. 'What do you want to do first?'

'Right now, I feel like I've been travelling forever and I would really like to have a shower and change into clean clothes.'

'Of course.' He leant back and beckoned the waiter. 'Are the tents ready?'

The man nodded. 'Yes, sir. We set it up just as you asked.' Tent? A shot of trepidation. She looked at the artfully tiled floor and stylised moulded walls. This was far too fancy a place for tents.

The 'tents' turned out to be canopied lodges, spread out in a circle around a central building. They faced outwards, so that you couldn't see the solar panels, water towers and practical buildings in the middle.

'That's my tent,' said Ben, pointing. 'And that's yours.'

Her tent was sparsely furnished, but contained everything she needed. There was a large double bed, with bolsters and drop-down mosquito nets. With the sides of the tent rolled up, you could lie in bed and watch the world go by. It would have felt very exposed if it wasn't for the fact that no one was around for miles.

Eager to rinse the heat and tiredness off her skin, Kumari had a shower – supplied by a water tank that stood on a tower behind – in the bathroom, which was housed in a low-slung building adjacent to the tent. And once she'd put on the cotton shirt she'd thought too fussy when she was packing, with a pair of cotton trousers, she felt much better.

When she got back to her tent, she found Ben lying on her bed, wearing his glasses and reading a brochure. He had changed into shorts and a cotton shirt. It made him look ridiculously colonial. She noticed for the first time that he had very muscular legs. Nice.

'There's about twelve different trips we can make, depending on what animals we want to see,' he said.

She flopped down on the bed next to him. It felt like the most natural thing in the world to be lying next to him on a big bed, looking out at the open savannah. He opened his arm and she snuggled in next to him, her head on his shoulder. 'What do you fancy?'

'They all look pretty good.' She breathed in the smell of him. Even out here, he reminded her of woodland and summer.

'I wouldn't mind going to see if there are any birds. Try out my new camera.'

'OK. That sounds good. Let's do that.' She was suddenly incredibly tired. She tried to focus on the brochure and read the information, but she couldn't.

'There's a few safari trails we could try,' Ben said.

But she wasn't listening. She studied his profile. The familiar line of his straight nose, the dip below his lower lip. She changed position so that she could kiss his cheek. He lowered the brochure and smiled. 'Hello, you.'

She tapped the bridge of his nose. 'How come you don't wear contacts?'

'Can't stand putting things in my eyes,' he said. 'How come you like my glasses so much?'

She changed position and rested her chin on his shoulder. 'I've always have a thing for men in glasses.'

'Really.' His eyes sparkled. He really was gorgeous. With or without the glasses. And he liked that she teased him. Wow.

'Uh-huh. I think glasses on a handsome man are ... sexy.'

'Very wise.'

'I know, right.' She reached up and pushed the spectacles to the top of his head so that she could kiss him properly.

Very early the next morning, they were bouncing along in the back of an open-sided safari truck. Kumari and Ben were in the back, sitting close together in the middle of a seat designed to hold four. In the front were their guide and the tracker. Also in the front was a radio and ammunition for the guns that were in the cab. She had asked why they needed a rifle on board if they weren't hunting and they'd said, cryptically, 'For safety.'

Behind them another jeep carried several armed men, including Dave. Ben seemed to have mastered the art of being polite and friendly to Dave while simultaneously ignoring him most of the time. She didn't know how he did it.

Kumari yawned. Her body wasn't entirely sure what time zone she was in, but it knew it was too early. The sky was lemon and pink with dawn. Around her the details of the landscape were coming into focus.

'Look at all that sky,' she breathed. It astounded her, the unbroken expanse that arched from horizon to horizon. In London the sky was only available in patches – hemmed in by trees and buildings, sliced up by vapour trails. Even in Yorkshire, the sky was parcelled up by the hills.

Ben was fiddling with his camera. He looked up. 'Yes,' he said. 'It's beautiful.' He pointed the camera at her and took a picture. Checking the screen on the back he said, 'Nope,' and deleted it.

She watched him. Every time she looked at him, she felt the pull of him, that deep-felt urge to give something of herself, to form a connection. But she had been there before. Wonderful though it was to surrender to love, she also knew what it was like to see that love wither with neglect. To lose that bond. To watch the dreams of a future together dwindle to nothing but dust. As much as she wanted to take a chance on him, she was afraid to. She didn't think she had the strength to go through heart-break again.

A flock of birds took to the sky from a thicket not far away. The vehicle slowed. The tracker said, 'Shh.'

The guide, who was driving, slowed the vehicle and they crawled towards the thicket. Kumari leant forward. Now that the noise of the jeep was gone, they could hear the animal sounds and, in the distance, birdsong that was carried to them by the breeze.

The tracker put his finger to his lips again and slipped out. He walked forward, crouching a little to look at the ground. The guide killed the engine, unzipped the gun bag and pulled out a rifle, moving quietly.

Kumari frowned. She objected to guns in general, but this was probably not the time to get into an argument about it. One of the many lessons she'd learnt working in the vaccination camp was that things weren't always how they seemed.

The tracker froze. He started to raise his hand, then his whole body tensed. What had he seen? Kumari strained to see. Behind her, she could feel Ben stretching to see past her. His chest was warm and solid against her shoulder.

Suddenly the tracker shouted something, turned and ran back towards the jeep. A loud crack rang out and he pitched forward.

'Kumari, get down.' Ben pulled her backwards and somehow pushed her into the footwell while simultaneously grabbing a handgun from the front. The guide was on the radio, shouting into it. More shots. Repeated gunfire came from the jeep behind and was returned from the thicket. Ben took aim and shot at the trees. Kumari cowered, making herself as small as possible and keeping out of the way. In the front, the driver crouched down and radioed for help.

Dave had appeared from somewhere and was trying to pull Ben down. Ben shrugged him off and took aim again. Dave, who probably knew his boss pretty well, joined in, angling himself so that he was kneeling in front of Ben.

Kumari, even with her arms wrapped over her head, felt the shots reverberate around her. The guide dropped the radio and grabbed the rifle.

A few minutes later, she heard another noise. An engine whine. A plane? The shooting stopped abruptly and from somewhere there was the sound of a powerful engine starting. The plane swooped and shots rang out again. They were shooting at the attackers. As the sounds receded, Ben lowered his gun. 'Kumari, are you hurt?'

'No.' She lifted her head and looked at the three men in the vehicle.

Ben had a cut on his forehead that was bleeding, but didn't look too bad. Dave and the guide seemed unhurt. She sat up and looked beyond them. The tracker lay on the ground, crying and moaning. If he was crying, that was a good sign. He was conscious.

'First aid kit,' she said.

The guide pulled out a tiny kit. This would have things for cuts and bites, but nothing useful. She grabbed it and made to get out of the vehicle.

Ben caught her arm. 'What are you doing?'

'He's hurt. I'm going to help him.'

'But you don't know if it's safe. If one of the poachers was injured, he might have been left behind and still be armed.'

'If he's injured,' she said, 'I'll help him too.'

He stared at her for a second, as though trying to make her see sense. She met his gaze.

'Fine,' he said. 'Dave.'

The men went ahead of her, guns at the ready. Moving like they were trying to watch all directions at the same time. She ignored them and rushed to the injured man. He was bleeding heavily from one side. She found the bullet wound in his stomach. The first aid pack contained one bandage. She used it as a dressing and pressed it against the wound. She couldn't see where the bullet had gone and didn't dare move him to find an exit wound. Blood seeped onto the bandage, but it didn't soak it immediately. She needed something to keep this in place.

'Hold this,' she instructed Ben. He put his gun down and did as he was told. She took off the man's shirt, pulled it tight over the bandage and tied it, binding the dressing to the wound. All the while, she talked to him, her voice low and calm, until he stilled enough to talk to her and tell her more about the pain.

Once she was sure he was stable, she left one of the men with him, with instructions to keep talking to him, and went to check on the others. The second jeep had caught most of the gunfire. Its side was full of holes and the tyres were in shreds. One of the other men had taken a shot to the shoulder. Kumari stabilised it and bound it using someone's shirt.

It seemed an age until the plane returned. Soon after that a convoy of vehicles arrived. A stretcher was produced and the injured men were carried off to be flown to the hospital.

The manager of the campsite, who had arrived with the backup, gabbled his apologies, but Kumari, bloodstained and suddenly exhausted as the adrenaline drained out of her, ignored him and let Ben guide her back to one of the new jeeps. Ben tried to talk to her, but she shook her head. They sat close together in silence, bloodstained hands tightly clutched, all the way back to the lodge.

It was the most welcome shower she'd ever had. Sometime during her shower, as the tracker's blood washed off her, she realised how lucky they'd been. She still felt shaky. It was the first time she'd heard real gunfire or come anywhere close to death. The enormity of what could have happened struck her with some force.

The poachers had concentrated on the heavily armed jeep rather than the one with the tourists in it. The rangers in the armed vehicle had been well trained, as were Dave and Ben. If the guide hadn't kept his head and radioed for help, if they had been any closer when the poachers opened fire ... there were so many ways in which things could have gone much worse. And Ben. He had put himself in front of her. He could literally have taken a bullet for her.

They could have both been killed.

Kumari put clean clothes on and tied her hair up in a bun. It would dry out creased and frizzy, but who cared. She was alive. How had she forgotten what a joy it was to be alive? And Ben. He liked her. She knew she liked him back, but she was fighting it. Why? Because she was afraid of what would happen if it didn't work out? Was she so mad as to throw away the chance of something wonderful on the off-chance that it might not go well? Life was, she decided, too short for playing games.

She checked her boots, put them on and walked the short distance between her tent and Ben's. Everything seemed brighter and sharper, as though her senses had been dialled up to maximum sensitivity. The world was an astounding place. How wonderful to be alive in it.

Ben was sitting on the porch in front of the tent, where an awning provided some shade. He was fiddling with his camera again. He lifted his head and raised his sunglasses to the top of his head when she approached. He had a small butterfly bandage on his forehead where he'd been cut.

'Hey.' He stood up. 'How are you feeling?'

'Much better now, thanks.'

'You were amazing out there,' he said. 'Most women would have screamed the place down.'

She stepped up to him and touched his cheek. 'I told you. I'm not most women.'

'No.' He looked into her eyes, want burning in his expression. 'You're incredible.'

She rose on her tiptoes and kissed him. His breath hitched. She pressed closer and he returned her kiss. His arms pulled her hard against him. She ran her hands into his hair. His mouth moved from hers and his kisses travelled down her jaw to her neck. She let her head tip back and breathed him in.

'Are you sure?' he whispered in between kisses.

She opened her eyes and smiled. She had never been so sure of anything in her life. 'Yes.' She pushed him gently towards the opening of the tent. He took her hand and led her inside.

They were sitting on the porch of his tent, with a hurricane lamp on a table between them. The staff at the park had zipped down the sides of the tent and lit lamps while they had been at dinner. Lemon and eucalyptus candles floated in bowls in an attempt to keep the bugs at bay. Ben had turned the lamp down low, so that their eyes could adjust to the darkness and see the shapes of the trees around them. Above them, the astounding sky was full of stars.

'Ben?'

'Yes?' His hand found hers in the gloom. His thumb stroked across her knuckles.

'I really like you,' she said. She did. He made her feel a sense of contentment that she hadn't had in years. It was almost as though her life had been ever so slightly askew and needed him to put everything into balance.

Ben's thumb stopped moving. He leant forward. 'Why do I feel there's going to be a "but" next?'

'How is this going to work? I mean, it's all well and good out here, with no one around, but when we get back ... how can we possibly date like normal people?'

He didn't reply. He was quiet for so long that she said, 'Ben?' to check if he was OK.

'I'm thinking,' he said.

Kumari leant across and, with her free hand, raised the wick so that the flame in the lamp rose higher. In the warm light, she could see Ben's frown.

'I've never had what you'd call a normal life,' he said solemnly. 'My parents tried very hard to keep things normal for us. You know, prep school and playtime and holidays where it was just us . . . I mean, there was security, and nannies, of course, but that was fairly normal compared to how it could have been. But I'm not so out of touch that I don't realise how different my life has been. When I was in the army . . . I was one of the guys. I liked that. But it was always made clear to me that it wasn't a long-term thing. I would always have to give up and come home to take on royal duties. It's . . . the rules.'

He'd mentioned the rules before.

'Tell me about them – these rules.'

'Um . . . let's see. Well, I don't have as many rules as my sisters, obviously, because I'm a bloke. Helena, my older big sister, she's the second in line to the throne, so she has a crap ton of rules to follow. She's very good about them, actually. Never knowingly broken a rule in her life. Takes after our dad. But then, he's the heir, so maybe it's an heir thing. Anyway. She has a lot of rules. Her husband was on the shortlist chosen for her. She's fond of him and he's a nice enough chap, so that's all good.'

'Chosen shortlist? Like an arranged marriage?'

'I suppose, in a manner of speaking. She could have chosen someone else, but like I said, Helena's fairly old school in some ways.'

Kumari pulled a face. Most people thought 'arranged' meant forced. She knew that it meant a parent-sanctioned shortlisting service. She'd never had an arranged marriage suggested to her. Partly because she'd met Shane when she was nineteen and got engaged by twenty, but also because her parents themselves had eloped to be together, so they couldn't exactly suggest it.

'My other big sister, Ophelia, she has similar rules, but people are slightly less bothered, especially now that Hel's got kids and Ophelia isn't likely to succeed to the throne.' He smiled. 'Ophelia's pretty daring, compared to Helena.'

Ophelia was the one with the fuchsia coat, Kumari remembered. Lucy liked her better than Helena. 'And you?' she asked.

'Well, like I said, I'm a bloke. That gives me far more freedom in many respects. And being the youngest means I can get away with misbehaving a bit and blaming it on youthful high jinks. Also, I'm only sixth in line, so people don't much care who I date or live with, but I do need my grandmother's permission to get married.'

Kumari squeezed his hand. 'I don't really fit in to your rules, do I?'

'I don't know, in all honesty.'

'I'm not an aristocrat. I have no power. I'm not rich. I'm not well connected. I'm divorced. I'm not a Christian. I'm not even white,' she said. 'There is no way your family is going to approve of me.'

When he said nothing, she said, 'And don't even *think* about suggesting I be your concubine, or whatever.'

He laughed. 'Wouldn't dream of it.'

'Good. Because . . . I may not be from money, but my parents gave me everything to get me where I am today and we have our pride.' To her surprise, her voice cracked. She had barely given a thought to her parents until now. They would be totally out of their depth with this.

When she had first introduced them to Shane, they had worried about everything, over and over. Would he be good to her? Would he support her career? Would two careers be conducive to having kids? With Shane having one English parent and one parent from India, would any kids have to straddle three cultures and end up not fitting in anywhere? How often would they get to see her? Would he take her away from them? And when things went wrong with Shane, she had gone home to be fed and hugged and looked after until she felt better.

What would they make of Ben? A guy who was trained to kill people, whose job was a bit like being a celebrity, one who supported a lot of good causes, admittedly, but still . . .

'Hey, come here.' He tugged her to her feet and pulled her to him, so that she was sitting sideways across his lap.

'This is all new for me too,' he said. 'I admit, in the past, my family wouldn't have even considered this to be a plausible match. But now . . . nowadays things are different. Everyone has to modernise a bit. The royal institution—'

'You mean your family.'

'No. I mean the institution. We may embody the institution, but we're still people,' he said, his voice more severe than she'd ever heard before. 'The royal institution has to modernise, but we also have to tread a fine line with tradition. That's not easy.'

She ran the words through her head again. 'That's a good speech, but what does it actually mean?'

'It means, it's complicated.'

'Doesn't it just boil down to the queen giving her permission?'

Ben laughed and she felt the urge to snuggle in closer to the heart of him. 'In some matters, yes. In others there are rules that even the queen has to keep to. Most of the rules and traditions are there for a reason.'

Shane had asked her dad's permission to marry her. Back then, when it was her first marriage, it had been a big deal. Her parents had been most concerned that she married well, with very low risk of her marriage breaking down. They had been impressed by Shane, with his charm and his secure career. But the marriage had broken down anyway. So her parents' judgement wasn't any better than hers. 'I'm pretty sure the only person in my family who needs to be impressed is me,'she said, almost to herself.

He kissed her shoulder. 'And how am I doing, impressing you?'

'It's early days yet,' she said. Which was a good point. She had only known Ben for a short time and she was falling for him. But you always thought you were in love at the start of a relationship, didn't you? It was only weeks later that you realised you'd mistaken arrogant for decisive and careless for laid-back. She tightened her arms around him, as though she could hold on to these days of innocence by sheer force of will.

'Kumari,' he said, 'I know it's only been a few weeks, but I've never felt anything so right before.'

She moved her head so that she could look at his face. No matter what her doubts were about the future, she couldn't doubt how she was feeling now. This man, with his sparkling blue eyes and laugh that belonged to a giant, made her feel like a queen. And when she lay her head back against his shoulder and breathed him in, she felt like she'd come home.

'I'm not given to huge declarations of affection,' he said. 'But I think we have something here. Something worth giving time to.'

Unexpected tears prickled in her eyes. She nodded.

For a moment they held each other in silence. No words were necessary.

Finally, Kumari said, 'So what happens now?'

'I'm not sure. I think we should see each other again, but ... quietly. Under the radar. I need to prepare a few people.'

Kumari gave a little snort. 'For the fact that you're going out with someone who's the wrong colour?'

'It's more complicated than that.' There was another intense silence.

'Are you still OK?' he said. 'It's not going to be the easiest thing to do. We'd have to fit around your work and mine, and try to meet without anyone seeing us.'

'The alternative is not seeing you at all,' she said. Even after such a short time, she knew she would hate not being with him. 'So, I'm OK. Let's do this.'

'Excellent.' He squeezed her to him. 'That's what I was hoping you'd say.'

The remaining days in Namibia passed in a daze. They never made it out to see the birds or to go horse riding. Instead, they went for walks, always trailed at a distance by Dave and a colleague. They ate meals by the light of hurricane lamps and sat out in the dark, spotting constellations in the sky.

At night, they lay in bed and listened to the crickets and bats. And they talked. And talked. By the time they thanked the staff at the camp and set off for the long journey back home, Kumari felt they were so steeped in each other that she could barely tell where she ended and Ben began. She felt like she'd known him all her life.

They went up to Kumari's flat because Ben insisted on walking her to the door. Dave went ahead, radiating alertness like a leopard on the hunt. Kumari was so tired she could barely keep her eyes open. Dave stood to one side, so that she could put her key in the lock and let them in.

Lucy's coat was on the hook. Kumari put a finger to her lips. Ben crept in and put his hands on her waist. 'Goodnight, gorgeous.'

She turned in his arms. 'Thank you for a wonderful few days.'

'It was my pleasure.' He kissed her. 'I'd better go.' But he didn't release his hold on her.

She stroked the side of his face gently. 'You'll have to actually leave, you know.'

He gave a mock groan. 'I know. I don't want to.' He kissed her again.

Someone turned on the light. 'You're back. How was—?'

Kumari turned to see Lucy, in her scratty pyjama shorts, with her hair stuck up on end, standing in her doorway, her mouth an 'O'.

'Oh,' Lucy said, recovering. 'Hello.'

Ben glanced quickly at Kumari and turned to her housemate. Kumari could almost see the transition as relaxed-on-holiday Ben turned into Prince Benedict. For a second she wondered if they could get away with Lucy thinking he was a regular guy.

He smiled.

Lucy squeaked. Her mouth opened, but no words came out. Nope. There was no way Lucy didn't recognise Ben.

'Hi, I'm Ben.' He offered her his hand to shake. Lucy squeaked again and curtsied.

'You don't have to do that,' said Ben, a little sharply.

A small sound made Kumari look at the door. Dave had miraculously appeared inside the flat. Lucy didn't seem to have noticed, she was too busy staring at Ben.

Ben looked at Kumari. She understood and stepped up next to him. 'Ben, this is Lucy. She's my flatmate.'

'Lovely to meet you,' Ben said smoothly, as though they were meeting socially.

Lucy squeaked, 'Yes.'

'Um . . . look, Lucy. It's quite important that you don't tell anyone that you saw me here,' said Ben. 'Is that OK?'

Lucy nodded so hard her hair vibrated.

'Thank you. I really appreciate it.' Ben looked at Kumari. 'I'll see you later, Kumari.'

She nodded, suddenly self-conscious. 'Bye.'

The two men left, Dave checking in front and Ben following as though it was the most natural thing in the world.

She locked the door behind them. Lucy still hadn't said anything. Kumari turned slowly. Lucy seemed to unfreeze.

'You . . . you're going out with Prince freaking Benedict!'

Nothing on earth could have stopped the grin that spread on Kumari's face.

Lucy puffed out her cheeks. 'Prince Benedict was in my house.' She looked down at herself. 'And he saw me dressed like this?!' She clapped her hands to her head. 'I want to die.'

Kumari laughed. 'Don't worry about it.'

'Ha. Easy for you to say. He hasn't seen you in your horrible pyjamas.'

Except he had. Admittedly, they were her nice, silky PJs. And they hadn't stayed on very long.

Lucy rubbed her eyes. 'I have *so* many questions.'

'Maybe we should wait until morning to answer them . . .' Kumari yawned, which set Lucy yawning too.

'OK,' said Lucy. 'But I'm waking you up early tomorrow so that you can tell me *everything* before I have to go to work.'

Kumari yawned again, suddenly exhausted. 'Deal.'

Chapter 7

Pinnacle News

Prince Benedict shoots to win

Prince Benedict watched a young basketball team train yesterday. The charity Shoot for Change helps young amputees regain their sense of independence by immersing themselves in a team sport. The thirty-two-year-old prince, who was looking tanned after a recent holiday, had a go on the court with the team and said it was a delight to be outshone by the youngsters.

When asked about his love life, the playboy prince, who has not been in a serious relationship since he was twenty-seven, laughed and joked that he was about as successful there as he is on the court.

Photo caption: Near miss. The young players commiserate with the prince when he misses his shot.

'I didn't dream that, did I? He was here?' said Lucy.

Kumari had just walked out of her room. Lucy pushed a mug of coffee across to her. Kumari grasped it gratefully.

'Yes. He was here.'

'No wonder you didn't want to tell me where you were going.'

'I'm sorry, Lucy. I did want to. But it has to be a secret. For now, at least. Ben has to ... do some groundwork before anyone can know about it.'

'Why, exactly?'

Kumari looked at Lucy. 'Well, I'm not exactly princess material, am I?'

Lucy shrugged. 'I don't see why not.'

'How many reasons would you like?' She listed the same reasons she'd given Ben, counting them off on her fingers. 'I'm not an aristocrat. I'm not well connected. I'm divorced. I'm not a Christian. I'm not even white.'

'In this day and age, though, are any of those going to be a problem?'

'Yes. Of course they are. Can you imagine what would happen if the press finds out?'

'What does ... *he* ... think about it?'

'Ben,' Kumari said pointedly. 'Ben thinks that things could be difficult, but he's willing to try and so am I.'

'He's got very little risk,' said Lucy. 'If it all goes wrong, he can always claim playboy prince high jinks. You, on the other hand ...'

'I know,' said Kumari. 'I know.'

'When are you going to tell your mum?'

'Not sure. You can't say anything. To anyone. You understand how important that is, right?'

'What do you take me for? Of course I won't.' Lucy rolled her eyes.

'Sorry. No. Of course you won't.'

Lucy stared at a spot behind her for a moment. 'We should probably take my postcard down though.'

Kumari turned to look at the board of hotness on the wall with the pictures of Hugh Jackman, Chris 'Captain America' Evans and Prince Benedict pinned to it. Lucy took the postcard of Benedict down and handed it to her.

'It's a bit weird for my fantasy boyfriend board to have a picture of your actual boyfriend on it.'

'Thanks.'

'I can't believe you're going out with Prince Benedict,' Lucy said. 'Prince actual bloody Benedict.'

Kumari flushed.

'Oh, you have some messages, by the way,' said Lucy. She found the notes stuck to the fridge. 'Here you go.'

One was from the committee secretary from Better For All. The other was from Ruby. Both asked her to call them back. 'What did Ruby want?' Kumari frowned at the piece of paper. She hadn't spoken to Ruby since that first date with Ben.

'Dunno.' Lucy sliced open a bagel and fed it carefully into the toaster. 'She was intrigued about where you were though. She asked when your shift ended and I said you weren't at work, you were away and she asked if it was with a guy.'

'And you said . . . ?'

'I said yes,' said Lucy. 'I didn't realise it was a problem. She'll never guess who it is though, will she?'

Since Ruby knew she'd met Ben, she might put two and two together.

'Is it a problem?' Lucy looked worried now.

Ruby set up the first date . . . so it probably wasn't a big deal that Ruby knew now. She'd probably feel a sense of achievement at successfully matchmaking anyway. 'No, I just hope she has the sense to keep it quiet,' said Kumari.

Kumari returned her phone calls during breaks at work. She left a message with the committee secretary. Ruby, however, answered her phone.

'Oh, hello, Kumari,' said Ruby. 'I guess you're back from your break, then. How was it?'

'Lovely, thanks. You left a message for me to call you back . . . ?'

But Ruby was not so easily distracted. 'Did you go with anyone special? Someone you had a blind date with perhaps?'

Kumari laughed. 'That would be quite a whirlwind romance,' she said. 'Listen, Ruby, I'm at work and I've only got a couple of minutes.'

'Oh. You're not giving me the brush-off, are you, Kumari?'

'No. I genuinely am at work.'

Ruby gave a theatrical sigh. 'I called because we're announcing the shortlist and I'd like a quote from you. We're trying to get some publicity from the "We listen to our volunteers and staff so that we can be sure our funds are going to practical causes" line. So if you could tell us your story about Hopeful and her kid, that would be ideal.'

'Oh, sure. Would you be able to use what's in the slides? Or do you need me to write something up especially?' She processed what she'd just heard. 'Does that mean my project made the shortlist?'

'Yes. Didn't you know? Someone was supposed to call you.'

'I didn't know. That's brilliant!' She did a little dance on the spot before remembering herself. 'Who else is on the shortlist?'

'A project to build small wind turbines, the 3D-printing limbs guy and Greg Frankish,' said Ruby. 'Those are all very visual projects. We have great images from them, but we need something with a bit of pizzazz for yours. We can't use a picture of you, for obvious reasons. People will only remember the newspaper coverage of you fawning over Prince Benedict.' She paused. 'If you ended up with Prince Benedict . . .' she said.

Kumari knew the other woman was fishing for information. She felt a bit bad that she couldn't share her news with Ruby, but Ben had been very insistent on privacy. Lucy finding out was an accident, but she couldn't tell anyone else. 'I'll send you the pictures that I used in my slides.'

'Yes, please do that.'

'Of course,' said Kumari.

Kumari said her goodbyes and hung up. She punched the air. Yes. Her project had made the shortlist. She phoned Victor.

'We did it! Made it onto the shortlist!' he said. 'Now we just need to persuade them that we're the better cause.'

'The 3D-printed prosthetics project is a good one.'

'Yes. But we need to be awesome. The feedback says that they feel we'll need a few days with a UK-based project coordinator as well as a local one. They're probably right. So we need to redo the numbers.'

Kumari sucked her teeth. 'That's a significant change.'

'We could do it,' said Victor thoughtfully. 'We'd need to work out how much extra it would cost. There's some leeway in the costing, so we could go up a bit . . .'

Victor worked in the funding office of Better For All. They knew exactly how much everything cost. When Kumari had first come up with the idea, she had approached him to help her cost it. As part of the funding application process, Better For All had allowed each pitch a few hours of funding coordinator time, so that they could ensure they were asking for the right amount of money. Victor had worked on the project with her outside of the allotted time, focusing on how to get everything they wanted to fit into the budget they were applying for, while Kumari honed the application to make sure the pitch hit all the keywords and aligned with the charity's objectives.

Kumari had the vision and wrote the proposal. Victor had the number-crunching expertise. If the project got funded, she would take on the role of project coordinator. If the project didn't get funded, it meant Kumari's involvement in the charity would go back to being a voluntary consultant for a few hours a month, helping review ongoing projects. It would be such a loss for Kumari and the women she hoped to help. 'Can you do the numbers again?' she asked.

'That's the problem,' said Victor. 'I don't think I can. I've got too much on. I've got a few personal things coming up too, so I can't help outside of work hours. I'm so sorry, Kumari.'

Kumari could hear from his voice that he was stressed.

'Don't worry, Victor, I'm sure I can deal with it,' she said in her most reassuring voice. 'You've helped me so much already.'

She chewed the inside of her cheek. She had been relying on Victor's help. Could she do the work herself? She didn't have the expertise and it would take her longer to find the information, but maybe . . .

'There's a temp here at the moment, Rita. She's been covering a funding coordinator role,' said Victor. 'I could ask her if she fancies having a go at this. I know she's been wanting something more substantial to work on. If it gets funded, it'll look good on her CV, especially if she wants to keep working in the sector.'

Oh, thank goodness. 'Would she mind?

Victor laughed. 'I shouldn't think so. She's bright and I think she'll find it interesting. I'll ask her.'

'Thank you Victor, you're a star.'

'You're welcome, Kumari. You know I think this is a great idea. It could make such a difference.'

She told him about Ruby's ideas for publicity and then, glancing at her watch, realised she had less than two minutes left of her break and quickly said her goodbyes.

As she speed-walked through the hospital corridors to get to her ward, she couldn't help smiling to herself. Things were looking up.

Chapter 8

The Daily Flash

Has the prince finally met his perfect match?

The most eligible bachelor in the nation, Prince Benedict, was seen out with pop sensation Jenny Dawes-Green (27) at the after-party for the Radio Music Awards last night. The prince (32), who has been single since he broke up with his last girlfriend, Posy Wilberforce, is no stranger to partying. He has been keeping a low profile of late, a change from his wild partying days, prompting speculation that he is once again seeing someone.

Dawes-Green, the lead singer in the chart-topping indie band Herculean, was seen talking and laughing with the prince, who is currently sixth in line to the throne. Aside from being a talented musician, Dawes-Green is known to be a formidable business manager too. Could she be the mysterious new girlfriend who has tamed the party prince? At five years younger, is she too young for the thirty-two-year-old prince?

Photo caption: Prince Benedict returning to his party lifestyle?

'I should get a haircut.' Kumari poked a wayward lock of hair. 'It's getting to the unmanageable stage.'

'Relax, you look fine,' said Lucy.

They were in the ladies' loos attached to the doctors' restroom. They didn't often get time to talk at work, but one of Lucy's theatre patients had been cancelled, so she was taking a quick breather before going in to prep for the next one.

Lucy did a quick check to see the cubicles weren't occupied, before saying in an undertone, 'Besides, he's seen you first thing in the morning. A bit of mad hair is hardly going to bother him.'

'Yes, but next week we're going out,' said Kumari.

Lucy looked confused. 'And the last couple of months you've been . . . ?'

'I mean actually out,' said Kumari. 'We've mostly been meeting at his place so far . . . so it's kind of a big deal.'

Realisation dawned. 'Oh!' Lucy's eyes were huge. 'Does that mean you're official now?'

'No. Not at all. It's just that he thought it would be nice to see how it went. We're going to some private club or other. He's going to introduce me to his best friend. It should be reasonably quiet.'

'Do you mind all the cloak and dagger stuff?' asked Lucy. 'It must be weird being the guilty secret. Like being the other woman.'

Kumari shrugged. She hadn't thought of it like that. In fact, she liked the clandestine nature of her relationship with Ben. It was completely different to any of her previous relationships, even the one with Shane. She put it down to the fact that they were both that much older. They both had obligations, and they both took their work very seriously. It was nice that he respected hers.

'I miss you,' Lucy said suddenly.

Kumari looked at her friend. They didn't see much of each other now – between their varied shifts and her being away in Ben's apartment all the time, she and Lucy tended to communicate via text more than speech nowadays.

'I'm sorry,' she said. 'I didn't mean for things to turn out like this.'

'I know,' said Lucy. 'And I don't begrudge you your fun for a minute, but . . . y'know. I miss hanging out with you.'

Kumari gave her a hug. 'I miss you too.' She released her friend and said, 'I was thinking of asking Ben if he could invite you round to his place in Kensington at some point. I don't know if it's feasible . . . he has to run it past the security people, but . . . if you're up for it?'

'What do you mean, if I'm up for it? You *know* I'm up for it!'

'I'll ask him then.'

Lucy gave the sort of squeal that could only be heard by dogs and bats.

Another doctor walked in. 'What are you two so excited about?' she asked.

'Neurotoxins,' said Lucy.

The other doctor rolled her eyes. 'Anaesthetists.'

The car dropped Kumari off at the entrance nearest Ben's apartment in Kensington Palace. The butler, who was called Mr Forrest, even by Ben, let her in and greeted her as Dr Senavaka. She ran up the stairs like she belonged there.

Ben's idea of a clandestine relationship involved her being picked up by specially arranged cars and brought to Kensington so that they could spend time together in his apartments. Or, as he called it, his 'flat'. The fact that her actual flat would fit comfortably into one of the reception rooms in his place seemed totally irrelevant to him.

She wasn't complaining about the low-key nature of their relationship. Her days of going out and partying were behind her now. Spending time at Ben's place meant quiet nights in and home-cooked meals, there was no pressure to be sociable. He was a better cook than she was, she was eating better than she had ever done while single. They had slipped into cosy domesticity with surprising ease.

'Hello, you,' he said when he opened the door.

'Hi.' She sniffed the air. 'Something smells amazing. What's cooking?'

He took the carrier bag she offered him. It contained two slices of cheesecake from a bakery near her flat. He preferred to make savoury meals, so she always picked up something for pudding. 'I'm making roast chicken with Moroccan-style vegetables,' he said, heading back to the kitchen. 'It's a bit random, but Ophie had this jar of harissa that she didn't know what to do with, so she gave it to me. I'm using that up.'

Ophie being Princess Ophelia. Not the heir. The other one. Ben talked about his sisters with fondness. Being an only child, Kumari had nothing to compare his experience to, but, as far as she could tell, he and his sisters squabbled and loved each other just like any other siblings would.

Kumari took her shoes off, partly from habit, partly because she loved the feel of the thick carpet under her stockinged feet, and followed Ben into the kitchen. It never ceased to amaze her how far you had to walk to cross the room. There was so much space between the items of furniture.

Ben poured a glass of wine and pushed it across to her.

'Actually,' he said. 'I need to talk to you about that.'

She gratefully took a sip. 'About what?'

'About my sisters.' He opened the oven door and frowned at the chicken inside. 'One sec.'

She waited while he fussed around with the food and wondered what he could want to talk to her about. The tension she had felt easing away returned to her shoulders. Until now, it had been about just them. They had both avoided bringing the outside world, including their families, into any discussions. Oh, they'd talked about growing up and how they fitted into their families in the abstract, but they'd never discussed them specifically. How could they? His family were the royals, directly descended from the current queen, while hers were a teacher and a nurse from Yorkshire, first generation immigrants from Sri Lanka. If she ever needed a reminder about how mad this relationship was, that was it.

Ben closed the oven again and came to stand next to her.

'So, what about your sisters?'

He twizzled the stem of his wine glass. 'We've been seeing each other for over two months now,' he said slowly. 'And I really, really like you.'

She didn't say anything, but was suddenly aware of her own breathing, the pounding of her heart.

He finally raised his eyes to meet hers. 'I'd like to introduce you to my sisters.'

Which would make her officially his girlfriend. Eeep. She wasn't ready for that yet. Was she? What did that mean for her? For him? For her family? For work? She stared at him, too overwhelmed to speak.

'Kumari?'

'I . . . I'd love to meet them but does that mean . . . ?' She gestured to the two of them.

Ben smiled and leant forward. 'Well, yes. It would mean telling them we're a couple. Which rather makes it official.'

She should have been deliriously happy, but all she could think of were the questions. She picked up her glass and took a large sip of wine. Her hand shook.

Ben stopped smiling. 'Oh.' Carefully, he removed her glass from her hand. He took her arm and led her into the sitting room, where they usually watched telly. He sat her down.

'I'm sorry. I didn't think. I should have led up to this a bit. I was so excited about the whole thing that I forgot how this must feel for you.'

'I'm sorry too,' she said. 'I don't know why it hit me so hard. I know who you are. It's just that . . . Ben, it's going to change things, isn't it? If I'm formally with you.'

'It is, yes.' He took her hands in his. 'I love you. I know it's only been a short time but I have never been surer about anything in my life.'

'I love you too.' She did. Thoughts of him filled every moment she had to herself. A life without him was unthinkable. But . . . 'This is a bit scary. Tell me. Tell me what to expect. Let me work things out.'

Ben let out a long breath. 'OK. Well, once this goes public, you're going to become famous, practically overnight. I don't mean small-time Internet famous. I mean proper, intrusive famous. The press is going to start following you around. People will start digging up things about you and your family. The first thing we'll have to do, once we tell my family, is to arrange for you to meet someone from my press team, so that they can work out if there's anything they need to be aware of. We'll have to arrange security for you, maybe. People you barely know will claim they're your best friend and talk to the papers.'

'I don't like cameras.' Her mouth felt dry. 'I'm not sure how I feel about that.'

'Trust me, I don't like them either.' His face was grim. 'But they are a fact of life around here.'

She had a sudden memory of photos of him, taken at his mother's funeral. Even in the most private of grief, he and his sisters had been photographed.

She felt the tightening in her chest. 'Will they hassle my parents too?'

Ben nodded. 'I'm sorry. We'll do what we can. Talk to the local police, get the press office to keep an eye out for the worst, but yes, they will attract some interest too, but nowhere near as much as you will.'

She let that sink in. 'I'll have to warn them.'

'Yes, that would be wise. It may be an idea for them to go and visit friends or something for a couple of weeks when the news comes out. News tends to become "old news" eventually. Hopefully, if they're not easy to find, the press will lose interest after a while.'

She thought about her family and their quiet, lower middle-class life. It was hard to imagine their routine being disrupted by anything, but he was right. They would need to do something to protect themselves from the spotlight.

'And what about my work?'

'While we're only going out,' he said carefully, 'then probably nothing needs to change. There'll be a few weeks of spotlight, but it's likely to be manageable.'

The emphasis on 'while we're only going out' didn't escape her. She narrowed her eyes. 'And if we become more serious? Like get engaged?'

His face told her everything.

'I'm not giving up work,' she said flatly. 'It's my career, Ben.'

'But it's a public-facing career. It will be difficult to maintain.'

'Other people manage. Your brother-in-law is a lawyer.'

'A lawyer with a very expensive law firm. Not many members of the public can walk in and talk to him on a whim,' said Ben. 'Unlike the hospital.'

She knew what he said was true, especially when she worked in A & E. 'But it's my career. I worked my arse off to get to where I am. I'm good at what I do. You can't ask me to just drop it and become . . . a royal housewife or whatever it is your people call it.'

'My people?' Ben's voice took on a sharper edge. His face reddened. 'My people are the British people.'

'No. Your people are the royal family. Trust me, that is not the same thing.'

'Fine,' he snapped. 'Well "my people", as you call them, would not expect you to be a housewife – although there was nothing wrong with being a full-time mother the last time I checked with anyone.'

'That is not what I meant and you know it.' Her voice had risen. She took a deep breath and forced herself to calm down, just a notch. 'What I meant is, that I can't not work. I would go mad. My work is important to me. It's my career. My livelihood.' She threw up her hands. 'If I stop working, I will be entirely dependent on you! How will I ever find a job when we break up?'

Ben recoiled as though she'd struck him. He stood up from the sofa and backed away from her.

She realised what she'd said. 'Ben . . .'

'When?' he said. '*When* we break up?'

'I'm sorr—'

'You don't even have faith enough to say *if* we break up?' Now his face was bright red. 'Is that what this is to you, Kumari? A brief fling? Some fun times before you go back to life the way it's always been? A . . . a game?' He put his hands to his head. 'Well, it's not a game to me.'

Kumari stood up too. 'Isn't it, Ben? Think about what you're asking me to do. You're not risking anything. But, me? I'd be risking my career, the lives of my family, everything I hold dear. Excuse me for not rolling over and accepting it.'

When he didn't turn round, she felt a leaden weight settle in her stomach. He thought she wasn't serious about him. That she had been playing with his affections simply for fun. Nothing could be further from the truth, but if that's what he thought then perhaps this argument had been for the best. 'I think I should go,' she said quietly.

He didn't turn around. He was still angry with her.

She walked away from him, past the kitchen where the dinner was still cooking, through the reception room with the carpet so thick it tickled. With each step she could feel the connection between them stretching. It was a pain that was almost physical. Her eyes hurt with the effort of not crying. She found her boots, stepped into them and knelt down to zip them up. They swam in front of her as her eyes filled with tears.

'Wait.'

She turned, blinking back the tears. Ben stood in the doorway at the other end of the room. His face was a mask of misery. 'You're right,' he said.

She straightened up, still kneeling. She might as well hear what he had to say. If she walked out now, she wouldn't see him again. All he'd have to do is block her from his private phone and then, snip. End of connection.

'You're right about the risks and sacrifices I'm asking of you,' he said. 'I was so wrapped up in how I felt I didn't stop to think about how you might feel.'

She nodded, the weight in her chest shifted a bit.

'Thank you.'

He took a small step towards her. 'Can we talk about this? Will you stay for dinner?' He gestured towards the kitchen. 'There's far too much food for me to eat by myself.'

Could they talk? The pain in her heart made her want to stay. The stubborn, bloody-minded side of her was still smarting and wanted to leave. Her hands hovered over her boots. If she left, there would be no more Ben. No more teasing about her having a spectacles fetish. No more evenings sitting on the sofa talking about how they would change the world. No more comparing notes on humanitarian causes they both supported from their very different vantage points. No more laughter. It would be a future bleached of all things good.

'I've made you roast chicken,' Ben said weakly. 'I was going to make Yorkshire pudding. The sort that's from frozen.'

That was what did it. He'd remembered.

She stood up and pushed one of her boots off her foot. She glanced over at Ben. He gave her a hopeful smile. She kicked the other boot off and turned just in time to face him when he scooped her up in a hug.

She buried her face in the side of his neck and breathed in the woodland and summer smell of him. How did she think she could ever live without him when his arms felt so much like home?

He caught her face in his hands and kissed her.

'I think we have a lot we need to discuss,' he said.

'We do.' She bit her lip. 'For what it's worth, I don't see this as a short-term thing. But I'm scared and over-whelmed and I can't see how this can possibly survive the real world.'

He gathered her close again, squeezing her against his hard body. 'It will,' he said. He laid little butterfly kisses on her eyelids. 'We'll make sure of it.'

Chapter 9

The Aurora Post

Horsing around at Badminton

The evening events at the Badminton Horse Trials are always a great place for youthful antics and gossip. Here are a few people we ran into at the gala dinner.

Prince Benedict was seen laughing and joking with millionaire heiress Gwyneth Ellesmere-Jones. The prince and Ellesmere-Jones have been linked before, hardly surprising as her big brother Rhodri Ellesmere-Jones is the prince's best friend. Has the prince fallen for his best friend's sister? These pictures would certainly suggest that romance is on the cards.

Picture caption: Prince Benedict and Gwyneth Ellesmere-Jones laughing at a private joke.

The first thing to do, they decided, was to tell their families. Once the royal household was told, things would be set in motion that would take up most of Kumari's time when she wasn't at work, so the first chance she got, she drove home.

It was late afternoon by the time she got there and the sunshine cast long shadows across the cul-de-sac.

Parking her car, she remembered to put it into gear and give the handbrake an extra heft to stop it from rolling down the hill. She got her bag out of the back and waved at the net-curtained windows of number one. Old Mrs Webb would have heard the car and come to check who it was. No one ever came in or out without her knowing. She was a one-woman Neighbourhood Watch.

Kumari walked down the street that she'd grown up on. Her mother kept her up to date with what was happening with everyone. Kumari had been a pre-schooler when they'd moved here and though they'd lived there for nearly thirty years, they were still 'that new family'. Everyone else knew each other from old because either they or their parents had lived here since the houses were built.

Her parents' neighbours, Albert and Betty, were in their tiny front garden, taking in the last of the day's sunshine with their cups of tea.

'Hello, love. You back home for a holiday?' asked Betty.

'Just a flying visit,' said Kumari. 'How're you? Keeping OK?'

Betty proceeded to tell her about her various aches and pains. Kumari listened and suggested that she see her GP about the recurring cough. It was a good few minutes before she could carry on to her house.

It was the sort of neighbourhood where people knew everything about each other. Her father used to say that you could blow your nose in your own house and by the next morning everyone in the street would be asking about your cold.

She let herself into the house and shouted, 'Hello.' The place smelt of spices and air freshener. Her mother, always self-conscious that the house shouldn't smell of curry, tended to cook in the daytime, with the back door open, despite the cold, so that the worst of the smell of frying spices escaped into the hillside. Kumari had always known when it was batch-cooking day because she came home from school to a house where the gas fire in the living room had still not managed to take the chill off the room.

Tonight, though, the house was warm.

'Kumari!' Her mother bustled out. She was still in her nursing uniform and cardigan. Unlike Kumari, her mother was petite, but what she lacked in height, she made up for in presence. She worked as a nurse and had the uncanny knack of making cranky children do as they were told.

Kumari turned from hanging up her coat to give her mother a hug and then bowed quickly, palms together, for a blessing. Her mother leant forward and kissed the top of her bent head.

'Come, come. Let me get you some tea. You must have driven straight up without stopping.'

'Actually, I did stop, but tea would be lovely. Hello, Thatha.' Her father was sitting at the kitchen table, doing his marking. He beamed at her. She noticed that he looked older now, there were more lines on his face and more white at his temples and in his moustache. She bowed in front of him and received a blessing and a kiss on the head from him too.

There were a few minutes of bustling around and generally catching up before Kumari was sitting at the table, opposite her parents, clutching a mug of tea.

Her parents exchanged a glance. She knew that look. It was her parents gearing up to act as a team. After thirty-odd years of marriage, they drew up the rules in a single glance. Kumari realised that in her time with Shane, she'd never reached that level of understanding. She liked to think that with Ben, she might actually get there.

'So,' her mother said, 'what was so important that you had to rush up here?'

There was no point beating around the bush. 'As you know, I've met someone,' she said. 'His name is Ben . . . he's, well, I think he's wonderful.'

'Darling, that's fantastic,' her mother said. 'Oh, I'm very pleased to hear that – aren't we, Sena?'

She still called him 'Sena', short for Senavaka, which was his nickname at university. He called her Ruki, short for Rukmali. Kumari loved that.

There was a pause for general congratulations before her father picked up the conversational baton. 'So, tell us about this man. This Ben. Who is he? What does he do?'

Kumari took in a deep breath. She had practised so many different ways of telling them, but none of them seemed adequate.

'Kumari?' said her mother. 'What is it, darling? Is something wrong?'

She shook her head. 'No. Nothing's wrong. Um . . .' There was no other way to tackle it. 'Who he is and what he does . . . are pretty much the same thing. His name's Ben, but you know him as Benedict. Prince Benedict.'

There was a silence. Her parents looked at each other again. For once, it seemed that neither of them knew what to say.

'He's the . . . grandson of the queen,' Kumari supplied.

'Yes.' Amma frowned at her tea. 'So that's why you didn't tell Lucy or me where you were going when you went away with him. Security reasons?'

'Yes.'

'And that's why you've not been home when I called. You were out with him?'

'Yes.'

They looked at each other. 'The prince,' Amma said, her voice bordering on awe.

Thatha gave a little laugh. 'At least we don't need to ask where his family's from.'

Amma giggled. 'Or where they live.' She turned back to Kumari. 'That's . . . incredible. How did this happen? How did my girl end up meeting a prince? Is it when you fell into his arms? Did he fall instantly in love with you?'

'Come on now, Ruki. Don't be silly.' He said it with a groan, but Kumari could see he was burning to know too.

Kumari grinned. 'It started there,' she said. She told them what had happened. When she recounted it, it dawned on her how fast things had moved. It was a whirlwind romance. She stopped smiling. She had grown up not trusting whirlwind things. She was a measured, sensible sort of person. But then, her first relationship had been all about measured and sensible and that hadn't turned out well. Besides, being with Ben felt right in a way that being with Shane hadn't.

'Oh, well that's wonderful,' said her mother. 'It'll be nice for you to go out and have some fun! And you could meet some amazing people.'

Her father cleared his throat, serious once more. 'Are you sure about this, Kumari? You are clearly worried about something. What exactly is bothering you about him?'

'It's not him. He's lovely. I genuinely like him. It's just . . . everything else.'

'Genuinely like him?' her mother said. 'Is that all you feel for him? Are you not sure? Are you being pressured?' She reached across and put a hand on her daughter's. 'Darling, just because he is a prince, doesn't mean he can tell you what to do.'

'Oh no. It's not that.' Kumari smiled. 'I love him. I adore him. But it's complicated.'

The words 'love him' had a strange effect on her parents. Two concerned faces looked back at her. She realised that they had assumed that seeing Benedict was a temporary thing. But now that they realised she was serious about it, they were less relaxed. The worry lines made her want to cry. She waited for the all-too familiar questions, but they didn't come. Her parents looked at each other and looked sad.

'Aren't you going to give me a lecture about us being from two different backgrounds? Or about being sure? Like you did when I told you about Shane?'

'Come now, Kumari. You're not stupid. Even you can see how different your worlds are. Even if you were a standard white, middle-class girl, you wouldn't have anything in common with this man. He's a prince. And one who likes his wine, women and parties, at that. Are you sure you're not just a novelty to him? A PR stunt?'

'Definitely not a PR stunt,' she said. 'We've been very careful to keep it secret. As for the other things, I don't think much of that is true. Not unless he's a really convincing actor.'

Another worried glance between them.

'A lot of the stuff in the newspapers about him – it's made up. Not all of it, obviously. He's told me about what he went through in the army and I'm not surprised he drank a lot when he came back, but the girlfriends . . . most of those were just women he happened to speak to and if someone got a picture of them standing together, they reported it as though he had a new girlfriend.'

Her parents didn't look convinced.

'I've spent a lot of time with him over the last few months,' she said. 'He drinks less than I do and clearly doesn't spend a lot of time partying either.'

'You are an adult now,' her father said. 'And we have to let you make your own choices . . . but, darling, think about this. This man's lifestyle – it's very public. If things go wrong, everyone will know about it.'

He didn't need to say 'and we think it will go wrong', it was obvious in his tone. Anyway, hadn't she herself assumed that a few days ago?

'You were so upset when things went wrong with Shane,' said her mother. 'We'd hate to see that happen to you again. Prince Benedict . . . he's not a reliable sort of person, is he?' She threw a glance at her husband. 'And some members of the royal family are a bit' – her voice dropped to a whisper, as though she was afraid of being overheard – 'much.'

'But you love the royals!' Kumari said. 'You and Lucy talk about them for hours.'

'Their public personalities, yes,' said her mother. 'In real life, I don't think anyone would want that life. Nothing is sacred. When their mother died, there were cameras everywhere those poor children went. It's not a life you'd want to lead.'

Slowly and carefully, Kumari explained what she and Ben had discussed the night before.

When she'd finished, her father said, 'I see. And what are you asking us today?'

'I'm not sure,' she said, which she knew was a perfectly acceptable answer. 'Permission. Advice.'

They looked at each other. Then her mother said, 'Darling, permission – you don't need our permission. You're an adult now. If this man will make you happy then you have our permission implicitly.'

'Advice then. I love him. I want to be with him, but it's so complicated. I don't even know where to start.' That feeling of thoughts whirling round her head was back. There were so many things to think about, it was hard to work out which thought to follow first.

'Start with the basics,' her father said. 'Does he love you back?'

'Yes.' She was surprised at how certain she felt.

'How do you know this?'

'He wants me to meet his family.' Which was a big deal for him, she knew.

There was a moment of silence before her mother said, 'The . . . the queen?'

'Eventually, but his sisters – Princess Helena and Princess Ophelia – to start with. And the Prince of Wales, his dad.' She grinned. 'That sounds so weird saying it out loud.'

Her mother tried not to smile and failed. 'Yes, well.'

'Nevertheless,' said her father sternly. 'Coming back to the conversation. This man, he is a military man, yes?'

'Former military, yes.'

'And how does that sit with you? You are trained to save lives. He has, essentially, been trained to shoot people.'

She was shocked by this. 'Thatha, he doesn't shoot people! The army is about much more than that.'

'But that's what he was trained to do. He was in active service. I'm not saying he's not a good man in civilian life, darling, but he has been trained to kill. What will happen when you have to listen to phrases like "collateral damage" and not react? Can you cope with that?'

'We share the same ideology about making the world a better place for people . . .'

'Do you share the same view of acceptable ways of going about that?'

'Yes.' They hadn't discussed that. All their conversations were about the good causes that they supported. If they supported the same causes . . . surely that meant they agreed. 'I think.'

'And what about diplomacy?' said her mother. 'What happens when you have to sit down to dinner with some crazed despot in the name of diplomacy? We brought you up to stand up for what you believe, how will you deal with that?'

Kumari sighed. That was going to be a problem. She did tend to shoot her mouth off without thinking. 'Ben says there will be training. If we get engaged.'

'Training?'

She nodded. 'Actually, there will be quite a lot of people involved in getting me up to standard with the royal stuff.'

She listed the things Ben had mentioned. 'Etiquette, protocol, style, diplomacy, security and there were some others I've forgotten . . . not to mention all the actual engagements and visits and stuff.'

'That sounds like a lot of work,' her mother said doubtfully. 'I have no doubt you'll learn everything, you've always been good at that, but . . . what about your job?'

'That's the other thing. I would have to give up my job.' Her parents were so horrified, they both physically moved back a little. She knew that feeling. She had spent her entire life working towards being a doctor. Her parents had poured everything into getting her there – her mother working extra weekend shifts and over the Christmas holidays, her father plugging away at the same school, despite being passed over for promotion because the headmaster still pretended that Mr Senavaka's practically non-existent accent was too strong for the students to understand. Everything had been focused towards getting Kumari through university and into a successful career as a doctor. Even taking a year out to go to work in Lesotho and her putting together the Boost Her! project proposal had been partly couched as a way of improving her CV, as well as being a chance to do good at the sharp end of a humanitarian crisis. To give all that up for a man, even if that man was a prince, was a bitter pill to swallow.

'That's . . . that's a big thing to ask,' said her father.

'I know.'

'How do you feel about that?' Her mother leant forward again.

'I . . . honestly, I don't want to stop work. My job makes a difference, you know. I don't want to give that up . . . But Ben's right. I couldn't carry on working. It's . . . well, I wouldn't be able to do normal shifts and I wouldn't be able to be a member of a team. Then there's the security aspect of it all.' She lifted her hands, a small defeated gesture. 'I can't see how I can do it. I would have to choose between working and being with him.'

Everyone was silent for a few minutes, each lost in thought.

'Perhaps . . .' her father said. 'Perhaps this man isn't the right man for you.'

She stared at him. 'But I love him.' The minute the words came out of her mouth, she realised how true they were. 'I really love him.'

'You thought you loved Shane,' her mother reminded her.

'I was so young when I met Shane. I didn't know what love was. I thought it was hearts and flowers and grand gestures. I forgot that when that phase has passed, you need to be able to live together and do dull things. With Ben . . . it feels comfortable. Like finding the perfect chair or the jumper that fits. When I'm with him everything seems like it was meant to be.'

They exchanged glances again. 'We're just worried about you getting hurt. Even if you and he were fine . . . and I'm sure you are,' said Amma. 'Even if all that was fine, the press intrusion would make your life miserable.'

She had rehearsed the response to this one. 'Prince Benedict is fairly popular. He thinks the press would largely be on his side.'

Her mother gave a little laugh. 'Your tone when you say "Prince Benedict" is different to how you say "Ben",' she said. 'It's almost as though you're talking about two different people.'

'I am,' she said. 'Ben . . . my Ben, is different to the guy you see on telly and in the newspapers. He doesn't drink nearly as much for a start.'

'Well, I must admit that is a relief to hear,' her mother said.

'And he's nice. You'd like him.'

'Can we meet him?' Her father's frown was back. 'I suppose we'll have to come to London.' He cast a glance around their small house. It was cosy and comfortable, but very small. 'He can't come here.'

'No. We'd have to go to him. To Ben's place in Kensington Palace, maybe.' She paused to look at their faces. They both looked a little stunned. She grinned. 'I'm sorry, you both look so surprised. It's funny.'

'Well,' said her mother, 'we can't all throw around phrases like "Prince Benedict's place in Kensington Palace" in everyday conversation.'

Kumari smiled. 'Obviously, I don't need to tell you not to tell anyone,' she said.

'No,' said Amma. 'Of course not.' She caught Thatha's eye. 'Can you imagine?'

He smiled. 'Imagine if Sonali Aunty found out.'

Amma started to laugh. 'She'd want to come and visit immediately. You'd have a hell of a time keeping her out of Kensington Palace.'

Kumari could picture her Sonali Aunty and the tide of other aunties swarming in Ben's big apartment, investigating everything, taking pictures so that they could tell everyone that they knew Prince Benedict personally, and had been to his house. 'No,' she said. 'Definitely don't tell anyone. Especially the aunties.'

At the end of the evening, before she went to bed, Amma said, 'Remember that we're always here for you if you need us. No matter what happens, there will always be a safe place for you here.'

While Kumari really hoped she wouldn't need to take them up on that again, it was still nice to know. 'I'll remember that,' she said.

'We just want you to be happy.'

Kumari gave her mother a tight hug. She had been right to come home and talk to her parents. They were in her corner no matter what happened. It made everything feel more manageable.

Chapter 10

Adorable pictures of Princess Francesca as she turns five!

Buckingham Palace has released official photographs of Princess Francesca's fifth birthday. The young princess is pictured in a formal pose with her parents, HRH Princess Helena and the Duke of Tewksbury, and her grandparents. The photograph that will melt the nation's hearts, though, is the one of Princess Francesca holding the hand of her eighteen-month-old sister, Princess Maria. The two princesses are third and fourth in line to the throne respectively.

Photo captions: The birthday girl with her sister. Photo caption: Informal photograph of the younger royals, Princess Francesca sits in between her mother, Princess Helena, and her aunt, Princess Ophelia, while little Princess Maria is on the shoulders of her uncle, Prince Benedict.

'Are you sure this looks OK?' Kumari checked herself in the mirror yet again. She was wearing a long, cream skirt and a loose-fitting blouse, gathered at the waist.

Ben appeared behind her, dressed in jeans, a shirt and a jumper. He looked impeccably groomed, like a catalogue model for Boden. He put his hands on her waist and kissed her cheek. 'Relax, you're going for tea, not a ball.'

She side-eyed him. 'Easy for you to say. They're your family. To me, they're the famous people I've only ever seen on TV before.'

'So was I, until you got to know me,' he said. 'I'm not so bad, right?'

'No. Fine. OK.'

He picked up the bottle of wine and the small pack of gifts that Kumari had got for the children.

'It's nothing fancy,' she said, now worried about the gifts. 'They're just things that my friends' kids like.'

'Helena's kids get all kinds of expensive nonsense that they're not interested in. The last time I went over, we played a ridiculous game involving lining marbles up on the weave of a wicker chair. I don't think they care about how expensive toys are.'

'But their mother might.'

'Nah.' He ushered her out of the apartment.

'So, is this bit of Kensington full of apartments and houses belonging to members of the royal family?' she asked, as they wandered through the building.

'Yes. And some of the staff.' He said hello to a butler who let them out through a side door. 'There are comm— regular people's apartments on the other side.' They were in a small quadrangle now. A man in uniform who was having a smoke hastily extinguished his cigarette and saluted. Ben acknowledged him. They walked across the quad into another building.

'So it's like some sort of royal enclave,' she said.

He gave her a stern glance. She smothered a giggle. 'Oh, come on, Ben. You've got to admit it's funny. It's like those places in Sri Lanka where the patriarch has built several homes on the same humongous piece of land and everyone there is related to each other.'

'If you say so,' he said. His eyes twinkled, but he didn't laugh. The further they got from the apartment, the more tense he seemed to become.

More corridors. Kumari felt the odd sensation that someone was following them. She turned to see that Ben's bodyguard, Dave, and a colleague had appeared behind them. How did he do that? Dave nodded to her.

They finally emerged through a side door into a kitchen garden. He led her through, nodding to the gardeners, who all paused in their work to greet him. An opening through a high box hedge led to a lovely enclosed garden where a table was set with a white tablecloth and food. There were finger sandwiches and plates filled with little square cakes. It was a proper afternoon tea. A few chairs were dotted around. A little girl, around five years old, was being chased around by a toddler. As soon as the older child spotted Ben, she changed course and ran straight to him. 'Uncle Ben!'

Ben handed Kumari the bottle of wine and scooped up the little girl and, meeting her sister halfway, scooped her up too.

Feeling a little lost, Kumari followed him as he walked across the lawn, a child in each arm.

Princess Helena stood up. 'Hello, Benedict.' She offered her cheek for him to kiss, then turned to Kumari.

'And you're Kumari. I'm so pleased to meet you. Benedict has told us so much about you . . .' She glanced at Ben. 'Actually, that's not totally true. He's kept you very much to himself until last week, and he hasn't stopped talking about you since. So I suppose it evens out.'

Kumari curtsied as she'd been taught.

'Oh thank you. Presents for the children,' she said, noticing the parcels Kumari was carrying. 'How lovely. Ben, put the girls down so they can open them.'

Ben put the children down. Princess Helena introduced them – princesses Francesca, the older one, and Maria, the toddler. Kumari bent down to their level and both children solemnly shook hands with her. She gave them their gifts and after a swift glance at their mother to check it was OK they opened the little bags. Kumari watched self-consciously as they each pulled out a toy made of a stick with paper furled around it so that when they 'threw' it, the paper unfurled into a cone and then shrank back again. It took a couple of goes before the older one managed it with a shriek of laughter. Princess Helena helped the toddler with hers. Soon the kids were running around 'throwing' the paper cones at everyone.

Ben put his arm around Kumari's waist as they watched them.

'Well, that should keep them happy for a while,' said Princess Helena. She had the strange upper-class accent that made words sound like they had odd vowels in them. 'Please sit down, Kumari. Let's have a cup of tea.'

They sat at one of the tables that had been set and the princess poured tea. 'How do you take it?'

'Milk, no sugar,' Kumari said.

'See that, no sugar, Benedict.' Helena raised her eyebrows at her brother. 'You should listen to the good doctor.'

He rolled his eyes.

'So, Benedict tells me you worked in Africa vaccinating children, Kumari,' she said. 'Tell me more.'

Kumari told her about the vaccination programme and the plight of women and children there. Helena listened to her, seemingly very interested. Every so often, she would ask a question. Kumari wondered if effective listening was something else the royals were trained in. Ben did it too. A sort of intense concentration, as though they could think of nothing better than to hear what you had to say. Surely no one could be that interested in anything. She made a note to ask Ben about it.

After a few minutes, Ben slipped off to play with his nieces, leaving Kumari with the princess. She watched him leave. When she turned back, Helena was watching her.

'My brother is very taken with you,' she said carefully. What was she supposed to take from that? 'Oh. Thank you,' she said politely.

'More so than I've ever seen before,' she added. 'He is, I believe, in love with you.'

Kumari felt the colour rise in her cheeks.

Helena leant forward. 'How do you feel about him?'

That was easy. 'I love him.'

Helena's eyes searched hers. 'Tell me, Kumari, how do you like the life here in Kensington? It must be different to the life of a doctor.'

'I am still a doctor,' Kumari said. 'But life here is very different to what I'm used to.'

'Do you think you could become used to it?'

Kumari's eyes strayed towards Ben, who was throwing the younger child in the air. 'To be with him . . . yes.'

'That's good.'

Kumari got the impression that Helena didn't approve of her. Or rather, that she hadn't made up her mind whether Kumari was an acceptable match for her brother or not. Ben cast a worried glance in their direction. This afternoon was more important to him than he let on. Kumari took a sip of tea from the delicate china cup. All she could do was be herself. If the princess didn't approve, then she and Ben would have to handle it as best they could.

The little Princess Francesca ran up to her mother.

'Can I show Kumari the new pond?' she asked.

'Of course. You must. You can show Uncle Ben too.'

'Oh.' Kumari put down her tea and took the pudgy little hand that was offered to her. The little girl reached for Ben with her free hand and walked them both down to the end of the picturesque garden.

The pond was slightly raised, with brand new brickwork.

'The gardeners put frog spawn in it,' Francesca informed them. 'So we'll have frogs to look for soon.' She pointed out various bits of interesting greenery, that meant very little to Kumari. Like Ben, she feigned interest. He kept shooting glances at her over the golden head of his niece.

Finally, when Francesca had exhausted the delights of the pond, she announced she would race them back and set off at a run. A nanny, who had been hovering not far away, set off after her.

Ben took Kumari's hand. 'How did it go with Helena?' he asked.

'She's very polite, but I don't think she likes me much.'

'Oh, she's very protective of me. It's a big sister thing. Give her time, she'll defrost.'

Kumari nodded. She didn't have big sisters, so maybe this was normal.

'Don't be too hard on Hel.' Ben looked at his feet. 'When our mother died, Hel was seventeen. She . . . stepped up. Worried about me and Ophie. Helped Dad keep us in line. Made us feel loved and looked after.' He cleared his throat. 'She's a bit formal, but I think she finds the ritual helps. She's a kind soul underneath.'

They walked a few steps in silence. Kumari tried and failed to imagine a world where she didn't have her parents as her safety net. Ben had been thirteen when his mother died – cancer didn't care who you were. She squeezed his hand.

Ben's other sister arrived a little later, with their father and stepmother. Ben introduced them all to Kumari. They were a lot warmer towards her than she'd expected.

'It's splendid that Benedict has finally met someone,' the Prince of Wales said, smiling. 'Yes, yes, Francesca. I'm coming.' He gave Kumari an apologetic shrug as he and his wife were dragged off by Princess Francesca to see the new pond.

'And this is my other sister, Ophelia,' said Ben.

Ophelia was a whirlwind of energy and fashionable colour. She kissed Kumari on the cheek and said, 'So you're the mystery woman who's got our Ben all loved up. So lovely to meet you. I've never seen him so loopy over anyone before.'

Ben gave Kumari a look that said he was mortified by this description. Kumari liked Ophelia immediately.

'You must call me Ophie.' Formality was dismissed. Ophelia was much more like Ben in her attitude. She sat down next to her sister and was immediately sat upon by the toddler princess, who was given Ophelia's clutch bag to play with. 'Oh, there's nothing in it,' said Ophelia. 'Just a hanky and some cough sweets.' She shifted the child into a more comfortable position and leant across to Kumari.

'So, how are you finding it? Is it frightfully stiff around here for you?'

'It . . . er . . . is a bit of a learning curve,' Kumari said diplomatically.

'I bet it is,' Ophelia replied. 'A lot of the stuff we're used to must look like complete nonsense to an outsider.'

'Ophelia.' Helena gave her sister a stern glare, which she ignored.

'So you and Benedict met at a charity thing, is that right?'

'I fell in love with her pretty much at first sight,' said Ben. 'But she was a little distracted at the time and I had to do a bit of work to get her to come on a date with me.'

'And then?' said Ophelia, expertly manoeuvring around her niece to pick up her tea.

Ben sat on the arm of Kumari's chair. 'Then I had to work even harder to get her to agree to meet me again. And the rest . . . worked out pretty well.'

Kumari looked up at him and smiled. Ophelia was so friendly it was hard not to relax. She could see that they were more similar in outlook than the austere Helena, despite Helena and Ben being similar in looks. Mind you, Helena was the oldest and would have been groomed to be heir at some point, whereas the other two were, as Ben had once put it, 'the spares to the heir'.

They were still talking when Ben suddenly jumped. He swore loudly and doubled up, a hand clutched to his eye.

Francesca, who was just running back from the pond, was horrified. 'Mama, Uncle Ben said—'

'Yes, yes, darling. Ben, what is the matter?'

'Blasted thing flew into my eye.' More cursing.

Kumari stood up. 'Let me see.'

He pushed her away, still muttering.

Without thinking, she slipped into doctor mode. 'Please can someone get me some plain water?' She turned to Ben. 'Sit down. Let me look.' She turned him so that there was a chair behind him and pressed him down firmly. He sat.

She spoke softly and soothingly. 'It's OK. I won't hurt you. Let me see.' He stopped swearing and let her move his hand away from his eye.

'Look up.' She pulled his eyelid up, keeping up a steady monologue in a soothing tone. There was a small insect in his eye. Someone handed her a glass of water. She glanced at it to check that it was OK and used it to rinse the bug out of his eye. He pulled away from her.

'Don't rub it.' She caught his hand. With her free hand she cupped the side of his face. 'Now blink. That's it. Now, how is it?'

He blinked carefully and looked up at her with a look of such pathetic gratitude that she melted just a little. She gave him a quick kiss. 'OK now?'

Ben mouthed, 'Thank you,' and put his hand over hers. Somewhere behind her, Ophelia said, 'Well, she seems a practical sort. Let's keep this one.'

Chapter 11

The Times Echo

Is Prince Benedict finally settling down?

Prince Benedict, the liveliest member of the royal family, is well known for his love of a good party, but keen Benedict-watchers will have noticed that he hasn't been in the news for some time. The prince who, in the past, has been linked to a series of high society ladies, and been a familiar face at top-end nightclubs has been keeping a low profile of late. Rumour has it that the prince has finally found love.

But who is this mystery woman who is said to have captured the prince's heart?

Photo caption: Prince Benedict dances at Cowes last year.

Kumari checked the address on the page she'd ripped out of the message pad in the kitchen. Yes, this was the place all right. It appeared to be an ordinary townhouse with a white door. She ran up the steps and rang the doorbell. She was let in by a man wearing a suit and gloves. He took her name and asked for some ID, which he checked against a book on the desk behind him. Clearly, he found her name there because he said, 'May I take your coat, Dr Senavaka?'

She handed over her coat. To her surprise, she was also asked to hand over her mobile phone. A sign on the wall told her that mobile phones were prohibited. She sighed and handed it over and filled in the small card to go with it. The man gave her a receipt with the model of the phone and the phone number written on it.

He led her through to a lounge with faded, cloth-covered sofas and William Morris wallpaper. She was reminded of a well-used stately home. 'The gentlemen are waiting for you in here, madam.' He indicated a door, through which she could see a polished bar.

Ben was standing at the bar, with his back to her, chatting to another man in a suit. When she walked in, the other man's head rose.

Ben turned. 'Kumari.' He came over, kissed her cheek and wrapped an arm around her. 'This is Rhodri, a friend from university,' he said. 'Rodders, this is Kumari.'

'Delighted,' he said. And he really did look delighted. 'Glad to meet the woman who's finally made an honest man of Benedict.'

Kumari smiled. 'Thank you. I do like a challenge.'

Rhodri laughed. 'I'm sure you do.' He gestured to the barman. 'What can I get you?' he asked Kumari.

'Diet Coke, please,' she said.

'No ice,' said Benedict.

Rhodri raised an eyebrow. 'You know the little lady's tastes already.'

Benedict winced.

'I'm not a "little lady", I'm a doctor,' Kumari said. 'But yes, no ice. Thanks.'

Rhodri's eyes moved from one to the other. The tips of his ears went pink. 'Er . . . right.'

The barman placed the drink on the bar. Kumari took it and thanked Rhodri again. He nodded. There was an awkwardness in the air now that hadn't been there before. Kumari felt it was her fault.

'Shall we sit down?' said Ben.

They moved to a table that had worn baize armchairs around it.

Rhodri coughed. 'Look . . . er . . . I didn't mean to be patronising there . . .'

Kumari looked at him, surprised to hear him apologise.

'Oh, don't worry about it. I'm sorry I snapped at you like that. I've just had a day of being patronised by a consultant at work. I shouldn't have taken it out on you.'

'Truce?' said Rhodri.

'Truce.' They shook on it.

Out of the corner of her eye, she saw Ben relax.

'So,' she said. 'This place . . . ?'

'Home from home,' said Ben. 'Nice, quiet place to come and socialise without any risk of being caught by an errant mobile phone.'

'I stay here whenever I'm in London for business,' said Rhodri. 'It's nice to have somewhere where the staff know you, if you see what I mean.'

'I imagine it is.' Kumari sat back in her chair and let the stress of the day drain out of her shoulders.

Ben and Rhodri resumed their conversation about cricket. She tuned out and let the tranquil atmosphere wrap around her instead. A few other people came in and the bar gradually got busier, but it wasn't exactly noisy or bustling. She could see why Ben liked it. It wasn't as empty as his apartment, but not so busy that he needed to put his guard up.

Every so often someone would come by to say hello. Most of them called him 'sir', but a few seemed to know him well enough to call him Ben.

Eventually, a waiter came in and whispered something to Ben, who nodded. Ben stood up and offered Kumari his arm. 'Dinner?'

The waiter rang a bell to say that dinner would be served. Since they had a head start, Ben and Kumari were first into the dining room.

'Is Rhodri eating alone?' said Kumari. 'Should we ask him to join us?'

Ben looked back to the door where people were filing in, caught Rhodri's eye and pointed to a table.

'Are you sure you two don't want to eat alone?' said Rhodri. 'Since you said you didn't get to go out often . . .'

'No, we eat alone all the time,' said Kumari, even though they only met a few times a week. 'It's nice to meet one of Ben's friends.'

'Well in that case.' He sat down.

Kumari grinned. 'Maybe you should tell me all about what Ben was like at university.'

'Hang on,' said Ben. 'I'm not sure I like this idea so much now.'

Rhodri laughed. 'All the more reason, eh, Kumari?'

It was a surprisingly enjoyable evening. Kumari wasn't sure what she'd expected – something more old-boy network maybe. The club had a relaxed atmosphere and Rhodri was genuinely good company. More than anything, she liked how Ben seemed relaxed and happy. She was starting to realise how much of himself he held in reserve when he was out in public. Always smiling, never a misplaced phrase, never a scowl. The perfect mask of civility at all times. It was a bit like . . . well, a bit like being a doctor. She always thought of her professional manner as a cloak that fell into place as soon as she saw a patient. It was like a switch was flicked in her head and the internal monologue of Kumari was replaced by the calmer, more sensible voice of Dr Senavaka. How else could she face the blood and tears in A & E?

Perhaps it was the same with Ben. When he was in front of the public, he was Prince Benedict. Bastion of royal etiquette. With her, in private, he was Ben – charming, slightly goofy and adorable. Here, he was somewhere in between. Closer to Ben than to Benedict. It was nice to see. He laughed at something Rhodri said and Kumari fell in love with him just a tiny bit more.

After dinner there was tea in another room, where the leather in the armchairs was worn down to butter softness. There was a fire in the grate – a gas one, judging by the lack of smoke. Warmth, good food and the aftermath of a day at work made Kumari's eyelids droop. She sank into the cushions of her armchair and let it soothe her.

She must have fallen asleep because she was woken up by Ben touching her arm. 'Sorry,' she muttered, forcing her eyes open.

'Come on, let's get you home,' he said.

She was given her coat and her mobile phone, which she gratefully pocketed. 'It did not ring, madam,' the concierge solemnly informed her.

Ben shrugged on his big coat. 'The usual exit please,' he told the concierge.

A few minutes later, they were escorted down a corridor to a side door. Kumari was fast learning that celebrities had access to all sorts of secret side entrances. Dave was waiting by the door. Ben opened the car door for Kumari and smiled. As she slid inside there was a flash of light. Someone took a photograph. Everything sped up. She dived into the car. Dave bustled Ben in and shut the door. The car was already moving when Dave jumped into the front. Shapes ran past the windows.

Dave looked into the back. 'Are you OK, sir? Madam?'

'Yes. We're fine. What the bloody hell happened there, Dave? I thought the club was secure.'

'So did I, sir,' said Dave grimly. 'I checked everything. They must have been lying in wait outside.'

'But how would they know we were here?' said Kumari.

'I don't know,' said Ben. 'They could have been waiting on the off-chance. I'll get Anton to look into it.'

Anton, Ben's private secretary, was another person that Kumari was getting to know quite well. He kept Ben's diary and made sure that Ben was fully briefed on whatever event he was attending that day. He was sharp and efficient and had a sense of humour that he kept well hidden most of the time. Kumari liked him immensely, but could see that an angry Anton would be a very frightening creature.

'It may be advisable to return to your apartment, sir, rather than Dr Senavaka's place. We are being followed.'

Kumari looked out of the back window and couldn't tell which of the cars was following them. It looked like normal traffic to her.

Ben looked at Kumari. 'Is that OK? You don't want people finding out where you live. Lucy won't get any peace once they know.'

She sighed and nodded. She had a change of clothes at Ben's place. 'I'll text Lucy and let her know.'

The feeling of warmth and well-being was gone. She felt alert and on edge. She texted Lucy and told her she couldn't come back that evening.

The response came: *I haven't seen you in ages. I only get to see you at work.*

Kumari texted back. *I'm sorry. Something happened. Paparazzi moment. Can't come home in case they follow me*

There was a long pause before Lucy said: *OK. See you when I see you, then. Night.*

She turned her phone off and settled back in her seat. Ben's warm hand found hers. She looked across at his face, painted in moving shades of light and dark as they drove through the city. He looked worried.

'You OK?' she asked him. He nodded slowly.

'Sure?'

Ben rubbed a hand over his eyes. 'My mother was popular with the press. We were always being photographed, but mostly at a respectful distance. We went about our business, and if we were in public, they took photos and wrote about us. That was OK. But once my mother was ill, they were everywhere. One even tried to sneak into the hospital to see her. Even for us, it was too much. She wanted to die at home, quietly. She didn't want any pictures of her looking ill to get into the press. We had to smuggle her home in the middle of the night, like we were fugitives. They couldn't let her have her last journey with dignity.' He sighed. 'I can't stop the press being interested in what my sisters and I do, but I don't have to like it.'

She tried to imagine what it must have felt like to be a thirteen-year-old boy, dealing with his mother's mortality and trying to keep some semblance of privacy. 'Oh, Ben.'

He gave her a small smile that broke her heart. 'I had hoped to protect you from this a bit, but I think our period of peace and quiet is at an end.'

Since she wasn't working the next morning, Kumari joined Ben in his morning meeting with Anton.

Anton showed them a photograph taken in the dark. It showed her bending forward to get into the car. Her face was partially obscured by her hair. Benedict, standing beside her, was clearly visible and the way he was looking at her made it obvious that they were together.

She looked at Ben. 'What do we do?'

Ben chewed his lip and glanced at Anton. 'Well . . . it had to come out sometime. We've had six months of relative quiet.'

'We could let the thing run its course,' said Anton. 'It's not the first time you've been linked to mystery young women, sir. I dare say this will blow over.'

'Except the normal photographs are of me talking to some woman at an event. In broad daylight. With very little evidence of anything,' Ben pointed out. 'This is us leaving a private club that I'm known to be a member of and . . .' He gestured at the paper.

'And your face says it all,' Kumari finished for him.

'Are you ready for this?' he said. 'You have no idea the crapstorm that's going to be unleashed when the press works out who you are.'

'I'll have to face it some time.'

Ben sighed. 'I've got to go on this tour of Scotland for the next few days. That should keep the press off your case for a bit, but after that . . .' He rubbed his hands over his face. 'I'm sorry, Kumari. This is not how I expected to ask you to move in with me, but would you consider moving in with me, or, at least, close to me?'

She stared at him. 'I'm not scared of some reporter. They can't force us to take our relationship at a different pace.' She put her hand over his. 'Let's see how this pans out, shall we? If they find out who I am and start showing up at my flat, I'll have you guys on speed-dial anyway.'

'We can let the local police know,' said Anton cautiously. 'So that they know to respond immediately if anything is reported in the building.'

'There,' said Kumari. 'It'll be fine.'

Ben brought her hand up and kissed her knuckles, but he didn't look convinced.

* * *

The Daily Flash

Who is Prince Benedict's mysterious girlfriend?

Sources close to the prince claim that he has not been seen at many social functions lately. Could this be because he has a new love interest keeping him closer to home? Who is the mystery woman who was seen leaving his private members' club with him last night? The dark-haired beauty does not appear to be anyone known in the prince's usual circles. Yet, the look on the prince's face suggests that she's someone very special indeed. The prince's office declined to comment.

Inside: Prince Benedict's ex-girlfriends, where are they now?

'Sources close to the prince?' Lucy put down the newspaper. For the first time in ages, they were both in the flat at the same time, having a leisurely morning off.

'Ben has no idea who they are. He thinks they were probably making that bit up.' Kumari was sitting on the sofa, her legs curled up underneath her. 'Hopefully, he's right.'

Lucy peered at the photograph again. 'They're right about the way he's looking at you, though. That's the look of a smitten man.'

Kumari's cheeks warmed at the thought. She loved that he looked at her like that. Did she look at him the same? She didn't, did she? She asked Lucy.

'I've not exactly seen the two of you together, have I?' Lucy said pointedly. 'But you do go all moony when you talk about him.'

'I will take you to see him one day, honest. I was going to check with Ben and Anton to arrange a date, but then this happened and put the kybosh on everything.'

Lucy put the newspaper down and sat back. 'What's it like?' she said. 'Are his sisters nice?'

'Ophelia's lovely. Helena is . . . more formal. Very nice, though.'

'Oh, come on, you've got to give me more than that! You guys have been together for months now and you haven't given me any gossip. You know I won't tell anyone.'

'OK, OK!" Kumari laughed. 'What do you want to know?'

'His sisters,' Lucy said firmly.

She ordered her thoughts. 'They really are nice. But they have this . . . self-control thing going on. It's like they've been trained to have a pleasant, smiling face. They can listen like nobody's business. When it first happens you think, oh yes, they're interested in what I'm saying, but after a while you start to wonder whether they really are, or whether they're actually thinking about what's for dinner.'

'Which is it?'

'I think – and I could be wrong – they actually are listening. It's part of the job.' She leant her head against the back of the sofa. 'Ben certainly sees it as a job. A role that needs filling.' She rolled her head sideways to look at her friend. 'You should see the amount of reading they do before they go to anything. If Ben goes to see someone from a charity, you can bet that Anton will have given him notes on what they do, where they do it, how the prince can help. He doesn't need to tell them he knows, but he does know. It's a special skill knowing everything about something for an afternoon and then forgetting it.'

Lucy absorbed this. 'Wow.' She blinked and gave Kumari a strange look.

'What?'

'Are you and Ben serious?'

'I've told my parents about him. He's told his sisters . . . so yes, I guess we are.'

'But how is this even going to work?'

Everyone wanted to know that. Including her. She thought of her argument with Ben about her career. About Helena's frostiness. About the huge, rambling set of apartments where you could go for hours without seeing anyone but staff who scurried about being busy. Without warning, tears threatened. Could she live a life like that? Without her job and her friends, what was left?

Kumari looked down at her hands. Ben had not tried to sugarcoat the truth. These evenings of sitting in her own flat with her friend, sharing a tub of cookie dough ice cream, were a luxury she would soon long for. Her hands blurred.

'Kumari?' Lucy moved to sit next to her and put an arm around her. 'Oh. Hey. I didn't mean to upset you.'

Kumari wrapped her own arm around her friend. 'But it's true. If I move in with Ben . . . all this is gone. I won't be able to work. I won't be able to see you. It'll be awful.'

'But you love him.'

'I do, but—'

'Then it's worth it.'

'Is it? It's a gilded cage. You have to follow the rules. Maintain protocol at all times. You can't just go out if you fancy a takeaway, you need to check with security.'

'But you could have whatever you wanted.'

'No. I couldn't.' Kumari's tears fell hot and fast now. 'I can't have this. I can't slob around in tracksuit bottoms and a T-shirt with you. I can't just go where I want. And I can't do my job. I worked my arse off to qualify and get a

136

job, and now it turns out I have to give it up to marry the man I want. It's so unfair I could scream.'

'At least you can do more stuff for the charity?'

Kumari's lip wobbled. 'I'm not sure I can. In the short term, maybe, but, apparently, it could be seen as being partisan to support a single charity above all others. Anton – that's Ben's private secretary – said it would be an argument to have with palace officials. It will be such a fight. Everything will be. It's already exhausting.'

'Oh, honey.' Lucy's arms tightened around her. 'I'm sorry.'

'The worst bit . . . the worst bit is that it's so seductive. I can sit in Ben's apartment with its lovely high ceilings and sometimes it feels pretty good. At those times I hate myself for what I'm turning into.'

Lucy let her cry for a bit then left her to find some tissues.

'OK. Tough love time,' she said solemnly. 'I understand where you're coming from, but you can't have it both ways. You're going to have to choose between him and your career at some point.'

Kumari sniffed. 'I know.'

'And given that you were fed up enough to take a year out to work in a vaccination clinic, I'd have thought it was a no-brainer that the job is the thing to go.'

'Yes, but it wasn't a year out from being a doctor. I was doing work, treating people. Plus, I'm not cut out for public life. I hate being in front of cameras. I need to be doing stuff. Making a difference in the world.'

'Maybe you still can. Have you had this conversation with Ben?'

'I've tried. We end up arguing.'

There was a short silence. Kumari could almost hear Lucy trying hard to avoid saying something.

'What?' she said. When Lucy didn't respond, Kumari said, 'You may as well tell me.'

Lucy sighed. 'Don't hate me, but are you sure you and Ben are right for each other?'

'Yes. We are. I know what you're saying. If there was some way I could remove Ben from the trappings of his birth, he would be just perfect. But I can't.'

Lucy giggled. 'So, you're saying that . . . if your handsome prince was less of a prince, you'd be happy?' She smiled. 'You are such a weirdo.'

'That is pretty much what I'm saying,' said Kumari. 'It's not just me that it affects.' She looked at her friend, lovely, kind Lucy. She hated the idea that her romance had the potential to harm Lucy too. 'If the press works out who I am, it could make things difficult for you too.'

'What? Everyone from work will buy me drinks to find out the gossip.'

'No.' Kumari explained what Ben and Anton had said about the press intrusion. 'I don't think you'll be in any danger if I'm not here,' she said.

'But you won't be here. I'll be all alone!' said Lucy.

'It's not that bad.'

'And what do I do with your post and stuff . . . stuff like what that your friend Ruby dropped off for you?'

'Wait, what stuff ?'

Lucy hauled herself off the sofa and found an envelope. 'This. She's popped round a couple of times in the past few weeks. Once because she was in the neighbourhood and wanted to talk to you about something. Once to drop this off.'

Inside the envelope were a couple of press clippings about the charity's Change From Within fund, listing the Boost Her! proposal, and a tri-fold leaflet where Kumari's vaccination programme was mentioned. 'That was nice of her,' said Kumari.

Lucy made a sceptical sound in her throat. 'I think she just wanted to gossip about you and Benedict. She kept talking about how hard it was not to tell anyone and I was the only other person she could talk to about it. At one point I thought she was never going to leave.'

Kumari frowned. 'I wonder how she knows about Ben. I didn't tell her.' She shrugged. 'Since she set us up in the first place, it's not surprising that she worked it out. I'm guessing we can rely on her to be discreet though.'

'How come you didn't tell her?' asked Lucy. 'I mean, like you say, she set you up.'

'I don't know. I didn't really want to tell anyone. A secret isn't a secret if you tell people.'

Lucy shook her head. 'You Brits are crazy.'

Making Waves

Chapter 12

Pinnacle News

Scoop! Prince Benedict's secret girlfriend identified!

A source close to the couple has revealed that the woman seen with Prince Benedict is Kumari Senavaka. You may know her as the woman who fell into the prince's arms during a royal visit. The prince was so impressed by her exotic beauty that he asked her out. Our sources reveal that the couple have been dating for a few months now and that Prince Benedict has already introduced her to his sisters and his father.

Photo caption: Kumari Senavaka clasps Prince Benedict's hand at a charity event. [Photo credit: Greg Frankish]

Photo caption: Prince Benedict leaves his private club with Kumari Senavaka.

What we know about Kumari Senavaka:

· She's a junior doctor at St Kildare's Hospital. She spent a year as a medical volunteer in Lesotho, where she was involved in a vaccination programme run by Better For All.

She's thirty years old and divorced from her first husband, a fellow medic.

Her parents are originally from Sri Lanka, but are now British citizens.

Senavaka was born in Yorkshire and lived there until she moved to Bristol, and then London for her medical studies.

She is an only child.

Kumari trudged up the steps out of the underground station, coffee in hand. It was her second long day shift in a row and she was starting to feel the tiredness in her bones. As she reached street level, her phone buzzed and pinged several times. Odd. She wasn't normally this popular. She crossed the street in a crowd of pedestrians and pulled her phone out once she was on the other side. There were seven text messages and three voice messages.

The first was from Lucy saying: *Have you seen the papers?*

Kumari looked up. No. She hadn't seen the papers. Perhaps she should pick up a copy from the newsagent kiosk. She wouldn't get to read it until lunchtime. And if she went into the kiosk they were bound to have chocolate Hobnobs on special offer . . . which would be a terrible temptation when she was feeling tired.

She was still thinking about biscuits when she reached the main approach to the hospital. Her phone started to ring. Just as she answered it, she heard someone say, 'There she is!'

Suddenly there were clicks and whirrs as people with cameras swarmed towards her. 'What the—'

Someone thrust a camera in her face.

Kumari set her sights on the entrance to the hospital and pushed through. Behind her, an ambulance turned on its siren.

Inside the hospital, people kept staring at her. Rather than wait for the lift, she walked up the stairs and arrived at the ward hot and out of breath. Her phone rang again. She ducked into a corridor to answer it. 'Ben?'

'Thank goodness. Where are you? Are you OK?'

'I'm at work. Ben, what's happening? There was—' She looked up as a nurse went past, eyeing her curiously.

'There was a small mob outside the hospital waiting for me. Photographers and some reporters, I think.'

'Already? I'm afraid this morning's papers had a clear picture of us. They know who you are. I was hoping that the time of day would put them off.'

'What?' It was a quarter to five in the morning.

'Never mind. The thing is, are you safe where you are?'

'I'm going into A & E in a minute.'

'That doesn't answer my question.'

'I know, but that's the only answer I have. I'm working, Ben. I have patients to see. I don't have time for this.'

'What time does the shift finish?'

'In twelve hours.'

'I'll send a car to get you after your shift. Is there a side entrance you can use?'

The concern in his voice made her bite back the sarcastic comment that immediately sprang to mind. 'Yes. Gladwell Street. There's a small courtyard with bins in it.' It was where the smokers went. She'd been out there once to cry when she lost a patient. It was a place that was small enough and miserable enough to be empty in the middle of a busy day.

'We'll find it. I'll see you later. Have a good day. Stay where you're safe, OK? Don't go outside.'

'I will.'

She put her phone away and changed into her scrubs.

It wasn't until late morning that the first comment came. She was assessing a man who had had a suspected heart attack. The nurse helping her had been called to another patient, so she was taking a blood sample herself. She talked to him gently, while she located a vein in his arm. His wife was sitting next to him on the bed.

'Sharp scratch,' Kumari said, as she pushed the needle into the vein. She watched as the blood flowed into the Vacutainer.

'I suppose you're not allowed to say "just a little prick" anymore?' said the man.

Kumari smiled. 'Not really, no.'

'Pity. Used to make me laugh, that.'

'OK.' She withdrew the needle and pressed a cotton ball to the puncture mark. 'Can you hold this please, firm pressure.' She turned, double-checked the labels and bagged it to send to the lab. 'We should have the results back within the hour. Are you feeling well enough to sit in the waiting room? It'll be at least forty minutes before we call you, if you want to go and get a cup of tea.'

The man nodded. 'I am feeling a lot better now.'

'But we need to work out what happened. If it was a heart attack, we'll have to get you seen to.' She smiled and stood up to leave.

'Um . . . Doctor?' said the wife.

She turned, expecting a medical question.

'You're her, aren't you?' the woman said, her face going bright pink. 'You're the doctor who's dating Prince Benedict.'

She didn't know how to respond. 'I . . . have to get this to the labs.' She grabbed the blood sample and ran, leaving a nurse to usher the couple out of the bay.

Kumari kept working, focusing on the cycle of briefing, examining and updating the computer file. She worked through one break and was told off by one of the senior nurses and shooed out of the room on the second one.

She went into the break room, where two nurses and another doctor were standing over a table, looking at something. Oh no.

Kumari got herself a glass of water and a cup of tea and sank into one of the plastic chairs. One of the nurses came up to her and pulled up a chair. 'What's he like?'

'What?' She really hoped they weren't talking about Ben.

'Prince Benedict. You're a dark horse, aren't you? All this time and none of us knew.'

Kumari rubbed her face. 'It's not exactly something you can go around talking about.'

'I would!' said the younger one.

'Maybe that's why you're not going out with him,' said the other. 'No discretion. Kumari went out with him for months and not a peep. That's how it's done.'

'Is he as dishy in real life as he looks on telly? Have you been to his place yet? Is it huge?'

'Never mind his house. What else is huge?'

'Guys,' Kumari said weakly. 'I'm knackered. Do you mind?'

'Oh, come on!'

The doctor redid her ponytail, in the manner of someone going back into a fight and said, 'I've got to go back in now.' She pointed at Kumari. 'You're going to have to tell me all about this when I see you next.'

The two nurses had apparently just started their break. They looked at her expectantly.

She sighed. She wasn't going to get out of this. 'Yes, he is as handsome in real life as he is on telly. And he's really nice. He's . . .' The phrase, 'a little bit goofy' drifted into her mind, but luckily she was not so tired as to say it out loud. Ben probably didn't want to be the goofy one. 'He's kind and sweet.'

The younger nurse sighed. 'Imagine that. Going out with a prince.' She perked up. 'Has he given you some fab presents?'

'Not really.' He had given her a couple of thoughtful gifts. A scarf, some audiobooks, things she'd actually use. Nothing frivolous. Unless you counted the insane holiday to Africa . . . that she couldn't mention. 'A few things, but nothing major.'

'No jewellery? What's the point of going out with a prince if there's no jewellery?'

Kumari laughed. 'You're right. I feel cheated. I'll have to work on that.'

The other women laughed too. 'So, is it serious? Have you met his family?' The younger one was clearly a huge fan.

'I . . . I don't think I can answer that yet,' Kumari said carefully. 'Sorry. I know you wanted more juicy gossip, but I can't really tell you anything.'

'What? Did you have to sign the Official Secrets Act or something?'

'No, but . . .' she said. 'Discretion, you see.'

'Aww.'

Kumari took a sip from her tea. She had a sandwich in her bag, but she was too tired to go and get it. She was really wishing she'd been able to buy that packet of Hobnobs now.

By the time she ended her shift, she felt like she'd been fielding questions about Ben for hours. Whenever she had two minutes between patients, someone would try to pump her for some gossip. She made her way down to the back of the hospital and, after checking that no one was following her, stepped out of the building. There was a car with darkened windows waiting in the small space. She took a step towards it.

What if it was a trap?

She hesitated, half scared, half amused by her paranoia. The front window of the car rolled down and Dave waved at her. She had never been so relieved to see anyone in her life. As she approached, the back door pushed open.

She hurled herself in and straight into Ben's arms.

Dave shut the door behind her and the car pulled out. For a few minutes, Ben just held her. She said nothing and breathed in the woodland and summer smell of him.

'You're shaking,' said Ben.

'I'm just tired.' Except it wasn't that. It was the strain of being asked questions. It was knowing dozens of reporters were piled up outside the hospital, blocking the entrance to A & E, and all to get at her. It had suddenly brought home to her just how far she'd come from her normal life. Until now, being with Ben had been a lovely secret. A fairy tale. But now . . . people knew. She wasn't going to be able to

149

slide between his world and hers anymore. Shit had just got real. She wanted to curl up in his arms and hide, but, she reminded herself, she was made of sterner stuff than that.

She took a deep breath. 'What now?'

'Seat belt?' said Ben.

'Right.' She strapped herself into the middle seat, so that she was as close to him as she could get.

'We can't use that exit again,' said Dave. 'We were spotted.'

Ben cursed under his breath.

'Where to, sir?'

'I'd like to go home, please,' Kumari said.

'You'd be safer at mine.' Ben took her hand. 'Are we being followed?'

The driver, someone Kumari hadn't seen before, said, 'Yes.' He slowed to a stop at some traffic lights. 'I can try and lose them.'

'Yes, please.' Ben turned his attention back to Kumari. 'Kumari, please. If they figure out where you live, there won't be any peace for you at home. Or for Lucy. Come back to mine. I'll send someone over to check on Lucy and pick up anything you need.'

She wanted to argue. That flat was her home. Lucy was her friend. If the paparazzi were invading there too, she needed to know that Lucy was OK, but what Ben said was true. If she went home now, she was sure to give away where she lived. Whereas Ben's apartment – well, they knew he lived there. As much as she hated the idea, it was a practical suggestion. And she was always practical.

She nodded. Inside, a little bit of her died.

'Thank you,' said Ben. 'My place, please, Dave and Joe.'

Chapter 13

Cause Celeb Magazine

Is that the sound of a million hearts breaking?

Prince Benedict has long been the nation's most eligible, and most determinedly difficult to catch, bachelor. His poster has adorned many a teenager's wall. But it seems that Prince Benedict has finally fallen in love. This rumour was prompted by a photograph of the prince solicitously helping an unknown woman into his car. His expression, as he holds the door for her, is nothing short of adoring. Just look at it. What girl wouldn't want a man to look at her like that!

The mystery of the identity of the woman had whipped social media into a frenzy. Now, finally we have an answer. Dr Kumari Senavaka – junior doctor and humanitarian. She was at the Golden Globe Awards last year, raising awareness for better healthcare for girls in the developing world. Dr Senavaka is thought to have met the prince at a pitch event where she caught the public's imagination by being so taken with him that she fell into his arms. Clearly, the prince felt the same way.

Prince Benedict's former girlfriends have included high society 'It girls', a popular Swedish actress and several women of aristocratic descent. Kumari Senavaka is a clear departure from the glamorous women the party-loving prince usually dates. At the same time, he seems to have taken on more royal duties and we haven't seen photos of him leaving nightclubs in some months. Perhaps this new girlfriend signals a more serious and mature phase for the prince.

Kumari was still lying in bed, half asleep, when the phone rang. She didn't recognise the number so she sat up in an attempt to sound more awake when she answered it.

'Dr Kumari Senavaka, please?'

'Speaking.'

The voice was male and familiar. Someone from the hospital, not one of her colleagues.

'This is Francis McGregor, Deputy Director of St Kildare's Hospital.'

Ah. Yeah. That was who it was. She had met him a couple of times.

'I'm phoning about what happened yesterday.'

'I'm so sorry about that. There was nothing I could do about it though. I—'

'It's happened again today. We have had to call the police in to escort some press people off the premises. This is a hospital, Dr Senavaka, not a resort.'

'I know that. I didn't *ask* for any of this.'

There was a pause at the other end of the line. When he spoke again, his tone was slightly softer. 'This is a difficult time,' he said carefully. 'We think it may be best if you stay off work for a few days, until the furore has died down. We've reallocated your shifts for the next two weeks—'

'Hang on, am I being disciplined? But I haven't done anything wrong. I turned up to work. I did my job. You can't—' Her throat closed up.

'I have to,' McGregor said. 'I have to put the needs of the hospital first. I'm sorry. There has been no criticism of your work, Dr Senavaka, but we can't let the situation continue. Ambulances and patients can't get to the hospital easily and the triage nurses have reported a large increase in spurious visits to A & E. We can schedule a time next week to discuss your return. Consider it . . . compassionate leave.'

'But you're short-staffed. You need me at work.'

'This is true, but we also need to be able to function properly to begin with.' He paused and cleared his throat. 'Don't take this the wrong way, this is not a threat or anything of the sort, but if in due course you decide to hand in your resignation, we would consider letting you off your notice period.'

'What—No. You can't do that.'

'As I said, it's just a suggestion. Not a threat to your employment or anything like that. It's just that given your . . . circumstances, if you decide you no longer want to work . . .'

White-hot fury made it difficult to breathe, let alone speak.

'I'm sorry,' McGregor said. 'Someone will contact you next week to discuss your return. If I don't speak to you again, best of luck with . . . everything.'

Kumari made a noise. It might have been a growl. McGregor hung up.

She threw her phone to the end of the bed and screamed.

There was the sound of pounding footsteps and Ben practically skidded into the room. He was wearing a pair of tracksuit bottoms and a sweaty T-shirt. He must have been in the gym (of course, the apartment had a gym!) doing his morning workout. He looked flushed and hot and amazing. If she took a photo now it would probably be worth a fortune.

'Kumari.' He looked around wildly, as though expecting to see assassins in the room. He relaxed a fraction when it was clear there weren't any. 'What happened?'

'The hospital just called. They've taken me off the rota for the next two weeks. Because of the press. And he dared to suggest—' her jaw clenched so hard it made her teeth grate.

Ben put his hands up in front of him and walked towards her, as though approaching a fierce beast. 'OK. That sounds . . . difficult.' He sat down on the side of the bed. 'Start from the beginning.'

She explained what had happened. He listened carefully, but to her surprise didn't seem as indignant as she was.

'Hopefully, the press interest will die down in a week or so,' he said.

Kumari crossed her arms. 'You're not being very supportive.'

'What can I say, Kumari? I can see the man's point. He has to think of the hospital first.'

'There must be something you can do. Your grandmother is queen, for heaven's sake. Order them to leave the hospital alone.'

Ben looked offended. 'I can't ask her to intervene in something like this.'

Kumari glared at him for a few seconds, before the small voice of common sense piped up that he had a point. 'But it's not fair,' she said.

He took her hands in his. 'I know it's not. There are a lot of things that won't seem fair, Kumari. What we're doing, you and me . . . When I told you it wasn't going to be easy, this is what I meant. We're asking a lot. From my family. From yours. From you.'

Anger and frustration made her eyes water. 'What are we asking of your family? They're not giving up anything.'

'Aren't they?' he said. 'It may not be a big deal to you, but tradition is a huge part of the institution. Our job, if you like. There are rules older than living memory that we have to adhere to. To break them was once unthinkable. My grandmother is a pragmatic monarch. She is relaxing the rules slowly. But people need the institution to symbolise certain things and we have to be careful how much we take away from them each time we change the rules. My immediate family like you and I'm not likely to ever take the throne, but even so . . . The institution is bigger than any of us.' He looked at her sadly.

The sadness in his expression leached the anger out of her. 'I'm sorry. I should have thought.'

'I don't mind,' he said. 'Because I want to be with you.' He kissed the back of her hand. 'But I guess I didn't understand the magnitude of what I was asking you to do. Are you sure you want to be with me?'

She loved her job. Oh sure, there were times when she wanted to jack it all in and open a cake shop, but honestly, she chose this profession. Even when she took a sabbatical, it was to go and do the same sort of thing in a different place. She studied Ben's worried face. This man needed her to give it up. If she wanted to be with him, she would have to let go and be absorbed into his world. Could she do that? Did she love him enough?

The alternative was that she got to keep everything in her life as it had been and lose him. Her heart squeezed extra hard in her chest. That was unthinkable.

She let go of his hand to stroke his cheek. 'I love you. And I want to be with you.'

He made a face. 'You had to think about it a bit.'

'You're asking me to stop being a doctor. I had to give it due consideration.'

He stared at her for a few seconds and then laughed. 'I guess I can be sure you're not just saying things to please me.'

'When have I ever done that?'

He cupped her face in his big, warm hands. 'Kumari, when you said you wanted to be with me . . . would you marry me, if I asked you to?'

She frowned. 'Are you actually asking me to?'

'Since we're giving due consideration before replying to questions today . . . I should point out that Prince Benedict has some things he has to do before he can ask you to marry him. So no. I'm not asking you right now.'

'What about Ben the guy. Y' know. My boyfriend.'

'Oh him? He'd marry you this afternoon if you said yes.'

Laughter bubbled up in her chest. 'I think I prefer that Ben guy,' she said. 'And I'd definitely say yes, if he asked. Which he hasn't.'

Ben laughed. 'You have no idea how much I love you.'

He kissed her, gently at first, then with more intensity, until she forgot about everything apart from how it felt when his skin slid against hers.

Ben had to go to a charity event, so Kumari was left rattling around in the apartment by herself. She checked the time and called Lucy, hoping to catch her before she went to work for the afternoon shift.

'It's me,' she said, when Lucy answered.

'Who? I've forgotten what you look like,' said Lucy.

'Don't be like that. Are you OK?'

'I am. Are you? Rumour has it that you had to be rescued by your prince in an incognito car.'

'Something like that. It wasn't as glamorous as that.'

'So, what's going on, Kumari? It's madness outside the hospital. McGregor got the police to come in and threaten to arrest the press people for . . . something. The place was really busy and it was a nightmare getting in.'

'Oh God, I'm so sorry.'

'Ah, it'll blow over. On the plus side, I'm suddenly *really* popular. Even dishy Dr Rohit came to talk to me today.'

'Cool. Did you ask him out?'

'No. Of course not. He's, like, amazing and I'm just me. He's way out of my league.'

Kumari started to laugh.

'Oh, yeah. I forgot who I was talking to,' said Lucy. 'How are things going with His Royal Hotness?'

The laughter fizzled out.

'Kumari?'

'McGregor's taken me off the rota for two weeks. He says my being there is disrupting the hospital's normal function. If the fuss doesn't die down, he wants me to resign.'

'Can he do that? He can't force you to resign.'

'Well, OK. What he actually said was that if I chose to resign, he'd let me off the notice period because it would be better for the hospital that way.'

Lucy listened to it all and said, 'I hate to say it, but he's right.'

'I know he is. Doesn't mean I have to like it,' Kumari wailed. 'I'm stuck in this apartment and it's really boring. I don't want it to be like this for the rest of my life. I'll hate it and I'll end up hating him. It's not a sound basis for a marriage.'

There was a gasp from the other end of the line. 'Has he asked you to marry him?'

'No. God, no. I just . . .' He hadn't actually proposed. He had checked what her answer would be so that he could do what protocol demanded of him. Ben was negotiating difficult waters with their relationship going at such speed. His grandmother's powers might be 'complicated', but she had ultimate say in whom her grandchildren could marry. Besides, Kumari had to be careful what she said. Idle gossip was now newsworthy. 'No,' she said firmly. 'He hasn't asked me to marry him. I'm just being hysterical and over the top. I'm staying here until the furore dies down. I can't come back to the flat because they'll find out where I live and then they won't leave you alone. I don't want to put you through that. So Ben's got me some accommodation at the other side of Kensington Palace. I'm going to get keys to it this evening.'

There was a pause as Lucy absorbed this. 'OK, so how long are you going to be away?'

158

'About a week, all being well.'

'I'm not much enjoying being the only one in the flat,' said Lucy.

'I know. I'm so sorry.' She seemed to be apologising to everyone at the moment. There was nothing going right. Except Ben. Ben was a beacon in the confused mess that was her life at the moment. A lighthouse in a storm. She had to keep him in sight.

'I miss you,' she told Lucy.

'I miss you too, honey.'

After hanging up, Kumari decided that she needed to know what was going on in the outside world. The Internet was a no–no. She had uninstalled Twitter from her phone the night before when the first death threats appeared. Ben had suggested she do the same for Facebook. She had just removed it from her home screen for now. She didn't dare look at that either. There was something about nameless, faceless people sending her hate mail that was . . . terrifying.

Nope. No Internet. It would have to be the newspapers. She pulled on her coat, grabbed her keys and made her way downstairs. The butler of the floor met her at the bottom of the stairs. She still wasn't used to staff.

'Can I help you, ma'am?'

'You don't happen to have a newspaper, do you?'

'Why, certainly. I'll bring a selection up for you.'

'I can come with—' She was going to suggest she go to get them herself, but the look on his face warned her not to even suggest it. 'I'll just wait upstairs in my rooms, then.'

She trailed back upstairs, reflecting that the place was beautiful and comfortable, but very much a gilded cage.

The butler showed up a few minutes later with a tray of newspapers. He looked mildly concerned. 'Ma'am, are you sure you want to read these? They may be a little upsetting.'

'All the more reason to read them then, don't you think?' She took the tray from him. 'Thank you so much Mr . . . ?'

'Lewis, ma'am.'

'Thank you, Mr Lewis.'

He hesitated a moment before bowing and moving back so that she could shut the door. She threw herself down on the sofa and looked at the pile of papers. *The Sentinel*, her paper of choice, was on the top of the pile. The tabloids were at the bottom. Thoughtfully, she put her arm underneath the pile and flipped it over. She picked up the first tabloid and turned it over. It was immediately obvious why Lewis had been worried.

Nearly all the papers had the same two photos. The first was the one she'd seen before, of her and Ben as they got into the car. The other one was new. It was of her, climbing the steps to the club. She could tell from her clothes it had been taken on the same evening as the blurry photo of them leaving, but this had been taken at the start of the evening. It was a good photo, with her face clearly visible in the light from above the door. Since she hadn't noticed a photographer when she went into the club, this must have been taken with a long-range lens, or they must have been hiding close by. The photographer had either taken photos of everyone who went in that night, or had known she was going to see Ben.

Remembering Greg's name under the photo of her shaking hands with Ben months ago, she looked for the photo credit. None of the papers had printed one. But they all had the same photo. Whoever it was, was getting a decent amount of money. She frowned. If both photos had been taken by the same person, why would they release them at different times?

Money, she decided. They'd teased people with a shot that didn't show her, but showed clearly that Prince Benedict was in love with the woman he was with. Then, when the papers were all desperate to find out who it was, they'd sold them the answer. Sneaky, but clever. Kumari sighed. Since she couldn't avoid it any longer, she picked up a tabloid and looked at the headlines. Oh, good heavens.

The Daily Watch

Is this what the royal family will look like in 100 years?

According to a prominent commentator, the decision to relax rules about who can marry into the British royal family could lead to a family of increasingly mixed lineage. We asked an anthropological modeller to predict what the family might look like three generations from now. As you can see, the ethnicity of future royals would be ambiguous. Are we ready for a black queen?

The Paragon Record

Concerns over the fate of the royal lineage

The latest link between royal grandson, Prince Benedict, and an immigrant doctor from the north of England has caused outrage among aristocratic circles. 'We know that the royal family are keen to

*be seen as more in touch with the average popu-
lace, but this is taking things too far. They've sac-
rificed poor Prince Benedict at the altar of political
correctness, probably because he is far enough
away in the line of succession that there is no
real chance of his children ever succeeding to the
throne. We expected better.'*

*The outburst of concern was caused by pictures
of Prince Benedict seen arm in arm with Sri Lankan
immigrant Kumari Senavaka. Senavaka, whose parents fled war-torn Sri Lanka in the 1970s, has taken
advantage of the British education system and is
now a qualified doctor working in the NHS.*

* * *

'Well most of that's plain wrong,' Amma said down the
phone. 'We're not refugees from the civil war. That didn't
even start until after we left.'

'I know, Amma, I know.' It was late afternoon now. Ben
had phoned to check Kumari was OK. She had told him
she was watching Netflix. She had, in fact, turned on the
TV, but seeing pictures of herself on the rolling newsfeed
had been enough to make her turn it off.

'And you're not Sri Lankan, you're British. You were
born here,' her mother continued.

Kumari sighed. She was sitting in the apartment's
kitchen, trying to eat her sandwich and talk to Amma
on her mobile at the same time. The newspapers were
stacked in a pile on the same tray that Lewis had brought
them on. She had read every article. All wild speculation

162

and half-truths, none of them had made her happy, even those that had put a more positive spin on her story.

'Why are they telling such ridiculous lies?' her mother demanded.

'I don't know. Everyone loves Prince Benedict. I suppose I'm not who they'd choose for him.'

There was a thoughtful silence at the other end of the line. 'Kumari,' Amma said. 'Are you sure about this? Going out with this man could have some very serious consequences for you. Are you sure this is a good thing?'

Amma didn't even know about what had happened at work. Kumari thought about Ben. 'I'm sure,' she said. 'I love him.'

'Does he feel the same way? Because if you break up, he will carry on with his life, but yours could be very difficult to rebuild.'

Despite the fact that she'd said exactly the same thing to Ben herself, Kumari felt herself bristle. 'I really think he does feel the same,' she said. 'And besides, I'm an adult. I can make my own mistakes. I recovered from breaking up with Shane, didn't I?'

'It's not the same, Kumari, and you know that. Don't be facetious.'

She deserved that. She didn't say anything.

'Have you spoken to him about all this?'

'Yes. Not about today's papers, but about the press intrusion in general.'

'And . . . ?'

'He warned me about it before. When we first started going out.' She sighed. 'Amma, it's going to be hard. I know. But I really do love him. And I think he's worth it.'

'In that case,' said Amma, 'you'll work something out. You've always been a very determined person, Kumari, and what you want, you will strive for. In all honesty though, I didn't expect you to want to marry a prince. You weren't exactly a princessy girl.'

'But you called me Kumari. My name literally means "princess".'

'That was your father's idea. You were a princess to us, always.'

Suddenly, there was a lump in her throat.

'If anything goes wrong,' Amma said, 'you know that you can always come home. To us. This will always be your home.'

'Thank you.' She remembered what he had said about their security. 'Amma, you and Thatha need to be careful. It's possible that people might figure out that you're my parents and come and hassle you. If that happens, can you tell me? Ben said he'd pay for security to be placed at the house.'

'Don't worry about us, darling, we'll be OK. Why would they want to bother us? We don't have anything exciting or photogenic about us.'

'I don't think that's how it works. It may not come to it, but please, don't answer the door to people unless you know who it is. Don't confirm anything if they manage to catch you to talk to.'

'Don't worry. We'll be careful.'

There was a moment of silence, where unspoken words hung in the air.

'Anyway,' said Amma. 'How is Ben?'

This was her way of trying to make everything sound normal again. Kumari relaxed a little. Eventually they circled round to talking about his family and how they were reacting to her.

'They've been really great,' she said, even though she'd barely seen any of them. Cautiously, she told her mother a bit of what Ben had told her that morning.

Surprisingly, Amma understood. 'It's not surprising,' she said. 'They have all those generations of tradition weighing down on them. Saving face and maintaining proper status is important.' She gave a little laugh. 'I imagine he's having the same sort of conversations I had with my parents before I eloped with your father.'

Kumari was startled. She'd known about how her mother, the rich Colombo girl, had fallen in love with her brother's friend, the poor scholarship student at the university. Her parents had been furious and done everything they could to keep them apart. Her father had got a job in England and they had married in secret and literally run away to be together. Reconciliation had taken years. In fact, her mother often said that it was Kumari's birth that had mended bridges. She was the first grandchild and it was the threat of not seeing her that had mended the rift between Amma and her parents. It had never occurred to Kumari to draw parallels between the two situations, but Amma was right. It was the same emotions, just with much bigger stakes.

'It must be hard for him,' Amma continued. 'He's a prince. You're just a regular person. You don't understand the conflicts that affect him and he won't understand the conflicts that affect you. My parents felt that your father wasn't right for me until we proved them wrong. He wasn't from the same station in life as them. He wasn't known in their circles. Things that were important to them and their social circle weren't important to him. They wanted me to find someone who would fit seamlessly into their lives and the plans they had for me.' She sighed. 'It's never fun when your family are disappointed in your life choices.'

Disappointed. That was such a loaded emotion. Suddenly, the weariness in Ben's voice made sense. No wonder he was hurt. And here she was giving him grief about *her* work.

'I hadn't thought of it like that.'

'When I used to cry about missing my family, your Thatha used to say to me that people cling to the things that give them meaning. Ben's family have had power and money for generations. In the past they will have married to make sure of more power and money. Just like my family did. It is what is expected of them, by everyone around them.' She sighed. 'It took my family years before they accepted change. They didn't even meet you until you were ten years old. At least Ben's family are trying to help you fit in, rather than trying to push *him* out. It seems to me they've come further, and faster, than would have been possible thirty, or even twenty years ago. Maybe they're trying their best.'

'Do you think it's reasonable, that if Ben and I stay together and get married, I'd have to give up my job? I can't give up my job. I've worked so hard to get here, I'd feel like I was throwing it away.'

'I don't know, darling. Only you can decide that.'

That was no help at all. 'When you had to choose,' said Kumari, 'how did you decide?'

'I tried to imagine myself in the future. A future without your father was too painful to contemplate.'

'Have you ever wondered what would have happened if you'd chosen differently?'

'Of course I have and no, I don't regret it for a minute. I have you and I have your father. My family came round eventually and now I have them too.'

Kumari could hear the smile in her mother's voice. She knew that her choice was already made.

There was the sound of her father speaking in the background.

'Thatha says, "What's the most important thing about being a doctor?"' Her mother passed the message on.

'Healing people. Making the world a better place for the sick and the suffering.' That was easy. She'd had to think about this a lot when she applied to work with Better For All.

'Maybe that's what you should focus on,' her mother suggested.

They were still chatting when Ben let himself in. Kumari said, 'I've got to go, Amma, Ben's home.'

'Oh, say hello to him,' Amma said. She used to say that to Shane, back in the day. It was her way of saying she accepted him.

'I will. I love you. Bye.'

Her mother repeated the blessing she always did, '*Thunsaranai.*' It meant 'three blessings'. A Sinhalese Buddhist blessing that was a comfort, even though Kumari was firmly agnostic. Her father often pointed out that being Buddhist and being agnostic were not mutually exclusive, but Kumari had never given either much thought.

'My mum says hello,' she said to Ben while she hung up.

'We should get them to come down and visit.' He kissed her. 'How have you been?'

Her gaze drifted towards the pile of newspapers.

'Ah,' he said. 'You saw. I asked them not to deliver the papers today. I didn't want you to get too upset.'

'I'm not a child, Ben. Anyway, I went downstairs and asked for a paper.'

He pulled her to him and held her for a minute. 'Oh, Kumari. I hate that this is happening.'

'Me too.' She buried her face in his shoulder and breathed him in. Her conversation with her mother was still resonating in her mind. She had assumed that he had nothing to lose by being in a relationship with her, but maybe she had been short-sighted.

'Ben,' she said, 'are your family giving you a hard time about us . . . well, about me?'

He drew back, frowning. 'What makes you say that?'

'Just wondering.' She caught his gaze and held it. 'Tell me.'

She could see that he considered lying to her but then he seemed to dismiss the thought.

'They were a bit surprised,' he said. 'But considering some of the insane things I've done in the past, I think they were just relieved. Why? Has anyone been nasty to you?'

'No. They've been the epitome of good manners,' she said.

He raised an eyebrow at her, which was kind of sexy.

'Good manners can be wielded like a weapon in skilled hands. I've seen Helena eviscerate a man with a well-aimed remark.'

'Don't think so,' she said. 'I'd have noticed.' A moment of doubt. 'Wouldn't I?'

'You. You would know. Some incredibly dense people might not, but you would.'

'Thanks. I do try not to be incredibly dense.'

He laughed and kissed her nose.

'So,' he said, letting go of her. 'Want to come and see the rooms I've secured for you?'

'Sure. Let me just put my stuff in a bag.'

A few minutes later, they were walking out through the entrance to Ben's building. He had suggested that walking around the outside would give her a better idea of where it was. They walked past the road that led to the gatehouse and around the building. When they reached the entrance to the gardens, now devoid of tourists, Ben produced a key and let them in, locking the gate carefully behind him. They walked hand in hand through the dark, silent gardens until they came to smaller gate that led to a wide walkway, with green hedges to one side and a tall wall on the other. Kumari realised from the traffic noise that beyond the wall was a busy road. She tried to mentally position herself on a map.

They came to another gatehouse and another building that was a less grand version of the one Ben lived in.

A concierge sat behind a desk. He sprang to his feet when he saw them.

'Hi. Is there a packet of keys for me to pick up?' Ben asked.

The concierge found an envelope containing keys and paperwork and handed it over. Ben thanked him and ushered Kumari up the stairs.

The corridors were less opulent here, but still plush. Ben took her to a door on the third floor. It had a keypad next to it. 'Here we are,' he said. He opened the envelope and tipped the contents into his hand. Three keys slid out. 'OK,' he said. 'These are yours – two garden gate keys and the keys to the great door. Your rooms will have a passcode that should be . . . aha. Here we are.' He keyed in the code and the door clicked open.

Kumari stepped into a small sitting room. There was a desk, some shelves and a small table with two comfy chairs pulled up in front of a gas fire. Having got used to Ben's rooms, this place looked tiny, but Kumari reminded herself that her own flat was pretty much the same size as this.

'That's the bedroom,' Ben said. 'And there's a toilet just there. It's not brilliant, but it's safe and warm and I hope it'll do.'

Kumari crossed the room and checked the bedroom, which was through a thick oak door. It was a nice room. Cosy. There was a double bed, a wardrobe and a small dressing table. It was, essentially, a small flat. It was like an old-fashioned, two-roomed set with all the dark wooden panelling, but it was more 'normal' than Ben's huge apartment.

'What do you think?' he asked.

'It's lovely,' said Kumari. She sat on the bed and looked around. 'I like it.'

'There are shared kitchen facilities, I believe,' said Ben. 'But really, if you need anything, you can always get it from mine.'

'It's only for a short while,' she said.

He nodded. 'Thank you for compromising. I know you didn't want to move in here.'

'It's OK. It was the sensible thing to do.' She smiled and held her hand out to him. He took it and she pulled him onto the bed next to her.

A slow smile spread across his face. 'Cheeky,' he said and brought her in close for a kiss.

Chapter 14

The Witness Reporter: Comments

Black-and-blue blood!

Prince Benedict has turned his back on the high-born ladies he normally dates and is now dating Sri Lankan émigré, Kumari Senavaka. The two met at a charity event that went viral when the petite doctor was seemingly so overwhelmed by meeting the prince she fell into his arms. Clearly, this piqued his interest so much that he asked a friend to arrange a date with the exotic doctor soon after.

Sources close to the couple say that they have not been out of each other's presence since. 'They are apart only when one of them goes to work,' a close friend said. 'They seem joined at the hip. I've never seen infatuation like it.'

Senavaka comes from West Yorkshire, an area with a large South-East Asian population. Not somewhere a prince would usually tread.

Kumari jumped when the doorbell rang. She was in Ben's flat after having come round for breakfast. As Ben had left earlier, he'd said, 'I told Ophie you were bored. She said she might come round later this morning. Hope that's OK.'

Even though it was unlikely to be anyone else, Kumari checked through the peephole before opening the door.

'Hello, darling.' Ophelia breezed in, bringing a waft of something pleasant and expensive with her. 'Ben tells me you're bored out of your lovely little mind. I'm free today, so I thought we could hang out a little.'

'Er . . . sure.' She followed Ophelia into the first reception room.

'Oh,' said Ophelia, looking around. 'You haven't added any touches to this place at all.'

'I don't actually live here,' Kumari said

'I'll see if I can send some flowers over. You need something to make it less . . . blokey.'

Kumari looked at the old-fashioned sofas. They didn't look even remotely blokey to her. She shrugged.

Ophelia put her hands together with a clap. 'I thought it would be nice for us to get to know each other better. I've booked us both into my favourite spa to be pampered for a bit. I gather you've had a beastly time with the press. You'll need something to take your mind off things for a bit.'

'Oh. Right. Thank you. That sounds . . . very nice.' She didn't remember the last time she'd been to a spa. Actually, she did remember. She and her two bridesmaids had gone to a spa for the weekend for her hen do. It had been a tipsy, fun affair. But she'd known the girls very well. One of them was Lucy. She eyed Ophelia, with her impossibly glossy hair and permanently perky smile. She barely knew this woman.

Ben had once told her that Ophelia, underneath that upbeat smile, had a mind like a steel trap. Kumari assessed her chances of second-guessing what was going on. Not

173

great. She was out of her depth with the social politics game. So she went for the straightforward approach. 'What's this all about?' she said. 'I'm sure you've got better things to do than babysit me. So why?'

Ophelia put her head to the side and gave her a thoughtful stare. The perkiness dimmed by a few notches, but remained in place. 'OK. Since you want a direct answer . . .' She took a step towards Kumari. 'Contrary to whatever you might have read in those,' she said, pointing towards the newspapers, 'I love my brother. He is determined that you and only you can make him happy. And making you happy, makes him happy. That being the case, I want to help him. There is an ulterior motive here, Kumari. That is to make you a little glossier, a little brighter, a little bit more . . . establishment. Think of it as armour. You've done pretty well so far. Daddy likes you. That's not an easy thing to have managed. But you need help. There will be a lot of people who will offer to help, but you don't really know any of them or the games they're playing. Whereas with me, you can be sure of one thing: I will never, ever do anything that will hurt my brother. You can trust me on that.'

The first thing that Kumari noticed was what Ophelia didn't say. She hadn't offered any assurance that she wouldn't hurt Kumari if it meant it would protect Ben. That was oddly reassuring. So long as Ben loved Kumari, Ophelia would be on Kumari's side. The moment Ben no longer needed her, she would be out. At least Ophelia was telling her the rules of engagement upfront. It was more than she was going to get from anyone else.

She smiled. 'Let me grab a jumper and a coat.'

Ophelia beamed. 'Wonderful,' she said. 'I can see we're going to be great friends.'

Funnily enough, Kumari thought so too.

Kumari lay in a flotation pod, in the dark. The air and water in the tank were at blood temperature. The salts in the water made her float. It was like lying in nothing. Weightless. Ophelia had assured her that it was the most relaxing experience ever. Right now, it just felt weird. It was a good job she wasn't claustrophobic.

She closed her eyes against the darkness and listened to the watery thumps and bops in her ears. Her conversation with her mother from the day before floated into her mind. What was it that Thatha had asked? 'What's the most important thing about being a doctor?'

She genuinely believed her answer was an honest one. She did want to make the world a better place for the sick and the dispossessed. To lift people out of suffering. She did that every day at work – relieving pain, giving someone the means to cope with an injury until it got better, sometimes simply stitching broken skin back together. In Lesotho, she had done it in an environment where the effect was more obvious. The child whose fever broke when the antibiotics took effect. The mother who wept when her poor, dehydrated baby came back to life after being on a drip for a few days. These individual highs made up for all the sleepless nights and long hours and aching feet. She, Kumari, had made someone's life better.

But then she thought of the queues that never got shorter, the patients who had to be seen in corridors because there were no rooms to see them in when A & E was too busy. One night, a few years before, she'd lost a patient. A young woman who could have been saved if only she'd been seen earlier. That incident affected Kumari deeply and made her question her place in the world. It was that, more than anything, that had made her join Better For All. That young woman had suffered because there weren't enough people to help in time. There weren't enough people because there wasn't enough money. People wanted to help. There just weren't enough resources in the right places. In some ways England and Lesotho suffered from the same problems.

The point of getting Benedict to come to the pitch event at Better For All was to get more media attention. To get more people to see the charity, so that more people would give and there would be more money to send resources to people who needed it. Raising awareness. Letting in the light so that the hidden problems were seen. That's what Benedict did. In his charity work Benedict firmly believed that he was making a difference.

She moved her head and the water in the tank sploshed in the dark. The movement made her body rock gently. Shaking her and lulling her. Did Ben's work alleviate suffering? It almost certainly did. They had often talked about the causes they felt strongly about. Hers were humanitarian and medical. His were to do with mental health, postwar reconstruction and looking after those damaged by war, be they soldiers or civilians.

She supported her charities by giving a few pounds when she could. He could support them with far more tangible grants. He could make the people who ran the initiatives account for what they spent. He could walk into a room and bring the attention of the world in with him. If she was with him, she could do that too.

Ben's mother, when she had been alive, had been a great humanitarian. She had understood the power of a photo opportunity. The right photo of a delicate British princess, crouching to help a refugee child pull on a pair of warm gloves, with the war-wasted landscape in the background, spoke to people in a way that a million words couldn't. Advocacy. Scrutiny. Diplomacy. These were powerful weapons too, in the right hands.

She opened her eyes. That's what Ben had been trying to tell her. She had more to give than her medical skills. She could make this work. Yes, this world that Ben lived in was scary and full of complex rules she didn't understand, but it was just a system to learn. She hadn't been born knowing how to set a broken arm. She'd learnt it. She could learn this too. She breathed in a lungful of warm air and breathed it out again. Her breath sounded loud and made the air move above her.

All right then. There was still time left for her to be in this tank. She knew she merely had to knock on the lid and they would open it for her. But Ophelia had paid for an hour. No point wasting it. She closed her eyes again and gave in to the sensation of being held. Eventually, she may even have fallen asleep.

'Thank you so much, Ophelia. It's been a lovely afternoon. I really appreciate it.' She meant it. They were sitting in the kitchen of Ben's apartment, because he had agreed to meet them there. She had offered Ophelia tea, and then had a momentary panic about tea sets before deciding that Ben's usual teapot and cups would do. She had offered to bring it out into the sitting room, but Ophelia had followed her in and pulled up a stool at the breakfast bar, as though she was completely at home with the place. Since it was her little brother's house, she probably was.

'Oh, don't mention it. It was a pleasure. I love a good project.' Ophelia got out her phone and started tapping at it.

Kumari looked up from where she was filling the teapot. 'Project?'

Ophelia nodded. 'Of course.' She looked up and caught her eye. 'Did you think I was just being friendly?'

Kumari laughed. She liked Ophelia's directness and acidity. She knew already, from spending an afternoon with her, that Ophelia was a force of nature. She managed to always be breezy and outspoken, but moderate what she said so that people got the impression that she was being completely straight with them, even when, really, she hadn't told them anything.

'You mean you weren't enjoying my company?' Kumari said. 'I'm wounded, I am.'

Ophelia grinned. Not the polite princess smile, but the full-on charisma blast. 'I must admit it wasn't as much of a chore as I feared. I always take Benedict's girlfriends, at least the ones he introduces to us, to the flotation tank the first time I hang out with them because if they're truly dull, I get an hour's break in the middle. Although only one of them has been dull, really.' She nodded towards the tea. 'Milk, please, no sugar.'

Kumari put a bit of milk into the empty cup, ready for when the tea was brewed enough to be poured.

'I have to admit,' said Ophelia. 'I'm pleased with what we've achieved today.'

Kumari touched her face. She wasn't wearing make-up, but her skin had been steamed, scrubbed, massaged and smeared to submission until it glowed with good health. Her eyebrows had been shaped into delicate arches, still thick, but much better behaved. The 'hair technician' had somehow taken her thick black hair, that she normally wore in a ponytail because it was too long, and made it a glossy, bouncy affair that skimmed her shoulders. Everything about her had been polished and somehow elevated to a different level of elegance.

'Your face, when I told you about the tank. Priceless,' said Ophelia. 'You were wrong though. It was relaxing, right?'

'OK. Well, I may have been hasty in my judgement. Although, I'm still not convinced by all that guff about removing toxins.'

'Oh, you science people take all the fun out of things.' They were still sipping tea and laughing when Ben came home. He kissed his sister's cheek in greeting and went over to stand next to Kumari.

'Wow,' he said. He stood back to admire her.

Feeling a little giddy, she did a twirl for him. 'What do you reckon?'

'Very . . . glossy,' he said. He kissed her cheek and put his arm around her waist. 'I think you're beautiful with or without the gloss.' He turned to look at his sister, who was looking pleased. 'I take it this is the "Ophelia checking out the new girlfriend" session. Judging by the fact that you're both still talking to each other, I'm guessing it went well.'

The women looked at each other. Kumari saw the laughter dancing in Ophelia's eyes. She genuinely liked Ben's sister. 'I think it did.'

Ophelia placed her teacup delicately on its saucer. 'I had better get going. I know it's my day off from duties, but there's just so much to do.'

'Oh. Stay for dinner,' said Ben.

'I'd love to, darling, but I must away. I have some friends coming round for drinks. I have to go and get changed into something less suitable.' She hopped off the stool, bestowed kisses on cheeks and whooshed out of the kitchen.

'I'll call you later in the week, Kumari.' Ophelia's voice drifted behind her as she disappeared into the hall. The door clicked shut.

In the silence left behind, Ben and Kumari looked at each other.

'I like her,' Kumari said. 'She's very . . . direct.'

Ben laughed. 'She certainly speaks her mind.'

'So, one sister down. One to go.' Kumari got out another cup and poured him a tea.

'Helena will be fine. Don't worry. She's not nearly as severe as she makes out.' He perched on the stool his sister had vacated, towing Kumari along to join him.

They sat so close their knees interweaved and chatted, catching up on each other's days. Eventually, they got round to discussing the day's press coverage.

'I had a briefing from Anton,' said Ben. He rubbed his hands over his face. 'It's been . . . worse than normal to be honest.' He looked at her sadly. 'I hate that you have to face this.'

Kumari shrugged. 'I've taken Twitter and Facebook off my phone,' she said. 'Some of it was nice, but some of it was horrible. I figured, I didn't need to know.'

He nodded. 'That's wise.'

'But social media's a huge part of how I communicate with my friends. Especially the ones that I don't see very often.'

He hugged her. 'I know. It must be very difficult.'

'You've never been on social media?' She didn't know why she was asking. She could clearly see how impossible that would be to manage.

'A luxury I'm not allowed to have,' he said. 'Too risky.' He thought for a moment. 'And frankly, seeing the bile that seems to pour out of people on it, too upsetting.'

'It's fun on a social level,' she said. 'Provided you know everyone you're talking to.'

'Exactly. You're famous now. The rules have changed.'

'Um . . . speaking of rules. I need to talk to you about something.'

He put his cup down and turned to her. 'Go ahead.' He had his formal listening face on.

She closed her eyes and opened them. 'If I were to leave my job . . . what would I be able to do?'

'In the first instance, we could arrange for you to do some work with charities. Not necessarily at the sharp end, like you're used to, but in the background. You could do some of the formal visits with me. If we were married, you could take on formal engagements – with me and by yourself. Does that answer your question?'

'Sort of.' She had worked most of that out for herself, but confirmation from him helped. Benedict did a lot of work with charities for wounded soldiers and war-bereaved families. She wanted to do a lot for health-related charities, childhood mental health and showing the importance of educating women so that it improved the lives of children. Already, she could see the areas of overlap.

'Kumari?'

Ben had been speaking to her and she hadn't been listening. 'Sorry. I was miles away.'

'I said, what's this all about? What are you thinking?' He looked worried.

She paused a moment to get her thoughts in line. 'I'm thinking . . . I thought you were asking me to give up my career and stop helping people if I wanted to be with you, but you're not, are you?'

He said nothing, but she could see the worry giving way to hope. The 'listening face' had dropped away. This was her Ben now, when he wasn't being perfectly schooled Benedict. She could read him with no effort at all.

She said, 'You're asking me to learn to do things differently.'

'I wouldn't ask you to give up your principles. I fell in love with you because you felt so strongly about your project. You were clearly petrified, but you cared so much that you got on and gave an impassioned speech. I don't want you to change from that to a clone-princess, but yes, you can't operate in exactly the same way as before either. It wouldn't be practical.'

The phrase 'fell in love' snagged her attention. It made her so happy. She smiled at him and pushed a lock of hair off his forehead.

He smiled and did a half-shrug. 'You know I'm in love with you, right? I might have mentioned it?'

She dropped her hand to his shoulder. 'You might have. And I might have mentioned how I love you too.' She ran her thumb along the line of his clavicle.

He grinned. 'I think you're just perfect.' He dropped his hands to her waist, his palms warm through the cotton blouse, and pulled her closer, so that she was standing between his thighs. 'I love the way your eyes light up when you talk. I love the way you argue with me. I love that you can ignore a plate of salad in favour of steak.' He kissed the side of her neck, causing a thrill to run through her. 'I love the way you laugh, the way you fit so perfectly into my arms when we're on the sofa.' His mouth was so close to her skin that his words were punctuated by his lips moving against her neck, sending a rush of sparks through her body. It was exquisite.

Kumari closed her eyes. His lips made it up to her ear, and he paused for a second, so that the world hung in stasis, his warm breath tickling her newly styled hair. Her pulse galloped. She didn't want to move, to disturb this moment of exquisite tension, but, at the same time, she was desperate for his touch. She dropped her free hand to rest on his thigh. He took her ear lobe gently between his teeth and gave the tiniest of tugs. Kumari moaned.

She drew back and her mouth found his. She couldn't think straight for wanting him. All she knew was that she never wanted to let him go.

Chapter 15

They stood outside the closed double doors leading to the room where the queen had requested their presence. Benedict had to present her to the monarch formally. Kumari had dressed smartly, in a fitted dress and a jacket that Ophelia had lent her. She hoped it gave the right impression.

'Ready?' Ben asked.

Kumari checked her dress and nodded. 'As I'll ever be.' Ben nodded to the – what was he? Butler? Man-at-arms? Whatever – the man knocked, opened the doors and announced them.

The old lady was standing by the tall window, looking out at the garden. Sunlight poured in, illuminating the polished floor. In the middle of the room, there were two sofas, facing each other, with tea laid on the small table between them. As with most rooms, there were connecting doors, but the doors had been shut, making the space feel more intimate. There was a faint smell of honeysuckle, from the enormous flower arrangement by the door.

The queen turned. She was dressed in a peach dress and low-heeled pumps. 'Ah,' she said. 'Benedict.'

He bowed and gave her a kiss on the cheek. Kumari curtsied. She was getting the hang of the curtsy now and could manage it in high heels. The queen acknowledged her with a nod. 'Kumari Senavaka,' she said. 'Let me look at you.' The old lady gave Kumari a once-over.

Kumari was suddenly reminded of her own grandmother, her mother's mother, sitting in a wicker chair in a garden in Sri Lanka, looking at the ten-year-old Kumari with the same assessing glare. She held her head up high, just as she had done then.

Two little dogs, who had been sitting at the queen's feet, came over and sniffed Kumari's hands. She wondered if she should ignore them. One of the dogs licked her hand. Without looking down, Kumari stroked its head. The queen clicked her tongue and the dogs went back to her.

'Hmm.' She went over to one of the sofas and sat down, effortlessly adopting a graceful pose, feet crossed at the ankle.

'Come,' she said. 'Sit.'

She indicated that Kumari should sit on the sofa opposite. Ben sat beside her. The queen raised an eyebrow at him. He grinned at her. She shook her head with the ghost of a smile.

Kumari realised that Benedict's grandmother adored him. Judging by the conspiratorial look they shared, he adored her right back. She allowed herself to relax a fraction.

A lady-in-waiting appeared and poured tea. This was a more formal occasion than tea in the garden with the princesses. It was an audience.

'So, you work, is that correct?' the queen asked her.

'Yes, ma'am. I'm a doctor.'

'Commendable profession. You will miss your work, when you take on duties with Benedict.' It wasn't a question. It was a statement of fact.

'Yes, ma'am. I will.'

'Benedict tells me you want to heal the world.'

'Or at least a significant proportion of it, yes.'

The queen picked up her tea and said, 'It's good to care. The world needs people who care, right now.'

'Kumari spent some time in Africa, running a vaccination programme,' Benedict chimed in.

'Indeed? Did it make a lot of difference to the area?' It was asked with genuine interest.

She would have liked to have said it solved everything, but that was not true. 'We made a significant impact. But there's a lot of work still left to do. We were curing patients and sending them back to the same conditions, so they were likely to fall ill again with something else straightaway.'

Shrewd blue eyes studied her. 'And if you had the power to influence those who made the decisions, what would you have them do?'

Kumari was momentarily taken aback. She looked at Ben, who gave her an encouraging smile. She had thought about this, argued with Ben about it, many an evening.

'If I had sufficient power and funds I would improve sanitation and get the food moving again so that people had enough to eat. With sanitation and food, the children might have a chance of surviving to adulthood. Then I'd invest in educating girls, with projects like the Boost Her! proposal. Well-informed girls grow up to become well-informed mothers. It only takes a generation or two to raise welfare levels.'

'That would be a good use of influence, yes.' The old lady nodded. 'And one has heard of your involvement with charity work. Also commendable.'

Kumari didn't know what to say. 'Thank you, ma'am.'

The queen drew a deep breath and released it. 'Well,' she said. 'The dogs like you.' She looked fondly down at her pets. 'And Benedict likes you.' She glanced at her grandson, as though seeking confirmation.

'Very much so,' Benedict said.

'In that case, you must be all right.' The queen smiled. There was mischief in that smile, the same sparkle that was in Ben's.

'You will have a lot of work ahead of you while you learn to fit in. The very best of luck, my dear. Not least because you will have to keep my grandson under control.' She put down her teacup. 'Now, Benedict. Tell me what you've been up to.'

Ben launched into a discussion about one of his charities and how he was hoping to help them increase literacy in deprived areas. Was that it? she wondered. Was the ordeal of 'being seen' by the queen over?

Ben made a lame joke and his grandmother laughed. She put her cup down and smiled fondly at Ben.

'It's good that you are embracing your duties, Benedict. We were worried about you.' She smiled at Kumari too. 'And it has been a delight to meet you, Kumari.' She rose. Their audience was at an end.

Ben and Kumari rose with her. As they took their leave, the queen looked at Kumari and said, 'Rebels are a product of their time. Benedict's mother was a woman ahead of her time. Perhaps you are more in tune with yours.'

Kumari didn't know what to say to that. She glanced at Ben, who looked pleased. So she said, 'Thank you, ma'am,' and hoped that was the appropriate response.

Afterwards, they left the sitting room and walked side by side down the corridor.

'That went well?' Kumari said, not entirely sure it had.

'It did. The dogs liked you, which is always a good sign,' said Ben. He put his arm around her and pulled her close. 'Grandma is a big softie at heart, really.'

'That's not what you said yesterday.'

'That was before I knew she liked you.'

Chapter 16

The Daily Watch

Letters – have your say: When political correctness affects the royal family, it's time to start worrying.

The royal family has often been accused of being out of touch with the British public. They've been working hard on their image, but making Prince Benedict step out with an immigrant northerner is taking things a bit too far. Of course, it makes great headlines. They found a girl with charity-work credentials and a Twitter account, no less. A clear bid to gain sympathy from the modern hipsters who value a social conscience over tradition. Harnessing her following – the Internet-savvy young generation to whom the royals appear irrelevant – may well boost the popularity of the young royal. It would certainly do no harm to the young lady in question.

In an age where fake news and fake celebrity liaisons are commonplace, we could have expected at least the royal family to have some integrity, but it appears even they have succumbed.

Thankfully, the prince is sufficiently far enough away from the throne to pose any real threat to the royal bloodline. In any case, I fully expect this 'relationship' to blow over in a matter of months after which the heartbroken royal will find solace in a more suitable match.

Sceptical from Kent

'I spoke to the hospital today,' Kumari said. 'The press intrusion seems to have died down now. I was wondering if I could go back to work.' They were in the kitchen of Ben's apartment, cooking. Or rather, Benedict was cooking, she was grinding garlic, salt and pepper in a stone pestle and mortar to help. Though Ben had mentioned marriage and she'd agreed to give up work if they got engaged, in the meantime she could go back to the hospital.

Ben paused in his chopping. 'What did they say?'

'McGregor wanted to check with the security office before he committed to anything.' She ground stone against stone. 'I think he's torn, to be honest. They need the staff. They might manage to pull in some locums after a few weeks, but, generally speaking, they can't just lose a doctor and carry on like normal.' She stabbed at a big piece of garlic that had escaped and dragged it into the mush.

'Do you want to go back?' He had put the knife down now and was wiping his hands on a cloth. Like everything else in this place, the tea towels were laundered and replaced while they were out. Kumari was at a loss as to how the housekeeper knew when to jump in and do things. Kumari herself had only been out for a couple of hours when she went for a run and back to her rooms for a shower. She had come back to find the place spotless.

'I'm bored,' she said. 'I need to be doing something.'

'Maybe you should see if your parents want to come down to see you,' he said. 'I'd like to meet them, and the schools are still off, so your father's not working. Plus, you going back to work now might be too soon.'

She stopped grinding things. Amma had mentioned several times that she would like to meet this man she'd heard so much about. They had to meet at some point. Why not get it done sooner rather than later? Like ripping off a plaster – it would be better done fast.

'But what's your schedule like?'

He pulled his phone out of his pocket. 'Not too bad. Most evenings are free.'

'OK.' She gave the garlic paste one last grind and passed it across to him. 'Shall I call them now and see if they can make it?'

He nodded, picked up the kitchen knife again and resumed chopping.

She picked up the white phone that was hanging on the wall, dialled nine to get an outside line and phoned home. To her surprise, her mother answered the phone after one ring.

'Hi. It's me,' Kumari said.

'Oh. Kumari. Er . . . can I call you back? We're waiting for the police to phone us back and I don't want to miss them.'

Questions about why and what was going on crowded her mind, but the tension in her mother's voice was enough to tell her that getting off the phone was more important right now. 'OK. Call me as soon as you can. On my mobile.' She added, 'Are you OK?', but her mother had already gone.

She briefly caught her father's voice before the connection cut out.

When she turned round, she saw that Ben had paused mid-chop. 'What's up?'

'She said she's waiting for the police to call her back. She didn't say why – she was anxious to get off the phone.' She pulled her own phone out of her pocket and sent a text asking what was happening. 'Hopefully, they can answer my text while they wait.'

Ben frowned. He strode over to the phone and dialled a number. 'Anton. What's happening at Kumari's parents' house? Find out, please.' He listened for a bit. 'OK. Keep me updated. I'll be here.' His gaze flicked to Kumari. 'She'll be here too.'

Kumari stared at her phone, willing it to buzz with a text message. Anxiety began its slow burn in her chest. Ben came over and put his arm around her.

'Anton thinks the press may have found out where your parents live. He's been working with our legal team to squash some defamatory headlines and articles from going out, but we can't stop them publishing facts.'

'Will they be OK?' She thought of the shock of suddenly being mobbed and kept in her workplace. Were her parents trapped in their house? Were they sitting in the living room with the curtains drawn?

Her phone finally buzzed. The text from Amma read: *We are fine. Photographers and a TV van outside the close, getting in the way. There were people in the back garden. Police on their way to clear things up. We are both fine.*

She felt some of the panic drain away. They were OK, just inconvenienced. 'It's not fair,' she said quietly. 'I'm the

192

one they should be harassing. Not my parents. I'm hiding here while my parents and the hospital are being mobbed. It's not right.'

Ben's mouth was a compressed line. 'No,' he said. 'It's not right.'

Kumari retrieved her drink and tapped her fingers against the work surface while she watched her phone. Ben cooked, his movements more precise and controlled than normal. He kept looking over at her phone, as though he too was waiting for it to ring.

When it finally rang, Kumari was setting the table. She raced over to the breakfast bar and grabbed it.

'Are you OK?' she said, without preamble.

'Yes, yes. We are fine,' said her mother. 'The police have made the press people go away now, and Mrs Webb offered to get her grandson to go to the shops for us if we need anything. The police said they'll have a patrol car come round every so often.'

Kumari breathed out slowly. 'That's good. So, what happened?'

Ben waved at her, wanting to know what was going on.

'Amma, would you mind if I put you on speakerphone? So that Ben can hear you too?'

There was a pause, then, 'Of course. It would be nice to speak to him too.'

She put the phone down, speaker phone on. 'OK.'

'Hi,' said Ben. 'This is Ben. It's nice to speak to you.'

'Hello,' said Amma. 'Um . . . Your Highness?'

'Oh, no need to call me that. Just Ben will do.'

'OK . . .' Kumari could almost hear her fighting the urge to add 'sir' at the end.

'So, what happened?' asked Kumari, anxious to get the conversation back on track.

'Well, I went to work this morning. Everything was normal then. Your father went into town mid-morning and stayed until it was time to pick me up. When we came home, there were people – not many, just a cluster of people – at the top of the road and they started taking photos. We had to get the shopping out of the car and these two men, one with a microphone and the other with a camera, came up and started trying to talk to us about you. They asked if we were your parents. I said yes. Then Thatha said not to talk to him and we went inside. They banged on the door . . . and there have been people banging on the door every so often all evening.'

Kumari glared at the phone. How could they harass two innocent people like that? She looked up at Ben and saw that his jaw was clenched so hard that a muscle was twingeing in his cheek.

'Was there anything else?' he asked quietly.

'Um . . . a couple of men jumped over the fence into the back garden and tried to look in through the windows. I opened the curtain and there were two cameras pointing at me. We called the police again and they said this time they could do something.' Her voice got tighter and tighter, until, by the end of the sentence, she sounded high-pitched.

Kumari sensed there was more.

Thatha's voice came on. 'Kumari, are you safe? If it's like this for us, I dread to think how much they're hounding you.'

'I . . . I'm not at home. I've rented a room so that they leave Lucy alone. I'm staying in Kensington. It's very safe here.'

If her father had any opinions on that, he didn't voice them. 'There's all sorts of people talking about you and us on the telly. There was even a bit on *North News*. There are people claiming to know us who I've never heard of.'

Kumari looked up at Ben, who had gone very still. His eyes were narrowed and focused. He looked a little scary. His gaze met hers briefly.

Ben said, 'I'm sorry you've been put through this. I genuinely am. I'm going to see if I can call in some security to keep people off your close, at the very least.'

'There was . . . something else,' said her father. 'Sometime while we were out, someone put things through the letterbox.'

'Things?' said Kumari.

'A racist note . . . uh . . . and some poo.'

'*What?*' Kumari bit back the swear word that first came to mind. Thirty years of not swearing in front of her parents and she wasn't about to start now.

'Did you hand it over to the police?' asked Ben.

'Well, not the poo . . . we put that in the bin.'

'Perfectly reasonable,' said Ben. He caught Kumari's eye and seemed to be asking something. She frowned, puzzled. Ben did a small eye roll.

'I was wondering,' he said carefully, still maintaining eye contact with Kumari, 'would you like to come and visit us?'

Finally Kumari understood. This would get them away from their home. People would lose interest in a few days. It would also allow Ben to get to know them.

'In . . . Kensington Palace?'

'Yes,' said Ben. 'I have access to rooms you can stay in.' There was silence from the other end of the line. They must be thinking about it.

'Maybe, if you have a conversation about it and speak to Kumari,' Ben said. 'I think it might be a good idea for you to get away as soon as possible and stay out of the public eye for a few days.'

'Thank you,' Thatha said. 'That is a very kind offer. Let us get back to you.'

Ben excused himself and Kumari took the phone off speaker and spoke to her parents alone.

'He seems very nice,' her father said. 'Your mother wants to know if you've spoken to Lucy.'

'Not since yesterday.' Oh God. If they'd found her parents, what if they'd found Lucy too? 'I'll call her as soon as I've finished speaking to you.'

By the time she hung up, she could hear Ben on the phone in the kitchen. He was asking Anton to arrange security for her parents, as promised. Then he started talking in hushed tones and took the phone with him into the bedroom and shut the door. What was that all about?

She quickly called Lucy and was relieved to hear all was well with her. When she'd finished, she heard Ben say, 'I know it's not protocol, but I must insist.'

She stepped out into the corridor, wondering whether she should really be eavesdropping. While she dithered, half in, half out of the kitchen, he said, 'What, now? OK, yes. Informal, yes? Thirty minutes.'

She took a step firmly into the hallway, so that she was standing outside the room when he marched out.

'What's in thirty minutes?' she asked.

'We've got five minutes to spruce up and then we've got to get across to the main palace. We're going to see Grandma.'

Kumari gave a little squeak. She was in jeans and a button-down shirt. 'I can't meet the queen dressed like this!'

'You have to. She has a window in her schedule. She's willing to meet us. We won't get this chance again.' He went back into the room and ran a comb through his hair and tucked his shirt in.

Kumari hastily did the same.

Ben was practically jumping up and down with impatience. He grabbed her hand.

'Do we need coats?'

'Grab one, you can put it on in the car.' He pulled the door shut behind him and set off at a pace. The car was waiting for them at the gatehouse.

When they got to Buckingham Palace, Ben jumped out and rushed in, barely stopping to acknowledge the staff, as he normally would. Kumari had to almost jog to keep up. They speed-walked through corridors, which all looked identical to her.

Eventually, they arrived at the foot of the enormous main staircase. She had seen this on TV.

A man in a suit stood at the top, looking at his watch. 'Two minutes to spare, Your Highness,' he said to Benedict. 'Well done.'

Both Ben and Kumari were breathing heavily from having run there. Ben raised his hand to ask for a minute, then said, 'Is she able to see us?'

'Yes.' The man turned and walked away. Kumari followed Ben up the wide stairs, fighting the overwhelming urge to stare at the opulence of it. The man led them into an oak-panelled room with two sofas and an enormous flower arrangement in it.

'Please. Do take a seat.'

Kumari sat and tried to catch her breath, willing herself not to break out into a sweat.

'I hate that guy,' Ben muttered. 'He's incredibly efficient, but he still treats me like I'm ten.'

'Ben, what's going on?'

He looked strung out. Nervous in a way she'd never seen him before. 'I'm asking for a formal statement to be made asking the press to stop the more racist aspect of their reporting and to give you and your family a break. Before I do that, I need my granny's permission to . . . well, formally be associated with you.'

'You say the most romantic things.'

He managed a tiny smile. 'I'm sorry. I realise it's weird. Some things, just are.'

She nodded. 'It's tradition. Right?'

Before he could answer, the door to the adjoining room opened and the same man as before came in. 'Her Majesty will see you now.'

The room was lined with books from floor to ceiling. There was a fireplace, which had another enormous flower arrangement in it. There were a couple of comfy chairs. At the far end of the table was an huge desk. The queen sat behind it, reading paperwork. She smiled when they entered.

Benedict bowed. Kumari curtsied.

The dogs came up to greet them. One of them put his paws on her leg so Kumari could scratch his head, as though he knew she was an old friend.

The queen seemed to note this with some amusement. She didn't ask them to sit, so they remained standing. Clearly, she intended this to be a formal meeting. She picked up her pen and said, 'So, Kumari. How are you finding your time in Kensington?'

Caught off guard, Kumari glanced at Ben before saying, 'It's very nice, thank you, ma'am.'

'Nice? Anything more?'

She took a deep breath. Well, if she was going to be pushed on it. 'Very safe and secure. But also a little restrictive.'

She nodded. 'I don't disagree.' She put her pen down and levelled her gaze at Kumari. 'Tell me, my dear, what religion are you?'

Next to her Ben winced and closed his eyes.

'I don't have one, ma'am. Although I was brought up Buddhist.'

'Atheist, eh?'

'Agnostic. I don't have enough faith to be an atheist.'

Ben gave a soft groan.

The queen glanced at her grandson. 'Not enough faith to be an atheist?' she said.

'To be an atheist I'd have to believe that there isn't a God. As an agnostic, I'm not sure either way. I'm ambivalent about the existence of a God and I don't much like the trappings of organised religion.'

'But you've chosen Benedict. He is the grandson of the Defender of the Faith.'

Kumari shot a glance a Ben. 'I don't hold that against him.' There was a moment of tense silence. One of the dogs huffed. The queen's mouth twitched. 'I see Benedict has chosen a partner in the image of his mother.'

Out of the corner of her eye, Kumari saw Ben breathe out and smile. She had clearly passed some sort of test. She smiled too.

The queen's gaze turned to Ben. 'Your suggestion, Benedict. We have here the message you left. This is unorthodox, but given the circumstances . . . a good idea.' She turned her attention back to Kumari. 'It has been a pleasure to see you again, Kumari.'

'Thank you, ma'am.' Was she being dismissed?

'If you would wait in the next room for two minutes, please,' she said. 'We would like a word with young Benedict.'

'Of course.'

The dog, who had settled at her feet, yapped at her. She gave it a quick pat and left the room.

The anteroom was empty, so she sank into one of the sofas and tried to work out what had just happened. Whatever it was, it had gone well. She looked at her hands and saw they were shaking. The beads of sweat that had been threatening since she got there broke out and trickled down the nape of her neck. The door opened and Ben reappeared. He closed the door quietly, took a few steps towards her and grinned.

Kumari stood up.

'You were amazing.' He closed the space between them and hugged her.

'Thanks.'

He took her face in his hands and kissed her fiercely.

'Marry me?' he asked.

She laughed.

'Actually,' Ben said, as he took her hand in his. 'I'm not joking.'

'Oh.' Kumari's heart galloped in her chest. Was this it? Even though they'd joked about it, part of her hadn't really believed it could happen.

Ben cleared his throat and went down on one knee. He was still holding her hand. His eyes met hers. Kumari felt her knees weaken.

'I don't have the ring ready yet, but, Kumari Senavaka, will you marry me?'

'Yes, yes,' she said. 'Yes, of course I will.' She leant forward and kissed him. He stood up, still kissing her back. It was a few minutes before they parted. Kumari felt as though her whole body was made of bubbles. Happiness fizzed and popped in her veins.

A discreet cough made them pull apart. The same man as before was standing in the doorway.

'Yes, yes, we're going,' Benedict said. He paused. 'Just one second.' He rushed back and, despite the protest from the man in the suit, opened the door and popped his head round it. 'She said yes,' he said.

Kumari heard the queen laugh and say something. Benedict returned, grinning. 'Her Majesty says congratulations,' he said. He slung his arm around Kumari and drew her close. Together they walked back to where the car was waiting for them.

Chapter 17

Fast Light News

'Leave my girlfriend alone,' says prince

Prince Benedict has released a statement to the press saying that he is increasingly alarmed by the racist nature of press coverage relating to his girlfriend, Kumari Senavaka. Like his decision to date the divorced doctor, this statement is a break with tradition. The prince explained that he felt it was warranted due to the intrusive nature of the press's behaviour towards his girlfriend and her family and friends. 'The level of intrusion and the tone of reporting has been indefensible. These people should be allowed to live their lives,' he said.

[Link: Read the statement in full]

The Times Echo

Prince Benedict's unprecedented request to the press to stop harassing his girlfriend

A statement released by Kensington Palace on behalf of the prince, who is sixth in line to the throne, requests that the press and public respect the privacy of those connected with the thirty-year-old doctor, who was unable to go to work due to the disruption caused by press and members of the public attempting to get a glimpse of her outside St Kildare's Hospital.

Dr Senavaka has had to close down all her social media accounts because of the number of abusive messages and death threats she was receiving.

'These people should be allowed to live their lives,' the prince said in his statement.

Princess Ophelia was asked by well-wishers how she felt about her brother's new flame. She smiled and said she was simply delighted. Speculation is rife that there may be a royal engagement very soon.

'I can't believe you live here,' said Lucy. It had been a few days since Ben's announcement to the press and Kumari was finally having Lucy round to her rooms. They had ordered a takeaway, which was delivered to the gatehouse, and were sitting in her living room sharing a tub of ice cream for pudding.

'I don't, really. I'm just staying here for a few weeks.'

Lucy gave her a knowing look. 'You keep telling yourself that.'

Kumari lowered her spoon. The mouthful of ice cream meant she couldn't speak for a few seconds.

'What's happening with work?' Lucy asked. 'People are asking about you.'

Kumari sighed. 'I spoke to McGregor. I . . . I resigned.'

It had felt awful, but it was inevitable. She would have had to resign as soon as she was formally engaged to Benedict. She and Rita were still writing the proposal for the Boost Her! project. If it got funded, she wouldn't be able to publicly support that, either. She couldn't tell Lucy any of this, because it was meant to be a secret until the formal announcement.

'McGregor offered to give me unpaid leave for longer, but I couldn't really carry on like that,' she said.

'I'm going to have to look for a new housemate, aren't I?' said Lucy. 'I mean, the man made a statement to the press, effectively declaring that he loves you. You guys will be getting married fairly soon.'

Kumari made a non-committal noise. She felt bad about not telling Lucy, the only people she had told were her parents. They had been delighted for her, and their fears that Ben would abandon her with a broken heart somewhat alleviated.

Lucy took the sound to mean scepticism. 'The royals don't talk about their relationships in any official way until they announce an engagement. All the other girlfriends, even the fairly long-term ones, have been known in the press, but never formally acknowledged like you have.' She grinned. 'Besides, anyone can see that he's completely in love with you.'

Kumari would have scoffed, but she didn't really disagree.

'If he asked you, would you say yes?' said Lucy. It was a mark of their friendship that she even asked. Lucy had seen the aftermath of Kumari's marriage breaking down. She knew that getting married again was not something Kumari would take lightly.

Kumari smiled. This she could answer without giving any secrets away. Finding Ben had been like finding a missing part of her soul. 'Yes,' she said. 'I would definitely say yes.'

Lucy gave one of her high-frequency squeaks. 'Awesome!' She bounced around in her seat. 'I get to be the woman who used to share a flat with the princess. I'm going to dine out on that one for years.' She paused. 'I get to come to the wedding, right?'

'There isn't a wedding yet!'

'Good point.' Lucy picked up another spoonful of ice cream. 'It's only a matter of time, though. I'll have to buy a hat.'

'You do that.' Kumari looked at her watch. 'Ben said he would pop by on his way back to his place. He's at some formal dinner for one of his charities this evening.'

Lucy looked up. 'It's a different world, I tell you. I mean, even this place. You call it your room – there are two rooms and a bathroom. It's not a room, it's a flat.'

Kumari laughed. 'You should see Ben's place. It's a three-bedroom apartment, but there's a sitting room, an office, a dining room that he never uses and another sitting room he uses as a gym.' She looked around. 'And everything is bigger than this.'

'Different world,' said Lucy. There was a knock on the door.

'That'll be Ben,' Kumari stood up.

'What do I do?' asked Lucy, suddenly looking panicked. 'Do I curtsy? What do I call him?'

'Relax. You've met him before. Just call him Ben.' Kumari checked through the spyhole and let Ben in.

He grinned at her and gave her a sound kiss. He looked amazing in a full dinner suit. He turned to Lucy.

'Hello, Lucy, it's good to see you again.' He shook hands with her and kissed her politely on the cheek. Lucy's cheeks flushed a little.

'I see you've got stuck into dessert. I've brought wine,' he said. Kumari handed him a glass from her small cupboard.

Ben pushed a chair next to Kumari's, but didn't sit down.

'So, how are you, Lucy? I hope you've not been hassled by the press. We had some security posted nearby, but there didn't seem to be too much activity.'

'No. It's been fine. I guess they knew you and Kumari weren't there.'

Ben fetched a bowl and a spoon and dug a serving of ice cream out of the tub.

'Hey,' said Kumari. 'Didn't they feed you at this do?'

'That's coming out of your share,' said Lucy. Apparently, seeing Ben steal ice cream was enough to get her over any sense of awe.

Ben grinned at them both and tucked in.

It didn't take long for the atmosphere to settle into one of relaxed friendship. Kumari realised that she had missed these cosy evenings with Lucy. The realisation that she might still be able to hang out with her, albeit on slightly different terms, made her ridiculously happy. The fact that she could share them with Ben too, made her happier still.

It was late by the time Lucy stood up to leave. Kumari and Ben walked her back to within a few yards of the gatehouse and Kumari hugged her friend. 'We'll have to do this again, it's been really nice. I've missed you so much.'

'Me too,' said Lucy. She shook Ben's hand. 'It was really nice to get to know you, Ben. I can see my friend is in safe hands.'

'Thank you,' said Ben. 'I'll take that as a huge compliment.' He kissed her cheek. 'It's been nice getting to know you too, Lucy.'

'Although, one question. Now that you guys are "official", why don't you get engaged? I mean, you've done the difficult part and got her past the queen, so what's the hold-up?'

Kumari looked at Ben, willing him to let her tell Lucy. Ben laughed and said, 'Have you been talking to Ophelia?'

'No. Why?'

'I guess that means both of us have a bossy person in our lives,' Ben said to Kumari. 'Ah look, here's your car, Lucy.'

Lucy looked like she was going to insist on an answer, but thankfully, she didn't.

After she'd gone, Ben and Kumari walked back to her rooms. Ben seemed to be preoccupied. Kumari gathered up the bowls and Ben opened a window to let the smell of food dissipate.

'It was really nice to see Lucy again,' said Kumari. 'I've missed her.'

'Yes, I could tell.'

'I hate not being able to tell Lucy,' she said.

'I'm sorry,' Ben said. 'We can't tell anyone until it's official. Apart from your parents, obviously.'

'But getting engaged is a big deal. It's so odd not telling my friends.' She stopped talking. Ben was looking at her with a goofy smile on his face. 'What?'

'Since it was done in rather a hurry last time . . .' he said. He reached into the pocket of his dinner jacket and pulled out a small box.

'Ooh. The ring arrived,' she said. She looked up at him. 'A handsome prince in a tuxedo, carrying an engagement ring . . . it's like my very own fairy tale.'

He opened the box and held it out to her, 'Be my princess?'

She laughed. 'Of course I will.'

He slipped it onto her finger. The ring had a large diamond set in a cluster of pale sapphires. It had been sized perfectly to fit her.

'It's beautiful,' Kumari said, admiring it. 'Oh, Ben. It's gorgeous.'

'The sapphires are from Sri Lanka. Ceylon sapphires. The diamond . . .' He cleared his throat. 'The diamond was my mother's.'

The catch in his voice made her look up. He was gazing at the ring with a faraway expression. 'She had this diamond bracelet,' he said. 'It was her favourite piece of jewellery. I remember she used to stir the tea and the light would catch the bracelet and scatter into dancing points all over the room. We used to love that as kids.' He turned her hand so that the diamond caught the light. 'When she died, none of us could bear to look at the bracelet so our dad had it broken up and made into smaller pieces so that we could each carry something of her with us. The two girls have earrings, Dad and I have cufflinks.' He looked up, his eyes dim. 'I wanted you to have something of hers too. I . . . she would have liked you.'

Without a word, Kumari pulled him into her arms and hugged him. She held him close, listening to his heartbeat. Ben held her tightly. 'She would have liked you,' he whispered again into her hair.

Kumari held him tighter. She didn't say anything, because there was nothing more to say. He had given her the highest compliment he could bestow.

Chapter 18

The Northern Paragon

Northern village rallies against harassment of royal girlfriend's parents

The residents of a quiet cul-de-sac near Leeds have formed a neighbourhood watch to keep an eye out for intrusive members of the press who try to sneak in to catch a glimpse of Harsha and Rukmali Senavaka. The Senavakas have lived in the street for nearly thirty years, ever since they moved there with their baby daughter. That baby daughter grew up to become the girlfriend of national heartthrob Prince Benedict. Ever since the identity of the prince's girlfriend became public, there has been a media frenzy with reporters and 'citizen journalists' trying to find out every last piece of information about the thirty-year-old doctor.

'They're nice people,' said Mrs Gloria Webb, of number 1 The Close. 'Never had any trouble from them. Always had a good word for everyone. Mr S taught my grandson English. Half this street has been treated by Mrs S at some point. They may be foreign folk, but they're our folk.' Mrs Webb was the first person to call the police and report suspicious behaviour outside the Senavakas' house.

*'They didn't take me seriously at first,' she said.
'The Senavakas were out and this man came and
put summat through the letterbox. Turned out it was
hate mail and something disgusting. Then all these
people with cameras and microphones turned up.
We had people jumping over fences into gardens.
This is a nice neighbourhood. We've never had
nowt like this before. We're not standing for it.'*

*The neighbourhood has arranged a round-the-
clock watch. Anyone not already known to people
on the street is approached by one of the residents.
If they don't have legitimate business in the street,
they are asked to leave.*

The local police have declined to comment.

Ben proposing to her suddenly kicked everything into
a whole new level of activity. She couldn't wear the ring
until the engagement was formally announced, but now
that Ben had made her presence official, something had
changed. The palace machinery swung into action – she
was now a part of it. The first thing that happened was that
Ophelia informed her that she was coming round with
'some people' and minutes later the room was full.

'OK, introductions,' said Ophelia. 'Kumari – this is my
dresser, Mrs Pilding. This is her assistant, Sinead. This is
my personal assistant, Julia. I've suggested that Julia and
I help you with your arrangements in the short-term. We
need to get you a PA to help with all of this. I would ask
Anton but . . . I can just imagine his face.' Ophelia rattled
off names, conducting the room like it was an orchestra.
Kumari tried to smile and keep up.

Eventually, everyone sat on the sofas. They all seemed to be looking at her. Kumari tried hard not to fidget.

Ben's housekeeper, Louise, arrived hot on the heels of the guests, with a trolley of tea and cakes. She gave Kumari a friendly smile. Ever since she became 'official', people like Louise and Mr Forrest had become a little friendlier towards her. Stepping out of their discreet shadows to make themselves visible. Kumari smiled back and mouthed 'help', which made Louise smile as she hurried away.

'I think we'll start with making a list of everyone whose help we're going to need,' said Ophelia. 'Kumari, would you mind standing up, please? Walk up to the top of the room and back, if you don't mind.'

Warily, Kumari did as she was asked.

'Hmm,' said Mrs Pilding. 'Posture, decorum.' Next to her, Sinead tapped furiously on an iPad.

Kumari gave Ophelia a quizzical look. She knew she would have to have some training in order to fit into this world, but how much?

Ophelia gave her a sparkling smile. 'Effortless grace like this isn't achieved without actual serious effort,' she said, gesturing to herself. She was wearing jeans and a button-down shirt. She looked cool and casual at the same time. It was only if you looked closely, as Kumari was now doing, that you saw the careful, barely there makeup, the precisely tailored shirt that hung on her shape just so, the hair that was pinned carefully to achieve the feeling of a careless updo.

'I've had years to learn all this,' said Ophelia. 'You'll have to get it down in a few months.'

'Etiquette,' said Mrs Pilding. 'Although, we have most of what's necessary already in place, from what you say, ma'am.'

Ophelia nodded. 'Just the finer points, I should think.'

Kumari silently thanked Amma's pernickety lectures on table manners.

'Hair, passable,' Mrs Pilding continued. Sinead's eyes flicked to Kumari's hair. Kumari tucked it behind her ear, nervously.

'Wardrobe, we'll leave for later.'

'Wardrobe?' Kumari said. She looked down at her own faded jeans and T-shirt. 'Fair enough. I think I'll be needing that.'

'I was thinking traditional outfits, elegant and simple dresses. In colours that would suit the darker complexion, of course,' Mrs Pilding said. 'The alternative is to use saris for all formal occasions, but really, I don't think that would convey the right message.'

Kumari narrowed her eyes. 'What message would that be, Mrs Pilding?'

'That you have been welcomed to the royal family, of course. Besides, you couldn't have all that midriff showing. It's not modest.'

Sinead looked like she was about to say something, but shrank back again after a warning glare from Mrs P.

Interesting. Kumari wondered if the young assistant had less traditional ideas than her boss. 'Sinead. What do you think?'

Ophelia's lips twitched and she gave Kumari the smallest of nods. There was a brief expression of triumph on her face before she hid it. Kumari felt like she'd passed some sort of test.

Sinead studied her, concentrating hard, her freckled face serious. She was a neat young woman, with straight, black hair and porcelain-white skin. Her face was a mixture of Chinese and Caucasian features. Kumari guessed that, given her name, she was part Irish, part Chinese.

'I think you could wear strong colours, ma'am, which is wonderful. We could do so much with that.' She glanced at Mrs Pilding before continuing. 'And with your South-East Asian background and height, we could easily incorporate some traditional prints, perhaps, into a very modern wardrobe. Something vibrant.' She smiled at the vision that only she could see. She made a balancing motion with her hands. 'We could go for an East-meets-West, old-meets-new vibe.'

Mrs Pilding was glaring at Sinead, who noticed and subsided into an awkward silence. Apparently, she had overstepped her mark. Kumari's eyes narrowed again. She raised her hand. 'I have a question.'

All four women looked up at her.

'What does "East meets West" entail, Sinead? Saris with modern tops? The top from a salwar kameez set over jeans?' She'd never worn a salwar kameez in her life. Or a kurta, for that matter. She'd worn a Kandyan sari to her first wedding and an Indian sari for parties, but really, she'd spent more time in jeans than any other item of clothing.

Sinead looked at Mrs Pilding again, as though asking for permission. When given the nod, albeit reluctantly, she fiddled with the iPad then turned it round to show Kumari. 'I did a bit of research,' she said, her eyes shining. 'I was thinking traditional-style, high street dresses paired with tailored jackets with subtle embroidery reminiscent of more traditional Asian styling.'

She passed the iPad to Kumari. There were a series of beautiful dresses, mostly with the clean, unfussy lines that she liked, but with detailing at the edges, like a sari. She flicked through and came to a set of slides where someone, Sinead presumably, had taken some suit dresses and coats and hand drawn detailing that turned something plain into something ever so slightly different. A splash of colour here. A bit of embroidery there. Nothing over the top, but just a trace of difference. She nodded. 'I like it,' she said.

Sinead glowed. 'I was thinking we could incorporate the diversity element without losing the traditional standard mentioned in the brief,' she said.

Kumari didn't miss the warning look Mrs Pilding shot her assistant.

'The brief?' Kumari said. 'What brief?'

The other women looked at Ophelia, who sighed. 'Even princesses have to answer to someone,' Ophelia said. 'On the one hand, I have a lot of leeway in which designers I use. On the other hand, everything has to be in keeping with the general standards. Have you ever seen any of us make a massive fashion faux pas?'

Kumari shook her head. She might not have noticed, but Lucy would have.

Ophelia nodded. 'That's because we have people like Mrs Pilding to make sure we don't step too far from the guidelines. The institution, you see, is bigger than any one of us.'

Ben had said that too. Kumari opened her mouth to protest, but Ophelia's eyebrow went up a fraction. It was enough to tell her that now was not the time. She closed her mouth again. She would have to talk to Ophelia about it when these other people weren't around.

She muttered, 'All right.'

There was a moment of uncomfortable silence. 'Moving on,' said Ophelia. 'I believe we've already started working on security.' She looked at Kumari. 'Dave is training up a CPS officer. You'll meet her soon enough.'

'CPS?' said Kumari.

'Close Protection Service,' said Ophelia. 'A bodyguard. There's a small team, but one assigned to you in particular. Like Dave is for Benedict.' She turned back to Mrs Pilding, changing position elegantly. 'What's next on the list, Mrs P?'

'Elocution,' said Mrs Pilding.

Kumari frowned. 'Wait a minute. Elocution? Why?'

Mrs Pilding's eyes narrowed. 'How can I say this, ma'am . . . your accent . . .'

Kumari turned to face her and crossed her arms. 'I'm from Yorkshire. This is a Yorkshire accent.' It wasn't even a particularly strong one anymore. Years of living in London had worn it down.

'Precisely, ma'am. People may . . . struggle to understand you.'

'Rubbish,' said Kumari. That wasn't the word she wanted to use, but swearing at this woman was not going to help.

Ophelia gave her an exasperated look. 'Kumari, darling. Remember what I just told you five minutes ago?'

Kumari frowned. 'No,' she said. 'This is not about the institution. This is about identity. You want me to be a nod to the people you don't touch at the moment. This is how I identify.' She held up a hand and counted off her fingers. 'First, I'm a doctor. Then, I'm a woman. Then, I'm British. And then, I'm northern.' She lowered her hand. 'But all you seem to be seeing is brown.'

The silence in the room told her everything. Even Ophelia seemed to be lost for words. Kumari sighed. It wasn't like this was a new thing. She'd had it all her life. From the dinner lady who claimed she could never understand her, despite her accent being exactly the same as everyone else's, to the patients who said, 'Isn't your English *good*' in surprised voices. This happened all the time. Why was she surprised to find it *here*?

Ophelia rallied first and said, 'To be fair, darling, that is what everyone else will be seeing too.'

Mrs Pilding gasped. Ophelia rolled her eyes. 'Oh, not us,' she said, gesturing vaguely behind her, as though her family were standing just by her shoulder. 'We're just glad Benedict's happy. I mean everyone else. You will be a public figure, Kumari. You're going to be seen by thousands of people. Millions, even.'

At least Ophelia didn't bother sugarcoating it. Kumari took a deep breath and looked at the other women in the room. Fine. If that was the way it was going to be, she would deal with it the way she'd always dealt with it. Firmly.

'OK,' she said. 'I understand that this is the way things have always been done, but we've got an opportunity to change things here. Shake up a few things. Ophelia – people who see me as brown first will inevitably underestimate me. How can we use that?'

The three other women turned to look at Ophelia, like they were watching a tennis match.

Ophelia's eyes narrowed and then she smiled, a wicked, mischievous smile. 'Oh, I like the way you think. If you're up for it, Helena will think of lots of ways to use that.' She clenched her hands in a little excited motion. 'I like it.'

'For the clothes, we can move one step away from the "safe" options. Maybe even use some designers who you wouldn't normally use . . . or even throw in a sari.' Kumari gestured towards Mrs Pilding. 'With an appropriately modest blouse that covers up all the midriff.' She opened her hands in a widening gesture. 'For special occasions.'

'Splendid,' said Ophelia. 'Within reason, of course.'

'Of course.' She couldn't believe how well this was going down. 'And we won't erase my accent because all the people who believe you're snobbish and out of touch will love that I have a regional accent.'

'But . . .' Julia spoke for the first time. 'I believe Mrs Pilding makes a good point about being understood. While most people in the UK will understand you perfectly well, it's possible that those from around the world may not.'

Mrs Pilding gave a triumphant nod.

Kumari thought about the times she'd had crosswise conversations with Lucy before Lucy got used to her accent. OK. Maybe that was a fair point. 'All right, how about a compromise. I'll learn to soften my accent. I'm not moving over to received pronunciation, but I'll make an effort. Does that work?'

There was no disagreement.

'I like Sinead's ideas for clothes,' Kumari said. 'I'm not sure how this works, but I'd like to explore that, please.'

Sinead glowed. Mrs Pilding looked less pleased, but didn't say anything.

'As for the rest – what was it? Deportment? Protocol . . . all of that. Bring it on.' She was bright, she knew that. She'd never shied away from work. She could do this.

'Excellent,' said Ophelia. 'Julia will liaise with you to organise your diary. Mrs Pilding and Sinead, will you be able to get in touch with Julia to arrange timings for your meetings with Kumari?'

'Of course,' said Mrs Pilding.

'I'm still doing some work finalising a proposal for one of the charities I work for,' said Kumari.

'If you let me know when your meetings are, I will make sure to work around them.' Julia made a note.

'Wonderful. Is there anything else anyone needs?'

'No. I think we have everything we need,' said Julia. She glanced at the others. There was clearly a pecking order among the support staff too and Julia seemed to be somewhere near the top in this room. Kumari felt a kick of nerves. Hierarchies were everything in this place. She had to find where she was in the order every time she walked into a room. She didn't know who to trust. Ophelia, maybe. At least she knew that Ophelia wouldn't do anything to harm her brother.

The other women did their curtsies to Ophelia and left the room. Ophelia stood up. 'I think that went well,' she said.

Kumari felt adrenaline draining out of her, leaving her feeling hollow. 'Did it? I didn't come across as too bossy?'

Ophelia laughed. 'Of course you did. But a top secret princess tip for you: don't be afraid to be bossy if it gets things done. In this place, where things have run along the same worn tracks for generations, you're different. You're upsetting the order of things. As you say, we are at a point of change. Own it. Do what you need to do.' She smiled. 'Our mother tried, you know. She had ideas about how things could evolve, but this place couldn't change then. It wasn't ready. But now . . . we may not be able to change everything, but we can make a start.'

'Are you sure it's ready now?' said Kumari. 'To change, I mean. People like the old-fashioned values and the pomp and ceremony. Lucy's family come over just to gawp at the palace from the outside.'

'We're more useful than that,' said Ophelia. 'You'll be surprised what a well-placed hint here and there can do.' A frown flitted across her features. 'We'd never interfere with government of course, that's not allowed. But in international affairs and humanitarian causes, we are useful.'

Kumari didn't doubt that. 'Well, thank you. For arranging all of that. It's a really steep learning curve for me.'

'Oh, think nothing of it,' said Ophelia. 'It's nice to have a project.' She picked up her handbag. 'Now, my darling, I must run. Was there anything else you needed?'

'Actually, yes. Sinead, the assistant. Is there any chance I could have her as my dresser? It would . . . allow Mrs P to devote her full attention to you.'

'And I do need a lot of attention,' said Ophelia cheerfully. 'I shall have a word in the appropriate ear.' She planted an air-kiss centimetres away from Kumari's cheek. 'Later, dear heart.'

Chapter 19

The Vista Post

Is Kumari set to become a new style icon?

Prince Benedict's girlfriend, Kumari, has yet to set her own style, but commentators are already speculating on the effect of having a woman of ethnic heritage linked to the royal family. Both of the princesses are known for their distinct styles: Princess Helena's tailored and traditional and Princess Ophelia's more vibrant and youthful. Up-and-coming designers will be clamouring to catch the eye of the newest addition to the young royal posse. Princess Ophelia, for example, has made the career of many a young designer by choosing to wear one of their creations.

From what we have seen, Kumari's taste oscillates between a sari for formal occasions and high street styles for informal. Time will tell which of these two style choices will come to the fore.

Photo caption: Kumari at the charity event where she first met the prince. [Photo credit Greg Frankish]

Photo caption: Kumari and the prince seen going into Harrods. Kumari wears a Marks & Spencer coat and jeans from Next. [Photo credit Farnaz Masud]

Kumari looked out of the car window at the gathered press and slipped her sunglasses on.

'Ready?' Ben asked. He too was wearing sunglasses. He was in cricketing whites because he would be playing later to support one of his educational charities. Kumari was in a lemon and white dress, with styling that hinted at Indian paisley patterns. Sinead had paired it with a scarf and a lightweight blue jacket and white shoes. Everything had been altered so that it fitted perfectly. Kumari wasn't sure which one of them had been more nervous about this, her first public outing as the prince's girlfriend. The Annual Krantz Solutions Fundraising Cricket Match wasn't the biggest event in Benedict's calendar, but it was sizeable enough to be scary. As the engagement hadn't been formally announced, she didn't wear the ring. It was still a precious secret.

There was a barrage of camera clicks as the car door was opened for Ben first, then her. Ben came round and held a hand out to help her out of the car. He managed to give the impression of being solicitous without ignoring the cameras. She stepped out and there was another flurry of clicking. They walked down the slightly muddy red carpet to the VIP entrance. Once they got inside, Ben squeezed her hand. 'Well done. First pap walk accomplished.'

They were met by someone involved in the charity and ushered into the VIP enclosure. Kumari had the surreal experience of people photographing her on their phones as she went past. She held on to her clutch bag. When she'd asked for a bag she could sling on her shoulder, Sinead had said that having something to hold was important. Now she realised why. It gave her something to do with her hands and, as Sinead had pointed out, it was a good shield to stop people from touching her. Choosing Sinead as her dresser had been a stroke of genius. Mrs Pilding's training meant that Sinead knew exactly what was expected, but she was new enough to be flexible. She was also very talented. Exactly what Kumari needed.

She shook hands almost mechanically. All these people wanting to speak to her and Ben felt vaguely oppressive. Turning her head, she caught sight of Dave, never more than arm's length away. Before they set off, Dave had introduced her to another CPS officer, a middle-aged lady called Danielle, who was just behind her, watching her in the same manner as Dave watched Ben. She had thought that having a bodyguard would be an off-putting and intrusive experience, but now realised that it was incredibly reassuring. She didn't know if Danielle would be her permanent bodyguard, or if they'd get to the level of ease that Ben and Dave had reached, but she was grateful to have her.

Thanks to the training she'd been having of late, she found small talk wasn't too taxing. She asked people about the work that the charity did, which was genuinely interesting. Ben, not too far away from her, did his thing, making it look effortless. She couldn't help noticing the variety of responses people had to her. Some people's gaze was frank and curious, a few of the younger women gave her looks of animosity, most of the aristocratic and super-rich (she was amazed to find she could now tell the difference between aristocrats and people who were just plain rich) just ignored her unless she was right next to Benedict. It was a clear message that she was there only at the behest of the prince. On her own, she was nothing.

Well, bugger that. No one was going to make her feel insignificant. She stamped down her insecurity, stood a little straighter and smiled. 'Own it' Ophelia had said. Own it she must. She beamed at the next person who came to talk to her. Thankfully, it was someone wanting to compliment her on her dress.

Finally, after what seemed like ages, they sat in the VIP enclosure to watch the cricket. She knew the basic rules. She had spent a lot of her childhood watching cricket on TV. Or rather, her father had watched the cricket, while Kumari read a book and glanced up occasionally to watch the replay of an exciting shot.

Ben disappeared off to play. He walked onto the pitch to cheers. He raised his bat to Kumari and she waved back.

'You're Benedict's new girlfriend, are you?' said the elderly lady, a dowager marchioness, who was sitting next to her. The seats in the VIP area were evenly spaced, so that everyone had decent elbow room.

'Yes,' said Kumari.

The older woman pulled out a pair of glasses, put them on and peered at Kumari. 'Yes, so I see,' she said. She put her glasses away. 'Tell me, young lady, do you ride?'

The question was so random that Kumari was taken aback. 'Not really,' she replied. 'I had a few lessons when I was young, but not since.'

The lady leant forward to look past her at Ben. 'Well, I dare say Benedict will fix you up with lessons before long.'

He had suggested it, as it happened. So had Ophelia. It was on her list of things to do, but she was damned if she was going to let that tone pass.

'Or,' Kumari said pointedly, 'not.'

The lady's bright-eyed gaze moved to her. She looked her up and down. 'Yes,' she said, stuffing about three vowels into the word. 'I don't suppose it's your sort of thing.'

Kumari gritted her teeth and smiled. She knew how to deal with this. It was the same as when dealing with certain matriarchs in Sri Lanka. They liked to goad you to see if they got a reaction. Deflect. Don't react. 'How about you? Do you ride?'

'Not anymore,' said the old lady. 'My hips won't allow it. But I do have a few horses. Racers, don't you know.'

'Oh, lovely. How are they doing? Any winners among them?' Yes. She was getting the hang of this.

The lady launched into a list of horses and races and times. Kumari kept up her interested face. She could do this. She could do this.

Later, when she went for a drink, she was cornered by a gent who insisted on telling her about his time in India. She couldn't get a word in to say that she'd never been to India, she was Sri Lankan.

Suddenly, a voice said, 'Dr S, how lovely to see you again.'

She turned and was relieved to see a familiar face.

'Rhodri.' She was so happy to see him that she nearly hugged him.

He air-kissed her cheek, his hand stopping just short of touching her elbow. 'How's it going?' he asked quietly.

She gave a small shrug.

'You're doing great,' he said in an undertone. He turned to the man she'd been listening to. 'Rhodri Ellesmere-Jones, sir.' He shook hands with the man who looked taken aback.

'Benedict's girlfriend and I were just discussing India,' the gent informed Rhodri.

'I'm sure it was very informative,' said Rhodri. 'Especially as Dr Senavaka here is from Sri Lanka.'

The gent huffed. 'Same thing,' he said.

'It's really not,' Kumari said.

'If you'll excuse us a minute. I need to introduce Dr S to someone.' Rhodri guided Kumari away.

'Thanks,' she whispered.

'I actually do want you to meet someone.' He gestured to a girl, beautifully groomed and surprisingly like Rhodri.

'This is Gwyneth, my sister. Gwyn, this is Kumari, Ben's girlfriend.'

Gwyneth gave her a friendly smile. Kumari recognised her from the hours she'd spent looking up people on the Internet. Gwyn occasionally got linked to Ben because they were at the same parties. Ben had told her that they were friends and that Gwyn was definitely not interested in him because she had a girlfriend she kept hidden from everyone in the family, apart from her brother.

They did the air-kissing thing. 'Rhodri's told me so much about you,' Gwyn said in her lilting Welsh accent, that was stronger than Rhodri's. 'Apparently, Ben's potty about you. About time he met someone nice.'

Kumari laughed and decided she liked Gwyn.

'Rodders!' Ben appeared, looking hot. The two men greeted each other with a handshake and hug combo.

'Out so soon?' said Rhodri.

'Never was much good at cricket.'

Ben kissed Gwyn on the cheek. 'Hello, Gwyn. What are you up to these days?'

'Oh, this and that, you know how it is,' said Gwyn.

'We're just monopolising your lovely Dr S here,' said Rhodri.

'For which I'm profoundly grateful,' Kumari said.

'She got trapped talking to old Lord Postie,' Gwyn told him.

Ben grimaced. 'He's easy to talk to,' he said. 'Just keeps going. Doesn't actually require any input from you.'

'So I gathered,' said Kumari drily.

'So, Rodders,' said Ben. 'What have you been up to?' They chatted for a bit. Rhodri and Gwyn were friendly and fun. They made Kumari feel insulated from the frosty reception of the others.

A floppy-haired young man with a clipboard edged towards Ben and Rhodri. 'Um . . . Your Highness,' he said.

Ben turned, smiling.

'I've been asked to escort you and Dr . . .' he paused to look at his clipboard ' . . . Se-na-va-ka, to the stage.'

'Oh, right. Yes,' said Ben.

Kumari took a step forward. The intern didn't move. He looked expectantly at Rhodri. There was a moment of confusion. Kumari rolled her eyes and stepped up, so that she was standing next to Ben.

Rhodri gave a bark of laughter. 'Oh, you poor boob,' he said. 'I'm not Dr Senavaka. She is.'

The boy went bright red. Kumari sighed. All this training and etiquette lessons and nothing had really changed.

The day dragged on. Even 20/20 cricket matches took a long time. The crowd in the VIP tent thinned. Kumari excused herself to go to the toilet and on the way back, she spotted someone familiar. Ruby? She did a quick double-take. Yes, it was Ruby, standing next to Greg Frankish.

Should she say hello? She changed course to go towards them. As she approached, she realised that they were holding hands. Something about this nagged at her. She stopped to work out what it was.

Ruby was going out with Greg. One by one things clicked into place. Ruby was going out with Greg. Greg was a photographer, not above doing something like ... waiting for Kumari and taking photos of her using a long-range lens when she was entering a private club. Lucy had mentioned that Ruby kept popping round. Kumari had a sudden image of the message pad in the kitchen of the flat. She had written down the name and postcode of the club and the date and time. She hadn't bothered to hide it. Why would she? If Ruby had been in the flat, she could have seen it.

The timeline fell into place. Ruby, who was the only other person to have reason to suspect that Kumari was seeing Benedict, must have told Greg when and where she would be meeting Ben. Greg had taken several photos. One as she arrived and one as she and Ben left. He had deliberately released the blurry photo first to whip up interest. And then, when everyone was wondering who she was, he sold the clear photo. Since every newspaper then reprinted his original photos of her and Ben at the charity event, he must have been paid for those again too.

Because of the greed of two people, she had been chased out of her home and her parents had been harassed. She stormed towards them.

'It was you,' she said, coming to halt beside Ruby.

Ruby jumped. 'Kumari. Hi.'

'It was you, wasn't it?' Kumari hissed in an undertone. 'You told him and he revealed my identity to the press.'

Greg turned. 'Hello, Kumari. Nice to see you.' He smiled. 'Surely, you don't begrudge me the chance to make a little money by doing my job. I am a journalist first and foremost.'

She bit back a comment on what else he was and focused her attention on Ruby. 'I thought we were friends.'

Ruby had the decency to look uncomfortable. 'I went to so much trouble to line up PR for the charity event and all the papers wanted to talk about was you. No matter what I did, your story stole the limelight.'

'So you thought you'd get your own back? By throwing the full horror of the media spotlight on me? Have you any idea what you've done?' said Kumari. 'We hadn't got the security arrangements in place when it broke. My parents were harassed. They had to be rescued by their neighbours. I had to leave my job and move out of my flat. Lucy had to have security on standby. What the hell did you have against my parents? Or Lucy?'

Ruby's mouth opened and closed a couple of times. 'I didn't—'

'You didn't think!' said Kumari. 'To you it was just a game. A stupid tit for tat.'

'Don't be such a sanctimonious cow,' Greg hissed. 'So, you had to move out of your place and into a luxury apartment at the royal family's expense. Oh boohoo. You're going out with a prince, sweetheart. The press goes with the territory.' He grinned. 'Speaking of which . . .'

Before she could react he had lifted his camera and taken her photo.

'You—'

'What?' said Greg. He took a step closer to her.

Danielle stepped up so that she was between Kumari and Greg. She didn't say anything, but her mere presence made Greg step back.

Kumari's gaze went from Greg to Ruby. 'I hope you're pleased with yourselves,' she said. She nodded to Danielle, turned and walked away.

A few seconds later, she heard a breathless, 'Kumari.' She turned to see Ruby, looking worried.

'What?'

'You aren't going to tell the charity, are you?'

Kumari looked beyond Ruby's shoulder and recognised the man who had come to wish Greg luck the night they did their initial pitch. The chairman of the Better for All board and his wife.

'How come Greg is so close to the chairman?' she asked.

'Alumni of the same school,' said Ruby. 'Greg did some portrait photos for the chairman's wedding anniversary and he invited us to this as a thank you.' She glanced over her shoulder, looking worried. 'Seriously, Kumari, are you going to tell them? Because it won't look good on me, but, more importantly, it's not right that a stupid mistake on my part should have an impact on Greg's project.'

'It's not just a stupid mistake on your part, is it?' said Kumari. 'I bet he offered you something. What was it? Did he offer to take you with him if he won?'

Ruby's face reddened, but she didn't reply.

'Oh, Ruby,' said Kumari. 'You know he was just using you. He made a lot of money from selling those photographs. And, if he got you to go around slagging me off within the charity, he would be making sure his project got funded too.'

'Don't be ridiculous,' said Ruby. 'Greg and I are in love.'

'You keep telling yourself that,' said Kumari.

'It's not relevant anyway,' said Ruby. 'What is relevant is what you're going to do.'

Kumari sighed. 'Nothing. I'm not going to stoop to your level. All the projects shortlisted are great causes. The proposals went in last week and if my project gets funded, it has to be on its own merit. So you're safe. Don't worry. I just wish I could say the same about my friends and family.' There was a cheer from the viewing stand. 'Now, if you'll excuse me, I have to go.'

She walked away again. This time, Ruby didn't follow her. Danielle fell into step beside her. 'Are you OK, ma'am?'

'Yes.' Kumari looked at the other woman and smiled. 'Thank you for intervening.'

'It's my job.'

'Even so,' said Kumari. 'I appreciate it.'

Danielle gave her a tiny half-smile and dropped back a step to follow her at a distance again.

Chapter 20

The Aurora Post

Prince and Kumari go to Frieze Art Fair, amidst rumours of an imminent royal engagement

Prince Benedict and his girlfriend, Kumari, have been to the opening of this year's Frieze Art Fair. They were seen together, unusually for a royal couple, holding hands. Kumari wore an orange and russet dress with Indian-inspired detailing designed by a relatively unknown designer, Sheena Kass, paired with shoes and a hat from the high street store Zara. The couple seemed relaxed and happy and were even spotted kissing.

Rumours abound that an engagement will be announced soon.

Amma and Thatha finally came to visit for the weekend. Ben had invited them to stay in his apartment, and Kumari temporarily moved into the smaller, third bedroom, so that she could be with them. They had decided against her staying in Ben's room, which is where she normally stayed. How strange that she still felt that way. She and Shane, as a married couple, had shared a bedroom when they visited her parents, so why would she feel odd about sharing with Ben? She shook her head. Best not to dig too deep.

Ben was out when they arrived, so Kumari had a few minutes alone with them before they met him.

They stood in the sitting room, holding their bags, looking hopelessly out of place in the large room. Kumari suddenly felt the immense awkwardness of the situation. It was so painful to see their discomfort that she wanted to cry. 'I'll show you round,' she said.

'This bag has food,' said Amma hesitantly, pointing to a large cool bag. 'I brought your favourite.'

The feeling of wanting to cry intensified. Her eyes hurt with the effort of holding back tears. 'I'll put it in the kitchen.' She grabbed the bag and carried it through. They followed her, padding quietly in their socks.

'Oh, my word,' said Amma when she saw the kitchen. This room, with the adjoining open-plan dining room, was as big as their whole house. Kumari had got so used to it now, she'd stopped noticing.

Thatha looked like he was trying not to touch anything. They both looked so uncomfortable. She had to do something. She put the kettle on. 'Tea? Was the journey OK?'

'Yes,' her mother said. 'It was very kind of Ben to send a car. Thank him for us.'

'He's at a meeting,' she said. 'He'll be back soon.' She opened the fridge and put the food in, packed carefully in Tupperware and used margarine tubs. The bag smelt of her years at uni, when her parents would swoop by to visit, bringing enough food to feed her for a week. Or when she was married to Shane, he was always delighted when she had food from home. And later, when she and Shane split up, she had always been sent home with a backpack full of food parcels that she froze to eat when she came back off

233

a night shift and couldn't be bothered to cook. Her entire life history was punctuated with these meals from home. And now, for the first time, she was in a place where they didn't fit.

She turned back to them and they were standing exactly where she'd left them. Still not touching anything.

'Are you OK?'

'Yes. This is very . . .' Amma waved a hand. 'Posh.'

'It is,' she said. Because it was. 'But it's OK.' She felt strange saying that. 'Please, sit down. Please.'

Her father seemed to snap out of his trance. He pulled a tall stool out for her mother and then took one himself.

Kumari made them tea, in mugs rather than teacups because they looked like they needed a proper cuppa.

They discussed the journey down and the arrangements that had been made to keep an eye on the house while they were 'down south'. Then the conversation slowed to silence. They sipped tea to cover up the gap where conversation would normally flow.

Kumari heard the buzz of the front door unlocking. She had never been so happy to hear anything in her life.

'That's Ben,' she said. 'I'll just go and check everything's OK.' She fled to the front hall.

Ben had hung up his coat and was pulling off his gloves. 'Are they here?'

She nodded. Her eyes filled with tears. Ben threw his gloves onto the side table and put his hands on her shoulders. 'What's the matter?'

'It feels so weird. They look so out of place and . . . it's weirding me out a bit.'

234

He looked puzzled, but made no comment. 'Let me come and say hello.' He took her hand. 'Come on. It's bound to be a bit strange at first.'

He was charming with them, like he was with everyone. He shook hands and made small talk, leaning against the counter. He told them a joke about the meeting he'd been in that afternoon. Kumari made him a tea and watched her mother be charmed. Her father, ever the thoughtful one, was reserved and polite. Slowly, slowly, the knot of tension in her chest loosened and the urgent need to cry drained away.

That evening, they decided to eat Amma's food. Kumari found dishes and helped her mother take everything out of the boxes to heat it up. Ben gave Kumari a curious glance when he saw the margarine tubs.

'Amma brought dinner,' she told him.

He popped the lid of one of the containers and peered inside. 'Home-made curry?' he said, eyes shining.

'Yes,' said Amma.

'Brilliant!' He opened another one. 'What's this one?'

'*Brinjal*,' Amma said. 'Sorry, you call it aubergine.'

He examined the tub. 'How did you make it?' He sniffed. 'Smells amazing.'

Amma launched into the basic recipe. Ben asked questions, his love of cooking coming to the fore. Soon they were discussing the merits of adding just a touch of puréed garlic right at the end of cooking.

Kumari glanced over at her father, who was watching Ben talking food with Amma. He gave her a small smile.

'Do we need cutlery?' Amma asked, when Kumari handed a stack of warmed plates to her father.

'Yes, of course,' said Thatha. He glanced at Ben. 'We should.'

'How would you normally eat?' said Ben. 'With fingers?'

Kumari nodded.

'Let's do that then. You'll have to teach me how to do it without making a mess.'

The Senavakas looked at each other. Kumari felt the deep discomfort returning. 'I don't know . . .'

'Oh, come on. I'm sure it tastes better when eaten the proper way,' said Ben.

Kumari hesitated. Her father said, 'It does actually taste better. Things get mixed better, if you see what I mean.' He made a mixing motion with his hands to illustrate.

Ben slipped into a chair. There was a brief moment of stasis when Kumari gestured to her parents that they should serve themselves first. They both glanced at Ben, who said, 'Excuse me a minute. I forgot to get some water for the table.'

Kumari suppressed a smile. It was a neat way to avert an awkward situation.

Amma served the rice for Thatha first and herself, just like she had done for as long as Kumari could remember. Kumari let Ben sort his own dinner out.

Ben had a good go at mixing the curries in with the rice.

'But how do you stop it falling apart?' he said, mashing his food together with a look of earnest concentration.

'Here, like this.' Amma demonstrated.

He took it in good spirit, being coached on eating technique by three people who had never had to worry about how to do it. He managed quite well, even if his place setting looked as if it had been attacked by a toddler by the end of the meal.

Kumari used her clean hand to rub his back. 'Pretty good going for a first-timer,' she said. 'You'll improve.'

'We're going to have to practise,' he said. He picked up his plate, that had been polished clean of any food. 'That was delicious. I thought I'd had curry before, but that was out of this world.'

Amma looked pleased. Ah Ben. Always so quick with a kind word. Kumari's heart swelled.

By the time they went to bed, everyone seemed to have unwound a little, although there was still a wariness about her parents and Kumari couldn't fully relax. She went to check that they had everything they needed.

'He is a very nice young man,' Amma said.

'I'm glad you like him.' It was a relief that they did. Amma didn't reply. Instead she took Kumari's face in her hands and pulled her down so that she could kiss the top of her head. '*Thunsaranai*, my baby,' she said. 'Goodnight.'

Kumari felt the urge to cry return.

Her parents were so ill at ease, it was clear that they didn't fit in. They would not be comfortable here. At the same time, Ben made no effort to take them round the palace. It was as though he sensed how misplaced they were and didn't want to make things worse. It occurred to her, briefly, that he might be hiding them from his wider family. Or perhaps protecting them. She couldn't be sure which.

The next evening he took them to a club for dinner. They had a private room. It was stiff and formal and strange. All in all, Kumari was glad when the visit was over. She loved her parents and she loved Ben. Seeing how far apart their two worlds were tied her up in knots.

When they called to say they'd got home safely, she asked Amma what she thought. Amma said, 'He clearly makes you happy. And he seems to love you very much. If this is what you want, my Kumari, you should take this with both hands.'

Kumari could sense the words that weren't being said.

'Amma. What's bothering you? Something is. I know.'

'We don't fit in that world, darling, you can see that. When you marry him, we will lose you. With Shane, we could pretend we were gaining a son-in-law, rather than losing a daughter . . . but with Ben, it's impossible. We will lose you.'

'But why? You can visit—'

'But you could never visit us. How would that work with the security necessity? We could come to you and stay in a room in your mansion and play with your children without ever meeting his side of the family. But your children could never come to stay with us. We would be the forgotten grandparents.' She sighed. 'Please don't misunderstand. I haven't got anything against Ben. Or your choice to be with him. I'm just pointing out what's bothering us. Because you asked.'

She had no response to that because she was pretty sure they were right. She said her goodbyes, hung up and put her head in her hands. Tears slid between her fingers. Ben found her like that, sitting on the bed. He gently gathered her up in his arms and held her until the sobs subsided.

When she explained to him what was wrong, he hugged her closer, but had nothing to say that would make her feel better.

Chapter 21

The Witness Reporter

Royals open new hospital for wounded service personnel

Princess Helena and Prince Benedict today opened a hospital with a wing specialising in physiotherapy and the rehabilitation of soldiers wounded while on active duty. The prince was shown the state-of-the-art physiotherapy suite and spoke at length with the mental health support team. The hospital is funded by the Princesses and Prince Foundation and by three charities that work together to support wounded members of the armed forces.

The princess, in her opening speech, spoke of the importance of coordinating medical services while her brother, himself once a serving soldier in the army, spoke about the key role played by mental health services in preparing soldiers who had endured trauma in battle to return to civilian life.

The evening after her parents left, Kumari called Lucy.

'Oh, hello, stranger,' Lucy said. 'How's life among the glitterati?'

Kumari sighed. 'Not as glittery as you'd think.' She looked around the kitchen in Ben's apartment. She had barely been out of this place for weeks. Even when she did it was with someone to mind her. She didn't need a minder.

'Do you want to meet for a drink?' she said. 'Please?'

'Are you allowed?'

'That's the very reason why I have to come out and meet you.'

Lucy didn't speak for a few seconds.

'Please, Lucy.' Kumari could hear the tears in her voice. She needed to see someone who understood her. To feel normal for one evening. No one knew her better than Lucy. She had neglected her friend lately. She really hoped Lucy could forgive her.

There was a small noise, like Lucy was clicking her tongue. 'OK, fine. Where?'

'Somewhere where I can sit in a dark corner and not be recognised.'

Lucy thought for a bit. 'Pub or cocktail bar?'

'Either.' Kumari tried to think of places she'd been to that would fit the bill.

'I know. Hang on, I'm going to send you a Google location for a pub. It's got a downstairs which has little alcoves. It's very cosy and private,' Lucy said. 'I'll be there in half an hour.'

'I'll have to sneak out, so it'll take a bit longer for me.' She went back to her rooms and put on her old jeans and a jumper. Just wearing her old clothes made her feel better. She pulled on a waterproof over her clothes. The drizzle outside gave her an excuse to keep her hood up. She pulled a beanie hat low over her forehead. There. She looked like anyone else. It took her a moment to think where she'd put her purse. She didn't need to carry money when she was with Ben. Things seemed to magically get paid for, although she suspected some of it was paid for by Dave and claimed back on expenses. She checked how much cash she had. Enough to get a cab one way. She'd have to get to a cashpoint before she went to the pub. She called and ordered a cab, giving the address of the gatehouse on the 'public' side of the estate. She checked the corridor and, remembering Ophelia's advice to 'own it', walked out with her head held high. No one challenged her. The cab was waiting for her by the time she walked down the drive to the sentry gate.

It was very strange being on the street without people noticing her. Kumari felt like she had a target on her back. She went over to the cashpoint and had to fight the urge to look furtively over her shoulder. Nothing out of the ordinary happened. She got her money and crossed over to the pub. In the basement, there were semi-secluded booths. People sat in small groups, chatting. She risked lowering her hood. Nobody took any notice of her. Looking round, she spotted Lucy sitting in a booth, waving to her.

Lucy had already bought a bottle of white wine and two glasses.

'Oh, you're a star.' Kumari handed over some money without needing to ask how much she owed. They had done this often enough in the past, albeit in different pubs.

'So, how's it all going? How's the ... er ... training going?'

'There's so much to remember,' said Kumari. 'Oh, hang on.' She rearranged her sitting position, scooting forward in her seat, pressing her knees and ankles together and placing her hands, one folded over the other, on the table. She raised her eyebrows. 'What do you think?'

Lucy peered round the side of the table at her legs. 'Nice. That's quite impressive, actually. You look taller.'

'I know, right?' She picked the wine glass up by the stem and took a delicate sip. 'The really weird thing is that his sisters have been doing this their whole lives, so they do it even when they're just chilling.'

Lucy smiled. 'Sounds interesting.'

Interesting? Yes, that was one way to describe it. There were plenty of other words too. Soul-destroying being one of them. Kumari put her glass down carefully. 'I suppose,' she said. 'But spending hours with different people who take apart everything you do and tell you how you've been doing it wrong all your life is not as much fun as it sounds.'

Lucy nodded. 'I know. Your mom told me.'

So Amma was still phoning the flat and talking to Lucy. While Kumari had been losing the things that defined her one by one, normal life carried on. Without her. She felt the tightness rise in her chest. She took a deep breath and found that her breath didn't go past her sternum. Even her lungs were rebelling.

'I gather the visit from your parents didn't go well.' Lucy put her hand out and covered Kumari's. 'Are you OK?'

Her sympathy undid Kumari. Another deep breath. This one was released as a strangled sob. She pressed her lips together to stop them trembling. Her eyes filled with tears. She shook her head.

'Oh, honey.' Lucy scooted over to come and sit next to her. She put an arm around Kumari and gave her a squeeze.

'Talk to me. Tell me all about it.'

It all came out. The pressure to conform, the way people ignored her unless she was standing right next to Benedict, the awful realisation that her parents would never feel comfortable in that environment, that she would never be able to work or just pop down to the shops without an escort. The suspicion of tokenism. And the terrible, terrible fear that everyone else was right after all. That she wasn't a suitable bride for a prince.

Lucy listened, interrupting occasionally to ask a question or to give her an extra hug. When Kumari had finally poured everything out and was steady enough to start drinking her wine, Lucy said, 'Do you feel better now you've spoken to someone?'

Did she? 'Not really. I mean, it's nice that all of it's not just echoing round in my head. But it's still there and it's all still crap.' She pulled a handkerchief out of her handbag and wiped her eyes.

'A hanky?' said Lucy. 'Fancy.'

Kumari stared at it. When had she acquired hankies instead of tissues? Ophelia had given her some as a gift. She opened it out, it had a K embroidered in the corner. Oh God, they were infiltrating her without her even realising. The ball of panic in her chest rose higher.

She turned to Lucy. 'I don't even know who I am anymore.'

Lucy looked at her gravely. 'Kumari, I hate to say this, but that is what you would be choosing if you marry Ben. You can't be as you were and be his wife at the same time in public. But you can still be you in private.' She pushed her hair back. 'I know it's not what you want to hear, but I'm afraid it's true.'

Kumari slumped back in her seat and laid her head back. At the back of her mind, Mrs Pilding tutted at the lack of decorum. 'So much for living the dream,' she said. She looked sideways at her best friend. 'You know, I'm sorry. This was your dream. I always feel a bit bad that I ended up with your dream boyfriend.'

Lucy laughed. 'I've heard some messed-up things from you, Kumari, but that is the stupidest thing yet.' She took a big sip of wine. 'Anyway, from what you've just told me, you're welcome to that life.'

They sat in companionable silence for a few minutes. Kumari wondered how long it had been since she was able to do that. Just sit. And think.

'Do you still love him?' Lucy asked suddenly.

'Yes.' She didn't need to question that. She never tired of his smile.

'Do you love him enough to stick with the rest of the crap?'

Her heart pounded in her ears. 'I don't know.' She raised her eyes to Lucy, begging for help. 'I don't know.'

'Then that is what we need to work out.'

They stayed in the pub and ate chips and talked, quietly, because you never knew who was in the next booth. No matter how they dissected the problem, there was no way around it. She had to give up her old life entirely if she was to make a new life with Ben. Eventually, exhausted, they changed topics and Kumari asked Lucy about work. Lucy gave her a run-through of the gossip. Of what people had been saying about her. About the dishy new surgeon who was even more attractive than the one Lucy had had her eye on before. All this made Kumari crave her old normality even more.

They were debating getting more chips, when Kumari's mobile rang.

'It's Ben. Where are you?'

A bolt of guilt shot through her. She had sneaked out. That probably wasn't allowed. 'I'm in the pub, with Lucy,' she said.

'In the pub? Where?'

'Central London,' she said cautiously.

Ben cursed. 'Seriously? Tell me where you are. I'll send someone over.'

'What? I don't want you to send someone over. I want to sit in the pub and have a drink with my friend.'

'Kumari . . .' She had heard that tone of voice before. She'd heard it that night when he stormed off and demanded a statement be issued asking the press to stop harassing her. Shit.

'Look,' he said. 'We can't have this discussion now. Please get yourself back to somewhere safe and we'll talk about it later.'

She didn't want to do either of those things. She wondered what would happen if she just hung up.

'Kumari, please. You've been the target of racist hate mail and death threats. You can easily be the target of a hate crime. Just tell me where you are and I'll send Dave over. Don't make me ask Dave to track you down.'

Lucy, who could clearly overhear what he was saying, mouthed 'go'.

Kumari sighed. 'Fine. We'll talk about it when I get back.' She gave him the name of the pub.

'Stay where you are,' he said. 'Dave will come and get you.' Kumari hung up and looked at Lucy, who stuck out her bottom lip and filled Kumari's glass up to the brim.

'How long have we got?' she said.

Kumari shrugged. 'Dunno. Dave's like some sort of ninja. I wouldn't be surprised if he could teleport.' They both looked at the door to the basement room.

'So . . . when you said you felt trapped. This is what you meant?' said Lucy.

'Yeah. It sounds so ridiculous to complain. It's a lovely place. Ben's so nice. I don't *need* anything . . .'

'But that's not who you are, is it? You're used to being your own person. Doing what you want, when you want. Being free . . . in the most basic sense of the word.'

'And work,' said Kumari. 'God, I miss work.' She looked sideways to Lucy. 'I even miss A & E.'

'Even puke nights?'

She smiled, it was surprisingly hard, like she'd worn her smiling muscles out. 'Well, OK, maybe not puke nights.'

Lucy looked thoughtfully at the wine bottle and started to pick at the corner of the label. 'If you were to do your dream job, what would it be?'

Kumari thought for a minute. 'I'd go back to Lesotho and run the training sessions for Boost Her! I don't know if it's been funded yet. They don't announce it for a few more weeks.'

Lucy looked like she was going to say something, but seemed to change her mind.

'What?' asked Kumari.

Lucy shook her head. 'Nothing.'

'Were you going to point out that I can't have that and be with Ben at the same time?'

Lucy continued to pick at the wine label. 'You know that already.'

Kumari felt the enormity of her choices. 'I want both. I love him and I love my work. Oh, Lucy, what am I going to do?' She put her head in her hands.

'Maybe you need a break. Go somewhere. Work things out.'

Chapter 22

Is this the beginning of the end for the monarchy?

Prince Benedict has officially announced his relationship with Asian immigrant Kumari Senavaka. Senavaka, a 'doctor' in the NHS, hails from near Leeds. She grew up just a stone's throw from the notorious suburb of Beeston, one of the worst car theft hotspots in Britain.

The prince met his future girlfriend at a charity event where onlookers say that Senavaka was openly flirtatious while speaking to the prince. Their next meeting was supposedly organised by mutual friends.

It's well known that northern women are more free with their sexual favours. It is not difficult to see how the prince could have been seduced by this exotic northern beauty.

Picture: Senavaka at the charity function where she lured the prince. [Photo credit: Greg Frankish]

Ben was waiting for her in the main stairwell when she got back. 'Thank goodness.' He gathered her to him in a hug. She hugged him back, and tried to make it convincing, but all she could think about was that she was stuck back here again. Ben thanked Dave and led Kumari back to her rooms. She marched into her bedroom and stashed her purse away. She had money now. Enough to get away if she needed to.

He followed her and sank onto the bed. 'Please don't do that to me again.'

'All I did was go out for drink, Ben.' She stayed where she was, fighting the urge to cross her arms.

'But you can't do that sort of thing anymore. Not without security.'

'*You* can't,' she said. 'Not me. I got there and nothing happened.'

'This time,' he said. 'Once we announce the engagement, the public interest is going to get worse. I'm sorry, but you have to take this seriously.'

She put her hands on her hips. 'Take this seriously? You want me to take this seriously? I gave up my job. I moved out of my flat. I'm letting people choose my clothes for me. I'm taking bloody elocution lessons. Tell me, Benedict, how is that *not* taking this seriously?'

He raised his hands. 'Kumari—' He sighed and dropped his hands onto his knees. 'This is how it has to be. I warned you. You knew what you were getting into.'

'I didn't understand the extent of it. Ben, my parents told me, when I first took that leap of faith to be with you, that I would always have a home with them. But that home has been under attack for weeks. And they genuinely believe that they will lose me to you and your family. And you know what? They're right. They'll never fit in here with the "darling, how many horses have you bought this week" set. We're not like you. This . . .' She threw her hands up in the air. 'This whole thing. It's completely ridiculous.' Tears sprang up again. Annoyed, she flicked them away. 'I can't do this.'

Ben stared at her, his hands gripping his knees. 'What do you mean, you can't do this?'

'This. All of it. I thought I could deal with it all. I thought loving you would carry me through it somehow.' She shook her head and fat tears rolled down her cheeks.

'But I can't. Being watched all the time. Being judged. Not being able to do any real work. I don't want to be some sort of parasite on the state, making speeches and cutting ribbons and living in a palace at other people's expense. I'm not used to being on this side of charity. I should be out there. At the sharp end of things. Making a difference to people's lives.'

For a second, there was silence. Ben's fingers flexed against his knees. 'Parasites?' he said quietly. 'Is that how you think of us?'

Oh shit. She'd just been really rude about his family.

'I didn't mean—'

'Yes, you did,' he said. He didn't look at her. His gaze was fixed on a spot at her feet. 'Let me tell you about being at the sharp end of things.' His eyes finally lifted and they were blazing. 'I spent two years on the front line. I saw my friends get shot. I saw places razed to the ground by bombing. I was at the sharp end of things and it didn't make a blind bit of difference to anyone's life other than make things worse. But Helena – you know, my sister who makes speeches and cuts ribbons – Helena was the figurehead for an official visit to the area. They had a state dinner that meant that two key figures in the region had to be in the same room together. They showed up and behaved themselves because they wanted to meet the princess. Six months later, they negotiated a ceasefire and UN access. That would never have happened if they hadn't met at that dinner. In one evening, just by being there, Helena made a difference to thousands of people and made their lives less miserable. Don't you *dare* call my family parasites.'

'I'm so sorry, I—' She brought her hands up to her face. They were shaking.

Ben let out a shaky sigh. 'Kumari, I understand that this has been a difficult few months for you. But if that's the way you feel about things then perhaps it's as well we found out now.'

She could feel the gap opening up between them. She could close it. All she had to do was pretend that she could cope. But she couldn't. Even if she pushed through it now, the pressure wouldn't disappear. It would come back, again and again, until it broke her. He was right. It was better they found out now, before they formally announced their engagement and it was too late to back out.

'I'm so sorry, Ben. I just can't do this. To be with you, I'd have to become someone completely different. I don't think I can.' She pushed down a sob. 'I'm so sorry.'

He dropped his gaze back to the floor and nodded.

'I know.' He rubbed a hand over his eyes. 'I can't keep you trapped here if you don't want to be here. I understand how it can feel oppressive. I don't have a magic solution to make it better.'

'I do love you . . .' she said.

'But not enough.'

They looked at each other and the gap between them widened. She wanted to reach out and hold him, but that was no longer allowed. Ten minutes ago, he had been her lover. Her Ben. Now he was a prince. Out of her league because she was just a nobody. A foolish nobody who had given up her job.

'So, I guess this is it,' he said. He sounded so sad, her already broken heart broke a little more.

'I guess so.' The tears flowed freely now. She made no effort to stop them. They dripped off her chin and onto her jumper. 'Ben,' she said. 'I didn't mean that about your sisters. Or you. You guys are great. I was angry and—'

'Yes.' He stood up and walked to the door. She took a step towards him.

'Look, Kumari, are you sure about this? Because if this happens, there's no undoing it. Once the press finds out they will hound you to find out why. I'll do what I can, but I can't protect you out there.'

She nodded. 'I know. I'll . . . go to ground somewhere for a bit.'

He looked at her with pain in his eyes. 'Where will you go?'

'My parents' place first,' she said. Because where else could she go but home?

'That's the first place people will look.'

'We'll be OK.'

He nodded. 'I'll do my best to keep it out of the papers for a while. In case . . .' He sighed. 'I won't try to contact you. But if . . . if you change your mind, call me.' His hand moved as though to touch her, but he dropped it back down to his side. 'Forrest will arrange a vehicle for you.'

Without another word, he opened the door and left.

Kumari sank down on the bed, fitting unconsciously into the warm place where he had just been. So that was it. The love of her life. Gone. She wrapped her arms around herself. She couldn't fall apart. Not yet. With a huge effort, she got back up again and pulled out the bag that Dave had brought from her flat all those weeks ago. She packed only the things that she'd originally owned. The rest didn't belong to her. Then she left her room for the last time and went to the main staircase, where Forrest had a car waiting for her.

It was well past midnight when the car turned into the cul-de-sac. The houses were all in darkness apart from her parents' house, where the downstairs light was on. They must have waited up for her, even though she had her own key and could have let herself in. She thanked the driver and lugged her bag up to the gate.

A window opened in the house next door. 'All right?' said the familiar voice of Alfred, the septuagenarian who lived there.

'It's only me, Alfred,' she said. She pushed the hood back off her head.

'Oh. Good to see you've not forgotten your home, lass.' She couldn't see him, but she could picture his face.

'I'd best get inside, Alfred. It's a bit cold out.'

'Right you are.' The window shut.

Kumari found her key and let herself in. Amma appeared before she'd locked the door behind her.

'Kumari.' Amma, dressed in her nightie and dressing gown, opened her arms. Kumari fell into them. Bending forward, she buried her face in the all-too familiar shoulder and breathed in the smell of Olay.

Suddenly all the effort of holding it together was too much and she burst into heartbroken tears.

Making Changes

Chapter 23

The Sentinel

Will having an Asian 'princess' in the palace make Buckingham Palace embrace diversity?

As the head of the Commonwealth, the queen is no stranger to the citizens of the East. Indeed, a large proportion of UK citizens identify their ethnic origin as Asian according to the 2011 census. Social attitudes towards interracial relationships have changed rapidly in the last thirty years, with less than twenty per cent of people expressing any fears about it. This number drops even further among the under-twenty-fives. Millennials, it seems, are entirely comfortable with unions that cross race lines.

If Britain itself is multicultural, the Royal Guard does not reflect this. Staff in the royal household are overwhelmingly white. Perhaps having a non-white member of the family will be the final push needed for widening diversity in palace staff.

How does the Asian community react to Prince Benedict's Asian girlfriend?

The royal family is generally popular among South-East Asians. It's part of what makes former Commonwealth citizens feel British. They were British enough to fight in the name of the king, so why not? As such, they're delighted to see some-one non-white on the arm of the prince. About time, they say.

The people who are most perturbed by Prince Benedict's non-white partner seem to be people who write for the media. Most papers discuss Dr Kumari Senavaka in terms of a second-generation Sri Lankan immigrant. But even the use of the word immigrant is misleading – the clue is in the 'second generation'. While her parents were economic migrants in the eighties, they became British citizens some years later. So Kumari Senavaka was born in Yorkshire to British parents. She has lived in the UK all her life. She is no immigrant, but as British as any of the prince's former girlfriends. More so, in fact, than his Swiss ex-girlfriend Leonie Baum. Yet none of those women have garnered as many column inches as Senavaka, with much of the speculation about the Asian community's reaction.

I live in Birmingham and my family hails from Bradford. I can tell you, the Asian community is delighted.

'Kumari. Come quickly,' Amma shouted from the living room.

It was late evening and Kumari was doing the washing up. She rushed into the living room, drying her hands on a tea towel.

It was a news clip showing Princess Helena visiting the opening of the Canham Prize for Contemporary Art. Helena was smiling and talking to some of the museum staff. She looked elegant and relaxed. How funny that she looked more at home on camera than in her own garden.

The news anchor's voice said, 'Some members of the press took the opportunity to quiz the princess about her brother's relationship.'

A clip of Helena showed her stopping to speak to members of the public. A voice off-screen said, 'What do you think of Prince Benedict and Kumari?'

Helena smiled. 'I'm delighted to see Benedict so happy,' she said, and moved on.

Kumari stared at the screen. Helena hadn't answered the question, but she'd conveyed the impression that she was delighted. What had Ophelia said? 'Helena is a consummate diplomat. We all are. But we try to be honest with family.' Helena may have been unsure of Kumari behind closed doors, but outside, to the world, she had just given her support.

'I thought you said she was frosty?' said Amma. 'She doesn't seem it.'

Kumari sat down on the sofa, next to her mother.

'I don't understand any of it,' she said. 'They live . . . it may as well be on a different planet.'

A day passed. Kumari was alone in the house. The post arrived, late afternoon as always. There was one window envelope, addressed to her parents, with the local council logo on it. This, she put on the coffee table, where the post usually went. The rest she approached with caution.

Her parents had shown her the box where they put the suspect letters, the ones they opened wearing gloves, or, if they were really worried, didn't open at all. They had taped the number of their police liaison officer to the wall above the phone. She came and took the hate mail away to be safely checked and destroyed.

One letter had 'Parents of Kumari' written on it in block capitals. She put that in the box to send to the police. There followed three postcards, two with the Union flag on the front. The third, incongruously, was a holiday postcard of Ibiza. They all had variations of 'Pakis go home' or 'Coming over here, sullying our royal family' on them. These, too, went into the box.

The remaining two letters had printed labels with 'Mr and Mrs Senavaka' on them. She stared at them. How did you know which ones were legitimate and which were hate mail? What did you do when it wasn't obvious?

She went to the back window and held the envelopes up to the light. Both had what seemed to be folded paper inside. One letter appeared to be considerably smaller than the envelope it was in. Kumari put that one in the suspect box too. Since she couldn't be sure what was in the last one, she threw that in too. Filing it in the hate-mail box meant that it would be a couple of days before it was opened. She hoped that, if it was legitimate, it wasn't something urgent.

She trudged upstairs to her room. Her phone buzzed in her pocket. She pulled it out and looked at the unfamiliar number. Who was this?

'Hello,' she said cautiously.

'Kumari? It's Sinead.'

'Sinead?' Why was Sinead calling her? She pulled herself together and put on her professional voice. 'What can I do for you?'

'It's just that . . . I was trying to make an appointment to show you the new fabrics I've found, but Julia is telling me that you're not taking appointments at the moment. I thought it was a bit strange. So I thought I'd call you?' There was a pause, as though Sinead had just remembered something. 'Oh. Are you on holiday? I didn't realise. I saw His Royal Highness yesterday, so I didn't . . . I'm sorry. I shouldn't have hassled you.'

'No. No, it's OK. Er . . . Listen, Sinead, it's fine.'

'No. I'm so sorry. Just let me know when you're back and I'll come and see you. Sorry. Bye.' Sinead hung up.

Kumari flopped down on the bed. She missed Sinead. Another person whose life she'd messed with. With her gone, Sinead would be out of a job. Of course, Ophelia would make sure she had a good reference, but Sinead had been set to be dresser to the prince's fiancée and she wouldn't be able to put that on her CV. She was already working on what Kumari would wear on the day the engagement was announced and was scouting for designers for a wedding dress. They'd agreed to try to give a boost to lesser-known British designers, especially ones with a minority background.

Oh God. She had let so many people down. She had left the man she loved, caused immense amounts of pain to him, to herself and to other people around her. Why? Because she couldn't handle the pressure? She had always prided herself in not giving up. Not running away from a fight. And here she was, running away. Hiding in her parents' house like a child.

Kumari lay on her back and stared at the ceiling. Had she been selfish? Probably. But the life she would have to lead at the palace would be so restrictive, she couldn't bear it. And what if her parents were right? What if she lost them? When she and Shane split up, it was pretty awful, but she always had this place to come to, to be safe. Her parents were always there for her. With Ben . . . it would be different, she knew. Amma and Thatha wouldn't have been comfortable going to the palace and she couldn't see Ben's family making any effort to see them. Apart from his sisters, none of them even bothered to see her. They had done their duty and met her. Acknowledged her in the barest terms. That was it. Ophelia did her best, for the sake of her brother, but her influence was still limited. But even to Ophelia, Kumari was an opportunity, a way to channel the things that she herself wasn't allowed to do. So the press wasn't too far off with the suggestion that there was a PR angle. But that was only because someone spotted an opportunity to use what was already there.

But what was she to Ben? She was a woman he loved enough to give his mother's diamond to. Not an experiment. Not a PR stunt. Just a woman he'd fallen in love with. Strange. The thought that he didn't love her had never occurred to her. He was the one who noticed her, he pursued her; when she first wanted to run away, he persuaded her to stay. She believed he loved her. And she loved him. But did she love him enough to stay and follow the rules?

There was a knock on the bedroom door. Kumari ignored it. Her mother came in anyway.

'Kumari, come and eat something. It's the evening and you haven't eaten anything since that slice of toast this morning, have you?'

'I'm not hungry.'

'Darling, you can't starve yourself. If you're so unhappy, why don't you call him and apologise?'

'Amma, you know why.'

Amma sat down on the side of the bed and touched Kumari's hair. Kumari shuffled over and laid her head on her mother's lap. 'So there are rules and traditions,' Amma said. 'You said to me that those didn't matter because you loved him. What changed?'

'They want me to give up everything – my job, my clothes, my friends, you.'

Amma stroked her hair gently. 'To be fair, they never asked you to give up your family.'

'They may as well have. Like you said, you'd never be comfortable or even particularly welcome there and any children we had would never be able to come and see you. I can't lose you.'

'You'll never really lose us. We'll always be your parents,' said Amma. 'I didn't mean to make you throw away your happiness just to please us.'

'I—' She frowned. Was she using her parents' fears as an excuse? Yes. Probably. Not only was she making Ben a laughing stock, she was making her parents feel guilty too. She was an awful person. She groaned.

Amma said nothing, just continued stroking her hair.

'What should I do, Amma?'

'I can't tell you what to do. You need to work that out for yourself.'

'If I go back, I'll have to deal with that stifling world again.' Tears pooled at the corners of her eyes. 'But I miss him, Amma. I miss him so much.'

'So perhaps you need to decide whether missing him is better or worse than being in the stifling world. Imagine yourself in a future without him.'

Right now, it felt worse. The absence of Ben was a smouldering hole in her chest. The embers of it threw out sparks from time to time and made her want to die.

'I'll tell you what, though,' said Amma. 'I don't think I've ever seen anything put you off your food before.'

Even that reminded her of Ben, asking her about steak and salad. The tears escaped and ran into her hair.

Chapter 24

The Northern Paragon

Prince opens new primary school

Prince Benedict opened a new school, St Crispin's Primary School, in Halifax. The new school caters for the catchment opened up by the new housing development.

When asked whether the fact that his new girlfriend, Kumari Senavaka, hails from Leeds had made him feel more affectionate towards the north, the prince replied, 'I've always been fond of the north. Who wouldn't be?'

The prince later sat with the Year 1 class and helped them do some collage work.

The Daily Watch

Is Prince Benedict going back to his old ways and does Kumari know?

Prince Benedict was seen emerging from a private party last night with a woman who wasn't his girlfriend. It appears that he took home Gwyneth Ellesmere-Jones, whom he had a relationship with several years ago. His new girlfriend, whose right to privacy he publicly defended two months ago, was nowhere to be seen.

Sources close to Kensington Palace have specu-lated that things may not be rosy with the unusual couple as Kumari has cancelled a lot of her appoint-ments with palace officials in the past week.

Kumari lay on her stomach on the living-room floor and stared at the paper. The picture had been taken as they were coming out of a doorway, Benedict's arm was behind Gwyneth, so it could have conceivably been rest-ing on her back. Or, more likely, not touching her at all. Benedict was half turned towards Gwyneth, speaking to someone behind her. Clearly visible over Gwyneth's shoulder was Rhodri. Kumari peered closer. Because she knew what she was looking for, she could just make out Dave in the background.

As far as she could see, Ben had gone somewhere with his friend and friend's sister. The stuff about Gwyneth was nonsense. The papers did like to make up things.

She sighed and found another picture of Benedict, sitting at a table, talking to schoolchildren. He was smiling, but he looked tired. She wondered if he was OK. If she had done any real damage. There would be fallout from her leaving. Embarrassment, at the very least. She hated that she'd done anything to hurt him.

She missed him so much it physically hurt her chest. It was as though there was a burning hole inside her.

Had she done the wrong thing? She had left because she felt trapped, her choices taken away from her. But now, she seemed to be trapped in her own home. People in the close were not likely to give away the fact that she'd come home, but she couldn't go into town without the risk of someone snapping a picture. With the press wondering what had happened to her, it was likely to spark another flurry of interest in her and in Ben. She didn't want that.

Her phone rang. It was Ophelia. Again. Ophelia had been ringing daily, sometimes more than once. Kumari had ignored the calls. She had considered blocking her number, but couldn't bring herself to do it. Weirdly, she missed Ophelia wafting in unannounced. She missed Sinead discussing the events she needed to go to and what impression they wanted to make. With a jolt, she realised that she'd been making friends.

She stared at the phone she was holding. She had to hand it to Ophelia for being persistent. She wasn't going to stop phoning.

Kumari sighed and took the call.

'About bloody time,' said Ophelia. 'What the bloody hell are you thinking?'

'I'm sorry,' Kumari said. Ophelia had been a friend in the cold, duty-bound corridors of Kensington. All she had asked in return was that Kumari didn't hurt her brother. And Kumari hadn't kept her side of the bargain.

'You should be,' said Ophelia. 'You bloody idiot. How could you do this to him? Seriously, Kumari, I thought you were made of stronger stuff than that.'

'I'm not. I'm sorry. It's all very well for you. You were brought up with all that protocol and etiquette, and people knowing exactly where you are at all times. It's all normal to you. But I'm not used to it. I've been making my own choices for so many years now. After that, it's so hard to go to a place where there are rules for everything. Where I have to check everything I do and say, and have someone watching my every move. I don't know how you can bear it, and frankly, I can't.'

'Well, that much is obvious,' Ophelia snapped. 'But why did you even try? If you didn't love Benedict enough to bend a little, why did you even start this thing? You know, if he'd wanted to, he could have just kept you and nobody would have said anything. He wouldn't have been the first prince to have kept a mistress. But no. Benedict wanted to marry you. Make you official. Now you've made him a laughing stock. Thank goodness the papers haven't got wind of it yet. There's going to be a shitstorm when they work out you're no longer together.'

The thought that she'd embarrassed Ben made her feel awful. As much as she hated being told off, Ophelia had a point. She hadn't been thinking about Ben. She had seen only the discomfort she was feeling. 'Is he OK?' she asked quietly.

There was a pause. 'He's ... not great,' said Ophelia. 'But I dare say he'll get over it.' She gave a sniff of mirthless laughter. 'He'll just take up drowning his sorrows again, like he did when he got back from the army. Maybe take up one of the more "suitable" matches that they keep waving in front of him.'

The wave of jealousy that coursed through her at that surprised even her. The idea of seeing photos of Ben standing on the famous balcony with some other woman made her feel physically ill. 'He would?'

'He'd have to,' said Ophelia. 'You don't understand, Kumari. We had a chance to change things. You blew it for us all.'

'I'm not a lab rat for your social experiment.' Lab rat. That was what it felt like. Being watched and tested all the time.

Ophelia swore. An incongruous sound when said in such a posh accent. 'It's not just about you, or us. Just think how you could have influenced things. You were a wild card. No one knew what you could have got away with. You could say things that I can't say and Helena can't even hint at. Your charities – educating girls, improving childhood survival rates in the Third World, better funding for midwives on the NHS. You could have influenced them all. Benedict wasn't offering you trappings. He was offering you genuine power, if you had the balls to take it.'

'I didn't want to be with Ben because of any of those things. I was with him because I love him.'

Ophelia gave a small huffing sound. 'And you're now running away from him because . . . ?'

Kumari had no answer to that. She still loved him. She knew that and so did Ophelia, apparently. She had screwed up.

'Hmm,' said Ophelia. 'Think about what you're doing, Kumari. We'll try to keep it out of the media for as long as we can, but it won't be long. You don't get a second shot at this.'

'Tell Ben—' She needed him to know she was sorry.

'No. I won't be telling him anything. He said he'd told you he wouldn't contact you. You can trust him on that. Ben never goes back on his word, stubborn muppet that he is. If you want to tell him anything, you have to tell him yourself.'

'I suppose that's fair.'

'Fair has nothing to do with it,' said Ophelia.

'Ophelia,' said Kumari. 'For what it's worth, I genuinely enjoyed being your friend.'

'Me too. Now think on it. Do the right thing.'

Kumari wasn't sure how long she sat there thinking, telephone in hand and newspapers spread around her. The sound of the post dropping through the letterbox made her jump. Wearily, she got up to fetch it.

There was more hate mail. She hurled it into the box. It tore at her that her parents had to go through this. They hadn't even told her the scale of it until she showed up at home. They were willing to put up with it for her happiness. Ben was probably putting up with a lot too. Being made to look like a fool didn't sound so bad, but when you saw it in the context where saving face was everything, it mattered a great deal.

She looked at the photographs on the mantelpiece. Her graduation photo, a picture of her with a stethoscope around her neck. A photo of her laughing in a teashop the weekend after her divorce went through. A photo of her and the team at the vaccination clinic. Even a newspaper clipping of her at the Golden Globes. Her parents collected photos of her triumphs. She had done all of those things. None of them had been particularly easy, but she'd lived through them and got things done. What had happened to her?

Ophelia was right. She had been given power and influence. She could use that to change the world. Wasn't that the plan she'd had with such clarity at the spa? How had she lost sight of that? But had she left it all behind because she was too chicken to fully commit to it? Because she was too concerned about other people's opinions to go and change the world?

She thought of the postcards. 'Go back to where you came from you Pakis.' No. She was better than this. She wasn't going to let them win.

Would Ben take her back? Would the rest of the royal family? Ophelia, maybe. Helena would probably stake her for hurting Ben, but, when it mattered, she'd be there for her. For all their talk about the institution of monarchy being bigger than any of them, Ben and his family knew when to take a stand. They'd taken a stand for her. All she'd had to do was stand with them.

She got out her phone and found a photo that she'd taken of Ben, sitting on the sofa reading, with his glasses on. He was looking at her sideways, amusement in his smile. She missed him so much she could barely breathe.

She couldn't call him. She wouldn't be able to get any words past her closed throat. She pulled up his number and texted: *Miss you.*

She stared at the text for a few seconds. After this, there would be no turning back. She would be stuck. Trapped in the palace, doing royal duties. But she would be with Ben. And she would be fighting from the inside.

She hit send.

She watched for a response for the whole day. There wasn't one.

Chapter 25

Society Waves Magazine

Official photographs from Princess Ophelia's 35th birthday

Formal photographs released from the palace show Princess Ophelia and the rest of the royal family, including the little princesses Francesca and Maria, and Princess Ophelia's boyfriend Dominic Heatherton. The pictures were taken by the royal photographer at a private garden party held in Buckingham Palace yesterday.

Prince Benedict's girlfriend Kumari Senavaka was conspicuously absent from the event, prompting rumours that the royal family are not thrilled with Prince Benedict's decision to discuss his private life in public.

Kumari was sitting in her spot on the sofa, watching the news with Thatha. Her parents had tried to get her to eat something, but she couldn't face it. All she could think of was the fact that she had texted Ben and he had ignored her. It was over. A flame of hope that she hadn't even realised she was carrying was snuffed out. There was nothing left but darkness.

Her parents exchanged worried glances, which she saw, but ignored. They tried to talk to her, to make her feel better. She ignored that too. She was only watching the news to see if she could catch a glimpse of whatever Ben was doing.

Her phone vibrated in her pocket. She felt a stab of hope and hated herself for it. It wasn't going to be Ben. Why did she torture herself hoping it was? She pulled it out anyway. It was from Ben. *Have been at formal event all day. Just got message. On my way.*

'Oh.' She sat up.

'What?' said Amma.

'Ben. Ben's coming.'

'What, *here*?' Amma said. 'When?'

'I don't know.' She texted back, but didn't get a reply. 'In a few hours, maybe. I don't know.'

Amma looked around. 'We have to tidy up. And I have no food to give him.'

'Calm down,' said Thatha. 'He's coming to see Kumari. Not to look at us or the house. Or to eat the food.' But he stood up too.

Soon they were all frantically tidying up. Amma insisted on cooking enough chicken pilau to feed a squadron, 'just in case'. Kumari helped, dicing garlic and ginger standing next to her mother, just as she had done in her teens.

It started raining around eight o'clock. Kumari had heard nothing from Ben since the text.

As it got later, Kumari helped Amma make up the bed in the small room for Ben. Around half past ten, her parents went to bed. Still no word.

Knowing she wouldn't be able to sleep, Kumari curled up in her old spot on the sofa and put the TV on low. She watched a rerun of a crime drama, barely noticing anything. Because the sound was low, she heard the car turn into the close. She shot out of her seat and pulled the edge of the curtain back to look out.

The car had pulled up between street lights, so that the man who emerged, his hood raised against the rain, was mostly caught in shadows. The man slung a backpack onto his shoulder and walked towards her house. She'd know that walk anywhere.

She opened the door in time to hear Alfred's, 'You need something, friend?'

Ben stopped and looked up. 'Um . . .'

Kumari stuck her head out of the door. 'It's OK, Alfred. We're expecting him.'

'Oh. Right you are, love.' Above her, Alfred's head remained where it was. Ben opened the gate and slowly walked to the door. Alfred said. 'It's not . . . ?'

'It's raining, Alfred.'

Ben looked up and gave Alfred a small salute. 'I appreciate the security.'

Kumari stepped back and let him step inside. Shutting the door behind her, she turned to face him. Ben was in her house. He was really here. She wanted to throw herself at him. Touch his beloved face, bury her face in the hollow of his neck and smell woodland and summer, to stroke him, to taste him. But she couldn't do any of that because she'd let him down.

Ben pushed his hood back. His face was wet from the rain. 'Kumari,' he said.

'You came.'

'I said I would, remember? I never break my word.'

Her hand moved towards him, all of its own accord. It took all of her strength to pull it back.

Ben sighed and shrugged off his coat. 'I think we need to talk, don't you?'

There was noise upstairs and Amma's head appeared over the banisters. 'Is he here? Ben, *putha*, do you need anything? We have food.'

Ben looked up, put his palms together and bowed his head to Amma. A small gesture of respect that cost him nothing, but made Amma smile. 'No, thanks. I'm fine.'

'I'll make him a cup of tea,' said Kumari.

Amma nodded and went back to bed. Kumari ushered Ben into the living room. 'Sit,' she said. 'Let me make you tea.'

She left the room and he followed her. He looked enormous in her mother's tiny galley kitchen. She put the kettle on and stared at him. He watched her and said nothing.

'I screwed up, didn't I?' she said.

'Yes. A bit,' he said.

'Only a bit?' She shook her head. 'No. I screwed up more than a bit. I hurt you. I embarrassed you. I let you down, I let Ophelia down . . . and Sinead . . . and . . .' She waved an arm, encompassing the world in general. 'I let everyone down.' Her eyes filled with tears. 'I'm so sorry, Ben.'

'Hey,' he said gently. 'I didn't come all the way up here to watch you beat yourself up. Like I said, we need to talk. First things first. Did you text me because you wanted to come back? Or some other reason?'

'What other reason could there possibly be?'

'Don't evade the question. Jeez. I should never have left you alone with Ophelia.'

'Yes. I want to come back. I . . . panicked. I thought I was losing everything, but I'm not, am I?'

He didn't say anything, as though he was waiting for her to work her way to the end of the sentence.

'I was gaining you. Us.'

Ben nodded. 'Yes. I was rather hoping that would be enough, but it is overwhelming, I understand. We – Helena, Ophelia and I – grew up with it and even we find it hard, so it must be so much worse for you. You told me you were scared and overwhelmed and I didn't do anything about it. I let you down too.'

They looked at each other across the two feet of lino that separated them.

'So what now?' he said.

'Will you take me back?'

'Wh—? Of course I will. Why do you think I'm here?'

She did what she'd been wanting to do all along and threw herself into his arms, buried her face in the curve between his shoulder and neck, and breathed him in. He held her tightly.

'One condition,' he said. 'You have to promise never to do this again. I don't think I could stand it. I had to go out and perform my duties and smile when all I really wanted to do was hide in a corner and feel sorry for myself.'

'I won't,' she said. 'Can you promise me you'll make an effort to make my parents welcome wherever we end up living?'

'I thought I did that already?' He loosened his grip on her so that he could move back and look at her.

When she shook her head, he said, 'OK. I will try harder. I promise.'

'Good.' She reached up and stroked his cheek, now lightly bristled with stubble. 'I've missed you so much.'

His blue eyes fixed on hers. 'I've missed you too,' he said. And kissed her.

The next morning, Kumari opened her eyes when she heard Ben's footsteps, unfamiliar and heavy compared to her parents' tread, going downstairs. She'd had only a few hours' sleep. She and Ben had stayed up late talking, planning their future and just being together. Could she just leave them to talk to each other and go back to sleep? She rolled over. From downstairs, she heard the murmur of voices. No. She needed to know what was happening.

She threw on some clothes and padded downstairs to find Ben sitting at the table talking to her parents. He had been given a mug of coffee and had a slice of toast in his hand. He looked over. 'Morning!' he said.

'Morning.' She fetched her own mug from the kitchen and poured herself a coffee. 'What are we talking about?'

'Just making plans,' said Ben. 'We were discussing the logistics of us getting married.'

'Oh.' Things had slotted right back on track, as though her running away had never happened.

'Your dad has agreed to give you away,' said Ben.

Thatha nodded. Kumari searched his expression and found sadness, but no regret.

There was a sharp rapping from the kitchen. The characteristic sound of Alfred's wife, Mary, tapping on the back door with a broom handle because she wanted to talk to Amma.

'That's the neighbour,' said Amma.

'Alfred saw Ben coming in last night,' said Kumari.

'He's been keeping a watch on everyone who comes down the path,' Thatha said. 'He's called the police a few times. If he thinks it's someone dodgy, he always phones and warns us.'

Kumari felt the need to defend the nosiness of the people she'd known all her life. 'He knew I was here the whole time and never told anyone.'

Ben looked thoughtful. The knocking continued.

'I think,' Ben said, 'your neighbours have been extremely kind and patriotic. How many houses are in the close?'

'Eight,' Thatha said.

'Is there any chance they could all fit in here? For a short time.'

Amma opened her mouth. Kumari could almost see the words 'but I haven't cleaned up' lining up to come out.

'What are you thinking of ?' said Thatha.

'I was thinking that perhaps it would be a good idea to thank them all.'

Amma's face was a picture of horror. Kumari jumped in with, 'It would be a bit cramped in here if we got that many people in. Maybe we could tell them to come into the close, just before we leave. We could shake hands and thank them and get straight into the car. I'm sure Dave would prefer that option too.'

Ben looked at the tiny living room. 'That sounds like an elegant and practical solution. Yes. Let's do that.' He looked at his watch. 'Are you OK to leave at ten?'

Kumari looked at her parents. 'Make it ten thirty.' Amma stood up. 'OK. Let me just go and tell Mary so that she can stop that knocking.'

Later, when Ben was upstairs having a shower, Kumari sat with her parents and explained how she was sure this time.

'I can make a change,' she said.

'To change an institution that old,' said Thatha, 'without damaging the good things about it . . . that will take more than a lifetime, Kumari. There's no going back on it once you get married.'

There was definitely a way to go back on a marriage, but she knew what he meant.

'I know,' said Kumari. 'Change takes at least a generation, often more. But it has to start somewhere. I have a chance to start something, and be with the man I love. It's not going to get better than that, is it?'

'In that case, good luck.' He put a hand on the crown of her head. '*Thunsaranai*, I'm proud of you.'

'I'm sorry if you feel like you'll be losing me. We will make an effort to make you feel included, I promise.'

Amma smiled. 'We know.'

Before she left the house, she knelt in front of her parents, asking for their blessing. They touched her head and gladly gave it. Ben too pressed his palms together in a namaste. They gave him their blessing too. Ben picked up Kumari's bag and his own. Kumari carried a bag of food Amma had packed for her.

Outside, the street was full of people, most leaning on their gates, waiting to see what was going to happen. Ben's car was parked at the top of the street. Dave stood beside it, radiating alertness.

Ben stood outside the gate and waved. 'I just wanted to say, thank you,' he said, his voice loud in the still morning. 'For all that you're doing to keep the Senavaka family safe. I really appreciate it. There has been a lot of nasty things that have happened to them – they're still getting hate mail, for example.' He pressed a hand to his heart. 'It means a lot to me to know that they are in such caring company.'

'It's just a few bad apples spoiling things for everyone,' Alfred said. He was wearing his Sunday suit, his hair combed back neatly.

'Exactly,' said Ben. 'It's wonderful that everyone here isn't like that.'

He went round, with Kumari following and smiling, and shook hands with everyone. It took a while. When someone got their camera out he asked them, politely, to please put it away.

'This is a personal visit, you see. Not official.' He smiled and Kumari watched the man he was talking to melt a little. 'You'll get me into trouble,' Ben said.

'Can't have that.' The camera was put away.

They finally made it to the car and Kumari relaxed into Ben, delighted to be by his side.

Chapter 26

The Sentinel

Women's Rights and the Royal Family

The royal family has always had rules. No one knows what they are, exactly, but we know they exist. Given that the top job, that of monarch, is equally attainable to both male and female heirs, you would think that the royals would be hot on equal opportunities.

But of the many, many charities that the royal family support, only a fraction are to do with women's causes. Perhaps Prince Benedict's girlfriend will change that.

Kumari Senavaka is a doctor and a humanitarian. She has been known to support causes such as improving education for girls and encouraging girls into scientific disciplines. She has had a very hands-on approach to her causes – volunteering to help in the background of events or, indeed, spending a year in Lesotho working as a doctor in a vaccination clinic. This is a woman who is not afraid of getting her hands dirty.

Unlike the prince's previous girlfriends, who have tended towards things like arts and finance, Kumari's eye is trained on science and medicine.

In fact, her latest cause, is a project bidding for internal funding from the Better For All charity to improve life for girls in the developing world. The Boost Her! project aims to train girls to become healthcare workers in their own villages, giving them status and salary while simultaneously improving the life chances of the villages in general.

If Prince Benedict were to marry Kumari, she would hold influence with institutions like the Princess and Prince Foundation that provides a platform on which several like-minded charities can get together and push forward agendas for change.

After she got back to London, Kumari invited Lucy round one afternoon to help keep a hint of normality to her life.

'When do you hear about the project proposal?' Lucy asked as she made herself at home on the the couch.

'Any day now,' said Kumari. 'I hope we get it. Rita worked so hard on it – I think she'd almost be more disappointed than me if it fails.' Even if they got the funding, she wouldn't be able to work on the project for much longer. She tamped down the nagging guilt that she hadn't told Victor and Rita that yet.

'I still can't believe you didn't tell the charity about Ruby,' said Lucy. 'She and that dirtbag deserve to be hung out to dry.'

'I didn't want to sink to their level. What they did was wrong, but if I sank Greg's project, I would be as bad as him. At least this way, even if we lose, I can be sure we did everything fairly.'

'That's very grown up of you,' said Lucy.

Kumari shrugged. 'You know how it is. With great power comes great responsibility and all that.'

'Don't tell me you're taking your life philosophy from *Spider-Man*.'

'There are worse philosophers than Stan Lee.'

Lucy rolled her eyes. 'And you get to be a princess. Nerd.' Kumari threw a cushion at her.

Kumari's phone rang. She apologised to Lucy and picked it up.

'It's Victor.' He sounded excited, his deep voice reverberating down the line. 'We did it. Or rather you and Rita did it.'

'Did what?' She could guess, but she needed to hear him say it.

'We got the grant! Boost Her! was funded!'

'Yes!' Kumari made a triumphant fist pump. She passed the message on to Lucy, who high-fived her.

'They chose the 3D-printed prosthetics project and ours. We can get things in motion within the next few weeks,' said Victor. 'I'm sorry I can't head it up, but you'll do an amazing job and with your new influence—'

'Victor. I can't be publicly involved in the project. I . . . don't think I'm allowed.'

'What do you mean you're not allowed?' said Victor. 'Why not?'

'No. The . . . er . . . the palace has asked that I step away from representing specific charities. I've started the process to get my name taken off any paperwork.'

'Oh.' He sounded so deflated that she felt a stab of guilt.

'But I was thinking, why not ask Rita to take the project coordinator job? Maybe you could head it if you had her to support you.'

'Rita?' He sounded puzzled.

'She's really diligent and very intelligent. I think she'd be really good.'

'She's very junior . . .' said Victor.

'But competent. She's bright and really impressed me.' She needed to know that she was leaving the project in good hands. 'Interview her. See how you get on. I know it's a bit of a wild card, but I genuinely think she'll do a good job.'

'Her contract will be coming up soon, the person she was doing maternity cover for is coming back,' said Victor. 'You're right. She is competent and keen . . . let me see what I can do.'

They chatted some more about timelines and plans. 'I'll sort out the paperwork in the next few days and send it to you,' said Kumari. She said her goodbyes and hung up.

Lucy was sitting cross-legged on her chair, looking like she was about to explode.

'So, we did it,' said Kumari. 'Without even having to drop Greg in the soup.'

'Yes! That's fantastic,' said Lucy. 'But more import-antly, the palace asked you to step away from represent-ing any one charity? What's that all about? Since when does the palace get to tell you what you can and can't represent?'

'Erm . . .' The engagement wasn't official yet. It was supposed to be a secret until the official announcement, which was only a few days away.

'Does this mean what I think it means?' said Lucy, lean-ing so far forward that she was in danger of toppling off her chair.

Kumari didn't reply, but the grin that rose on her face was answer enough for her friend.

Lucy leapt out of her chair and squealed. 'That's just the best!' She hugged Kumari, who laughed and hugged her back.

'Is there a ring? Can I see it? I promise I won't breathe a word to anyone.' She paused and gasped. 'Does your mother know?'

'Of course she does.'

'And she didn't tell me,' said Lucy. 'Oh never mind. Show me the ring. Show me. Show me.'

Kumari fetched the ring. Lucy looked at it in wonder and Kumari told her the story behind the diamond. Lucy listened to the end and wiped her eyes. 'That is so adorable,' she said. 'If you weren't my best friend, I'd hate you.'

Kumari didn't need to go to any formal visits until the engagement was announced. She threw herself into learning protocol and poise, a crash course in finishing school and learning to speak French. It would be a while before she could match even Ophelia for languages, but it was a start and learning new things kept her from getting bored.

The other thing that kept her sane was working on the second-stage plans for the Boost Her! project. She had to do most of the work by email. Until the paperwork went through she was technically still head of the project, and she was determined to make sure she did as much as she could before she had to hand things over. It was galling that the letters she wrote were sent on behalf of someone else, but this project mattered too much to her to let her own ego get in the way.

Sinead arrived pushing a clothes rail that took up most of Kumari's little sitting room. Kumari helped her move the mirror to where the light was better.

'I have three options for you,' Sinead said. She took them out and explained where each piece came from. There was a mixture of old designers, new designers and high street brands. 'You'll be standing up for the photos, mostly,' said Sinead. 'So we need something that hangs well.'

In the end Kumari chose something that was a mixture of high street dress, taken up and adjusted to fit her properly, a designer jacket and mid-range accessories. 'Something for everyone,' she said.

Sinead laughed. 'I will make a note of that. For reference. Also, I have a few roughs from prospective designers for the wedding dress. I approached a few that we discussed, as well as the mainstream ones.' She pulled out a portfolio case.

There was a brisk knock on the door. Kumari frowned, waved Sinead to stay where she was and answered it. Ophelia breezed in. 'Did I miss it?'

'Come in, Your Highness, why don't you,' said Kumari. She shut the door.

On seeing Kumari had returned to Kensington, Ophelia had said, 'Oh, excellent. You did the right thing. Welcome back, darling.' And that had been the end of that. They had slipped back into their friendship as though nothing had interrupted it.

Ophelia ignored her comment. 'Are these the designs? Oh good. What are we having?'

Sinead glanced at Kumari, who motioned her to go ahead. There was no point trying to stop Ophelia interfering. You may as well try to hold back the tide.

'OK,' said Sinead. 'I removed anything that didn't meet the modesty requirements or was too plain. So we've narrowed it down to these.'

She spread out six designs. All beautiful. Kumari stared at them. How was she supposed to choose?

Ophelia glanced sideways at her. 'It's your wedding, darling, you choose what you want. Of course, you may want to lean towards an up-and-coming designer. That would be entirely understandable.'

'As you say,' Kumari shot back. The hint was not lost on her. 'It's my wedding.'

'Quite so.'

Sinead watched the exchange with wide eyes. Kumari, who was learning fast what the limitations on her freedom were, noted that all the gowns had sleeves and a certain degree of simplicity around the skirts.

'I don't have to get married in white, do I?' she said. 'It's my second wedding.'

'Oh no, something pale will do,' said Sinead. 'I think red might be pushing it though. I know it's traditional . . .'

'Not really,' Kumari said. 'Sinhala brides wear white.'

'Same colour for weddings and funerals?' said Ophelia. 'Interesting.'

'I hadn't thought about it that way,' said Kumari. 'Anyway, for my first wedding, I had two ceremonies. A church one and a Sri Lankan one. Shane was Catholic you see.'

There was a moment of silence. She looked up and caught the other two looking at her. 'What?'

'Nothing,' said Ophelia. 'So, back to the matter at hand. Are you any closer to deciding yet?'

'I like that one and that one.' She pointed to two of the drawings. 'Tell me about them.'

Sinead whipped away the other sketches and pulled out fabric samples in pale pastel shades. It took them most of the afternoon to work out the details.

In the end, they picked a dress that had a bodice reminiscent of a delicately embroidered sari blouse and a wide skirt with a patterned base. The designer, an Indonesian–British woman from Brighton, would be invited to meet Kumari so that they could iron out the details.

Kumari took a photo of the concept sketch to show Amma. After Ophelia and Sinead had left, she pulled up the picture and looked at it. It would be the most beautiful, most expensive dress she had ever worn. She turned over her left hand and looked at the blue and white gemstones on the ring. Suddenly, it was all real. She was getting married. To Ben. She smiled at the picture of the dress. Somehow they had survived the nightmare. Now they would be all the stronger for it.

Chapter 27

The Times Echo

Prince Benedict engaged to Kumari Senavaka

The palace has announced the engagement of Prince Benedict to Dr Kumari Senavaka. The prince designed the ring himself and it contains Ceylon sapphires and a diamond that belonged to his mother. The couple met on a blind date set up by mutual friends.

The wedding date has not been set yet, but it is expected to take place in the spring.

The couple posed in the gardens at Buckingham Palace for their formal engagement photos, where they broke royal protocol by holding hands.

Picture caption: The Prince and Kumari pose for their formal photo.

Picture caption: The engagement ring

'Just relax,' the man from the royal press office said. 'There won't be any surprise questions. Just be yourselves. You'll be fantastic.'

They were in Benedict's living room, positioned on one of the sofas, with a prominent newscaster sitting in a chair opposite them. The cameras were positioned so that the interviewer would be just out of shot. If Kumari were to look straight at her, she could more or less ignore the camera. She was feeling light-headed and anxious. It wasn't as bad as everyone staring at her, but there were quite a lot of people in Ben's sitting room.

Ben sat next to her and adjusted his microphone. He caught her eye. She stared at him, feeling the panic rise. Slowly and deliberately, he winked at her. This popped the bubble of panic and made her giggle. She immediately felt better.

The newscaster who was interviewing them glanced up from her notes and smiled. 'It's not going to be an aggressive interview, I promise.'

Kumari smiled back, but it was an effort. She hadn't eaten anything all morning because she felt so ill. A woman checked her make-up. Benedict said something to Anton who was a few feet away.

'Your Highness, if you're ready?' the producer said.

'Of course.' Benedict cut short his conversation and shifted in his seat so that he was closer to Kumari. This, Kumari reflected, was the difference between classy and famous. Benedict was nervous as hell, she knew because they'd taken turns panicking at breakfast time. But he was unfailingly polite. To everyone. Always.

The only time she'd seen him show how riled he could get was with her or his family. She was one of the few people who saw the private man behind the public persona. She looked up at him. He took her hand and squeezed it.

'Ready?' asked the interviewer.

Ben waited for Kumari to say yes before saying yes himself. The producer counted them in.

The first question was about the proposal. Ben answered it. After a few seconds, Kumari's heart stopped roaring in her ears and she was able to join in. She kept her eyes on Ben or on their joined hands, to keep the panic at bay.

They talked about how they met. How they saw the world in the same way. How they wanted to help people.

'Children?' asked the interviewer.

They looked at each other and smiled. 'In good time,' said Ben. 'But, yes.'

'Family is important to us both,' Kumari said.

The interviewer asked, 'And, Kumari, how do you feel about giving up your career?'

That was the kicker. Ben squeezed her hand.

'I'm sad, obviously, to give up being a doctor,' she said. 'But, when I became a doctor, I swore to first do no harm. My presence at a public hospital caused problems once I was in the public eye and it was hampering my colleagues' ability to treat patients, so I had to leave.' She glanced at Ben, who gave her a tiny smile.

'I will also miss working with Better for All. That said,' she continued, 'my main motivation, with medicine, with the work I do with medical charities, is to help people. So I will be continuing to do that, but in a slightly different context.'

There was a pause. Ben stepped in, 'Kumari will be joining my sisters and me at the Princesses and Prince Foundation.'

'How wonderful,' the interviewer said. 'And how have you found the difference in your life from being a working doctor, to being, for want of a better description, a celebrity?' Expertly, she moved the conversation back to the topic at hand.

They talked some more about their story and their plans together. At one point the interviewer asked them if they were happy.

Kumari looked at Ben and caught his gaze. After all the ups and downs, were they happy? Yes, she decided, yes they were. He smiled at her. She put her other hand over his so that his hand was sandwiched between her own. And Benedict *glowed*. She had made him do that. She couldn't take her eyes off him. 'Yes,' she said. 'Very happy.' That was the image that ended up in all the newspapers the next day. The two of them, lost in each other's eyes, smiling like lovestruck teenagers.

'Omigod. You guys are so *cute*,' Lucy said. 'Just look at this.' She waved a front page with a photo of the two of them looking adoringly at each other. 'It's so perfect it's sickening.'

'That wasn't actually planned,' said Kumari. 'We were supposed to smile and answer questions.'

They were in her little apartment, a bottle of wine between them. Kumari had to sign the last of the paperwork handing over the Boost Her! project to Victor. She didn't think she could go through with it without extra support.

She fiddled with her pen.

'You're sure you want to do this?' Lucy asked.

'I'm pretty sure I have no choice,' said Kumari. 'It's not like I can go out there and oversee it all. Victor's a good guy. He helped me pull most of this stuff together. He'll do a good job. Plus he'll have Rita to help him. She's great.'

She tapped the pen, end over end.

'So . . .' said Lucy. 'Maybe you should just do it. One quick signature and you're done. Like ripping off a Band-Aid.'

Kumari took a deep breath and signed and dated it.

'There,' she said.

Lucy passed her the glass of wine. 'Well done, Dr Senavaka.'

Kumari sighed. 'I'm going to miss being called Dr Senavaka.'

'What are you going to be called?'

'Duchess of something. Depending on what ducal title Benedict gets given.'

'Oh,' said Lucy, sounding mildly disappointed. 'Not Princess Kumari?'

'No.' She giggled. 'Although Princess Kumari might be overkill – "Princess Princess".'

Lucy pulled a face. 'Seems a whole waste of marrying a prince if you don't get to be a princess.'

'Does a bit.'

She pushed the documents further away. Lucy, giving her a knowing glance, gathered them up and put them in her bag. 'I'll post them tomorrow morning.' She picked up her glass and clinked it against Kumari's. 'So, that's it then. All your "commoner" jobs handed over.'

'Yeah. Feels weird.'

'I bet. What are you going to do instead?'

'I'm taking a role in the foundation that Benedict and his sisters run. It's a really great idea actually. To pull together groups that work on similar things and have a big unified project delivered through all the different avenues. It has the potential to have a much bigger impact than the individual projects.'

'The whole being bigger than the sum of the parts?' said Lucy.

'Exactly!'

Lucy smiled. 'So you get to change the world anyway.'

Kumari grinned. Yes. She did get to change the world.

Being part of a royal foundation gave her far more influence and allowed her to do far more to help people than she could ever imagine. 'Yeah,' she said. 'That is rather cool.'

Chapter 28

The Witness Reporter

Nation gripped by royal wedding fever

Homes up and down the country are decked in red, white and blue as the nation prepares for the wedding of Prince Benedict and his Sri Lankan–British girlfriend, Kumari Senavaka. The pair, whose whirlwind romance is characterised by being unconventional (by royal standards) and good-humoured, are immensely popular with the British public. So much so that Kumari Senavaka, a doctor and vocal advocate of education for girls, is now mostly known simply as 'Kumari'. When asked about it in an interview, she said, 'You know you've arrived when people feel comfortable enough to call you by your first name.'

The couple have further extended their reputation for being better connected with the public than the rest of the royal family by making their wedding a public occasion and inviting two thousand commoners to the event. The couple invited the entire street where Kumari grew up, in recognition of the way the street rallied against vandals who targeted Kumari's parents in racist attacks. While the residents are in London, Prince Benedict has paid for security to watch their houses.

Later this week, Kumari will accompany the prince to an event encouraging young women to go into science. This will be her first formal royal engagement.

The crowd outside the event was sizeable. Kumari had been concentrating on what Anton was telling them about the initiative to get more young women involved in science. Since this was something Kumari had a good deal of personal experience in, they had all agreed that she should be the one to give a short speech and open the event. It was relatively small and, she felt, full of her kind of people – scientists. It was a good way to ease her into being a public figure. It had all seemed like such a good idea at the time.

She looked at her speech, it was getting a little tattered from being clutched in her hand. Ben touched her wrist. 'You're going to be fine,' he said. 'Trust me. You'll be wonderful.'

She nodded. She could do this. She was getting better at dealing with crowds. It was a matter of remembering that they were a collection of individuals. Focus on the person in front of her, rather than the mass as a whole. Ben had taught her that and it seemed to work.

The car came to a stop. First Ben, then Kumari, stepped out. The car behind them carried Danielle and some other security people. They were already out of their vehicle.

Kumari waved. Ben took her hand.

They were met by three women, who she was introduced to. She shook hands with them and sensed their nerves. They were nervous of meeting her? Seriously?

The older of the women, a physics professor, led the way, explaining about the project and how participation of girls in science was far lower than expected at all points in the education system, and that by the time they got to professional level, in science, technology, engineering and mathematics, only fifteen per cent of graduate jobs were taken by girls.

'We lose them at every stage,' she said, her hands moving to emphasise her point.

'Why do you think that is?' asked Ben.

'Partly, social conditioning. We are told in a hundred subtle ways that girls can't do certain professions. Partly because women interact differently to men. We are taught to placate; to compromise. But science is a very combative atmosphere. You are essentially always trying to prove or disprove something. There will always be conflict. And men are more likely to face that conflict with confidence – even when they're wrong. We need to give young women the tools to deal with that sort of atmosphere.'

'Yes,' said Kumari. She recognised a lot of that from medicine too, but she couldn't say that now. There was a lot of not-saying-things-directly involved in this public-facing role she had now. Everything she or Ben said would be analysed and spun to fit whatever world view the commentators held. Helena had been grooming her on the art of saying things that sounded meaningful while remaining carefully neutral. It was hard work. 'Is there any work on how that could be addressed?'

'It's essential that we retain the enthusiasm that young girls have and nurture it so that they don't lose it as they get older.'

By the time they got to the hall, Kumari was engrossed in the theories this woman was describing. Much of what she said chimed with Kumari's own ideas about educating women and enabling them to get back to work after taking career breaks to have families.

A few minutes later, she stood at the podium and looked at the faces turned towards her. Nearly all of them female. Most of them very young. She noted that there was a mix of skin tones. Good. She cleared her throat and leant closer towards the microphone. She focused on one face at a time and found her voice.

'A few years ago, I was like you,' she said to the girls who were standing solemnly watching her. 'I was a girl interested in science. There were plenty of people, mostly boys, sometimes other girls and women, who told me that "girls can't do science". They were wrong. That message is still there. The message is still wrong, but the difference is now we know that it's a lie. A myth, if you like. Women have been involved in pushing the boundaries of science for years, they were simply never talked about – Rosalind Franklin, Mileva Maric, Jocelyn Bell Burnell, the list goes on . . . You are the future. You will be those women who make new discoveries and invent new things and change the world. If every one of you inspires three others, soon the message will spread and no one will ever be able to say "girls can't do science" with a straight face again.'

She moved back and murmured, 'Thank you.' There was complete silence for a heartbeat. Then a wave of applause, a few whoops. She focused on individual faces of the girls in the front and saw the grins, the admiration. Cameras clicked all over the place, but she didn't care. She'd done it. She'd given her first speech and she'd inspired people.

She took a few steps away from the podium and went to stand by Ben, who beamed at her and took her hand again. Right now, she felt like she was the luckiest woman in the world.

They spent another half-hour walking around the exhibits, talking to the young scientists who were running the demonstrations. Kumari let her inner geek surface and asked a lot of questions, much to the delight of some of the adult volunteers. Ben, too, appeared to be taking a huge interest in what he was being told. They made DNA models out of jelly babies. They watched a strobe light make a water droplet seem to rise up while it dripped. They played with VR equipment.

Kumari was almost sad to leave. In her old life, she would have happily wandered around here for hours, although she would have worn more comfortable shoes. She was learning a lot about the wonderful world of high heels. Mostly that there was a reason she used to only wear them on special occasions.

They left the exhibition hall hand in hand. A path had been cleared for them to walk down, with people standing either side behind barriers. There were a couple of news cameras and reporters with microphones, not to mention the hundreds of smartphones.

Ben released her hand. She had a moment of free-falling fear, before she remembered. Focus on one person at a time. She and Ben walked down the corridor of people, one on either side. She shook hands, and smiled.

'Are you having a hen do?' someone asked.

'Oh yes. It's being organised by my friends,' she said, smiling.

A surprising number of people wanted just to touch her. She could see why Helena and Ophelia carried their bags like shields. If someone looked too grabby, she could sense Danielle stepping closer to her, that seemed to help dissuade people. Danielle was another member of her team who had become indispensable.

Someone offered her a posy of flowers. She took it, thanking the person, and carried it with her.

A man in a turban was standing by the barriers, carrying a little girl, who couldn't have been more than five. The girl was clutching a plastic Union flag.

Kumari stopped. 'Hello,' she said. The girl hid her face in her dad's shoulder and peered out at her.

'You're not shy,' said her dad, tickling her.

'That's a pretty outfit you're wearing,' Kumari said. It was. The girl was wearing a little blue sari.

Ben came to stand beside her. 'Oh, you're wearing Kumari's sari from the first time we met. How thoughtful.'

The child nodded.

'Her mum made it for her,' the father supplied. He indicated a small Asian woman beside him, who was practically vibrating with excitement.

'It's her favourite princess costume,' the woman said. 'She wants to be like you when she's big.'

The full realisation hit Kumari then. This little girl, with her brown skin and black hair, had come dressed as her. She, Kumari, was an icon. A princess to aspire to. More importantly for a small child, a princess that looked like her.

'You look beautiful,' she said.

The father tickled the little girl again. 'Say thank you.'

A muffled 'thank you' came from where the child was burrowing into his shoulder.

'Thank you,' Kumari said to the family. Both parents beamed at her. She carried on walking. As she neared the car, she turned around to look. The father had put the sari-clad little girl on his shoulders and she was waving enthusiastically.

Once they were safely back in the car, Kumari's hands started to shake.

'Hey,' said Ben. 'You did so well.'

'She was dressed as me,' Kumari said.

Ben didn't need to ask her what she was talking about.

'Yes,' he said. 'That was really sweet. You see. You're more than just you now. People are going to pour in their own vision of who they think you are. So long as you inspire people to be their best, then you're doing well.'

He leant across and kissed her. 'You did brilliantly with your speech. I'm so proud to be the guy marrying you.'

She side-eyed him. She was secretly pleased with her performance too.

Chapter 29

The Pinnacle News

Are you invited to the royal wedding?

Prince Benedict and his fiancée, Kumari Senavaka, will be inviting two thousand guests from a variety of communities to their wedding. The invitations have already been sent out. Those invited are believed to be neighbours from the area Kumari grew up in, several hundred members of the Windsor Castle, Buckingham Palace and Kensington Palace communities, a thousand young people who have been active in serving their communities, staff members from the hospitals and charities that Kumari worked in and selected others.

For those who aren't invited to the event itself, there is still the chance to see the royal couple after they are married as they will take a procession around the town of Windsor. It is thought that there will be an open-air concert in Windsor, with free tickets being made available on a first come, first served basis.

Prince Benedict and Kumari wanted to make this wedding a celebration of difference and unity.

Kumari sat in the limo with Lucy and Thatha on either side of her. Danielle, who was now officially her CPS officer, sat in the front. The dress rustled every time she moved. They had decided that she didn't need a veil, but her hairpiece had a loop of fabric that touched at her shoulders and blended with her train. Her dress was mainly pale blue, so light it was almost white, with bright blue and gold embroidery on it. When she walked, the folds of fabric at the base revealed flashes of cerulean blue. She had opted for a car, rather than carriage, for this first part. There would be a carriage later.

'Woah,' said Lucy, looking out of the car's tinted windows at the crowds outside, all of whom were standing behind crash barriers waving flags. 'I feel like royalty.' Lucy was wearing a long slip dress of same blue. There was a line of deeper blue just at the bottom.

She looked at Kumari. A hysterical laugh rose in Kumari's chest and burst out before she could stop it. Suddenly, they were both giggling like children. Thatha watched them, smiling indulgently.

As they neared the arch that led into the grounds of Windsor Castle, he shushed them. After a few seconds struggling, Kumari got herself under control. She didn't dare look at Lucy, in case it started again.

The car pulled up outside the doors of St George's Chapel.

Thatha said, 'Ready?'

Kumari nodded. He touched his fingertips to the top of her head, lightly, so that she barely felt it through all the hairspray. 'Be happy,' he said.

Kumari felt her eyes prickle. 'Don't make me cry.'

He smiled and she could see his eyes were already full. Someone opened Lucy's door for her and the roar of the crowds came in. A terrifying sound. Lucy got out and the door shut. Thatha got out next and held out his hand to help her. She gripped it firmly and stepped out. The noise intensified. Bells rang overhead. For a moment, she felt panic gallop through her. Lucy appeared next to her, fussing with the dress. Kumari turned and caught her eye. Lucy said, 'Benedict.'

That was what this was all about. Benedict. The people, the cameras, the staring, none of that was important. She straightened up, allowed her father to tuck her hand into his arm, took a deep breath and walked towards the chapel. As she walked, a gust of wind, as if on cue, blew her skirts, drawing out the darker blue detail. There was an audible 'ooh' from the crowd.

Someone had arranged the flower girls and pageboy in front of her. They paused at the door and she remembered to wave to the crowds. The cheer that greeted this was almost a wall of sound.

The 'Wedding March' rang out from the grand organ above the nave. A wave of murmurs preceded her. She was dimly aware of the flower arrangements that she and Ophelia had carefully chosen, the blue, white and gold decorations, the people in the seats either side of the aisle. There was too much to take in all at once. So she fixed her eyes on the two figures standing by the altar.

Benedict and Rhodri were both in their military uniforms. Benedict had explained to her the significance of all the bits of his uniform: the red-and-gold sash, the braiding, the working on the sleeves, the medals – they all had meaning. But, right now, all Kumari could remember was Ben carefully explaining to her and a giggling Lucy that aiguillettes meant a type of braiding, and weren't the same as a French white sausage. That was the man she was marrying. Ben, who faced the world with humour and compassion. He just also happened to be a prince.

As she got closer, she could see Benedict's hands, furling and unfurling with nerves. Rhodri glanced over his shoulder and flashed her a grin. She smiled and bowed her head.

When she drew level with the altar, Benedict turned. His blue eyes sparkled. Her gaze met his and all doubts burned away. This was exactly where she wanted to be.

Thatha squeezed her hand before he helped her up to the altar.

She and Ben repeated their vows, learnt by heart now, and exchanged rings. After the hymns, they went into the small room behind the altar where they signed the legal papers that made them husband and wife.

Once this was done, Ben sighed, picked up her hand and laid a kiss on her knuckles. 'I love you,' he said, a catch in his voice.

'I love you too.'

'You can have a sneaky kiss, you know?' said Rhodri.

'Mind the make-up,' Lucy hissed.

Kumari and Ben looked at each other. Ben leant in and gave her a light kiss on her lips. He moved back. 'Best not mess up your lipstick. There will be cameras everywhere.'

'See,' said Lucy pointedly. 'That's considerate.'

Rhodri rolled his eyes good-naturedly. Kumari laughed. She loved that there was a spark between her best friend and Ben's. 'Stop squabbling you two.'

'That's *our* job,' said Ben.

Anton, who had appeared from somewhere, checked the doorway. 'Ready?'

They went back into the body of the church to the sounds of fanfare. They went first to the queen, to whom they bowed. She gave them a happy smile. Then they turned and walked down the length of the aisle. Now, Kumari could notice people. Familiar faces of friends, her own grandmother and mother, standing together, resplendent in jewel-bright saris. Famous faces. Hats.

She walked carefully, so that she didn't trip up on her skirts, although given that tripping on her skirts was what had brought her here in the first place, perhaps that wouldn't be so bad. Beside her, Benedict muttered, 'Don't tread on the dress' to himself as he matched her step for step.

When they reached the outside, the cheering was deafening. They paused to wave.

The realisation that this was her life now hit Kumari square in the chest. She gasped. She had been the reluctant star beforehand. The potential bride of the prince. But now she was part of it. These people were her people too. For some reason this didn't frighten her as much as it had before. She was here now. Secure. With the man she loved. Nothing was going to faze her now.

By the time they had done a carriage ride around Windsor, waved to several thousand people and returned to the castle, Kumari's arms ached and she really needed a glass of water. She had to change clothes and prepare for the wedding breakfast in a bit. But first there was something else to do. She and Ben met Rhodri and Lucy at the door and followed them into a small room away from the other guests.

In the room, Amma and Thatha stood waiting, with Ben's father, stepmother and sisters. In the centre of the room was a tall lamp garlanded with white flowers. There was a small crowd of Sri Lankans – a single drummer, a *kapuwa* – who would have traditionally conducted the ceremonial part of the marriage – and three children who were all in traditional dress.

Since they were already married, they had dispensed with the marriage ceremony, but the lighting of the lamp was retained.

The *kapuwa* looked at his watch, waited for the auspicious moment and signalled that the drummer should start. Amma handed them a lit taper. Kumari took it in her right hand and Ben put his own right hand around hers. When the *kapuwa*, his eyes fixed on his watch, gave them the signal, they lit one of the wicks in the lamp together. A symbolic lighting of the way for their life together. The small choir of three sang a traditional song of blessing. Something Kumari had only ever heard at weddings.

Once they had lit the lamp, Kumari and Ben put their palms together and bowed in front of her parents and his father. Finally, the Prince of Wales broke into a smile and said, 'Welcome to the family, Kumari.'

Kumari grinned back. Now, it was done.

Making Merry

Chapter 30
(Present day)

Prince Benedict and Kumari prepare for their first Christmas together

They've been married for seven months now and the Duke and Duchess of Westbury, Prince Benedict and his wife Kumari, seem more in love than ever. The couple were spotted last week buying Christmas decorations at London's famous winter market in Hyde Park.

Prince Benedict tried on a novelty Christmas hat and Kumari bought several sets of wooden ornaments made by the Southall Woodturners' Guild.

'She was really interested in how they were made,' said Terry Smith, who was running the stall that day. 'All our ornaments are handmade using wood from broken or abandoned furniture. She particularly liked the traditional wooden baubles and bought three full sets of them.'

Kumari was well wrapped up against the cold in a Lucy Squire coat and matching hat and gloves from Burberry. She completed the outfit with a pair of comfy boots. The swing-style winter coat concealed the Duchess's waistline, sparking speculation that she might be pregnant.

Photo caption: Prince Benedict makes Kumari laugh by trying on a Disney Anna hat, complete with plaits.

Turn to page 12 for a selection of the best wooden Christmas tree ornaments.

First Light News

Kumari, Duchess of Westbury, opens new neonatal wing

The Duchess of Westbury, known to most as Kumari, will have one of her rare solo engagements today when she opens the new premature baby unit at St Kildare's Hospital. Since marrying Prince Benedict earlier this year, Kumari has taken on more and more active royal duties.

Despite initial scepticism in some parts of the media, the thirty-one-year-old British–Asian former doctor has taken to public life remarkably well. She seems to be popular with the public, particularly in her native Yorkshire where she is rumoured to be in the running for Yorkshire Woman of the Year.

There were those who predicted that an institution as old and revered as the monarchy would not be able to cope with a senior royal who was not white, but Kumari and Prince Benedict have navigated any difficulties with grace and charm. No one who has seen the two together can doubt that they are in love. Millions tuned in to watch their wedding and the royal family remains more popular than ever.

As she opens the neonatal unit today there is much speculation whether the fact that she is attending this event by herself, rather than in support of another senior royal, is a hint of pregnancy news to come.

Photo caption: Prince Benedict and his sisters HRHs Princess Helena and Princess Ophelia arrive at the US Embassy reception last week.

Kumari pulled on the tasseled cord to a smattering of applause, and formally opened the new ward. As she did so, she couldn't help but reflect on how much her life had changed over the last year. From Letsho to Los Angeles to London, from a doctor living in a small flat to a princess in a palace, at times she almost didn't recognise her life. She'd like to think she was getting used to this princess thing, but the last seven months had hardly been smooth sailing. Some days she missed her old life desperately. She was used to doing things directly, which the new rules governing her life no longer allowed. The rules drove her crazy. How many times had she burned to speak her mind, to declare herself for a cause . . . To say what she actually *meant* for a change, rather than being carefully diplomatic at all times? She stifled a sigh. Frustrating though all this was, it was what made it possible for her to be with Ben. And Ben was worth it.

Cameras flashed and Kumari smiled for them. The unveiled plaque announced that the new neonatal unit had been opened by HRH the Duchess of Westbury. She was fast becoming the go-to royal for opening hospitals. She didn't mind. She felt at home in the clinical setting.

She posed for the photos. The formal pose came easily now, after so many months of practice. Back straight, arms slightly away from body, tilt head, smile. She still had a way to go before she looked as natural as her sisters-in-law did, but she was getting there.

The photos were important. Wherever she went, she took the cameras and the world's attention with her. Thousands of people who had never heard about this unit would check out a page to see what outfit she was wearing and end up finding out all about the work they did.

Her favourite part was when she got to talk informally to the staff at the end.

One woman cheekily asked if she would be in need of maternity services soon. Kumari laughed it off without responding. The nation seemed to be obsessed with how soon she and Ben would have a baby. Let them obsess. She knew better than to comment, even in jest. Anything she said would immediately be reported in the national press and analysed in minute detail. She and Ben had agreed to leave it a year before they started trying. She was still getting used to the madness of being a public figure. She wasn't ready to tackle pregnancy as well.

The whole visit lasted less than two hours, but being 'on' the whole time, watching herself every minute, was tiring. By the time she got back to her car, she was exhausted. Her personal assistant, Annie, and private secretary, Barry, were both in the car. Barry handled her diary and formalities. Annie made sure she was looked after personally.

'Well done, ma'am,' said Barry. He had been assistant private secretary to Princess Helena before taking up the post with Kumari. With a track record in the military and then higher education, Barry was a little intimidating, but also, Kumari had found out, a really nice guy under the thick eyebrows.

'Thank you,' she said.

Annie had come from the charity sector. Like Kumari, she was still learning the ways of the royal household, which was something Kumari found comforting. Annie handed her a glass of water, which she gratefully sipped. 'That's it for now, right, Barry?'

Barry inclined his head. 'Yes, ma'am. Would you like to go through the rest of the notes from today while we travel?'

'There was a message on your phone, ma'am,' Annie interrupted. She passed Kumari her phone, which was always left with either Annie or Barry when she was on formal visits.

Kumari glanced at the screen. It was a message from Ben. *Quiet night in tonight? Race you to the bottom of the pile of Christmas cards to sign.*

She smiled. There was a lot she hadn't fully assimilated about being part of the 'senior royals'. One of them was the sheer amount of correspondence involved. People wrote to her all the time. She loved reading the letters, which were always vetted by Barry to check for anything dangerous or abusive. The letters she actually got to see were wonderful notes from people telling her how she had helped or inspired them. Sometimes people sent in pictures their kids had drawn. She would have liked to write back personally to all of them, but there was so much of it that she had to let Barry's team handle that. But she liked to scrawl a short note whenever she could.

Lately, there had been a huge number of Christmas cards to sign. Previously, she had assumed that only a fraction of the pile were actually signed by the royals themselves, but it turned out not to be the case. She seemed to have been signing 'Kumari' on cards for days. 'Netflix and cards?' was a standing joke between her and Ben now.

Other people got married and spent the first few years of their lives getting to know each other, slowly growing into each other's lives until they were a unit. She and Ben didn't have that luxury. They'd had a short honeymoon, but had been busy with royal engagements, and lessons – those endless lessons – for Kumari, ever since.

Where other people bickered about who put the rubbish out and whose turn it was to do the shopping, they argued about the rules – which ones she had to follow, which ones she could bend. There weren't many she could bend, really, but she tried anyway, because she hated being hemmed in the way she was. Ben was very happy with the rules now, but he hadn't always been like that either. She thought he rather liked arguing the toss with her, teasing her and making her laugh. She certainly wouldn't have had it any other way.

She texted back *You're on*, handed the phone back to Annie and turned to give Barry her full attention.

He handed her a folder.

'We thought you might like to respond to the top one personally.' Annie grinned.

Kumari opened the file, puzzled. On top was a cover note:

Dear Kumari,

Thank you so much for all you've done for us. Rita.

316

PS: You might recognise someone on page 2.

Below it was the first report from the Boost Her! project. Smiling, Kumari skimmed the first page – a description of the opening of the first Boost Her! health centre, there was a picture of the buildings, data on the number of patients seen already and the number they were expecting to cater for when they reached capacity. There was also an inset about the little cottage industries that had sprung up around the project – women who made extra money by providing lunch packets or laundry services for the staff and the trainee ambassadors. Boost Her! was already boosting the local economy simply by being there, which was an unexpected bonus.

Curious about the cover note, Kumari flipped over to page 2. There was a photo of a local Lesotho girl, in a pristine Boost Her! project tabard, with a toddler on her hip.

Kumari looked closer. She knew that smile. The last time she'd seen it, she had been a footsore volunteer. 'Oh my goodness, is that Hopeful?'

Hopeful, the original inspiration for the Boost Her! project. The little boy on her hip must be her son, Nimo. Kumari read through the description of how Hopeful was one of the first cohort of Boost Her! ambassadors to have completed her training. Nimo, the baby who had nearly died, looked happy and healthy.

Kumari stared at the photo and felt a sudden visceral longing for her old life, where she got to work at the bleeding edge of a health crisis and see the difference her work made on a daily basis. Even working in A & E, every patient she stabilised, even injury she bound up . . . everything made someone's terrible day a little better.

In the past, she'd have gone to an event for supporting women's health, or for the protection of battered women and she would have got involved, raised money for them, spoken out in the press about the cause, volunteered her services as a doctor even . . . but there was a rule for everything when one was a royal. Ye shall not support any one cause above the others was a pretty big one.

She stifled a sigh and reminded herself that she was still making a difference. Only now, she was doing it on a much larger scale. Raising money in hundreds of thousands, rather than mere thousands; forging links between charities so that they could amplify their impact; giving a voice to those who would otherwise go unheard. The trouble with scale, though, was it also needed distance and took time. She missed being up close to her work, seeing the impact she made daily.

She looked back at the picture of Hopeful and her son. At least with Boost Her! she could see the result of her hard work. She might not be able to head up the project like she'd originally hoped to, but the project was going great guns. She smiled. It was all good.

Even though it wasn't late, it was dark by the time Kumari got back home to Kensington Palace. She saw Dave in the corridor outside their apartments and smiled at him. He nodded back to her. If Dave was here, then Ben was home.

When they got married, Ben's grandparents had offered him a set of rooms, bigger than the ones he'd had before and on the ground floor, so that they had a private garden. Like all the apartments in Kensington Palace, the rooms had high ceilings and huge windows that gave them a sense of vastness. Kumari strode along and reflected that the sense of space wasn't just down to the high, decorated ceilings. It was down to the actual size of the rooms. It took several minutes to cross some of them.

It had been suggested to Kumari that she should redecorate it to 'make it their own', but apart from having it repainted, she didn't see anything wrong with it, so she'd left it alone.

This meant that all she had to do was decide what furniture she wanted. The apartments had been empty when they'd moved in. It turned out, the royals didn't buy furniture. They commissioned it, received it as a gift or inherited it. She had spoken to a designer and run through some ideas and the man had then produced a catalogue of likely pieces in the royal stores for her to choose from. Being still new to opulence, she had tried to choose the least delicate and most practical items, but her house was still full of priceless things. She had been paranoid about breaking something, until Ben had gently pointed out that there was a ton more of the stuff in storage and that everything could be fixed by expert restorers, if needs be. She was still a little obsessive about coasters though.

Kumari let herself in, knowing that her own CPS officer, Danielle, would join the rest of the security team watching the CCTV of the corridor and other exits as soon at the door closed behind her. Being constantly under surveillance was another thing she'd had to get used to. At least the security team could be relied upon to be discreet.

'I'm home,' she called. She hung up her coat. One of the things that she and Ben had insisted on was that they had some privacy, or at least the illusion of it. The security team had no surveillance inside the apartment. Although they had a housekeeper who kept things ticking over, they only saw her at their allocated appointments in the morning. The housekeeping staff came in and cleaned and prepped rooms while they were out. They also made sure there were fresh flowers in the main rooms every day, with a different colour scheme each day. Today, she noticed the colours were yellow and pink. Beautiful.

'I'm in here,' came Ben's voice. She found him lying on one of the sofas, his knees hanging over the arm of it. He had his glasses on and was staring at a tablet. He was still in a suit, but had removed his tie, leaving his shirt open at the neck. Kumari smiled. This was one of her favourite looks on him.

She took a moment to admire him. Her husband. She had been aware of him for most of her life. But it had never occurred to her that she could meet him in person. If someone had told her a few years ago that she'd be married to him – Prince Benedict, grandson of the queen – she would have thought they were on hallucinogenic drugs. And yet, here she was. No longer a doctor, working long hours in A & E, but a duchess, married to a prince. Some days her life didn't seem real.

Ben looked up and smiled. Her whole world lit up in response. If this was a dream, she didn't ever want to wake up.

'Hello, you,' she said, padding across the vast spread of Axminster carpet. The sitting room overlooked the garden and was cheerful in the summer. Now, with the heavy drapes drawn and the huge Christmas tree scenting the room with pine, it felt wonderfully homely.

Ben lifted up his head and shoulders so that she could sit down, then laid his head on her lap. She kissed his forehead.

'What're you doing?' Kumari peered at the screen.

'Looking for inspiration. I still haven't got any gifts yet.' He sighed. 'Harrods has nothing fun. I'm looking at John Lewis now. Cheap, cheerful and silly, that's what we need.'

'And you're looking at John Lewis?'

Ben tipped his head back. 'I've tried a load of other high street places, thank you.'

She grinned at him and kissed him again. 'Sure you have.'

He reached up and touched her cheek. 'Good day?' he said.

She shrugged. 'Yes. I think so.' She reached for the tablet. 'I have an idea, let me see that.'

He passed it over. 'Ophelia said she's coming down to see us, by the way. I've told security to let her through.'

'That's nice.' That meant that her sister-in-law would be showing up any second now. She tapped in the name of a website that she'd used when she'd needed to buy Secret Santa gifts, back in the days when she still worked at the hospital. That kind of normality felt like a lifetime ago now. 'Here we go. Try this place. It's very cheap and very tacky . . .'

'Ah. Perfect.' Ben took the tablet off her and scrolled through the gag gifts. 'Wow. This is great.'

'Are you sure about this?' said Kumari. 'It seems a little . . . disrespectful.' She still couldn't get her head around why a family who could afford almost anything, would insist on buying the cheapest, most ridiculous presents for each other.

'Yep. It's tradition.'

When she said nothing, he lowered the tablet onto his stomach and looked up at her. 'Think about it,' he said. 'If we were allowed to get expensive gifts for each other, where would it end? We're a very competitive bunch. It would get ridiculous really fast. This way, we're forced to think about what we buy, but in a good way.'

Kumari smiled. 'That makes sense.' She trailed her fingers through his hair, the way she knew he liked. 'Does this "cheap gifts only" rule apply to you and me?'

He closed his eyes. 'Do you want it to?' he murmured.

'I'd like ... a thoughtful present from you. Not an expensive one. Just a thoughtful one will do.'

He opened one eye and looked at her, a smile tugging at the corners of his mouth. 'I'll think about it.'

She laughed. He reached up to pull her to him.

The door buzzed and Ophelia wafted in. 'Oh. Not interrupting anything, I hope,' she said, without any sign of remorse. She threw herself into the sofa opposite. 'This month! My goodness. So much to do and so little time to do it in. It's mid-December already and I haven't got presents for anyone. Have you?'

'Working on it.' Ben picked up the tablet again and resumed scrolling.

'I haven't,' said Kumari. 'Lucy's coming next week. I'll probably try and sort something out.'

'Ooh, can I come?' Ophelia pulled out her phone. 'When is it?'

'Wednesday,' said Kumari. She was really looking forward to seeing Lucy. It had been months. She wasn't entirely sure she wanted Ophelia to be there too. Much as she loved her, she wanted Lucy all to herself for a bit.

'Ah, I'm in Surrey, at a gala thing,' said Ophelia. 'Oh, bother. Never mind.' She put her phone away.

'Is it always so busy at this time of year?' said Kumari. Her own diary had been booked solid for weeks, so had Ben's. Many of the charities invited the patrons to their end-of-year dinners. She tended to be invited as Ben's partner at the moment, but it wouldn't be long before she would be allowed to do the dinners solo. She wasn't sure how she felt about that, to be perfectly honest. She loved that they were able to support so many great causes, but she was bound by so many rules that she was in constant fear of getting carried away in her enthusiasm and becoming too involved. At least, with Ben there, she could take her cues from him.

'Always hectic at Christmas, darling,' said Ophelia. 'After all the dinners and speeches and letter-writing, it's almost a relief to get to Grandma's on Christmas Eve.'

Ben snorted.

Ophelia ignored him. 'Have you got your outfits sorted for Sandringham yet?' she asked Kumari.

'Erm . . . Sinead said it was all done. I'm meeting her next week to go over the final selection.' Lucy was coming to hang out with her while she and her dresser went through the outfits. It was the only time they could find that fitted around Kumari's schedule and Lucy's shifts at the hospital.

Ophelia gave her an appraising look. 'You did well, choosing Sinead,' she said. 'I like the style she's creating for you. A bit different, but still following all of the rules. Good eye.'

'Thanks,' said Kumari.

'All in all, you're taking to this rather well,' Ophelia continued.

'Like there was ever any doubt that she would!' said Ben.

Kumari's face warmed. It had been a steep learning curve, but she was relaxing into the role of duchess now, even if she still got the urge to giggle if she stopped to think about it for too long. It was hard to imagine that not so long ago, she was a hospital doctor, run off her feet looking after patients . . . and now she lived in this enormous apartment . . . with a housekeeper . . . and hung out with princesses after work. And she had a team. A *team*, whose jobs revolved around making sure she was properly dressed, informed and looked after at all times. No wonder she had to pinch herself from time to time. 'I've been very lucky with my team.'

'Hmm. You know, darling,' said Ophelia, looking pointedly at Ben. 'I could murder a cup of tea. Shall we call the housekeeper?'

Ben sighed. 'You are *such* a princess sometimes.' He sat up and handed the tablet to Kumari. 'I'll get it. Ophelia clearly wants to get rid of me so she can talk to you about something.' He gave Kumari a look of mock severity. 'I'm relying on you not to let her plan anything too heinous.'

'I've got your back,' said Kumari.

As soon as Ben disappeared, Ophelia said. 'I've got him the *best* present,' she said. 'Do you know what he's got for me?'

Kumari laughed. 'Nope. Because he hasn't yet. Even if he had, you know I wouldn't tell.'

Ophelia pulled a face. 'Ah well.' She leaned forward. 'Actually, Kumari, I just wanted to check that you were OK. The whole Sandringham thing can be a bit . . . overwhelming . . . when you first join the family. So I just wanted to say, if you're worried about anything, just tap me on the arm and I'll do what I can to help.'

Kumari blinked. The idea of spending time with all of her in-laws over Christmas was scary enough, but to do it in such a formal manner was a whole extra level of nerve-wracking. She was grateful for any support. 'Thank you,' she said. 'I'm probably going to take you up on that.'

Ophelia smiled. 'Do.' She looked like she wanted to say more.

There was a beat of silence.

Kumari waited. Ophelia sighed. 'Actually, there's something else,' she said, looking down at her hands. 'What are you and Ben doing between Christmas and New Year? Are you going to see your parents?'

Ah, so that was why she waited until Ben was out of the room to ask. She wanted to give Kumari the chance to say something without having to check with Ben. Ophelia might come across as overly breezy, but underneath it all, she was one of the kindest, most considerate people Kumari had ever met.

'Yes. They're coming over here for a few days before New Year. But otherwise, we were planning on spending some time here . . . together.' She frowned. 'Why? Aren't you spending it with Dominic?'

Ophelia gave a small one-shouldered shrug. 'No. He's going skiing with some old chums. He says there's quite an important business deal riding on it and ...' She sighed, then flicked a hand as though waving away the next thought. 'Anyway, I was wondering if you minded if I joined you ... for some of the time. All my other friends have commitments.'

Kumari stared at her sister-in-law, torn. She and Ben had both been so busy, they hadn't had much time alone together since their honeymoon, which seemed a very long time ago now. She had been hoping they could just laze around and enjoy each other in private for a few days during the holidays. She knew Ben was hoping for that too. But Ophelia was Ben's sister. She had been incredibly thoughtful in asking Kumari privately, so that she could give an honest answer.

Looking at Ophelia now, Kumari saw the worry lines, carefully concealed, and the sadness in her eyes. This was Ophelia with her armour down. It didn't happen often. Over the last year, Ophelia had become one of her closest friends. It was very rare that she needed anything. And now that she did, it wasn't in Kumari to deny her help. 'Let me talk to Ben,' she said.

'Talk to me about what?' said Ben as he came in carrying a tray with three mugs on it. 'Earl Grey for you, given the hour.' He passed one to Ophelia. 'And regular for you.' He passed Kumari her drink, took his own and sat next to her. 'So, what are we talking to me about?'

'About Ophelia spending some time with us between Christmas and New Year,' said Kumari.

Ben's eyes met hers. 'But—' He looked at his sister, who gave him a small smile. 'Oh.' He looked back at Kumari.

'Maybe some of the time,' she said apologetically.

'Ye-s,' he said. 'Yes. We're not going anywhere. We were planning to stay here, so yes. Come over. You could meet Kumari's parents again.'

There was a second of mutual understanding and Ophelia smiled, her full-wattage princess smile. 'Brilliant. That's settled then.' She clapped her hands. 'It will be a delight to see your parents again, Kumari. I haven't had so much fun discussing literature for ages.'

Kumari wanted to ask Ophelia if everything was all right with Dominic, but the moment had passed. 'My dad will be delighted too,' she said.

The following week, Kumari and Ben went to see a community centre where they worked with young people to prevent youth offenders from reoffending. After a good meeting, they did the walk back to their cars, each walking down one side of the line of people, shaking hands and stopping occasionally to talk to someone. A news reporter stopped her. 'Your Highness, are you looking forward to your first Christmas with the royal family?'

Kumari paused and smiled. 'Of course. It's my first Christmas with my husband too, so it's a very special occasion.'

'There are a lot of traditions involved in the Sandringham Christmas,' the man continued. 'Will you be adding any Sri Lankan traditions to the mix this year.'

She had been expecting this. She laughed. 'I'm sure everything is perfect as it is. If it isn't broken, why fix it?'

The man opened his mouth to ask another question, but Kumari firmly turned away from him to talk to someone else. Her CPS officer, Danielle, stepped up to prevent her from being hassled any further.

A few yards further down, Kumari spotted a familiar face.

'Victor!' She reached forward and grasped his hand. 'How are you?'

Victor's smile was crooked. He leant forward. He had clearly come there with the express intention of speaking to her.

'What's wrong?' said Kumari.

'I need to talk to you about Boost Her!' said Victor. 'We're having the funding pulled.'

Kumari stopped still. 'But why? I saw the first report. It's doing really well.'

He looked uncomfortable. 'They . . . All the projects are going to stop after a year. But the project needs longer to show results It was meant to be a five-year project and they're axing it after one.' His voice was tight and anguished.

'Oh no. That's terrible. They're just getting started. They can't assess the full impact until the ambassadors have gone back to spread the word.'

'Exactly!' said Victor. 'Please, can you help? You've got influence now.'

'Of course,' said Kumari, her mind already whirring. 'Of course I'll help. Let me—'

Beside her, an aide said sharply, 'Ma'am.'

Oh bugger, she wasn't supposed to make offers of help without consulting a million different officials first. She took a small step back and said, 'Victor, could you write to my office formally, please.'

Victor's face fell. He had assumed this was a standard brush off. Kumari's heart ached for him. She leant forward and whispered. 'I'll do whatever I can. We'll find you the money somehow.'

She gave him a reassuring smile and carried on walking. There had to be something she could do. She would have to ask Barry to investigate options as soon as she got back.

Chapter 31

Better For All boss doing better for himself?

The chairman of the international health charity Better For All has been suspended from his post at the charity pending allegations of corruption and money laundering. Funding for all the charity's projects have been halted pending the outcome of the investigation.

The Daily Flash

Kumari breaks royal rules and promises to help fund a charity

HRH Kumari, the Duchess of Westbury told a representative from a charity that she would help support them. The Boost Her! initiative, which aims to improve health and welfare in rural communities in Lesotho, was recently told that their funding would be curtailed due to a budget freeze. A representative of the charity project approached the duchess about it following a visit by the duke and duchess to a community centre in Hackney.

When she heard about the reduction in funding, the duchess, who was deeply involved in the project before she met Prince Benedict, appeared to be shocked and assured the charity representative that she would help. She gave the representative the formal response of suggesting he writes to her office, but then was heard to whisper, 'We'll find you the money somehow.'

The royal family do not donate to charities directly, so perhaps the duchess plans to take this through the Princesses and Prince Foundation, where she is newly a trustee? Or perhaps she plans to make a private donation from HRH Prince Benedict's considerable private funds? Or is this latest addition to the royal family throwing out the royal rulebook already?

Kumari stared at the headline in horror. After all these months of being careful, she'd slipped up. She didn't know who she was more annoyed with, the newspaper or herself. 'I'm so sorry,' she said. 'I was so shocked to hear about it.' She was in her office, having her morning catch-up with Barry.

She frowned. 'How did they know? Victor wouldn't go to the press. He's a friend.' Except she hadn't had any contact with him in a long time. She'd lost contact with a lot of her old friends. Her diary was so busy that she didn't have time to reach out to them and she wasn't allowed on any of her old social media accounts, which, in reality, had been the only way she'd been in touch with most of her friends.

'One of the news reporters picked it up on his boom microphone.' Barry gave her a stern stare. 'Your Highness, when in public you have to always assume that—'

'The mike is always on,' Kumari finished his sentence. She should have known better. All those months of training and she forgot herself for one moment, which just happened to be when a microphone was nearby. Ugh.

Barry was giving her his 'disapproving headmaster' glare. He sometimes had a tendency to treat Kumari like she was an errant cadet. She would have to put a stop to that.

She met his gaze. 'I made a mistake. I apologise. Now, what can we do to retrieve the situation?'

He stared at her a moment longer. She stared back. She lifted her chin. 'Major Smythe,' she said, in her sternest doctor voice. 'What can we do to limit the damage?'

Barry looked away. 'Well ... ma'am. The press office have prepared this statement.' He passed a sheet of paper over.

'Thanks,' Kumari muttered. This would be the official line that she was meant to follow. She twitched the paper straight and read the statement.

HRH Duchess of Westbury cares deeply about the education of women and the role it plays in improving welfare standards. She has requested that the Boost Her! initiative apply to the Princesses and Prince Foundation for funding in order to complete their mission. Their application will be considered alongside other applications for inclusion in one of the collaborative projects that are the core strength of the foundation.

It basically stated the facts and strongly hinted that Kumari was not personally going to support the charity, without explicitly saying so. Kumari sighed and handed it back to Barry. 'Is this really the best we can do? This is an initiative that could change the future for women in Lesotho! It could—'

'They have also asked me to tell you that in the past twenty-four hours, there have been three separate freedom of information requests submitted regarding charitable donations made through the Princesses and Prince Foundation.' He gave her a meaningful glare.

'OK. OK. Stick to the formal line. I get it.' She rubbed her eyes. Her new life was meant to have power, but it came with so many rules and limitations that it was almost as though she was even more powerless than before. At least before she was allowed to say what she thought! 'What if I get asked about it the next time I'm out?'

'The press office advises keeping things vague and perhaps discussing the importance of increasing girls' education opportunities both here and abroad. But in general terms only.'

'I can certainly do that,' said Kumari. 'Is there anything else?'

'Only that we have had an email approach from your colleague Victor Aye requesting more information already,' said Barry. 'They have been sent the full application pack for the Princesses and Prince Foundation grant schemes.'

He handed her a sheaf of paper. 'He also sent in this, for your attention.'

She scanned the document. Victor had sent her a summary sheet of which parts of the project would need to halt as soon as the funding ran out. Since Kumari had spent so long working on the project plans before she left it all to join the royal family, it only took a quick skim through for her to grasp the severity of the shortfall.

There must be more she could do ... 'Barry, who assesses the applications?'

'A full committee,' said Barry. 'You will be one of the people on that committee.'

Oh. Good. Perhaps she could—

'However,' Barry continued. 'Given your links with this particular charity, you would have to declare your interest and abstain from the discussion.'

Bugger.

'Also, the window for applications for this year closed a month ago, so any applications submitted now won't be discussed until next year.' He flicked through his notes. 'Given the information we have, there may be a gap between the fund ending and the new funding starting ... assuming their application is successful.' He looked up, his expression apologetic. 'I checked.'

Kumari sighed again. 'Thank you.' It just got worse and worse. Still, even if she wasn't in the room when the decision was made, she could have a quiet word with people and make sure they gave it proper attention. 'Can you get me a list of the people on the decision-making committee, please?'

Barry raised an eyebrow at her. 'Is this wise, ma'am?'

She met his gaze. 'There's no reason why I shouldn't know who my colleagues on the decision-making committee are, is there?'

Barry sighed. 'I suppose not, ma'am. I will get you the list.'

'Thank you,' she said again.

Barry made a note. 'This project won their original funding in an open competition,' he said without looking up.

'There's no reason why it wouldn't be supported if it went to the committee.'

That was true. It was a project with merit. It was quite likely to be funded . . . but the timing was not good. Kumari tapped a finger on her desk. She knew without asking that she couldn't ask the committee to extend the funding period backward to cover the shortfall. They'd had to refuse another charity who had asked for that the year before. So how could she help cover the gap? There must be something she could do. If she wasn't allowed to use her influence directly for that, then maybe she could just use money to help.

'Before we move on to the next item. What would happen if Ben and I were to make an anonymous donation from our private funds?'

They were Ben's private funds, really. She still hadn't got her head around the size of it all. Even the size of her clothing budget astounded her. The only way to keep sane was to think of her stipend as a salary and think of the rest as the cost of doing business. Which, in a way, it was. She could donate a portion of her stipend from now until the new funding round was announced. That would bridge the gap. Assuming they won the funding.

Barry frowned. 'Anonymously?' he asked.

She nodded. 'A one-off private donation.' She'd have to ask Ben, but it wasn't worth even going there if the rules didn't allow it.

'Technically, you could do that, ma'am, but I wouldn't advise it. Given what happened yesterday, people will put two and two together and then you'll be inundated with requests for support. The whole point of having a foundation is to allow your charitable donations to be channelled so that they have full transparency and maximum impact in the areas you focus on.' He was going into lecture mode again.

Kumari waved a hand wearily. 'Yes, yes. I know. I just thought I'd ask.'

Barry subsided.

'What's next on the agenda?'

As they returned to discussing what was going on during the day, the information Barry had just given her settled in the back of her mind.

There had to be a way. There just had to.

On Wednesday, Lucy arrived, bearing a bottle of wine. Kumari popped it in the fridge. 'No booze until after the clothes have been sorted,' she said.

'It's only, like, three days. Why would you need so many?' said Lucy, watching as Sinead wheeled in an overloaded clothes rack.

'Well,' said Sinead. 'There's the outfit for travelling in – needs to be comfortable but not likely to crumple because someone is bound to take a photo. There's the cocktail dress for early evening drinks on Christmas Eve. Evening gown for dinner. Outdoor clothes for church. Nice dress to go under it, so that you can go straight to Christmas Day lunch. Slightly more formal dress for Christmas Day evening buffet. Something casual for Boxing Day . . .' She flicked through the hangers as she spoke. 'So, I propose we go through them in chronological order.'

Kumari sat down on the sofa with Lucy perched next to her. 'It's like the most advanced version of making up looks with the mail order catalogue.'

'You never use a mail order catalogue,' said Kumari. 'You use the Internet, like everyone else.'

'Same thing,' said Lucy.

Sinead cleared her throat. 'According to the schedule I've got, the first event is drinks on Christmas Eve. We chose a cocktail dress. It has been altered to fit you, would you like to try it on?'

Kumari tried each outfit on while Sinead checked for fit and ticked it off her list. Lucy asked questions. When they got to the formal evening gown, Sinead said, 'I've requested these jewels for you to wear with it. The request has been approved.'

'Can I see?' said Lucy.

Sinead glanced at Kumari to check before saying, 'Of course.' She brought up the pictures on her tablet and passed it over.

Lucy whistled. 'Wow. Get a load of those.' She turned to Kumari. 'You get to wear the most incredible bling, you lucky thing.'

'It's not mine, I borrow it,' said Kumari as she came out from behind her changing screen, dressed in her dark-green evening gown. The dress had an embroidered sweetheart neckline. On Sinead's concept sketch, she had added an emerald necklace from Ben's mother's collection. The collection was full of amazing pieces of jewellery, as beautiful as they were precious. In her old life, she would have had to buy tickets to even look at them.

She stood still while Sinead checked the fit. The alterations meant that it fit perfectly.

'Just look at that dress. It looks amazing on you,' said Lucy. 'Can I touch it?'

Sinead reluctantly nodded. Lucy stroked the velvet skirt of the dress. 'So soft . . .' She shook her head. 'I can't believe you get to wear this stuff.' She pinched the fabric between finger and thumb, which made Sinead tut.

Kumari smiled. 'I think I'd best take this off, so it's in perfect condition for the day.'

Sinead unzipped it for her and she went back behind her screen.

'You really are living the dream,' said Lucy.

Kumari, who was now back in her dressing gown, ready for the next outfit, sat down on the couch and unbuckled her shoes. 'You know the best bit?' she said to Lucy.

'You can choose a best bit? It's all pretty amazing,' said Lucy.

'You'll appreciate this,' said Kumari. She lifted up the pair of shoes she had just removed. 'Made-to-measure shoes!'

'You are kidding,' said Lucy. For a second she was speechless. Lucy knew better than anyone the trouble Kumari had finding shoes to fit her long, thin feet.

'I know, right,' said Kumari. A bubble of hysterical laughter rose in her throat. 'I feel very special.'

Lucy's mouth twitched. 'Anyone would think you'd married a handsome prince . . . oh wait.'

They both started laughing. Sinead smiled patiently and gave them a few minutes before gently reminding them of the task at hand.

They were still going through everything when Ben arrived home and popped his head round the door to say hello to Lucy. 'How long will you be?'

'Another half-hour,' said Kumari.

'I'll go get the supper on, then,' said Ben.

'I'll come with you,' said Lucy. 'I never thought I'd have enough of fashion, but turns out I do have a limit. Who knew?' She blew Kumari a kiss. 'It was good to meet you, Sinead.' She let herself out of the door.

Kumari stood still while Sinead checked and pinned things. 'Sinead,' she said, 'are you sure about coming to Sandringham? I'm sure I can manage if you want to spend Christmas with your family.'

'Oh no, ma'am.' Sinead continued pinching and tucking as she spoke. 'It's your first visit to Sandringham. I don't want you to be there without me. Besides, I've never organised a wardrobe for the event by myself before and what if I've missed something? It would be so much quicker to sort out if I was there.'

'But you'll miss Christmas at home.'

'Oh, they'll be fine,' said Sinead. 'Anyway, I've booked my flight for the twenty-seventh already. There's no point trying to change it now.'

Kumari sighed. 'If you're sure . . .' she said. Although she felt bad about Sinead working over the holiday, she was also glad that she was going to be there. From what she'd been told, Christmas at Sandringham was a highly regimented formal affair with a bewildering number of outfit changes at specific times. Having Sinead there to help her get her hair and make-up ready before each portion of the event would be a great relief.

'I'm sure, ma'am,' Sinead said. She stood back and looked critically at Kumari. 'That's fine now,' she said and moved on to the next item.

By the time they'd finished with the clothing options, including drafting up options for events in January, Kumari was starving. She saw Sinead off and traipsed to the kitchen where Lucy was sitting on a bar stool, glass of white wine in hand, chatting to Ben as he stirred something on the hob.

Kumari paused at the doorway to savour the moment. Her best friend and Ben got on well. There had been an awkward few weeks when Lucy's short fling with Ben's best friend Rhodri had ended, but they seemed to have moved past that now.

Kumari smiled. The kitchen was her favourite room in the apartments. It was the only one with modern furniture. Everything was in glossy cream and dark granite. Tasteful to the extreme. As it would be, because the previous incumbent had been Ben's older sister Helena.

There was an aura of informality about this room. Ben had told her that when Helena lived there, he and Ophelia had often come round for dinner. He loved this kitchen too.

She stepped into the room.

Ben beamed at her. 'Hello, beautiful,' he said, and blew her a kiss. 'How did it go with the dress drama?'

'I think it's OK. Sinead is more nervous than I am.'

'Well, this is nearly ready,' said Ben. 'It's nothing fancy,' he said to Lucy apologetically. 'Just stroganoff and dumplings.'

'My favourite,' said Lucy.

They had a dining room, which they had yet to use. They preferred to take their meals informally in the kitchen, rather than go through to another room. Kumari set the table. She needed to talk to Ben about the ways in which she might help the Boost Her! charity, but it would have to wait until later.

'So, tell me about this jaunt to Sandringham then. How do royals spend their Christmas?' Lucy said over dinner.

'It's a family thing. Grandma likes to have all the immediate family round. Actually, she's very strict about that. We decorate the tree and do Christmas presents and play games, do jigsaws, that sort of thing. Regular family stuff,' said Ben.

'You make it sound like a normal family do,' said Kumari. 'It's so not. There's a timetable,' she said to Lucy. 'With times and venues and dress codes.'

'Like what?' said Lucy.

'Let's see . . .' said Kumari. 'On Christmas Eve there's a reception – for which we have to arrive exactly on time. Then cocktails, formalwear.'

'We do Christmas presents then,' Ben interjected.

'Right. Then a break and formal dinner, black tie.' Kumari glanced at Ben, who nodded. 'Christmas Day is breakfast, informal. Church, smart formal, followed by Christmas lunch. Then dinner, formal again, but not as formal as the night before . . . and then I think that's it.'

'There's the hunt on Boxing Day,' said Ben.

'Yeah, but we don't have to go to that,' said Kumari.

Ben paused, spoon halfway to his mouth. He lowered the spoon. 'Yes. We do.'

'But I don't agree with hunting,' said Kumari. 'You know that.'

'None of the Christmas event is optional. We have to go on the hunt. You don't have to shoot things, but we have to go.'

Kumari stared at him. She had just assumed that, as she and Ben both supported wildlife conservation charities, that they would both be exempt from the blood sport.

'Hunting is wrong,' she said. 'I'm not doing it.'

Ben rolled his eyes. 'It's just a pheasant shoot, Kumari.'

They stared at each other. Ben's mouth was set in a firm line. He had that determined look about him that Kumari hadn't seen in a long time.

'It's an important tradition,' he said quietly.

'I'm not going hunting,' she shot back, equally quietly.

They glared at each other over their meals.

'Er . . . guys,' said Lucy.

Oh. Kumari was jolted out of her staring competition. She'd forgotten about Lucy. She threw a quick glance at Ben. It wasn't fair to let this discussion ruin Lucy's evening. She glanced across at her friend, who was concentrating fiercely on her food. Ben gave her a tiny nod. Airing private grievances in public was not done. Not even in front of friends. They would discuss this later.

'I'm sorry, Lucy,' said Kumari. 'You don't need to get involved in this. Let's talk about something else.'

'Yes,' Ben said smoothly. 'What are you up to in the holidays?'

'I'm going home to Boston to see my family,' said Lucy. 'My brother and his wife had a baby, so I get to see my new nephew.'

'Oh, how lovely, when are you flying out?' Kumari asked. Now that they were on safer territory, the awkwardness passed.

They returned to the topic hours later when they were stacking the dishwasher.

'It's killing for entertainment,' said Kumari. 'I thought you supported animal welfare and habitat conservation charities.'

'Conservation, yes,' said Ben. 'There's a difference between that and animal preservation. Sometimes you need to control populations.'

Kumari opened her mouth to protest that this population was artificially maintained, but Ben forestalled her. 'We've talked about this, Kumari. I have to do it. It's tradition. It's important.'

'But I disagree with it.' This was important to her. All the other traditions, some sensible, some a bit strange, were mostly harmless, but this wasn't something Kumari could give in to. She had been brought up Buddhist, where not hurting others was paramount. She was pragmatic about it most of the time, but this, to her, was a clear-cut waste of life. 'I'm sorry, Ben, I feel really strongly about this. I don't want to have any part of it.'

'But—'

'And anyway, you and I, we're pretty much the antithesis of royal tradition. If your grandmother agreed to us getting married, I can't see her throwing a wobbly just because I don't want to go out and kill things.'

She saw Ben's pained expression and softened a little. 'I don't see why this is so difficult,' said Kumari. 'I'll leave early. You go to the shoot and join me later.'

'We can't do that,' said Ben. 'We can't leave early without a good reason. That's disrespectful to the monarch.'

'And we can't have that,' said Kumari, without rancour. Being 'disrespectful to the monarch' was a much bigger deal than it sounded. The queen commanded a certain respect even among her family. Kumari was constantly buffeting up against the limits of what she could and couldn't do. She was learning fast that while some boundaries could flex, there were others which had to be respected. Anything that appeared to snub the monarch was a definite no–no.

She carefully restacked the plates so that she could get one more in. She had huge respect for the queen, not least because she was an amazing lady, but this was important to her. They had a say in what she wore, what she said, where she went, what she did . . . she was damned if they were going to make her compromise on her moral stance as well. She straightened up. 'Nevertheless,' she said. 'I will not be party to killing creatures for sport.'

'Kumari . . .' there was a warning tone to Ben's voice.

'You don't understand—' Kumari began.

'No, Kumari, *you* don't understand.' Ben slammed the dishwasher shut so hard the glassware rattled.

Well. If he was going to be like that there was no point talking to him. Kumari turned her back to him.

Ben said nothing. She could feel him glowering. She began making two mugs of hot chocolate, smacking the mugs down and generally making more noise than was strictly necessary.

After a few minutes, Ben said, 'I don't think I've ever seen anyone make a warm and soothing drink so violently before.'

Kumari stopped moving and looked down at where she'd spilled some hot chocolate on the counter by stirring too furiously. The incongruity wasn't lost on her. She bit back a smile. 'Pass me a paper towel, would you?'

He came and stood next to her and wiped up the spill. 'I'm sorry I snapped.'

'And I'm sorry I don't understand,' she said. 'I want to, though. Explain it to me.'

He sighed. 'I'm not sure I can. It's important that I go.'

He put his arm around her waist and she laid her head against his shoulder.

'Please,' said Kumari. 'I don't want to see birds killed for no good reason.'

Ben sighed and pinched the bridge of this nose. 'OK.' He looked up. 'OK, how about this as a compromise? I'll tell Grandma that you're not coming out for reasons of moral objection and that I'm staying at the house to keep you company. In return you agree to come and make small talk at the lunch after the shoot.'

She would have preferred to not have anything to do with it, but she could tell from the set of his mouth that he had reached the limit of his negotiations. It was a fair compromise. 'Deal,' she said. 'Thank you.'

He smiled. 'If it makes you happy . . .'

'It's hard negotiating family and spouse,' she said. 'What we do this Christmas will set the pattern for later Christmases. Balancing it all is hard.'

'Especially with my family,' said Ben.

Kumari thought about her first Christmas with her ex-husband. 'Any family is difficult,' she said quietly. 'So long as we're still a team at the end of it, it'll all be fine.'

Ben pulled her closer and kissed the top of her head. Kumari sank into his embrace and forgot that there were other things she needed to talk to him about.

Chapter 32

The Paragon Record

Is Kumari ready for a royal Christmas?

In a few weeks Kumari, the new Duchess of Westbury, will attend her first formal Christmas at Sandringham. What can she expect?

The direct relatives of the queen must attend Christmas at Sandringham. The only reasons for absence are illness or being in service abroad – Prince Benedict, for example, missed Christmas celebrations when he was stationed in active service in the Middle East. The direct relatives include Her Majesty's children, grandchildren and great-grandchildren.

The royals arrive in strict order. The queen, who travels in her own private carriage which is attached to a regular scheduled train, is the last to arrive, so her family are waiting to greet her when she does.

The schedule over the Christmas period is strictly regimented and requires several changes of clothes. There are strict rules about what to do when. Kumari is in for a very interesting time. We are not the only ones to hope that the Duke and Duchess of Westbury will use the occasion to announce happy news of expansion to the family.

Turn to page 7 for a full run-through of the San-dringham Christmas schedule with dress codes and examples of what sort of food might be served.

Ben drove them in his own car. Two security vehicles followed them, but Kumari could easily ignore them and pretend it was just her and Ben, alone in a car, like normal people. Ben's car wasn't ostentatious. It would have passed for any other car. They had piled the presents, all carefully wrapped and labelled, in the back. Their luggage had been sent on ahead.

Kumari looked at Ben and smiled. She didn't often get to see him drive. They mostly got driven places in the company of serious security people.

Today, Ben looked more cheerful than she'd seen in weeks. It suited him. He wore glasses when he was driving. They suited him too. She'd always liked men in glasses, but with Ben it went to a whole new level. The glasses transformed him from the perfect prince that she'd seen on TV to her very own flawed but wonderful Ben. Sometimes it was nice to be able to forget about everything else and just enjoy being with the man she'd fallen in love with. She reached across and patted his thigh.

He gave her a smile that made her melt.

'Not far now,' he said. They drove up to some formidable-looking gates. The guard peered into the car. Ben gave him a cheerful wave. The guard touched his cap in a salute and let them through.

'Really not far now,' said Ben. His eyes sparkled.

'You're very excited about this, aren't you?' said Kumari. As her apprehension mounted, his excitement seemed to be increasing. She'd known these few days were important to him, but she hadn't realised quite how much.

'It's Christmas,' said Ben. 'This is what Christmas means to me. As kids, we always came here for Crimble. Regardless of where we were in the world, on Christmas Eve, we had to be back here for Grandma and Grandpa's Christmas bash. I'm excited because this year, I get to share it with you.' He grinned.

Kumari melted a tiny bit more. She often used to work the Christmas shift at the hospital, which wasn't exactly festive. If she wasn't working, she'd spent Christmas at home with Amma and Thatha – with lots of Christmas specials on the telly and the chance to catch up on much-needed sleep. Last year was the last such relaxed Christmas. Ben had said that Christmas was about family. There were only three people in the family she'd grown up in.

Ben's family, on the other hand, was huge. Besides, this was the full-on royal Christmas experience. The fear that she might do something hideously wrong formed a knot in her stomach. She took a deep breath. It would be fine. Ben would be there. So would Ben's sisters, father and stepmother, all of whom Kumari got on well with. She sighed.

A frown flitted across Ben's brow. 'You OK? You're not nervous, are you?'

'Well, I am a bit,' said Kumari. 'This is your family do. It would be scary enough even if they weren't the royal family!'

'You'll enjoy it once you get there. Grandpa, once he's had a good meal and a couple of cocktails, is a hoot.' He reached across and gave her hand a squeeze. 'And the food is always amazing.' He paused. 'I hope they have the crumble. I love the crumble.'

Kumari looked out of the window. Ben seemed so excited about all things Christmas and Sandringham, it was quite sweet.

She still needed to talk to him about Boost Her!, but she couldn't bring herself to puncture his Christmas cheer. She thought of her list of people who were on the decision-making committee at the Trust. Two of those people were Ben's sisters. Both would be there over Christmas, she was bound to be able to find a moment to chat to them.

Even though they had passed the outer gates, there was still quite a lot of land to drive through before you got to the house. Pasture rolled by, glittering with frost in the winter sunshine. The weather forecast had predicted snow, maybe even a white Christmas, but there was no sign of it so far.

'Here we go,' said Ben. The road curved and they were on the main approach to the house. Trees lined a straight avenue. At the end of the road, behind low, ornamental hedges, was Sandringham House, it's mismatched wings stretching out either side.

It was mostly made of red brick, with windows and the large central portico picked out in white. It wasn't symmetrical, more like an 'L' shape – the long main house and an extra wing on one side. Small domes and turrets dotted the roofline where different generations had added bits to the original building. She looked upwards. There were only three floors, not counting the dormer windows in the roof, but the place seemed to stretch for miles either side. She could well believe that it had over 700 rooms. They called it Sandringham House, but it was really a palace.

'Wow,' said Kumari. Even at this distance, it was impressive. 'That's amazing.'

Ben's grin widened. 'I love that you have that reaction,' he said. 'These places were built to inspire wonder.'

Kumari thought of the National Trust properties she'd been round on family holidays with her parents. Every year they had the debate about whether they'd visit enough places to make an annual membership pay for itself. Every year, they'd decided, quite correctly, that they wouldn't.

She had gone from that, to seeing palaces every other day. Prince Benedict, once one of the most sought after single men in Britain, was taking her to Christmas in Sandringham . . . with the royal family. It was like she'd left her life behind and stepped into a fairy tale.

They drove past the formal gardens. With topiary. How could you *not* be impressed by this? 'Are they just regular places to you?' she asked her husband. 'Don't you notice them anymore?'

'Not always,' said Ben. 'Every so often, I have a moment of "my goodness, that's a beautiful house". I suppose, if you were into it, you'd know about the architecture and histories that go with the houses. Now those are fascinating. My cousin, Georgie, went through a phase of spouting random facts about houses once.' He gave her a sideways glance. 'Do you remember Georgie?'

Yes, she remembered Georgie. She was a cousin. Some time ago, Kumari had been given a list of who was who, along with their formal titles and photographs. She'd scribbled down Ben's names for them along the margins. She was still more likely to remember their first names rather than keep track of who was duke or earl of what.

They arrived at the top of the drive, which then split off into the main sweep and a few side roads. Ben drove them round to a courtyard at the side, where a few other cars and four-wheel drive vehicles were parked around a neat square of grass. A couple of uniformed members of staff came running up. Ben jumped out and opened the boot for them to unload.

'Welcome back, Your Highness,' said one of the footmen, older than the others.

Ben said, 'It's Trent, isn't it? How are you?'

The man beamed. 'I'm very well, sir. It's a delight to see you.' He dipped his head in a bow. 'And you too, ma'am.'

'Likewise,' said Kumari.

'Shall we take these to the white drawing room?' said Trent.

'Yes, please,' said Benedict. He took Kumari's hand. 'Come on. I'll show you around.'

They crunched back across the fine, beige gravel to the main entrance where a butler was waiting for them. He took their coats. The entrance was a small, warm affair with pale, polished wood and lights in sconces. Ben ushered her through an arch into the saloon where people were sitting on the sofas or standing around chatting. There was a chorus of greetings. Everyone knew who she was, which wasn't surprising as she was the one who was new and, let's face it, her brownness stood out against the mass of white faces. Kumari had met them all at the wedding. Some she'd met again at various functions.

People had to arrive in order of 'seniority', which seemed to mean, roughly, that the higher in the order of succession you were, the later you turned up. Kumari and Ben had almost finished greeting everyone when Ophelia breezed in, resplendent in russet and orange. A few minutes later one of Ben's nieces hurtled in, heralding the arrival of Helena.

Ophelia greeted Kumari with an effusive hug. Helena, always more reserved, gave her a kiss on the cheek and a warm smile. Now that the children were there, the hum of conversation went up in volume a little.

Kumari finally understood what Ben had meant when he said they could kick back and relax. There was chatter and laughter as the various members of the family talked and teased each other. Two teenage boys – Ben's cousins – stood together looking awkward as their mother and aunt discussed their education. Cousin Georgie was sitting in one of the single armchairs, trying to look as inconspicuous as possible. Georgie's brother, Edwin, was talking to an uncle about something. Take away the antique furniture and the accents and it was pretty much the same as every large family gathering there ever was.

The Prince of Wales and his wife arrived. Soon afterwards a butler came in and rang a small bell. Everyone went quiet.

'Her Majesty and the Duke of Hereford will arrive in ten minutes,' the man said solemnly. There was a general drift to retrieve coats and go to the porch at the front of the house.

Kumari took her lead from Ben, standing next to him in the correct place. The rest of the royal family, even the children, knew exactly where to stand. She tended to have to count places until she got to where she was meant to be. It had been part of her training. She stood in between Ophelia and Ben, her warm coat buckled. She watched as Ben played with Maria, making the little girl's teddy pop up from behind her father. He was good with kids.

Helena caught her eye and raised her eyebrows. She glanced from Ben to Kumari and gave her a questioning look. The implication was clear. When are you going to have children? Everyone seemed to be obsessed with the subject – Ben's family, her family, the newspapers, even her mother's friend Sonali Aunty. Everyone wanted to know. Kumari rolled her eyes. Like it was anyone's business but theirs. Despite Ben being keen to have kids, they had agreed that they would give themselves a year to settle into life together before they thought about having children. She was glad he'd agreed to that, because there was so much of this life that was new to her, the thought of having to deal with pregnancy as well was just too much.

She watched as Ben made his niece laugh. He would make a great dad . . .

Her train of thought was cut short as the queen's car arrived. When the door opened to let the great lady out, all the men bowed their heads and the ladies, Kumari included, dipped a curtsey.

Her Majesty surveyed the gathering of her children, grandchildren and great-grandchildren and beamed. Her husband, the Duke of Hereford, came to stand beside her. He clapped his hands together. 'Well then, you lot. Let's get this party started.'

Kumari checked her dress in the mirror. Her hair and make-up had already been done for her by Sinead, who was currently getting out Kumari's jewellery. Given her minimal make-up style, it took relatively little time to do her face, but her hair, which she preferred to wear up, often took longer. The dress was a pink-and-blue shot silk cocktail dress with gold working on one shoulder. Her version was a little longer than the one the designer normally sold and had gossamer-light silk sleeves. It had been designed by an up-and-coming British–Nepali designer. Kumari smiled. One of the things she liked about being in the spotlight was being able to give smaller stores a helping hand.

Ben had asked early on that she try to wear British-made clothes wherever possible. This, she was happy to do. She put on a sapphire and diamond necklace that Ben had given her as a honeymoon present. It wasn't ostentatious and complemented her outfit.

Ben knocked on the connecting door. Sinead caught Kumari's eye. Kumari nodded. 'One second, Ben,' she said.

'Is there anything else you need?' asked Sinead.

'No. I think I'm OK,' said Kumari. She ran a mental checklist. Face, hair, dress, shoes, jewellery. All done.

'I'll be waiting when you come back up. I'll help you with the next dress.' Sinead bowed and left the room.

Kumari said, 'Thank you.'

She waited for the door to close and said, 'Come in, Ben.'

They had been given adjoining rooms, with a door linking the two. Both rooms had four-poster beds, covered with blankets, and a few other items of furniture, but no fireplace. Surprisingly, neither room was particularly big. After the acres of space in Kensington, the rooms felt tiny. But, Kumari reflected, looking around the room, still a good size.

With the curtains drawn, it felt dark, despite the lights. It was also a little chilly. There was a heater plugged into the wall, which wasn't turned on. Ben had assured her that the staff made sure the rooms were warm at bedtime, but had warned her that it took a while for the chill to lift in the morning. Kumari had asked her PA to pack her warmer pyjamas.

When Ben stepped into the room, Kumari did a little twirl. 'What do you reckon? Will I do?'

Ben grinned. He stepped closer and pulled her to him. 'Not a day goes by I don't marvel at how lucky I am to be married to you.'

She put her arms around his neck. 'You say the nicest things, my love.'

He kissed her nose. 'How are you doing? Are you still nervous?'

'A bit.'

'Well, you *look* fantastic.'

She stepped back from him and tweaked her skirt where it had been crushed. 'So what happens at this bit then?'

'We eat tiny cakes and sandwiches and catch up on the gossip. Grandma likes to have a good old natter about who's doing what and whose horses have foaled. She gets told all of this stuff anyway, but I think she likes to get a personal spin on things. Uncle Richard was saying he hasn't seen her outside of formal occasions since our wedding.'

He gave her his arm and they stepped out.

They walked companionably along the corridor, pausing to acknowledge the various members of staff they passed.

As they walked, Kumari started to worry about how she would fit in. Everyone had been wonderfully welcoming, but she'd made her first misstep two weeks ago. It was such a shame that it had happened just before she met the family again. Thinking of that reminded her of the Boost Her! initiative. She glanced at Ben. No time like the present. 'Ben,' said Kumari quietly.

'Mmm?'

'What would happen if we were to make an anonymous donation to a particular charity?'

Ben paused mid-step. 'Oh no, please tell me you didn't. Because we're in enough bother already with your unguarded comment to Victor.'

'That was an accident. I was just so shocked. I felt there must be something I could do. I promise I haven't done anything,' she said. 'I'm just asking what would happen.'

'I don't know, but I know it wouldn't be good. It's a case of, if it happens once, where would it end? We have systems in place for philanthropy, Kumari. They are there for a reason. I regularly pay into the running costs of the foundation. The foundation raises money and coordinates projects in a way that is open and transparent. Don't worry. It's a great cause. Something will come up.'

'But what if something is time-critical?'

'It can't be helped.'

'But—'

'There's a certain cadre of journalists who would love to get hold of a story that suggests that "the royal family are siphoning taxpayers money off to their cronies".' He made air quotes with his free hand.

'But I'm not talking about taxpayers' money. I'm talking about your private wealth.'

'I *know*, but it wouldn't make a difference. You can point that out until you're blue in the face, but no one will believe you. Don't you remember what you went through when they found out you were dating me? The tabloids . . . they're not after the truth. They're after scandal and any half-truth is enough for them to whip one up.' Ben stopped and took her hands in his. 'I'm sorry. We are not in a position to offer Boost Her! direct help, especially now that you've alerted people to the fact that you might try to. They will be watching everything that is connected to that charity now. *Everything.*' His eyes bored into hers. 'I thought you understood the gravity of this.'

'I do. But . . . there has to be something I can do! I can't let the project die before it's had a chance.'

'Kumari. The rules exist for a reason. Think about it. You're thinking you want to help someone who is doing a great job and happens to need some help urgently. You like them. You want to help, right?'

'Yes.' Was that so bad?

'Now imagine you're on the outside. You have a project, probably equally as worthy. You've tried to get the attention of a royal patron but haven't managed it yet. Or worse, you've met a royal and they've completely forgotten you exist. Then you see another charity being given special favours because someone in the royal family likes them more. How would you feel?'

She didn't have to think about it for long to know that he was right. It would look terrible. 'I see,' she said. She sighed again. 'I do.' They resumed walking down the corridor. 'It's just so . . . frustrating.'

'I know it's hard to stay neutral,' said Ben. 'But stay neutral we must.'

Even though she could see what he meant, the idea of sitting back and doing nothing made her feel so . . . trapped. What was the point of having power and influence if you couldn't use them to help people? All this softly, softly, carefully, carefully stuff was all well and good, but it wouldn't come through in time to save her project. As far as she could see, there was only one option – speak to everyone on the committee quietly to ensure the project got further funding and find a way to make a private donation to bridge the gap. There had to be a way of doing that without arousing suspicion. There had to be.

They had arrived outside the White Drawing Room. Voices spoke in plummy, aristocratic accents. Someone laughed. Kumari drew a deep breath. Here it was. Christmas with the family.

Ben gave her hand a squeeze. 'Are you OK?'

'Yes. I'm fine.' She pulled in a deep breath in preparation. 'Let's go.'

Ben leant closer. 'I love you,' he said. 'Even when you're nervous.'

She nudged him. 'Stop being corny.'

'But I do,' he said, batting his eyelids theatrically at her.

Kumari giggled, despite her nerves. 'I love you too, you goofball.'

Ben grinned at her. 'That's better.'

The White Drawing Room was . . . well, mainly white. White walls, white ceiling, white furniture with white upholstery. There was an enormous Christmas tree which appeared to have only lights on it. The heavy gold drapes had been drawn against the gathering darkness outside. Along one wall was a line of white-draped tables, with presents stacked in neat piles. As they walked past, Kumari noticed that each pile had a name label. Everyone had a pile.

She released Ben's hand so that she could accept a drink. She chose the non-alcoholic version.

Ophelia and Helena were sitting on a low chaise longue near the tree, with the two little princesses kneeling on the floor in front of them, looking through a box of decorations. Kumari went over to them. She pulled up a footstool and sat down, careful to keep her dress from being squashed.

'What have you got?' she asked Francesca.

The little girl looked up. She looked utterly adorable in her smock dress. 'I'm looking for my favourite one.'

Her younger sister, still barely out of toddlerhood, pulled something out, and threw it on the ground before diving in for another.

Kumari caught the next one as it came out. 'Maria,' she said gently. 'Be careful, please. Put each one on the ground like this.' She demonstrated, putting the bauble gently onto the carpet. 'It would be very sad if one of those broke because it was thrown on the floor.'

Maria looked thoughtfully at her.

Francesca rolled her eyes. 'She's always throwing things. She's such a baby.'

Seeing Maria's furious pout, Kumari said, 'No, she's not. She just forgot for a minute about being gentle. Right, Maria?'

Maria yanked another bauble out.

'Ooh. What's painted on that one?' said Kumari, leaning forwards.

Distracted, Maria peered at it too. 'Snowman,' she said.

Kumari glanced up at her sisters-in-law. They were chatting. Helena, who always had one eye on the kids, gave her an approving smile. Kumari had come to learn that from Helena, this was practically a hug and kiss.

She turned her attention back to the girls.

Francesca eventually found the teddy ornament that she was looking for and Kumari helped Maria find a new favourite for herself.

'Well then,' said a voice behind her. 'We can start decorating the tree.'

Kumari jumped. Ben's grandmother was standing next to her. She scrambled to get to her feet. The queen put a gentle hand on her shoulder to stop her.

'Now,' said the monarch. 'What shall we hang on the tree first.'

Kumari joined her sisters-in-law on the chaise longue and together they watched as the queen of England helped two tiny girls hang the first decorations on the Christmas tree.

At the other end of the room, the Duke of Hereford said, 'What, too old for decorating a tree now? Go on with you.' And soon the two teenaged boys ambled over and started to help.

Within minutes, boxes of decorations were being unpacked and handed out as various members of the family helped decorate the tree. The tree was gradually festooned with garlands and a random assortment of ornaments and a collection of gingerbread men that someone produced. There was no tinsel. When it was done, it looked like any other tree decorated with enthusiasm and love. A perfectly imperfect tree. The lower branches were festooned with clusters of baubles, while the higher branches, where the adults and teenagers could reach, were more balanced. A family tree, rather than a royal one.

Finally, Maria was asked to put the star on the top of the tree. She was hoisted onto Ben's shoulders and helped, with plenty of useless advice, to place the star in the 'right' place.

There was a smattering of applause from everyone else as Ben lowered his niece onto the floor. He took a bow.

A buffet was served at the further end of the room. Kumari brushed off her dress and got herself a couple of sandwiches and a tiny round Victoria sponge. She was delighted to see some squares of milk toffee, each with a cashew nut embedded in the top. She grabbed a few of those too.

She had learnt now that grazing was the way forward at these events. You ate just enough to take the edge off your hunger. Otherwise there would be no room for dinner.

Normally, if the queen was present, no one ate unless she ate, but tonight that rule didn't seem to apply. Kumari bit into her salmon sandwich and looked around as the family members wandered around, chatting. Ben, who had been talking to Georgie at the other side of the room, caught her eye and raised a questioning eyebrow. She smiled to let him know she was OK.

A movement to the side caught her eye and she turned to find the queen standing next to her, picking up a mini lemon tart. The old lady had so much presence that Kumari was always surprised at how small she was when you saw her close up.

'One shouldn't,' said the monarch. 'But we do love these.'

'I'm sure you're allowed at Christmas,' said Kumari.

The queen gave her an assessing look. 'Are doctors meant to encourage excess?'

'No, ma'am,' said Kumari. 'But sometimes we're pragmatic about things.'

'Yes,' said the queen, drawing the word out. 'To be pragmatic is a good thing ... when appropriate.' She smiled. 'And how are you, dear? Is married life agreeing with you?'

'Yes, thank you, ma'am.'

'Oh, please. No need to be so formal here,' said the queen. 'Come. Talk to me.' She made her way to an armchair. Kumari held her plate for her while she sank slowly into it. 'Thank you.' The old lady took her plate and indicated that Kumari should take a seat.

Kumari indicated the milk toffees. 'Thank you for including these. They're my favourite.'

'Ah. We asked if Chef knew any suitable Sri Lankan delights and he obliged.' The queen smiled. 'One of the benefits of the Commonwealth, you see. Recipes for everything.'

'Thank you,' said Kumari. 'I genuinely appreciate it.'

'It was our pleasure.' She popped a tiny lemon tart in her mouth and savoured it. After a few moments, she said, 'And how are you finding undertaking the royal visits?'

Kumari chose a straight-backed chair to sit in. 'They are ... harder work than I was expecting,' she confessed. 'But very rewarding. I'm enjoying them. I think I'm getting the hang of it.'

The queen gave her a shrewd look. 'Apart from that minor miscommunication the other week.'

Of course she knew about that. The queen, Kumari had come to realise, knew everything. 'Apart from that.'

'Have you come to terms with our need to be impartial?'

Nothing got past her, did it? Kumari considered bluffing, but realised that the monarch would probably see through it. She must get lied to all the time. Perhaps it was time to put all that training in how to say things without actually saying anything into practice.

'It's difficult,' Kumari said carefully. 'But I understand the need for it and I am sorry.' There must be some way she could help the charity and she intended to find it, but the queen didn't need to know that.

The old lady nodded slowly. 'You seem to be taking to public life very well. People love you and Benedict is very happy. I think you will be fine ... so long as you don't do anything rash.' Bright blue eyes flashed at her with amusement.

Dammit.

'Yes, ma'am,' said Kumari. Any action she took would have to be done very, very carefully.

Benedict, spotting his grandmother chatting to Kumari, came over.

'Ah, Benedict,' said the queen. 'Now I have both of you here ... when am I going to have another great-grandchild?'

'They've only been married five minutes, Grandma,' Ophelia butted in. 'Give them some time to enjoy themselves.'

'Children are not a burden,' said her grandmother. She glanced across the room where her husband was having an ostentatious game of hide-and-seek with the little princesses who were both, quite obviously, hiding behind the same curtain. 'Enjoying oneself and children are not incompatible.'

Benedict gave his grandmother a kiss on the cheek. 'All in good time, Grandma.'

'Don't leave it too long though,' said Benedict's Aunt Venetia. 'When I was your age, Ben, I already had Edwin and Georgie.'

'Don't listen to them, Kumari,' said Ophelia.

Kumari rolled her eyes and reflected that this was exactly the sort of thing she'd probably have had to put up with from her own aunties and grandparents, if she'd ever been in a position to see them.

After some time, the clock on the mantel chimed five o'clock. Ophelia nudged Kumari. 'Present time!' she said.

'You're almost as excited as the kids,' said Kumari.

'I can't wait for you two to see the presents I got you,' said Ophelia. 'I spent ages choosing them.'

It was quite a long, drawn-out affair as everyone had presents from everyone else. Since Kumari didn't feel she knew the queen well enough to buy her a full-on gag gift, she'd opted for asking Lucy to help her make a batch of fruit and cashew nut cake using Amma's recipe. Ben, on the other hand, had cheekily got her a set of 'granny racers' – a track with two wind-up toys of old ladies in wheelchairs, which you could race. She seemed delighted with this.

For Ophelia, Kumari had bought the brightest flashing Christmas tree earrings she could find. Helena got a set of fake tattoos with the names of a boy band on them. This made Helena smile. For Ben's father, she had picked up a set of glasses with wide-open eyes painted on. This made him laugh out loud. He had Ben's laugh, big and booming.

All around her, people were hooting with laughter or groaning in mock annoyance. Ophelia's present for Ben was a pair of pantomine dame glasses. He put them on to howls of laughter.

Kumari opened her own present from Ophelia, which was a commemorative mug with a truly awful image of herself and Ben on it and the legend 'Congratulations Prince Benedict and Kumar'.

'Kumar?' she said. She looked again at the picture, which was grainy and barely recognisable as her and Ben, and started to laugh. Ben took it from her and started laughing too. After that, everything was funny. It was the most wonderful evening.

Chapter 33

The Society Post

What do the royal family get each other for Christmas?

What do you get for someone who has everything? Choosing presents for the royals is always going to be tricky, so they opt instead for home-made presents or gag gifts. Here are a few choice gifts from last year:

Princess Francesca gave her great-grandmother a necklace made of pasta. Her Majesty is said to have worn it at lunch on Christmas Day.

Prince Benedict gave his brother-in-law, David, a T-shirt that said 'Property of She Who Must Be Obeyed'. He also gave Princess Ophelia a red, braided wig.

Princess Ophelia gave her grandmother a bottle of rhubarb gin, made with rhubarb from her boyfriend Dominic Heatherton's garden.

We don't know what presents will be exchanged this year, but we hope Kumari got the memo that cheap and cheerful is the way to go.

When Kumari got back upstairs, still flushed with laughter and liquor, Sinead was waiting for her, twitching with impatience.

'I'm so sorry,' said Kumari. 'I know I'm late.'

'We've got less than half an hour to get you sorted for the evening.' Sinead fussed around her.

Kumari smiled a little tipsily at her dresser. 'OK then . . . let's do this.'

She stepped out of her cocktail dress and stood in her shapewear while Sinead gently dropped the green gown over her head. Obediently, she raised her arms and turned so that Sinead could zip her up. The sweetheart neckline was heavily embroidered, but the rest of the dress was plain and form-fitted until it flared out slightly from her knees. The hem was embroidered the same way as the neckline. Translucent fabric covered her arms and shoulders.

Sinead nodded to herself as she tweaked the shoulders and hem so that everything sat just so.

Kumari stood patiently while Sinead checked whether her hair needed redoing, which it didn't. Thankfully, she could use the same shoes. She unhooked her earrings and necklace.

For the formal dinner, she had been lent a necklace from Ben's late mother's collection. She knew that Ben was wearing his diamond cufflinks made from her favourite bracelet. Helena and Ophelia, too, were wearing their mother's jewels. The necklace given to Kumari had emeralds in it, to go with her dress. There were earrings to match. They were so beautiful, she could have stared at them for hours. It was hard to believe she was actually allowed to wear them.

Putting them on, Kumari felt the weight of the jewels. Before she married Ben, she had always worn tiny stud earrings or none at all, so the idea that jewellery could be so heavy that it hurt had been a revelation. In the first few weeks after her wedding, she'd had constant headaches from the combination of necklaces, earrings and tiaras. It was easier now. Maybe her neck had become stronger.

She checked her reflection. The jewels looked lustrous against the smooth brown of her skin. Wow.

Her gaze travelled down to her stomach, which was flatter now than it had ever been, but still needed a good tug of spandex. She wasn't fat, as some of the papers liked to make out, she had a personal trainer who made sure of that, but no matter how toned she was, the newspapers found a way to comment on her 'curves'.

One day Ben had heard a visiting designer fussing about it and casually mentioned that he preferred a smooth arc to a harsh angle. The discussion about her becoming flatter had ended abruptly at that point. But designer dresses still demanded near concave stomachs, so Kumari wore shapewear. It was damned uncomfortable, but it made for much more flattering photographs.

'There,' said Sinead, carefully pinning the tiara into place. 'You look fantastic, ma'am.'

'All thanks to you, Sinead,' said Kumari. She smiled at the other woman. 'How are you getting on? Are you being well looked after here?'

There was a whole society 'below stairs'. It turned out that everywhere they went, the entourage staff were treated very well. But given the austere style of the main

369

bedrooms, Kumari was a little worried at the state of things for her team.

'I'm fine, ma'am,' said Sinead.

Kumari glanced at the heater and raised her eyebrows.

'We have those too,' said Sinead. 'And blankets. Mrs Pilding warned me, so I have brought my hot water bottle.'

'Very wise.' Kumari frowned. 'I wonder if I could have a hot water bottle too . . .'

'Oh yes,' said Sinead. 'It's already planned. Before you come up, one of the maids comes in and puts hot water bottles in the beds. It's a well-oiled machine, this house. I've never seen anything like it.'

Ben rapped on the adjoining door and walked in without waiting for a reply. Sinead, as always, snapped into a higher level of tension in the presence of the prince.

He was dressed in black tie. The cut of his jacket was such that it made his shoulders seem wider and his waist narrower. And, Kumari reflected, he never needed to wear spandex. 'Ready?' he said.

Kumari glanced at Sinead.

'All done,' said Sinead. 'Have a great evening, ma'am. Sir.'

'We will,' said Ben. 'These things are always great fun. I hope you've been made welcome, Sinead?'

'Yes sir, everyone is very kind.'

'Excellent.' He held out his arm to Kumari. 'Shall we, my love?'

This time they swept down the hall towards the ballroom, which was set to the side of the house. The walls were lined with paintings of battle scenes and a collection of antique weaponry.

'Your family likes weapons almost as much as they like their formal dinners,' Kumari commented as they walked past an impressive collection of knives.

Ben paused. 'Yes, I suppose we do,' he said. He tilted his head back and looked at the collection from top to bottom. 'The family have reigned for about a thousand years, and we created an empire based on conquest and trade . . . so yes. Warcraft and negotiation are what we do best. And both are better conducted on a full stomach.'

Kumari took in his profile, so familiar to her now, and saw for a moment the soldier he kept hidden. He was a man descended from people who had dominated a battle-field and ruled with absolute power. Here, in the home that he most associated with his family, it was clearer than any-where else. No wonder the hunt was mandatory. It was a symbol of the battles they'd won.

'You're different here,' she said quietly. 'You're more Prince Benedict than usual.'

He looked at her and his eyes softened. 'I'm sorry.' He raised her hand and kissed it. 'I didn't realise.'

'It's not a criticism,' said Kumari. 'I just like Ben the regular guy a bit better than the prince.'

Ben was silent for a moment. His gaze roved over the collection of weapons. 'Me too,' he said, eventually.

As they neared the ballroom, they were joined by Ophelia, who was striding along talking to the older of her teenage cousins.

'Oh, I say,' said Ophelia, looking at Kumari's outfit. 'You've got the emeralds.'

'It's fine,' said Ben, too quickly.

'What about them?' said Kumari. A flash of panic. Was she not supposed to wear them? Why had they been signed off, if not? 'Is there something I should know?'

'It's fine. Don't worry.' Ophelia glanced around to check for listeners, which, given the number of staff around, were a great many. 'Just don't be surprised if the pater gets a bit misty-eyed over them. He got them for Mummy as a present. I think they were a favourite.'

'Oh,' said Kumari. 'I didn't know. Sinead must not have either or—'

'Worry not,' said Ophelia. 'He'll be fine. Step-ma is pretty good at cheering him up.'

'She's very understanding about his grief,' said Kumari, as they fell into step with one another.

'She was widowed when she was pretty young, herself,' said Ophelia. 'Her husband came off his horse. Wasn't wearing the proper headgear and . . . it didn't end well. Anyway, she was wonderful when Mummy . . . you know. So when they finally got together a few years later, none of us were really surprised. They understand that they both loved someone else before and that grief and love never really go away. They just get muted with time.'

They arrived at the ballroom. Ben took Kumari's arm again and the cousin took Ophelia's.

The ballroom was opulently decorated. Unlike the saloon, which had a homely feel, this was more formal and looked like someone had gone mad with the gold leaf. The walls were covered with ornate silk wallpaper, which was warm and dark in contrast to the glints of gold on the mouldings. The high ceiling held two huge chandeliers. Everything seemed to glow softly in the light.

An enormous Christmas tree, decorated in red and gold, stood at one end of the room. The table was already set in formal silver and they were led to their seats by a footman.

Kumari was seated in between Ophelia and Helena's husband, David, while Ben was between Helena and cousin Georgie.

Dinner, all the many courses of it, was delicious. Kumari noticed that there was crumble and custard listed as one of the puddings. Ben would be pleased. She was now used to making small talk with whomever she ended up sitting next to, so with the good food and a glass of wine, she relaxed as the evening wore on. Helena's husband, David, in a clear attempt to make her feel at home, kept explaining this tradition or that to her. It had the effect of reminding her that she wasn't part of this close-knit set. Not yet.

After dinner, the ladies withdrew to one of the drawing rooms for coffee.

'The men get to go and have drinkies,' said Ophelia. She rolled her eyes.

'What if you wanted to have an after-dinner drink?' said Kumari. All she really wanted right now was coffee and a mint.

'Oh, there are ways,' said Ophelia. 'But if you just popped over there, Granny would have a blue fit. She's very laid-back about some things and a real stickler for tradition about others.'

The queen, looking splendid in a pale-blue gown, was in deep conversation with Helena. Kumari and Ophelia sank onto a sofa a little distance away. An aunt came to join them.

'How are you getting on, Kumari? Learning the ropes, I dare say.'

'I am, thank you.'

'You've done a splendid job choosing your dresser. She's made some inspired choices for you of late. Very impressive.'

This assumed that Kumari had no input into her dress choices whatsoever, but Kumari let it pass. 'I'll be sure to let her know you said so,' she said politely. 'It means a lot to her.'

'Benedict seems to be taking to married life well,' the woman carried on. 'We're all so glad to see he's settled down. He was such a tearaway when he was younger, we were all genuinely worried for him.'

'Yes.'

'How are you finding the traditions here at Sandringham?' She pronounced Sandringham with extended vowels.

'It's very interesting,' said Kumari. 'Classy,' she added in her strongest Yorkshire accent.

Beside her, Ophelia gave a snort of laughter, which she covered up with a cough. The aunt gave her a curious glance, then returned her attention to Kumari.

'Do your parents mind that you're not spending Christmas with them?'

'Not at all,' said Kumari. 'We'll be meeting them later in the week. We'll be spending New Year together.'

Her mother had always worked on Christmas Day while Kumari and her father usually had a quiet lunch together and watched the Queen's Speech before one of them had to go to pick her mother up from work. They did Christmas dinner whenever Amma had her next day off. If Kumari didn't go home for Christmas, that was accepted without comment. It was all very laid-back, because it was just a fun holiday to them. The New Year though, that was a symbolic new beginning. They always liked her to be home for that.

The aunt was still talking. 'Then of course there's the hunt on Boxing Day, when the extended family show up,' she said. 'I'm looking forward to that. It's a nice bracing walk. And it's always a good lunch and a catch-up.'

Kumari's gaze flicked towards the queen. Had Ben told her that she would not be going to the shoot yet? Unlikely, as it hadn't been mentioned. She wondered why he was so reluctant to talk to his grandmother about it. He hadn't hesitated to speak to her when he wanted to propose to Kumari and that had been a far bigger issue that risked his grandmother's disapproval. There must be more to this than he was letting on. She frowned. She needed to get to the bottom of it as soon as she could.

While coffee was a gentle affair, the level of noise went up considerably when the men rejoined them. There was a raucous game of charades, which Kumari threw herself into with gusto. She and Ben were so good at guessing each other's mimes that they were banned from playing on the same team. Ben had mentioned that the family were competitive, but she hadn't realised how much. As she watched them good-naturedly tussle to come out on top, she was once again reminded that this was a family that did not like to lose at things. Not even granny racing.

Kumari was fuzzy with drink and laughter and practically asleep on her feet by the time the evening wound up. It was around midnight. She and Ben made their way back to their rooms and found Sinead asleep on a chair outside Kumari's room.

'Sinead?' said Kumari. 'What are you doing here?'

Sinead startled awake. 'Oh. Oh.' She shot to her feet. 'I thought you might need some help with . . .' Her eyes darted to the jewellery and then to Ben, who had his arm firmly tucked around Kumari's waist. 'Oh.'

'I think we'll be fine,' said Kumari. 'You go to bed.'

When Sinead hesitated, Ben said, 'I'll make sure the right bits of jewellery go into the right boxes.' He gave Kumari a mischievous grin. 'I might even help her out of everything else.'

Kumari kicked his ankle. 'Ignore him,' she said to Sinead. 'Go to bed. I'll need you to be alert tomorrow, because I certainly won't be.'

Leaving Sinead to make her way to her own room, Kumari ushered Ben in and shut the door. 'Honestly, Benedict,' she said, with mock severity. 'Poor Sinead didn't know where to look.'

Ben turned her so that he could put his arms around her. 'Oh, come on. I'm sure she knows I'm capable of getting you out of your clothes without help.'

'She's just worried about the jewellery. If I lose something, she and I are both going to get it in the neck.'

'Can't have that,' said Ben. 'Let's get those packed up.'

She sat on the bed and he removed the tiara. The box was already laid out on the dressing table. While Ben put it away and locked up the box, Kumari removed her shoes and the rest of the jewels. Handing these to Ben, she rolled her head, trying to ease the tension in her neck.

'Still getting a sore neck?' he said, rubbing it gently.

'A little.' She yawned. 'I don't know how your grand-mother keeps going. I'm exhausted.'

'Oh, I don't think Grandma sleeps very much.' He carefully stacked the locked jewellery boxes.

She stood up and reached for the zip on her dress.

'Here, let me help.' Ben unzipped her dress slowly, making a shiver run down her spine. She shrugged the dress off her shoulders and let it slide to her feet. Now she was wearing only tights and shapewear. There was no sexy way to remove shapewear.

'Sorry about this,' she said and started to peel it off herself.

Ben sat on the bed and watched her with an expression of fascination and horror. 'I don't know why you need to wear that stuff. It looks bloody uncomfortable.'

'It is,' said Kumari, forcing the garment past her hips. 'But I have to, given that the newspapers are obsessed with the size of my midriff, in case I'm pregnant.'

'It's a very lovely midriff,' said Ben. 'I love your midriff.' He reached forward and touched the red lines where the spandex had dug into her skin. 'I could ask them to leave you alone,' he said. 'Again.'

'I think once was enough,' said Kumari. She finally peeled the shapewear off. 'Oh my God, that's so much better.' She stretched.

Ben pulled her closer and kissed her stomach. 'I wish you didn't have to wear those things,' he said. 'You're beautiful as you are. Soft.'

Kumari sighed. 'It would be nice,' she said. 'But the world demands skinniness.'

'The world doesn't know what it's missing,' said Ben.

She reached for the brushed-cotton pyjamas that had been laid out for her. Ben caught her hand and kissed it.

'Oh, come on, Ben,' she said. 'I'm cold.'

His gaze met hers and he gave her a slow smile. 'I'm sure I can think of a way to fix that.' He stood up and pulled her hard up against him. 'Might be able to help with the speculation too.'

Kumari laughed. 'You are so drunk.'

Ben chuckled against her collarbone. Suddenly, she wasn't quite so tired anymore. She snuggled into him and breathed in the familiar summer and woodland smell of him. 'God, I love you,' she said.

'Let's go to bed,' he said. 'Mine's bigger.' And he swung her up in his arms and carried her through the connecting door to his room.

Chapter 34

Cause Celeb Magazine

Princess shoutouts

It's Kumari's first Christmas as a royal. What does it mean to you? We took to Twitter to find out (Twitter handles redacted).

OMG, I love seeing a brown girl in the formal royal family photos! Princesses come in all colours!

When I was a kid, I wanted to be Princess Jasmine from Aladdin, but I didn't like the harem trousers she wore. Now my daughter wants to be Kumari . . . and she knows she can wear whatever the hell she likes. #PrincessKumari FTW

Love the pictures of Prince Benedict hamming it up in an Xmas hat to make #Kumari laugh. Could those two get any cuter?

Looks like Kumari is winning hearts everywhere. We totally adore her. Check out the special where our fashion editor comments on all the outfits Kumari has worn in public since she became the Duchess of Westbury.

They were woken up the next morning by polite knocking. Kumari didn't want some butler seeing her in her dishevelled pyjamas so she slipped out of bed and back into her room. As the connecting door closed behind her, she heard Ben tell the butler to come in. The maid had already been in her room. Everything was tidy and a tray with a lidded platter and a teapot with a tea cosy over it were on the bedside table.

Kumari poured herself a cup of tea and climbed into bed. Sitting back against the pillows, she closed her eyes and savoured a moment of contentment. She had navigated the family evening without upsetting anyone. Her husband loved her. And now she had a lovely cup of tea brought to her bedside. Things didn't get much better than this.

With the first sip of tea, she realised she was hungry. She thought about how she'd worked up her appetite and smiled. She could murder a bacon sandwich.

Kumari lifted the lid. Fruit. She looked at it with some concern. That wasn't going to keep her going until lunchtime, especially as there was a brisk walk to the chapel at eleven.

She popped her head through the door into Ben's room. He was sitting in bed with a cup of coffee, looking bleary-eyed.

'I have a plate of fruit in my room,' she said.

'Yes. The ladies get that.'

'What do you get?' There was no evidence of toast or any other breakfast on his side table. She remembered the gents were supposed to have breakfast a bit later. Downstairs.

'The full works,' he said.

'Can I come?'

He looked thoughtful for a second. 'Don't see why not. Ophelia used to come sometimes, if she'd been out riding.'

'I think I'm going to go for a run first. Want to come with me?'

Ben looked like he was going to refuse, but eventually he sighed. 'You're right. That is a good idea. OK. Give me a few minutes to get straight. Let's do it.'

After a pleasant run through the estate with Ben, Kumari showered and dressed in her formal church outfit: a simple woollen dress with a brooch at the shoulder as an accent. Given that she had to walk a fair distance, Sinead had paired it with chunky heeled boots. There was a coat, hat and scarf to complete the outfit, which she would wear later. Ben knocked on her door and they went down to the breakfast room together.

Ophelia was there, still in her riding gear. Apart from that, the room was full of men and boys, all tucking into a fried breakfast. Kumari loaded up her plate and sat down.

'Eating for two?' said David.

Kumari caught Ben's eye and saw him trying not to laugh.

'No,' she said. 'This is all for my little self.'

'Don't let him get to you,' said Ophelia. 'He's just getting his own back from all the pressure when he and Helena got married.'

David grinned. 'You think it's bad for you. Imagine being responsible for bringing the next heir into the world.'

'Well, it's not like you had the difficult bit, is it?' said Ophelia.

'Suppose not,' he said. He gave her an evil grin. 'I can't wait until it's your turn.'

'Hmph,' said Ophelia.

'Well, it must be coming around soon,' he said. 'You and Dominic have been together for a while now. He must be ready to pop the question soon.'

'All in good time,' said Ophelia. 'I'm not in a hurry.'

David was suddenly sober. 'Is he feeling the nerves? Would you like me to have a discreet chat, man to man?'

Ophelia didn't respond immediately, but finally said, 'No, thank you. It'll be fine. As I say, I'm not in any pressing hurry. You've done your bit producing an heir and a spare, rather takes the heat off me.'

They ate in silence for a few minutes. Ben's uncle sat down. 'Will you be joining us at the church today, Kumari?'

'Yes, I will,' she said. While she herself had no problem with going to the church service, she had made sure to check that Ben's grandmother and the local priest would have no objections to someone who didn't believe coming to the service. Neither had minded.

'You are . . . Buddhist?'

'Lapsed Buddhist, I guess. More or less agnostic.'

She braced herself for a predictable set of questions about how her lack of faith clashed with being married to one of the royal family, who were meant to be Defenders of the Faith.

'I see.' He ate a few mouthfuls thoughtfully. 'Fascinating religion Buddhism.'

'Yes.'

'I met a chap once who discussed the teachings of the Buddha in terms of atomic physics. Astonishing stuff, really. He was an astrophysicist and a monk, so I imagine he knew what he was talking about.'

Kumari was taken aback. She hadn't been expecting that. Ben's family had a habit of doing this. Just when she felt she understood what they were about, they threw a curve ball at her. The work they did was more than a mere task to them. They worked in such a wide variety of areas that sometimes they came across things that chimed strongly with them. So they all had sections of their work that they were passionate about. 'That does sound interesting,' she said. 'Do you remember who it was?'

'Not off-hand, but I'm sure I can get my aide to dig out the information for you. I read a couple of his newspaper articles – the more accessible stuff, if you like. Genuinely amazing.' He smiled at her. 'How are your projects going? You had an interesting project educating girls in Africa, I believe?'

'That one *was* going really well, actually,' she said. 'But it's just had its funding pulled. It's very upsetting.'

'I can imagine,' he said. 'I suppose they must wait for the next round of funding from the foundation now to get help.'

'Oh, is that the Lesotho programme?' said Ophelia.

Kumari brightened up. 'Yes,' she said. 'They're going to apply to the Foundation.' Ophelia was on the committee. This was the perfect chance to bring it to her attention. 'Did I show you the report they sent a few weeks ago? They're doing great work. Not only on the project, but in the local area too.' She gave them a quick outline of it.

'Sounds like it would be a real shame to see it close,' said Ophelia thoughtfully.

Kumari felt a spark of satisfaction. At least one member of the decision-making committee was on side. She glanced across at Ben. He would probably have to abstain from voting too, given that his wife was closely linked to the project. But what would he think of making a private donation to cover the gap between the end of one funding stream and the start of another?

If she went through with her plan of making an anonymous donation, she'd run the risk of someone finding out. If that happened, she'd have to beg for forgiveness, which, given the number of warnings she'd had, might not be given. Still, it would be worth it. Wouldn't it? What's the worst that could happen?

She glanced at Ben. The royal institution being annoyed with her, she could deal with, but she wasn't sure she could cope with Ben being disappointed in her.

Ben misunderstood her expression and patted her arm. 'I'm sure something will come up, my love.'

She gave him a half-hearted smile. 'Yes,' she said weakly.

It was a grey day with a sharp chill that bit at ears and noses. Even bundled up in her warm coat, hat, scarf and gloves, Kumari could feel the cold. The brisk walk and the hearty breakfast helped a lot. If she'd relied on the platter of fruit that was sent to her room, she'd have frozen to death by now.

People lined the path leading to the parish church, despite the chill in the air. The royal party walked as a big group, with Ben's father at the head. Kumari walked hand in hand with Ben. People waved to them as they went past and shouted Christmas greetings. Ben seemed to recognise some of them. Apparently, there were those who came every year. One, an old man in a wheelchair, was greeted by name by several members of the party. A retired employee of the 'big house'.

There was an atmosphere of good will. Kumari forgot her earlier preoccupation and smiled, feeling genuinely buoyed by the mood. The group reached the church and lined up, in the correct order, to greet the queen when her car arrived.

The service was not long. It was warm and moving. The family sat in the first few pews and the locals crowded the rest of the church.

After the service, they walked back. Ben's Uncle Richard started whistling. Ophelia bickered good-naturedly with one of the aunts. The two teenagers were having an involved discussion about a movie. Kumari shot a sideways glance at Ben, handsome in his buttoned-up great-coat. He looked happier and more relaxed than she'd ever seen him before in public. This is what Christmas at Sandringham meant to him. Not formality and fine dining. It was about being with his family and being at peace with who he was. Something that didn't happen automatically, even for princes. This was what 'family' meant to Ben. There were only three people in her family, so she hadn't understood it before. She squeezed his hand, happy that he was happy.

Thank goodness they had found a compromise around her not going to the shoot the following day. If they hadn't she would have been dogged by a sense of resentment for being forced to support something she found wrong. She would have hated for that to ruin Ben's Christmas.

And, given that what she did the first Christmas would set the pattern for later ones, ruin every single Christmas after that.

The adults went straight to the Christmas lunch – which was lavish, but informal enough for there to be no seating plan and no starters. It still involved starched, white napkins and silver candelabra on the table. The meal centred around a beautifully roasted turkey, which was carved at the table by the chef. There was every sort of side dish you could ask for – vegetables, potatoes (both roast and mashed), a variety of sauces. Ben, who liked pigs in blankets, managed to sit so that he was directly in front of them. Everyone ate sparingly because there was more to come. Kumari ended up seated next to Georgie, who shyly told her about her interest in virtual world-building.

At the end of the main meal, an enormous Christmas pudding was brought in by a steward, placed on the table and set alight. An involuntary 'ooh' went around the table as the blue flame caught. The steward cut the pudding and waiters distributed the portions. The whole thing ran like a choreographed dance.

'Are you looking forward to the shoot tomorrow, Kumari?' said one of the uncles.

Kumari shot a glance at Ben. He gave a minute shake of the head. Wait? Hadn't he told them she wasn't coming? Whyever not?

Though she was furious, she couldn't drop Ben in it, so the best she could do was be non-committal. 'Um . . .' she said. 'I'm not sure how I feel about it.'

'Ah. First time?'

'It would be, yes.'

'It's tremendous fun. You'll love it,' he said.

Thankfully, someone asked him to pass the brandy butter and he was distracted enough to move on.

Kumari quietly fumed that Ben hadn't told his grandmother yet. She had asked him days ago. He seemed to sense that she wanted to talk to him and avoided eye contact through the whole of the cheese course.

She tried to grab a few moments with him after the meal, but the whole family ended up in the drawing room again to watch the Queen's Speech on the large screen that had been wheeled in while they were having lunch. The only member of the family who wasn't there was the monarch herself, who, apparently, didn't want to hear what people had to say.

She leant in and whispered to Ben. 'Did you have the chance—'

He said, 'It's starting.' Someone else shushed him.

Kumari normally watched the speech with her father. They would each have a cup of tea and a mince pie and listen in silence until the end. Sometimes, Kumari would only watch the opening lines and then pick up a book.

Here, everyone stood up for the national anthem and settled back down again, glasses of port in hand. Every so often someone would comment on what they thought Her Majesty was referring to. Or point out what she'd left out. They would immediately be shushed by the rest of the family. Kumari looked around her at the roomful of people she had grown up seeing on TV and remembered with a jolt that she was part of this family now.

She glanced at Ben, who was watching his grandmother on the screen, a small smile on his face. She had married this man and now she was somehow spending Christmas with the queen. She was so busy with trying to keep up from day to day, that sometimes she forgot what it all really meant. She, who had been a relative nobody, now had access to powerful people. In fact, she *was* a powerful person. She thought about the Boost Her! initiative. A small part of her thought about Ben's explanation of how people might feel she was using her power to unfair advantage and felt a bit bad about it. If she were looking in from the outside, she would definitely have hated to see that. But what use was power if you didn't do good things with it? And where did you find the line that divided 'helping' from 'corruption'?

There was a small cheer and Ben nudged her. 'She said, "New additions and expanded horizons", that's us.'

Kumari smiled at him. Yes. Expanded horizons. She was only just realising where the limits of those horizons were.

Chapter 35

The Times Echo

Britain set for post-holiday freeze

Severe weather warnings are in place all over the country as the Met Office warns of snow, ice and blizzard-like conditions set to sweep across the country tomorrow. While all efforts are being made to keep the road networks open, police are warning against any unnecessary travel.

'If at all possible, why not extend your Christmas stay a little longer and avoid travelling on the 27th and 28th of December,' said a spokesperson for the RAC.

Widespread disruption is expected on the rail networks and air travel is expected to be delayed. If you are due to fly out on the 27th or 28th, please check the status of your flight before you set off for the airport.

Finally, there was time to relax and do as they pleased in this highly regimented holiday. She caught up with Ben and slipped her arm through his.

'Back to our chambers?' she said sweetly.

Ben side-eyed her. 'Sure.'

They walked off together, neither of them speaking. Even though she was almost rigid with anger, Kumari held it together until they made it to Ben's room. As soon as the door clicked shut, she rounded on him. 'You haven't spoken to the Queen about the hunt? You said you would. You've had plenty of opportunity, Ben. Why haven't you?' When he said nothing, she continued. 'I am not going on this hunt. If you're too scared to tell her, I will.'

Ben sighed and ran a hand over his eyes. 'It's not her . . . I'm not afraid of telling her. She will understand, I'm sure. She seems to like you.'

'Then what's your hold-up?' She put her hands on her hips. In the back of her mind, her decorum coach chided her 'a lady does not stand like a common soldier'.

'It's me.' He sat in one of the chairs and stared at the ground, his hands weaving over and over each other. 'You see, I'm trying to decide how I feel about the whole thing. On the one hand, you feel strongly about hunting for sport. I respect that. On the other hand, I don't have the same qualms about it as you do. It's just a way of life around here. And going on the shoot . . . I've been going out there with my dad and my grandpa for as long as I can remember. It's a touchstone. Something that doesn't change.'

He paused for a second, as though searching for the right words. When he spoke again, his voice was low. 'When my mother first fell ill . . . Christmas was terrible. She was trying to enjoy the holiday as if things were normal, but we all knew that she was dying . . . we were torn between the hope that something would save her and the knowledge that it probably wouldn't.' He gave a half laugh. 'Stupid as it sounds, I hoped there would be a Christmas Day miracle . . . On Boxing Day, she was exhausted and Daddy didn't want to leave her side, so Grandpa took us out. And for the first time in days, I was concentrating on something else . . . on shooting and spotting . . . and I forgot that things were bad. It was the only day in that awful time that I remember being normal.' He looked up. 'So the shoot isn't just a shoot to me. It's important. But so are you. And I feel I should support you and stay away . . . but I just . . . don't want to.' He sighed again. 'I'm sorry, Kumari. I can't explain it any better than that.'

Kumari let her arms drop. All anger evaporated. 'Oh, Ben.' She carefully knelt in front of him. 'I didn't know. I should have realised.' She took his hands in his. 'Listen. This is my issue. Not yours. You don't have to stay behind to keep me company. I understand.'

He looked into her face. 'But you're my wife,' he said. 'We're a team. Whatever your choice, I must support you. I want to.'

She rested her palm against his cheek. 'But being here, all this tradition, it makes you happy. I want more than anything for you to be happy. Let me talk to your grandma. I'll explain. And then I'll stay behind. I'll be here when you get back. See. No big deal.'

He stared at her for a long moment. 'Are you sure?'

'Of course. Just because we do some things separately, doesn't mean we're not a team.'

Kumari was still thinking about this when she went to her room for yet another change of clothes. This time it was fairly quick as it didn't involve a formal ballgown. It did involve jewellery, though. A simple necklace with a diamond pendant from the queen's collection. Sinead fussed around her, pinning her hair in place.

'It's lovely having all these beautiful things to wear, but I've forgotten what it's like to wear the same outfit for a whole day,' Kumari grumbled.

'It's tradition,' said Sinead. 'It's quite fun to do, as a design challenge. It's not often you have to work on a winter wardrobe that includes the outdoors and the indoors all in one afternoon. I helped Mrs P out with Princess Ophelia's wardrobe last year. She had the most incredible gown.'

Kumari cast an eye at her reflection. This dress was fairly simple, compared to the rest of the outfits. A soft-grey wool dress with burgundy accents, with tights, naturally, and burgundy pumps.

Sinead finished her hair with a clasp that was the exact same colour as the accents on the dress. She seemed to have something on her mind.

'Is something the matter?' Kumari said.

'I was wondering if you would be needing me later tonight?' said Sinead, her face colouring.

Kumari thought of the night before. 'I'm sure I'll be fine,' she said, smiling.

'I was . . . wondering if you would mind if I left this evening instead of tomorrow morning. My flight to Ireland isn't until the twenty-seventh, but it would be good to get some things done before and—'

'Oh, Sinead, of course!' Kumari remembered that she had a present for her. 'Wait a minute. I have something.' She went to the wardrobe where she had put the small bag she had brought with her. It was the only way she could think of to smuggle in a present without Sinead being the one to unpack it. She extracted an envelope. 'Here. Merry Christmas.'

Sinead took it, looking puzzled. 'But, ma'am, I've already had a—'

'That was your official present. This is from me,' said Kumari. 'Go on. Open it.'

Sinead pulled out a letter and a printout of the cocktail menu from a bar in London. She had once let slip that she and her best friend went there every month after payday and were working their way through the menu.

'It's a voucher entitling you to two of each of the cocktails on their menu and three super-secret ones,' said Kumari.

'You remembered . . .' said Sinead in an awed voice.

For a second Kumari was confused. Of course she remembered. Sinead was one of the few people she saw every day. She was a friend. But, she realised, to Sinead, she was just her client. Power was great, but it was also lonely.

'I called them myself,' she said, in case Sinead thought she'd got her PA to do it. 'Martin, the owner, seems like a lovely bloke.'

'Thank you,' said Sinead, a catch in her voice. 'This is so lovely.' She moved towards Kumari, as though she was going to give her a hug but stopped. 'Thank you,' she said again.

'Have a lovely Christmas, Sinead. You get off early. I'll be fine. Thank you again for working over Christmas.'

'Oh, it was a pleasure,' said Sinead. 'I've never been to Sandringham before. I've always wanted to see what it was like.'

'Good.' Kumari smiled. 'I hope your flight is OK on the twenty-seventh.'

Sinead tucked the envelope into her pocket and tidied up the last of the hair products. 'The weather forecast isn't great. There's a snowstorm coming that day. I'm hoping I'll be able to leave before it hits. Luckily, it's only a short-haul flight. Should be fine.' But her voice sounded anything but certain.

Kumari made a mental note to speak to someone about the travelling conditions as soon as she could. Her parents were coming down on the twenty-eighth, which put them right in the middle of the predicted snowstorm. It might be better if she could get them down to Kensington Palace a day or two early. She would much rather they were stuck in London with her, than snowed in in their house in Yorkshire. Although, when she stopped to think about it, they might prefer to be at home. Hmm. One more thing to sort out.

She waved goodbye to Sinead and let herself into Ben's room through the adjoining door. He was staring out of the window. Kumari allowed herself a second to admire him. Tall and broad-shouldered, he could really carry off a suit. It was just as well, really, considering he had to wear them so much. He turned. His blue eyes caught her gaze. He smiled, eyes softening, and Kumari couldn't help but smile back.

She held her arms out towards him. 'Ready?'

He crossed the room in a couple of strides and took her hands in his. 'Of course. Let's go and see Grandma.'

It wasn't going to be easy to catch the queen before they went into the hall and sat down. Once they were seated, it would be awkward for them to go up to the head of the table to speak to her, so they would have to talk to her at pre-dinner drinks. Kumari scanned the room as soon as she got there and spotted the monarch sitting with her dogs by the fire, seemingly deep in conversation with one of Ben's uncles. Kumari gripped Ben's hand and marched over.

Ben cleared his throat. The uncle looked up. 'Ah, Benedict. Kumari,' he said.

The queen, who seemed absorbed in scratching behind the dog's ears, said without looking up, 'Did you want to speak to us, Kumari?'

'Um . . . yes, ma'am. It will only take a few minutes.'

'Certainly,' she said. 'If you'll excuse us a moment Freddy.' She carried on petting the dogs.

It was awkward towering over the older lady, so Kumari knelt on the floor. So did Ben.

'It's about the Boxing Day shoot tomorrow,' said Ben.

'I don't . . . I won't be joining you,' said Kumari. There was no point tiptoeing around it.

The queen levelled a stern glance at her.

'I mean,' said Kumari, realising her mistake. 'I would like permission to not attend.'

'I see. And you have a good reason, one presumes?'

'I don't agree with hunting for sport, ma'am.'

The queen's sharp blue eyes, the same colour as Ben's, looked into Kumari's. 'A moral objection, then,' she said. 'Very well. We must live according to our conscience.'

Was that it? Was it that easy? Why had Ben been so worried? 'Thank you, ma'am.'

'Of course, Kumari. We know you have a strong sense of what is right and wrong. One is glad that you tackled the matter before the event.' The queen held her gaze. 'It is always advisable to ask for permission, rather than forgiveness. Don't you agree?'

This was a warning. She was being told that there were boundaries and the queen wouldn't take kindly to Kumari overstepping them. It was almost as though she knew what Kumari had been thinking.

'Yes, ma'am,' said Kumari. 'I understand.'

The queen nodded. 'And what of you, Benedict?'

'I'm coming out tomorrow,' said Benedict.

'You would abandon your wife and partake in an activity she finds abhorrent?'

Ben met his grandmother's gaze. 'No, Grandma,' he said deliberately. 'I'm giving my wife some space to herself while I go out hunting with my grandpa.'

The queen laughed. 'Of course you are. Your grandpa will be delighted that you're going. He always enjoys these romps.' She looked across the room at her husband. 'Even at his age,' she said, smiling.

The dinner gong rang. Ben rose to his feet and helped Kumari up. 'Shall I walk you in to dinner, Grandma?' he said.

Benedict offered her a hand to help her rise. She gave him a scornful look and stood up by herself. 'Oh no, thank you, Benedict. I believe Richard is doing the honours this evening.'

A few minutes later, Kumari walked into the dining room with Ben. 'What was all that about permission rather than forgiveness?' Ben whispered to her. 'What's going on?'

Kumari shrugged. 'Nothing, as far as I know.' And nothing could happen now, because the queen had effectively told her not to. Although how she knew was a mystery.

Chapter 36

www.glamourous.co.uk

Kumari breaks the Internet with stunning green dress

Just when you thought Kumari couldn't be any cooler, she rocks up to the most formal of formal occasions, Christmas Eve dinner at Sandringham, wearing a ball gown designed for her by the little-known British designer, Pema. Formal photographs released by the palace yesterday show the duchess standing next to her husband, Prince Benedict, looking radiant in dark green. She outshone even Princess Ophelia, normally the most exuberant of the royals. The only disappointing thing about this dress is that it shows that Kumari's stomach is so flat that it's unlikely she's hiding a baby bump. We're gutted because, just look at those two! Wouldn't they have the most gorgeous babies?

Princess Ophelia wore a pink ombre dress by Givenchy. Want details? We've got everything you want to know about those fabulous dresses, where to get the real thing or how to fake it with the closest high street equivalent in our fashion section on page 23.

The next morning, breakfast was a crowded affair as 'the wider family' arrived. Various lords, earls and ladies turned up, most of them dressed for the outdoors. After the fairly gentle atmosphere of the last few days, the larger gathering seemed loud and overwhelming. Kumari was introduced to so many people, she had given up trying to remember how they were all connected, and focused on names instead.

The saloon was crammed with people, all dressed for the outdoors. Children zipped around, playing a game that involved a lot of dodging and hiding. It was almost a relief when the gong went summoning everyone out for the hunt.

Kumari stood in the doorway with the others who were remaining behind, mostly the elderly and one or two children. The hunt truly was something one did not decline. The shooting party traipsed off, the large group stretching out into clusters as people got into their stride.

'Oh, thank goodness they've gone,' said a voice behind her. 'Now we get a few hours of peace.'

Kumari turned to find a small woman with brown hair smiling at the departing pack. Her foot was in plaster and she was leaning on a crutch.

'The only good thing about this wretched broken foot is that it gets me out of that.' She nodded at the departing hunt. 'I've never understood the fascination with shooting at things.'

'Me neither,' said Kumari. Benedict had pointed this woman out to her and suggested that she was someone Kumari might like to talk to. She remembered having met her before, at the wedding. She recalled rather liking her. In a world where the women tended to be tall and whip-thin, this woman stood out by being short and matronly.

'I'm not sure if you remember me. I'm Carla,' the woman said. 'Married to the Earl of Hythe.'

'I'm—'

'Oh, everyone knows who you are, darling,' said Carla. 'Your wedding caused such a stir.' She started to walk back towards the saloon, where tea and cake had been laid out for them. 'Tell me, darling. Do you miss being a doctor?'

She was getting used to this question. People asked her that often. 'A bit,' she said. 'But there's plenty to keep me busy.'

'I bet,' said Carla. 'When I was on the other side, I used to think the royals were the "idle rich". Ha! Shows how much I knew. Honestly, I read more reports now than I ever did when I was in corporate finance.'

Kumari did a mental jog to catch up. Oh yes. The Earl of Hythe's second wife. Once a high-flyer in corporate finance. They had met at a charity reception and fallen in love instantly, according to Ophelia. Kumari glanced at the woman standing beside her, who was staring thoughtfully at the tiny cakes.

'I recommend those tiny almond and raspberry ones,' Kumari said.

'Good call.' Carla picked up two of them.

'I am told,' said Carla, 'that I should ask you how your charity work is going as regards educating women and girls in the developing world.'

Kumari was taken aback. 'You were told?'

'Benedict told me. "Have a chat with Kumari, won't you, Aunt Carla," he said. "Talk about education for girls and healthcare stuff. She'd love that. She misses having someone to talk medicine to." . . . So here I am, darling. Ready to talk medicine.' She dropped her voice and said in a conspiratorial whisper, 'I did a biotech degree, you know. Before I got sucked into the world of money.'

Kumari laughed. She now saw why Ben had suggested she speak to Carla. They had some things in common.

'Well,' she said. 'Let me tell you about this one project . . .' She told Carla about the Boost Her! project. 'It seems like a small thing now, just raising hygiene standards and improving child survival rates in the villages, but over a few years, you end up with a much healthier and better informed population. If you want to make permanent change to people and culture, you start by educating the mothers, so that they influence the next generation.' She raised her hands in exasperation. 'I can't believe they have to shut it down without even giving it a chance to get started.'

'Oh, that does seem dreadfully sad,' said Carla. 'How are they meant to show any progress in that time? They need the first cohort to go back to the villages and then gather data on mortality rates for two years at least before they can show the effect. It's ridiculous that something so important is jeopardised by one man's greed.'

'Exactly,' said Kumari. 'It's so unfair. I've tried to think of ways that I could help, but it seems that the only course of action is to apply to the Princesses and Prince Foundation to be considered for next year's grants. There's an awkward gap between their current funding ending and the foundation's next round starting, so even if they were successful in their application, they'd have a struggle making it through.'

'Could you not have a quiet word with the funders?' said Carla. 'You are a woman of considerable influence now.'

'No. Apparently that would be frowned upon.'

'I see, the famous neutrality,' said Carla. 'That is . . . as my nephew would say, a total pisser.'

Kumari laughed, despite herself. 'Precisely.'

Carla looked thoughtful. She popped a little cake in her mouth. 'Mm,' she said, a minute later. 'Those are good. Tell me, darling, if you were allowed to donate money to a charity at will, what would you give to this charity you mention?'

Kumari thought about it. 'I'd fund it to the end.'

'That would be the ideal scenario,' said Carla. 'But if you were pressed for a minimum viable amount?'

'If I were being brutal about it,' she said, 'I'd check the costing hadn't changed from their original proposal . . . and I'd fund them for a year. This would give them the time to secure further funding and at least give the girls from the first cohort a year to make a difference.'

Carla nodded. 'And get metrics to show improved life expectancy for babies in those villages.' She chose another cake. 'How do you feel about mobile midwifery clinics?'

This was the sort of thing Kumari could chat about for ages. So, it turned out, could Carla. They were still chatting when the hunting party returned, looking windblown and red-faced from the cold. Ben kissed Kumari's cheek.

'Did you have a nice time?' He slipped an arm around her waist.

'I did, thanks. I spoke to Carla.'

'Excellent. I knew you'd like her.' He grinned. 'Now then, what's for lunch, I wonder. I'm famished.'

After lunch, they drove away from Sandringham, with Ben at the wheel as before. Kumari let out a long breath and felt the tension she'd been carrying over the past few days drain out of her.

'You survived your first royal Christmas,' he said. 'What did you think of it?'

Kumari didn't answer immediately. She had come expecting pomp and excess and ritual. There had been quite a lot of that, but there had also been an unexpected sense of warmth. It was about reaffirming family bonds and establishing new ones when the family expanded, as it had done when she'd married Ben. 'It was . . . nice,' she said. 'Your family are good fun when they let their hair down.'

Ben smiled. 'That's good. I knew you'd fit in beautifully.'

'I think that's pushing the definition of "fitting in" a bit,' said Kumari with a laugh. 'You're right, though. It wasn't nearly as frightening as I expected it to be.' After a moment, she added, 'You guys are a close-knit family.'

'We have to be,' said Ben. 'There aren't many people like us and if we have some sort of crisis, we need to be able to rely on each other.' He slowed down at the gatehouse and was waved out. 'I think that's why Grandma is always so insistent that we come to Christmas here. It's group bonding, if you like. She's reminding us that we have each other.'

Kumari let this sink in. A long time ago, Ben had told her that the rules around the institution of royalty had to be changed slowly and carefully, that to take away too much too soon would have repercussions. At the time, she hadn't understood. The past few days had given her an idea of what it really meant. All the ritual and tradition provided cultural touchstones. Something you could point to and say, 'Yes, it's mad, but it's a thing we do. It's part of what makes us different to everyone else.'

The mere existence of the royal institution was part of what made the UK united. People were attached to it, even while they complained about it. It was a way to hold on to who you were, when you were in danger of being absorbed into the homogenous mass of the world.

'Well, I'm glad I didn't break anything by refusing to go to the shoot this morning,' said Kumari.

'Grandma took it fairly well, I thought,' said Ben. 'I'm still puzzled by that stuff about asking for permission and forgiveness though?'

'I thought it was a warning not to push my luck,' said Kumari.

Ben frowned. After a few minutes he said, 'Hmm. might be.' He shot a sideways glance at her. 'Were you intending to push your luck?'

She didn't reply.

'Kumari? Were you hoping to do something for the charity you were upset about? Was that it?'

'I've tried every avenue I can think of – I'm speaking to members of the decision-making committee carefully, so that they're aware how great the project is, I've looked into other short-term grant sources, I've even looked into making private donations, but everything has some risk attached to it. And your granny seems to be able to read minds,' she said. 'I know when to give up.'

'Ah,' said Ben. 'Don't do that. I'm sure we can come up with something that doesn't break any rules and gives them a helping hand. Let's keep thinking.'

Kumari said nothing and looked out of the window. What else was there to say? The silence stretched between them.

It started to snow. It wasn't anything too bad yet, just light flurries which didn't seem to be settling.

'Looks like the promised bad weather is starting,' said Kumari, glad to have something else to talk about. 'I might see if my parents could come down tonight, rather than tomorrow. See if they can get here before the worst of it hits.'

'Good idea,' said Ben. 'If it's all right with them, just call my office and get a Land Rover sent over to them. That will get them here regardless of the weather.'

Kumari pulled out her phone and made the calls. Her parents were already concerned about the weather and were more than happy to be picked up early. She finally hung up. She had asked Ophelia to stay away that night, so that she and Ben could have an evening to themselves, but it couldn't be helped. It was safer to get her parents down early. She could relax with Ben some other time.

'All sorted?' said Ben.

'Yep, we should have a couple of hours at home before they show up. Thank goodness we had Louise make up the bedrooms before she went away for Christmas.' Kumari was still getting used to having all these members of staff, but she had to admit that her housekeeper Louise was a real lifesaver. Keeping everything ticking over by herself would have been impossible.

'It'll be nice to see them,' said Ben.

Kumari hadn't seen her parents since the wedding. She'd spoken to them most weeks, but her schedule had been too packed to arrange a visit. She wondered if Amma had cooked up a load of food to bring with her. That was, she realised, one of her own comforting touchstones – her mother's Sri Lankan meals in the freezer, ready to be heated up whenever life got too overwhelming.

Ben was clearly thinking along the same lines. 'Will your mum bring food?' he said, far too eagerly.

Kumari laughed. 'You've been doing nothing but eat for three days!'

'That's different,' he said. 'Anyway, I hope she does. You've got to teach me how to eat with my hands properly too. It's embarrassing not being able to keep up on the table manners front.'

'Oh, come on! It's not like anyone would judge you for using cutlery instead of your hands to eat curry!'

Ben twitched an eyebrow at her. That always made her smile and he knew it.

Kumari felt a sudden urge to throw her arms around him, but given that he was driving, it was best not to. 'I love you,' she said.

Ben took his eyes off the road for a second to beam at her. 'I love you too.'

Chapter 37

The Times Herald

Boxing Day shoot

What could be more traditional on Boxing Day than going out and shooting pheasant? Pictures released today, show the royal hunting party as they walk through the Sandringham grounds en route to the Boxing Day shoot. The queen and her husband, the Duke of Hereford, were seen taking it all in their stride as they walked down to the shoot with their grandson, Prince Benedict.

The ladies were seen at the hunting lodge, all dressed casually for the occasion. Prince Benedict's wife, Kumari, was notably absent. Speculation is rife as to whether the duchess was excused due to being in a delicate condition. It is equally possible that the duchess, who was brought up by Buddhist parents, was excused on moral and religious grounds.

Photo caption: HRH the Duke of Hereford keeping pace with his grandson HRH Prince Benedict, Duke of Westbury.

The Daily Flash

Letters: Kumari snubs the Queen

The Sandringham Boxing Day shoot is a royal tradition stretching back hundreds of years. No member of the royal family has missed it without having a good excuse. But this year, Prince Benedict's new wife, Kumari, deliberately snubbed the queen by refusing to attend. The left-leaning pundits would have us believe that Kumari's absence was due to her religious principles and abhorrence of hunting. But the duchess famously doesn't know how she feels about God. She has no religious principles. This is just another example of the erosion of the traditions of the monarchy. Whatever next? Selfies with the queen?

Photo caption: Princess Helena attends the Boxing Day shoot. She was five months pregnant with Princess Francesca at the time.

Kumari woke up far too early, considering how late she had gone to bed the night before. Ben was still fast asleep. She curled herself around him and tried to get back to sleep, but it was no use. She was wide awake. She sighed. There was no point lying here. She may as well get up and make herself a cup of coffee.

The apartment had an extra reception room and several guest bedrooms, which were further down from Kumari and Ben's bedroom, so that they and the guests had a modicum of privacy. The reception rooms, dining room and kitchen were all joined to one another by linking doors, just like the function rooms in the main part of Kensington Palace.

Kumari wandered barefoot into the kitchen and put the coffee on. A lot of the rooms had underfloor heating. It was a wonderful thing.

Her parents had arrived well after midnight the night before . . . or this morning, depending on how you looked at it. All they'd had time to do was put the food in the fridge and be shown to their room.

She opened the fridge door and looked in. Amma's food parcels, in their myriad tupperware containers and reused margarine tubs, were crammed in between the food that Ben and Kumari had ordered. Ben had planned to cook roast pork with all the trimmings as a sort of belated Christmas meal for the four of them that evening. He could have ordered it in, of course, but Kumari got the impression he needed some time to decompress and cooking gave him the chance to do that.

Soft footfalls made her look round. Her mother stood in the kitchen doorway, in her faded dressing gown. She looked incongruously careworn amidst the perfectly coordinated kitchen. When she had visited the first time, she had looked incredibly uncomfortable to be in such a posh place. Now, she seemed a little more relaxed. She was getting used to things too.

'I'm making coffee, Amma, would you like one?'

'That would be nice,' she said. She leaned against the work surface and watched her as she poured them a mug each. 'You look well.'

'Thank you,' Kumari said automatically.

'I'm glad,' said Amma. 'I know we speak to you often, but it is very reassuring to see you . . . in real life, I mean. Not on the telly.'

Kumari smiled. Amma still texted her whenever she saw her on TV. 'You're on the news' or 'Very nice pic of you in the paper today'. She liked that.

She stepped up to her mother and put her head on her shoulder. 'It's nice to see you too. I miss you.'

Her mother put her arm around her and gave her a gentle hug. 'How is it, this life? Are you coping as well as you seem to be?'

Kumari lifted her head. 'I am actually, yes. I'm getting used to it. There are rough spots, but in the main, I'm very happy.'

Amma's gaze met hers. 'So you made the right decision. That's a relief for me to know.'

'Yeah, I made the right decision.'

'And the Christmas holidays at Sandringham went OK?'

She had told Amma about some of her fears. 'Yes, it did. Everyone was very nice.' She pulled a face. 'Although, I could have done without everyone asking me when we were having kids. Seriously Amma, even the queen!'

Amma laughed. 'It's like that with big families. Everyone in everyone else's business.' Amma had come from a large family, but since she had been estranged from her family for a long time, Kumari didn't know many of them. 'You know,' Amma added. 'It does get harder the older you get . . .'

'Not you too.' Kumari groaned. She wasn't really annoyed. She expected it from Amma.

'Well, you are my only hope of having a grandchild.' Amma smiled at her over the rim of the coffee mug.

Kumari didn't answer for a second and looked thoughtfully at the rings on her hands.

'Is it that you're scared? Or does Ben want to wait?' said Amma.

'Oh, Ben would love to have kids. He wants to have about three. But it's a big thing. I dunno, I felt like I needed a bit more time to get used to things before . . .' She sighed.

Amma rubbed her shoulder. 'I understand,' she said. 'But there's never really a good time to have kids.'

'So now's as bad a time as any other?'

'Something like that.' Amma pulled her closer so that she could plant a kiss on the top of Kumari's head. She released her and took a sip of coffee. 'So, is that it? Or is something else bothering you?'

Ah, Amma. She always knew when something was up. Kumari explained about the Boost Her! initiative. Amma listened carefully. 'So . . . you can't offer to fund them directly, in case someone finds out. You can't publicly state your support unless it's in very general terms. You can't publicly criticise the funding body . . . it does limit your options a bit.'

'The queen effectively warned me not to do anything stupid, so I can't break any of the rules at the moment,' she said. 'It's very frustrating.'

'Is there any way you could help . . . off the record? Maybe mention it casually to someone with money who might take a hint and step in? Someone who's not a royal. Would that be possible?'

She thought about it. 'It would . . . except I don't really know anyone well enough to be able to be subtle about it. Maybe I should talk to Ophelia. She knows everyone.'

'I'm sure there will be someone,' said Amma. 'You're doing a lot for a lot of people,' she added kindly. 'Sometimes, you can't save them all.'

'I know,' said Kumari. 'But I have to try.'

Ophelia phoned just before lunch. 'Are they there? Can I come round yet?'

Kumari looked at her parents. Amma was chatting to Ben about something that required them to draw diagrams. She dreaded to think what that was about. Thatha was sitting on the sofa, reading a book. It was a scene of calm and tranquillity. Adding Ophelia would blow that apart. On the other hand, Thatha would be delighted to see Ophelia.

'They're here,' she said.

'Fabboo,' said Ophelia. 'I'll be there in two ticks.'

'Have you eaten?' said Kumari, even though she knew the answer.

'Oh no. I'll have lunch at yours.' The line clicked and the connection was lost.

Kumari shook her head and hung up. 'Ophelia's coming for lunch,' she told Ben.

'That's fine,' said Ben. 'It'll stretch.'

He thought nothing of his sisters showing up at random times and inviting themselves to dinner. That must be what it was like to have brothers and sisters. Kumari thought about Ben's comment: 'She's reminding us that we have each other.' They did. Whatever differences there were between them, if one of them needed something, the entire family would close ranks around them.

Kumari went to the window and looked outside. The snow was coming down heavily now and had settled in

411

a layer several inches thick on the windowsill. Through the white, she could see the glowing windows in the rest of Kensington Palace. She was part of this family now. And if she and Ben had children, they would be too. Maybe . . .

A sudden gust of wind threw a squall of snow hard against the window, making her jump. Goodness, it was getting wild out there. She hoped Lucy's flight had got off on time. She sent a quick text wishing her a safe journey.

The reply arrived almost instantly. *The airport is in total chaos. Flights cancelled. No accommodation. Should give up and make my way back to the flat, but scared of getting stranded somewhere on the way. Lucy.'*

Kumari frowned. The Land Rover that brought her parents here was still there. There would be a driver around too.

'Ben,' she said. 'Can I have a quick word?'

Ben excused himself and joined her. 'What's up?'

She showed him the text from Lucy.

'We can't leave her there,' he said. 'Let's send a car and get her home.'

Kumari thought of Lucy returning to the empty flat, where she'd have depleted the fridge and turned down the heating. 'I hate to think of her in the flat all alone. Do you think we could invite her here?'

He smiled. 'Since we've already got your parents and my sister, we may as well add Lucy into the mix. I'm sure we can fit another person in the apartments.'

'That's exactly what I was thinking,' said Kumari. She was about to dial Ben's PA, when she remembered that Sinead was supposed to be flying out today too. She texted

Sinead. *Did you make your flight? Or are you stuck in the airport? Which airport?*

When the reply came, it said that Sinead was in the same airport, but at a different terminal. 'Ben,' she said. 'Can we fit in Sinead too?'

Ben laughed. 'Sure, why not!'

She texted Sinead.

Am sending a car to get you. Will give you a time to meet them. Hang tight.

Her phone rang. It was Sinead.

'You don't need to do that, ma'am. I'm sure the flights will start again soon. It's your family time,' Sinead said, speaking really fast.

'Don't be silly,' said Kumari. 'I can't leave you stuck there in this. There's plenty of room here.'

'But I can't possibly. It wouldn't be right.'

'Sinead. It's my house. I get to say what's right.'

There was a small snuffling sound at the other end of the line.

'Sinead?'

'Yes, ma'am. Thank you.'

She told Sinead to await instructions of where to meet the car and hung up.

She answered Ben's quizzical look with, 'She's coming.'

He grinned.

'How about your team?' she said. 'Anyone likely to be stranded in an airport?'

He thought about it for a minute, then shook his head. 'No. Most of them were already off and the others are all local, so no, they should be fine. Any other waifs and strays you want to invite over?'

She couldn't think of anyone else who might not be somewhere safe and warm. She made a few phone calls and arranged for Lucy and Sinead to be picked up.

A few minutes later, Ophelia swept in. 'Hello, hello,' she said. She held up some bags, one of which clinked. 'I've brought things for your party.'

'Who said we were having a party?' said Ben.

'Well, I'm here, so it will be one anyway,' said Ophelia, waving a hand. 'Hello, Mr and Mrs Senavaka. How lovely to see you.' She bestowed kisses on cheeks. 'I read that book you recommended, Mr Senavaka. Fascinating.'

Kumari watched her father smile and murmur, 'Please call me Sena.' He had been thrilled to find out that Ophelia's English Literature degree had been more than a formality and that she was happy to discuss poetry with him for hours.

'I suppose I should go and check if there's enough food to stretch to two extra people for tonight,' said Ben.

Amma's head came up. 'Extra people?'

Ben rolled his eyes. 'Kumari's just invited a couple of people who were stranded in the airports to come and stay until this blizzard is over and the skies reopen. So we'll have more to feed than I expected.'

'Oh shut up, you love it,' said Ophelia.

Cooking was Ben's hobby. Having extra people to appreciate his creations was never going to be a problem.

'Come on, grumpy, I'll help you,' said Kumari. She and Amma followed him into the kitchen. Within minutes he and Amma were discussing ways to stretch the menu. In the living room Thatha and Ophelia settled into a discussion about poetry. Kumari leant against the doorway between the rooms and smiled.

Chapter 38

The Standard Times

Storm Humphrey hits Britain with a Vengeance

The country has woken up to a post-Christmas whiteout with heavy snowfall overnight. There are reports of up to three feet of snow in some areas of the north. There is widespread disruption on the railways and roads. Police are warning people to avoid travelling if at all possible.

Air traffic is also disrupted due to high winds and blizzard conditions. Many hundreds of travellers spent a miserable night trapped in airports as flights were cancelled and the airport hotels filled up. As the airport retailers ran out of food, several enterprising local establishments were given permission to set up 'pop up' food outlets. Local church groups have rallied to provide stranded travellers with blankets and shelter.

It is hoped that the bad weather will ease up during the course of the day and that there will be opportunity to clear snow from the roads so that people can travel home. The Environment Agency has warned that in a few days, when the snow melts, there is a risk of flooding and has warned people in flood-risk areas to prepare their houses for such an eventuality.

What's next for Kumari, the Duchess of Westbury?

What a year it's been. First there was the fairy-tale romance of the prince who fell for the humanitarian doctor, then the incredible wedding, and now Kumari is changing the traditions of the royal family by being the first royal wife who didn't attend the traditional Boxing Day shoot.

Kumari, who from day one has been vocal in her support for women's rights and better prospects for girls, is a breath of fresh air. While the Princesses Helena and Ophelia are respected and revered, Kumari embodies an 'everywoman'. She did the things we did. Dreamed the dreams we dreamed. She could have been any one of us. Seeing the love between her and the prince gives us all hope for a brighter future.

The inclusion of Kumari in the royal line-up is changing the world's view of Britain. The shadow of the empire is lifting. The lady herself has done much to increase the diversity within palace walls. Her dresser, Sinead Cho, is half-Chinese. Her assistant, Annie Shah, is Kenyan. Her clothes are often made by designers of BAME backgrounds.

Next year, Kumari and Prince Benedict will undertake a tour of the Commonwealth, presenting the new face of the monarchy to the world. We are so looking forward to what they achieve.

Photo caption: That photo from the wedding. Prince Benedict rests his forehead against his wife's as they share a private joke. Have you ever seen a couple more in love?

In the end there were nine people at the meal. One of Ophelia's friends had walked from Paddington Station where all the trains had been cancelled and Edwin, one of the cousins, who was staying in one of the other wings, had tracked them down and been invited in. Edwin helped Lucy work out how to extend the dining table while Kumari and Sinead hunted down extra tablecloths and napkins. The apartment was well supplied for entertaining, but Kumari still didn't know where everything was kept. She could have called whoever was covering housekeeping for Louise, but decided it was better to do it herself.

Ophelia had located the most important implement, the corkscrew, and was making sure everyone had a glass of something. Ophelia's friend, Wendy, a red-haired girl with an infectious laugh, was looking through Ben and Kumari's music collection. The whole place was full of noise and bustle in a way that it had never been before. It made the place feel warm and alive. Kumari realised that this was how the place was meant to be. Bustling. Full of voices and laughter. That was what made it home.

She came into the dining room, carrying two large tablecloths, to find that the table now took up most of the room. Ben shouted in from the kitchen that there were spare chairs in a cupboard in another room. Edwin went off to find them. Wendy finally settled on a CD of Bing Crosby singing Christmas songs. Kumari sang along as she, Lucy and Sinead sorted out the table.

'How much cutlery do you people own?' said Lucy, looking into the wide drawer. Kumari joined her. The cutlery was held in a purpose-built, extra-wide drawer. There were regular forks, salad forks, meat forks, fish forks, dessert forks and even garnish forks. Kumari knew the names and uses of all of these, thanks to the comprehensive etiquette lessons. Eating was an important part of diplomacy.

'I think we'll go for the simplest setting,' she said, grabbing a handful. 'A knife, a fork, a dessert spoon.'

'Which is the dessert spoon?' said Lucy, staring at the neatly sorted selection of spoons.

Kumari pointed them out. 'Can you grab some tea-spoons too,' she said. 'Those are the small ones,' she added with a grin.

'I know that!' Lucy grinned back.

They moved down the table together, setting the places.

'I've missed this,' Kumari said. 'You know, just hanging out with you.'

'Aw. I've missed you too,' said Lucy. 'The new housemate is nice and all, but nowhere near as much fun as you.'

'It's a shame things didn't go any further with you and Rhodri,' said Kumari. 'That would have been so cool if my best friend was with Ben's best friend. We could have gone on holiday together or something.'

Lucy pulled a face. 'I'm not sure that would be such a great idea. Rhodri's sweet, but that was just a best man and bridesmaid thing. We're not exactly made for each other.'

She smiled. 'I think we both realised that at the same time. It's all good. We're friends.'

'That's good,' said Kumari. 'I haven't seen Rhodri in ages. I keep inviting him round, but he never takes us up on it.'

'Are you talking about Rhodri Ellesmere-Jones?' said Sinead shyly.

'Yes, why?' said Kumari.

'Um . . .'

'Sinead, if you have gossip, you have to share it with me,' said Kumari. 'Please.'

Sinead glanced over her shoulder. 'Well, the rumour is that he used to have a huge crush on Princess Ophelia. He asked her out once, apparently, when he was about eighteen and she thought he was joking and laughed at him. He hasn't been to visit Prince Benedict in Kensington ever since. He always meets him somewhere else . . .'

'At the club,' said Kumari. 'Of course. I wondered why that was.'

'Well, that explains what happened at your wedding,' said Lucy. 'I was just his distraction.'

Kumari put a hand on Lucy's arm. 'I'm so sorry.'

'What for?' She grinned. 'It was fun. He was my distraction too.'

Ophelia came in carrying a bottle of red. 'What are we talking about?' she said.

'Rhodri Ellesmere-Jones,' said Kumari.

'Ah, lovely Rodders. How is he? I haven't spoken to him in ages. I saw him at your wedding, of course, but didn't get to talk to him. He was somewhat . . . distracted, as I recall.' She nodded at Lucy.

'You need a good distraction at a wedding,' said Lucy cheerfully.

'Oh, you do,' said Sinead. 'Definitely.'

All four women laughed. Kumari felt a little flutter of happiness. She couldn't remember the last time she'd been able to hang out with people and catch up on the gossip. It had been too long since she'd been as relaxed as this.

It wasn't long before everyone was sitting at the table. Ben had done his roast pork with all the trimmings, including Kumari's favourite, Yorkshire puddings. He had also made a dish of cheesy roast potatoes, which Lucy recognised with delight as 'funeral potatoes', a spare dish of honey-glazed carrots and Amma's devilled cauliflowers.

'Shall we say grace?' said Ophelia.

Everyone bowed their heads, even Kumari and her family, while Ophelia said a very quick prayer of thanks, then everyone dived in. After days of formal dining in Sandringham, it was a relief to be at a table where everyone talked over each other and the wine was passed to whomever wanted it, in whichever direction it needed to go. Ophelia suddenly said, 'Oh, I forgot. There are Christmas crackers!' She ran into the sitting room and returned with a dozen crackers. Soon everyone was wearing paper hats and reading out the dreadful cracker jokes. As the evening wore on and people relaxed in each other's company, the dining room filled with noise. Discussions started elsewhere continued. Occasionally there would be a burst of laughter.

Kumari finished her meal and looked around. Sinead and Amma were deep in discussion about an article that had appeared in *The Sentinel*. Ophelia was listening in and throwing in her own insight. Lucy was horrifying Thatha with a description of jello salad. Edwin, Ben and Wendy were discussing which fantasy writers could have influenced George R. R. Martin's world-building. People were having fun.

There were no presents, there wasn't even a Christmas tree in this room, but Kumari felt the warmth of the occasion. Having grown up an only child, with no extended family around her, she didn't have Ben's fondness of large family gatherings. But here, surrounded by family and friends enjoying each other's company . . . she finally understood how Christmas was supposed to be. She looked over at Ben, who gave her a small smile. She put her hand in his and squeezed. He leant across and kissed her cheek.

When the cutlery had stopped clinking and everyone had finished, Lucy groaned, 'I don't think I could eat another thing.'

Ben said, 'We have crumble and custard or ice cream for pudding.'

'I'm happy to prove myself wrong,' said Lucy.

Ben stood up.

'Before you go,' said Ophelia. 'I think we should raise a toast to Ben and to Kumari's mum Rukmali for a fantastic meal.'

Everyone raised their glasses.

'And,' Ophelia continued. 'I think we should also raise a toast to Ben and Kumari, for their kindness in taking in all us waifs and strays and letting us gatecrash what was surely meant to be a quiet family dinner.'

'Oh, it's no —' Kumari started to object.

'No point being modest about it,' Ophelia cut her off. 'I should add that I'm very impressed with my new sister-in-law. Not only did she navigate the formality of the infamous Sandringham Christmas like a pro, she managed to get out of the Boxing Day shoot without annoying Grandma, which has to be some sort of a record. I know it's been a difficult time for you, Kumari, and you were hoping to have these few days to spend time with Ben and your parents, so we are, all of us, very grateful for your kindness in letting us join you. Speaking for myself, I have to say, I haven't had this much fun in months.'

'Hear, hear,' said Edwin.

'Right,' said Ophelia. 'I'm done. You can go and get pudding now.'

Ben grabbed Kumari's hand, so she went with him.

'How much has Ophelia had to drink?' said Kumari when they got to the kitchen.

Ben shrugged. 'Who cares?' he said. 'What she said was true. You are truly amazing.' He pulled her close and gave her a kiss that melted her insides.

When he released her and made to move away, she held him close. 'Ben. I've been thinking.' She bit her lip. 'You know how I asked if we could wait a bit before we started a family . . . I'm thinking maybe we've left it long enough now.'

'Really?' Ben's grin lit up the whole kitchen. 'That's . . . there are no words.' He kissed her again, this time a kiss full of promise and excitement. 'That's the best present I could have had.' He gave her a hug, then pulled a face. 'I guess we should serve up pudding first, right?'

Kumari laughed. 'Probably best.' She kissed the tip of his nose and gave him a gentle push.

'Since we're doing presents right now,' he said. 'I have something for you.' He pulled out his phone and found something on it. 'Here,' he said. 'Read this.'

He released her and went to get the crumble out of the oven.

Kumari looked at the screen. It was an email to Ben from Lady Clara.

Dearest Benedict. I write this in haste, so I didn't have a chance to find your lovely wife's email address, whereas yours is in my address book. Please can you tell Kumari that I enjoyed our discussion yesterday and was so taken by her passion for her projects that I looked up the Boost Her! initiative that she mentioned to me. It seems like a very valuable endeavour and she is absolutely correct to be incensed at the withdrawal of funding. I, too, am very annoyed. So much so that I have decided to step in and fund it as a private benefactor for two years. Hopefully, this will buy them enough time to secure other funding to complete, and perhaps extend, the project. Will you please let Kumari know.

Merry Christmas,

Clara

Kumari read it twice before it sank in, then gave a squeal. 'Oh, Ben!' He put down the dish he was carrying so that she could hug him. 'You knew, didn't you? You knew she'd do something like that. That's why you made a point of making her speak to me.'

'I didn't want to get your hopes up,' he said. 'But I did think she might be sympathetic. She isn't bound by the same rules as we are so . . .'

She kissed him. 'I love you, you wonderful man.'

'Well, you wanted a thoughtful present. Will this do?'

'Of course it will do.' She hugged him close. 'It's the best thing you could have given me.'

He laughed and kissed her. 'Merry Christmas, my princess.'

Acknowledgements

A few years ago, I promised myself that by the time my daughters were old enough to read my books, I'd have at least one novel with a brown girl on the cover. It's important to be able to see yourself reflected in popular culture. I'm always thrilled when I spot a Sri Lankan character in a genre novel – the first time I spotted one was in Allison Pearson's *I Don't Know How She Does It* and I still remember the buzz from seeing that! I've always written Sri Lankans into my romcoms – written under my pen name, Rhoda Baxter – but usually as secondary characters. Now, finally, I have a novel, written under my own name, with a Sri Lankan main character and a heroine of colour on the cover. Yay! Princesses come in all colours.

This book was an unexpected gift that came about because of a chance conversation. So thank you to the team at Bonnier Zaffre for taking a leap of faith. With special thanks to my editor, Tara Loder, for all the support along the way. Federica Leonardis, you rock! Thanks for being a sounding board during the project and for being chief cheerleader to keep me going.

Thanks to Jen Hicks, who is always my first reader, for super-fast and useful 'gloves-off' feedback on my first draft. I really appreciate it.

The ladies of the Naughty Kitchen were instrumental in keeping me sane when the pressure got too much. It's also handy knowing people who can tell you where to find a calendar of high society events or just shoot the breeze about celebrity wedding dress designers. Cheers, ladies.

I owe a very special thank you to my family, who helped in so many little ways to allow me extra writing time. Thank you so much for understanding . . . and for pointing out useful headlines for me to look in to!

And lastly, thank *you*, the reader, for buying and reading the book. I literally couldn't do this without you!